Magnolia Hill

A Novel

Caroline Friday

Magnolia Hill

Published by Sixth Day Media, LLC

Marietta, Georgia 30068

www.sixthdaymedia.com

Graphic Sixth Day logo is a registered trademark of

Sixth Day Media, LLC

All rights reserved. Except for brief excerpts for review purposes, no part of this book may be reproduced or used in any form without written permission from the publisher.

This story is a work of fiction. All names, characters, and events are the product of the author's imagination. Any resemblance to any person, living or dead, is purely coincidental.

Unless otherwise noted, all Scripture quotations are taken from the King James Version of the Bible. (Public Domain.)

© 2012 Caroline Friday

Cover Art and Design: Sixth Day Media, LLC

Inside logo: Sixth Day Media, LLC

Author Photos: Sixth Day Media, LLC

ISBN-13: 978-1483974712
ISBN-10: 1483974715

Acknowledgement

A heartfelt thanks goes to my husband, children, and certain friends and extended family members who have supported my writing over the years. Your love and encouragement were essential to the completion of this work and continue to be so precious to me as I endeavor to write down all the stories and books in my head and heart. I particularly want to thank certain family members for helping in the editing of this manuscript. I will be forever grateful to all of you for helping me keep my dream alive! ♥

A note to my Brunswick County, NC friends: please excuse any details that may not be historically accurate and accept them as the offspring of my vivid imagination. In addition, all use of names, characters, and events are purely the product of my creativity and imagination and should in no way, whatsoever, be considered a reflection on any person or persons now living or dead.

To J.C., my prince, who pulled me out of the deep.

Part I

Chapter 1

North Carolina 1925

Cadie Hamilton crouched outside the little church steeple of the Gospel Church in her pressed calico frock, hanging on to every word coming from the mouth of the Reverend Averill Thomas. No one knew of her hiding place by the upper window ledge—not until today. Despite Cadie's objections, her older sister, Tessie, had insisted on coming along and was stooped beside her, squirming and fidgeting like a worm in a robin's beak. Tessie always had a way of messing up Cadie's plans and getting caught was not one of them. Of course, going to church wasn't wrong at all—Cadie's mama and daddy encouraged church attendance, even though they chose to sleep in most Sunday mornings. No, it was because this was "that Negro church," and as of that very moment, she and Tessie were the only white faces for miles around.

"Faith! Somebody say, 'faith!'"

"FAITH!"

"Hope! Somebody say, 'hope!'"

"HOPE!"

"Love! Somebody say, 'love!'"

"LOVE!"

"But the greatest of these is—love," the reverend added in a breathy whisper. Sweat streamed from his dark face and soaked the edges of his collar as he sang to his congregation, *"Glory, glory. Glory, glory, glory—Lord!"* in a soft voice. He repeated the lyrics over and over, enraptured in his own world as he swayed back and forth in front of the plain, wooden cross propped on top of a rectangular table decorated with nothing other than a white cloth and a glass vase filled with wildflowers.

Every now and again, Cadie saw the damp stains underneath the arms of his flowing, black robe that brought a twinge of guilt to her tummy, like she was peeking into his bedroom window. At the grown-up age of fifteen, she ought to know better, and she did. She was much too old to be climbing trees or onto rooftops, peering through window slats covered in dirt and peeling, yellowed paint, but she couldn't help herself. Ever since that Sunday last spring when she first heard him preach while gathering wild raspberries for one of Mama's pies, she couldn't keep away. Even the simplicity of its name, "The Gospel Church," enticed her like a bee to honey.

Reverend Thomas finished his song and drew in a long breath. "You know, when I preach like this and call out to the Lord—Jesus!" He closed his eyes and looked up at the ceiling, yelling with all his might, "Jesus—Jesus!" The ringing of this name was like an electric spark sizzling through the air, stifling the smallest movement, even from Tessie. Cadie had warned her to keep quiet and flatten her body against the base of the steeple where the shade of a live oak tree kept them hidden from view, particularly from a withered old man who everyone referred to as Old Man Jackson. Every Sunday, during the heat of summer and the cold of winter, he sat in a weathered rocker by the front door, rocking back and forth with his eyes closed, nodding his head in agreement. Cadie heard the slow and steady rock of his chair, along with an occasional "Amen" and "Yes, Lord." But after this unexpected outburst, the creak of the rocker stopped, and all was still.

The reverend leaned toward the congregation and spoke in a hushed tone. "If I don't have the love of God in my heart, then to His ears, all that preachin' just sounds like two clangin' garbage pails bangin' together, makin' some kinda awful racket." He lifted his worn, leather Bible up in the air and resumed his pace before the packed room, waving his arms about for effect. "And when I get up here and prophecy to you and explain this Bible here and impart all kinds of knowledge about God's Word and have faith in His miracles and blessin's—a faith that can move mountains even—if I don't have His love in my heart, then in His eyes, all that knowledge and all that faith are worth nuthin'!"

By now, Cadie was transfixed by more than the reverend's words. His height and muscular stature and the way his close-cropped hair fit his skull like a knitted, wool cap had her captivated—and of course, there were the white teeth that gleamed like pearls strung across a swath of black velvet. She often wondered how such a man could end up in this little church in Pleasant Oaks, North Carolina, a little crossroads of a town just a few miles south of Wilmington. It was hard to believe he was a native of Brunswick County, born and raised among all the other poor and underprivileged Negroes. But here he was, preaching up a storm, without a speck of dirt under his fingernails or a scuff on his shoes, so unlike many sitting in the congregation. Cadie noticed how his head was always raised up high as though his skin was the color of alabaster, just like a rare jewel tossed in a pile of rough-hewn stones waiting to be plucked out of obscurity into the realm of greatness. And yet, greatness didn't seem to be his desire, other than to preach like this, Sunday after Sunday.

There's somethin' about the reverend that isn't natural, Cadie could hear Mama say to the ladies in her sewing club. *And no one who has any sense in his head'll go messin' with it.* Cadie knew what that meant, as did everyone else, even if they refused to remember. It was now spring of 1925, just five years after her daddy had left the house one night with his shotgun, claiming to go on a turkey hunt. Cadie thought it strange, since it wasn't anywhere near turkey season, and besides, she'd never known Daddy to go hunting after sunset. And even stranger, he took some of Mama's good white bed sheets with him, which had created quite a ruckus, since they had been hand-embroidered by Cadie's grandma. When Cadie asked about it, she was told to "hush up" and "keep quiet," and that's what she had done. Her ten-year-old mind pretended to ignore the whisperings and guarded discussions afterward, including stories about the dark, shadowy figures that roamed the forest near Jackson's Creek—figures that could burn up a tree with one deep exhalation like a fire-breathing dragon. They were meant to scare her, and they did for a time, but eventually she realized how ridiculous they were. What did all of that have to do with Daddy turkey hunting at night with Mama's good bed sheets?

"Ca-dee," Tessie whispered in her ear. "Come on!"

Cadie hated it when her sister pronounced her name "Kay-Dee" in a slow, deliberate manner as though it was a set of initials for some leathery ole farm hand. "No!" she whispered back. "And stop your fidgetin'!"

"I'm not fidgetin'."

"Are, too. Now, stop it!"

Sweat beaded on Tessie's forehead, despite the breeze, making her wire-framed eyeglasses slide down the bridge of her nose. She pushed them back in place and nudged Cadie. "I've heard enough. Now, come on. Let's go."

"Shh!" Cadie glared, slamming her fingers to her lips.

Tessie mouthed, *We're gonna get caught.*

Cadie made a face, trying to ignore every twitch of her sister's shoulder and toss of her long braid. But as she turned back toward the reverend, a warning bell went off in her mind, and with it, the fear that Tessie's prediction would come true—that one day she would get caught peeking in like this. Then what would Mama and Daddy do? And what about the reverend? What on earth would he say?

A shiver ran up and down her spine as the reverend's eyes roamed around the room, looking for a place to rest. "You gotta have love in your heart. Love for God, love for yourself, and love for your neighbor. And that means all your neighbors. Not some, but all of 'em. Even the mean ones. Nasty as all get out. Just plain awful. Jesus said, 'Love your enemies and pray for those who persecute you, that you may be sons and daughters of your Father in heaven.' Now, who's he talkin' about, huh?"

His gaze wove through the congregation, down one pew and then the other, accompanied by a Cheshire cat grin—just waiting for someone to give him the answer he desired. A sneeze was heard here, a cough there, followed by the clearing of a throat. Obviously, no one had the confidence to speak up, because not a word was spoken. "Don't give me that look, now. Y'all know, don't you? Well, come on. Uh huh, yep, that's right. He's talkin' about those people livin' way on the other side of the river—in those big, clean, rich, white houses."

The reverend's long, dark finger pointed toward the set of opened windows, extending past Jackson's Creek toward a plantation on the banks of the lower Cape Fear River known as Magnolia Hill. Cadie visualized the dark faces moving away from the windows like a bee zipping away from a water hose, not wanting to interfere with the power of such a gesture. After a moment, his finger returned back to its place and gripped the Bible. "The ones who tell ya lies—that you're no good—you're stupid, poor, dirty, black, ain't got no future. Just an ole colored, Nigra ninny!"

Cadie sucked in her breath at the jolt of shame that always accompanied the utterance of this word. The room was now so quiet, one could hear a pin drop, but Reverend Thomas just smiled, like he had every right to say it. "God said, 'Love your enemies. Pray for those who persecute you.' Those are the people you gotta love. Those are the people you gotta pray for. Ain't that right?" A cloud of passion swept him up into a whirlwind of frantic pacing. "Oh, Lord, you gotta get this! You gotta get this today, you gotta get this!" The congregation's "Amens" and "Hallelujahs" rose in volume, but it wasn't enough for the reverend. He added a little spiritual jig to his pacing, working himself into a frenzy until the "Amens" and "Hallelujahs" built back up to deafening shouts. "So whatcha gonna do? You gonna hate 'em?"

"No."

"I didn't hear you."

"No!"

"You mean when Mr. Rich White Man, givin' out jobs right and left down at the lumber mill, tells you he ain't gonna hire ya just 'cause your skin is black and not white, and you barely have enough money to feed your family, you ain't gonna hate him?"

"No!"

Reverend Thomas ignored the congregation's response and leaned in on Jack Reynolds, a stone-faced man sitting in the middle of the front pew with his eyes cast to the floor. "No, sir," Jack muttered, shaking his head.

"Whatcha gonna do?"

Jack looked up, his eyes glistening. "Love him. Pray for him," he answered along with the congregation.

The reverend smiled and resumed his roam about the room. He honed in on two women who clapped and cheered in unison. The older one was Magnolia Hill's head cook, Matilda Goodwin, known to everyone as Mattie, and the younger was her teenage daughter, Zena, who was about Cadie's age. "You mean when Miz Rich White Woman won't give you a day off, works your fingers to the bone, tells you she don't want you comin' to church on Sundee 'cause she needs her silver polished or her ironin' done or her dawg washed, you ain't gonna hate her?"

Cadie felt Tessie's hard tug on her arm, and without thinking, she snapped back with a loud "NO!" that rose above the congregation's collective voice. Immediately, she wanted to grab it back and shove it down her throat, but the damage was done—it reverberated off the walls like a ball with no end to its bounce, causing the cadence of the reverend's message to tilt in an awkward manner.

A long silence reigned as he cocked his head and surveyed the congregation. But then suddenly, an unusual look came over him, and he looked up toward the steeple window. Cadie's breath caught in her throat, and she pulled away, feeling the whoosh of blood flow through her body. "Cadieee," Tessie whispered. But Cadie was frozen, unable to move.

Reverend Thomas resumed his normal rhythm while inching his way underneath the steeple window. "When she tells you she's gonna fire you if your collard greens are bitter or your biscuits are flat or your fried chicken ain't crispy, you ain't gonna hate her?"

"No," the congregation replied in unison.

"Whatcha gonna do?"

"Love her. Pray for her."

He stopped under the steeple window and called out in an extra loud voice, "I said, whatcha gonna do?!" Cadie slammed her eyelids shut and squeezed, waiting for the moment to pass. Her heart pounded and the blood surged once more from her cheeks down to her feet. Finally, his gentle voice called to her, "I'm talkin' to you, my child."

Cadie blinked hard, wishing she could disappear into the wood siding, but it was as if some unknown power took over, forcing her to turn and peek through the window slats where she met his gaze, head on. They locked eyes, and for a moment, the fear left her and was replaced with a desire for that *something* that was on this man. Cadie didn't understand it and couldn't explain it, but she knew it was there. A deep longing stirred within her until her eyes shifted, and she saw something else, something strange and ugly—the head of a mangled scar snaking under his collar like a serpent slithering through a bed of thick ivy.

As though on cue, Tessie let out a yelp and slid down the roof, threatening to fall flat on her backside. Cadie scrambled to her feet and grabbed Tessie by the arm, pulling her back up to a stable position so they could safely scamper down the live oak tree and make a run for it.

Once their feet hit the ground, they ran like the wind all the way to the edge of the forest that bordered a row of live oaks growing on the church's property. One of the trees had been burned from top to bottom and stuck up out of the ground like a spooky, blackened skeleton. As Cadie made her way into the woods, she couldn't help but turn back and look at a trail of dirty Spanish moss that hung from one of its charred limbs. She had seen it sometime before, thinking an old, shriveled-up snakeskin had gotten entwined somehow, but today it looked different. Back and forth, it swayed like the tail of a cat as the breeze blew through the trees, rustling the needles on the pines and the leaves on the gnarled arms of the neighboring live oaks. Cadie peered closer, watching it move, when suddenly she realized it wasn't Spanish moss or a snakeskin, after all. Why, it was nothing more than a frayed length of decomposing rope.

The wind sent the leaves on the surrounding trees into a wild, fluttery dance, but Cadie couldn't hear a thing except the eerie thump of her heart. She stared at the rope, unable to tear her eyes away as the reverend's voice permeated her senses. It was quiet at first but grew in volume until it rang out, loud and clear, "Love never fails! Love NEVER fails!"

Chapter 2

"Ca-die!" Tessie's voice echoed through the trees as Cadie raced away from the Gospel Church, past a row of dilapidated wooden shacks with sunken front porches and dry, overgrown lawns. A mangy dog sniffed through an overturned garbage can, and an old, scrawny rooster strutted across the dirt path that lead to a small, broken-down house where a pair of white eyes peered out of a dirty screened-window. From the outline of two dark pigtails tied up with bright red ribbons, Cadie knew it was Jack Reynolds' five-year-old daughter, Nettie. She flashed the little girl a smile and waved as she and Tessie streaked by, running with all their might.

Cadie reached the creek first and dashed across the rocks, working her way toward the middle of the creek bed. "Cadie, stop!" Tessie called once more, stopping short of the water's edge.

"Come on!" she called back, motioning with her arm.

Tessie shook her head and scowled as Cadie ventured further out. "We're not supposed to get our dresses wet!"

Cadie steadied her foothold and gave a big wave to her sister. She didn't give a hoot about her brown calico dress, since she hated it anyway. It wasn't the least bit fashionable for a girl her age to be seen around town clothed like a common field hand, but Mama said it was practical, and in the Hamilton household, practicality was the order of the day.

The water rushed through Cadie's legs and over her shoes, rising higher as she maneuvered the rocks and mounds of silt and mud protruding from the surface. For an instant, she lost her footing on a slippery stone and fell into the cool, muddy water, which was now chest deep. She laughed to herself, imagining the look of horror on Tessie's face, since they both knew what muddy water could do to calico material. *Oh, well,* she thought. *Maybe Mama'll buy some new cloth and make another set of dresses. Like a pink linen. Or a silky blue.*

A golden eagle screeched as it soared high into the clouds, causing Cadie to suspend all thoughts about her dowdy dress. She shielded her eyes from the glaring sun and watched it glide back and forth overhead until it flapped its long wings and disappeared into a clump of tall pines on the opposite creek bank. It wasn't until the sun went behind a cloud that Cadie noticed she, too, was being watched.

Mrs. Adelaide Stephens sat next to her husband under a shady gazebo and strained her eyes under the brim of a tulle and silk flowered hat that matched her coral chiffon dress to a tee. Cadie's heart froze in her chest as a sneer worked its way into Mrs. Stephens's expression. She leaned toward Mr. Stephens, nudged him in the side, and extended a gloved finger toward Cadie, but he never turned his attentions away from a smattering of well-heeled guests who meandered about the spacious lawn. Instead, he adjusted the brim of his bowler hat and pulled his gold pocket watch from his brocade waistcoat to check the time.

The scent of oleander and wild honeysuckle blew across the water, sending a wet chill over Cadie's drenched body. She hugged her arms to her chest, contemplating her stroke of bad luck. Even though she had been seen, she figured she might as well make the most of being this close to the goings on at Magnolia Hill.

Cadie waded upstream a ways and found a tall clump of river grass growing behind a row of purple oleander bushes where she could hide from view. She closed her eyes and pictured the canopy of magnificent live oaks lining the drive that led to the grand plantation house and its row of tall, white Corinthian columns. Magnolia trees and bright pink and white azalea bushes surrounded the front lawn, emitting a gentle fragrance that made the house warm and inviting, despite its size. Cadie loved the shiny black shutters that framed the front windows and the colorful, hand-crafted stained glass outlining the mahogany front door. Spiraling, boxwood topiaries stood on either side of the entranceway in perfect symmetry, their roots established in ceramic urns imported all the way from someplace far off—like Italy or Greece, maybe. But the most alluring feature of all was the porch that encircled the entire front of the house, with its fresh coat of white paint and matching wooden rockers. Cadie could almost hear them tilting back and forth in the cool breeze—

"Your behavior has become downright embarrassing," Mrs. Stephens hissed at her husband. "If you could see how ridiculous you look, gaping at a girl nearly half your age."

"Don't cause a scene today, dear," he replied coolly. He then rose to his feet and wandered into a crowd of young ladies as an elderly couple approached the gazebo, diverting Mrs. Stephens's attention.

Now that the coast was clear, Cadie quickly made her way up the steep hill towards the apple orchard that covered the entire length of the property. With a squish squash of her shoes, she roamed through the trees, straining her ears to listen to more gossip and observe the comings and goings of the Stephenses and their guests. Her senses delighted in seeing linen-covered tables adorned with sterling silver, crystal stemware, and fine china from England, all accented with magnificent centerpieces of colorful azalea blooms, hydrangeas, and wild roses. Familiar noises wafted from the kitchen and across the grounds like a pleasing smell, tantalizing her with expectation. Today, there was the soft clink of dishes, the gentle cackle of a woman, and the *whoosh* of a linen tablecloth as it spread across a long, serving table, indicating the meal was in the throes of preparation. And the food was always a sight to behold! She couldn't wait to see what emerged from the back of the house, whether it be platters of fried chicken, barbecued pork or braised beef, vegetable and fruit salads, biscuits and piping hot loaves of bread, and tall, frosted cakes adorned with little nosegays of roses and ribbons.

As for the guests, some of them she recognized from trips to town, but the others she saw only at the Stephenses' parties. One of her favorites was a beautiful blonde girl with porcelain skin and rosy pink lips whom Cadie referred to as "Pretty Lady." She flitted about like an exotic bird, gobbling up finger sandwiches and little cheese puffs and sipping from crystal stemware while she smiled at every man at the party, especially Mr. Stephens. A handsome, young gentleman with dark hair and eyes, whom Cadie called "Dashing," always hovered around Pretty Lady, vying for her affections. While he did seem to make progress every now and again, receiving the occasional bat of the eye and lilt of a laugh, Mr. Stephens was always there to whisk her away. Cadie often felt sorry for Dashing and hoped one day he would have the courage to be bolder with Pretty Lady. She imagined Pretty Lady loved him, too, certainly more than she did Mr. Stephens, who was stodgy and old and a married man at that.

Then there was Mrs. Williamson, who was large and round and reminded Cadie of an enormous stuffed sausage. She had a fat, double chin, heaving bosom, and wore a girdle that made a constant swishing sound as she waddled around the grounds. And not only that, she was mean and nasty and was in the habit of cutting people to the quick with her words. Cadie thought it a horrible waste of silk, ribbons, and lace to clothe a fat cow like Mrs. Williamson.

Safely hidden in the trees, Cadie scanned the crowd, thankful Mrs.

Williamson was nowhere to be seen today. Pretty Lady was all the way on the other end of the grounds with Mr. Stephens, but there was no evidence of Dashing. Cadie smiled to herself, imagining him wandering through the apple trees, intent on finding a pretty, young girl hiding there, full of wit and imagination—

Cadie's heart leapt with a warm sensation at the sight of a man in a black bowler kiss the hand of an elegant lady who wore her hair in a traditional updo. Another gentleman took the arm of a lovely girl sporting a short bob under a cloche hat and escorted her to the shade of a live oak, where they nibbled on food and sipped from sparkling tumblers. He said something clever, Cadie wasn't sure what, but it must have been witty and brilliant, because the girl tossed back her head and laughed in a way that sounded just like the tinkling of crystal prisms hanging from a chandelier. *I could laugh like that*, Cadie thought. *And if I had a nice dress and a hat, and my hair was bobbed in such a way . . .*

Cadie's thoughts ran wild as she grabbed a fresh apple from a low-hanging limb and sunk her teeth into its ripened flesh, letting a slurp of juice flow down her chin. Suddenly, the sound of voices resonated nearby, mingling with the hum of the party. She stopped in mid-chew and listened intently, thinking she heard something else, like a murmur, but the intonation was unclear. Then a movement caught her attention just yards away—it was a young man and woman tucked underneath a clump of apple trees.

Norman McLain, wearing plain, brown work trousers and a white shirt, was entwined in the arms of Molly Stephens, who obviously hadn't a care in the world that her silk, floral dress was being soiled by a bed of rotting apples. Cadie looked away, rolling her eyes in disgust. Norman had flirted his way through every girl in town until he made his way here with the Stephenses' only daughter, of all people. And to think, just a month ago, he had declared his undying love for Cadie and Cadie only. *Ha!* She couldn't believe she had almost fallen for his romantic sweet talk.

"Stop that," Molly said as she laced her fingers in Norman's and pushed his wandering hand away. He silenced her mouth with his own, trying once more. "I said stop it. You're messin' up my dress." Molly sat up and smoothed her skirt down, but Norman pulled her to the ground again, kissing her on the neck.

The giggles that followed caused an inward grimace to work its way through Cadie, but she couldn't resist sneaking another look. The sight was repugnant to her, and not because she was jealous. How Molly could stand Norman devouring her like a starving animal was a mystery, especially when there were men like Dashing at the party—Cadie was sure he would never kiss a lady in such a revolting way. She searched her mind, trying to understand it all. Molly Stephens could have her pick of any of the gentlemen here, or in the entire county even, but she lay under the sweaty weight of someone like Norman, soiling such a beautiful dress.

"I've gotta go," Molly said. "Mother's invited a friend of hers from Wilmington—"

"I don't wanna hear about rich, old men lookin' at you—not in that way."

"I can't," Molly said, trying to wiggle free from Norman's embrace.

"I'm not waitin' forever, and I mean it."

"Norman, please. Don't be like that." Molly nuzzled her mouth behind his ear, and in no time, the darkness lifted from his countenance like the sun emerging after a midsummer rain. "You will wait for me, won't you?" she purred. "Promise me you'll wait." But before Norman could answer, Molly gave him a quick peck on the lips and disappeared behind a curtain of leaves.

Cadie waited until the coast was clear before moving toward him, being careful to remain as quiet as possible. He slunk back to the ground and closed his eyes, shoving his hands underneath his head. A slight, upward curve of his lips revealed a lopsided smile that made her blood boil for some reason. She moved closer, tossing a few more apples into her dress pockets until she was close enough to kick him hard if she wanted to. Instead, she tugged on a ripe apple overhead, which sent a flurry of leaves and sticks tumbling down.

Norman sat up and shook the debris from his hair, smiling in that aggravating way of his. "Well, lookee here."

"Look all you want, it won't do you any good," Cadie snipped, continuing to pick more apples.

"Says who?"

"Says me."

He stood up and brushed off the back of his trousers. "I see you're stealin' apples."

"They're ripe. They need to be picked. It's a shame to let 'em rot like this."

Cadie noticed how his eyes devoured her wet dress and the way it clung to her waist and legs. "I'd say that's about right." He grabbed an apple from the tree and chomped down, smacking his lips like an old horse. "But you're not supposed to steal. You're gonna have to pay for that." He swallowed hard and brushed up beside her, breathing deeply. "Mmm. You smell good. Just like old, muddy, creek water."

She shoved him aside, but he grabbed her wrist and held tight. "Let go of me," she said, trying to wiggle free. He pulled her into his arms and ran his fingers through her soaked hair. "I said, let go."

"I knew you were there," he said, his grip tightening. "You like lookin', don't you?"

Anger rose up in her at the way he was making fun, as if he knew her heart and what was buried inside her soul. "At what?" she said.

In one sweeping gaze, he took in her eyes and mouth and said, "At this." His lips gazed hers, and instantly, an electric shock shot through her entire body, burning deep into her vital organs. She jerked away and tossed a few more apples into her dress pocket, acting as though she hadn't a care in the world—but inside, her heart raced and her breath came in shallow bursts that almost made her faint. Something had just happened, something she didn't understand. She had kissed him before, a peck on the cheek and, twice that she could remember, a soft kiss on the mouth, but nothing like this powerful sensation that left her weak in the spine and the backs of the knees. She wondered if this was what Molly experienced just minutes before.

"I know you're jealous—"

"I'm not jealous of you or anything you do, Norman McLain."

"She don't mean nothin', Cadie. It's just that her daddy—you know—this house and everything." He grabbed her hand, but the touch was tender this time. "You know you're the only one for me."

His thumb swirled across her palm, and the electric current shot through her again. She had heard these words so many times, but now they sounded different, and the rough, callused skin that often repelled her seemed different, too. She imagined his fingers belonged to the hand of a high-born Southern gentleman whose caresses were soft and silky smooth from a life of privilege. The fire in her settled into a smoldering flame deep within her belly, threatening to suffocate her with its luring thoughts—she could kiss him again if she wanted to, just the way Molly had done, hidden away in the trees. It would be so easy to close her eyes and imagine he drove a fancy motorcar with loads of servants at his disposal and wore a silk brocade waistcoat with a gold pocket watch tucked in the pocket.—

"You still love me, don't you?" he asked.

Immediately, the temptation disappeared. Cadie forced herself to look at him, long and hard, and she hated what she saw—a rugged, seventeen-year-old boy in a dirty white shirt and trousers ripped at the knee, his shaggy, brown hair due for a cut by at least two weeks, and his face streaked with sweat and grime. No matter how vivid her imagination, he would always be pain ole Norman McLain, son of a mercantile owner. Nothing more.

"You're a fool," she said with a sneer. "Just a nuthin', a nobody, and everybody knows it. Even Molly." Her eyes raked over him in disgust. "How could anybody ever love you?"

His face flushed deep red, and his fists clenched into a ball, which sent Cadie running as fast she could. She tore off toward the creek with him chasing her through the woods and down toward the creek bank until she reached Old Hargett's Bridge. Without hesitation, she crossed the dilapidated, rotting boards, balancing on the creaking wood and swaying pilings like she had done a hundred times before. She knew he would never follow, being the coward he was. Sure enough, he halted at the edge of the bridge and yelled, "You ever speak to me like that again—I'll teach you a lesson, I will! I swear it!"

"What? You gonna whip me?" she yelled back. "You couldn't whip a hog fly with a flat iron!" And with that, she turned and disappeared into the depth of the woods.

Chapter 3

Cadie kicked at a rock as she and Tessie wandered down the long dirt road that led to their farmhouse. It had taken less than an hour for her dress to dry in the hot sun, and now it was stiff and dirty and made a slight crunching sound with every step. Despite Tessie's objections, she had stripped down to her petticoat and draped the soaking dress over a row of low-lying hedges near a small, grassy clearing just a little ways down from Magnolia Hill—right where Jackson's Creek joined up with the Cape Fear. It was one of her favorite spots to watch the boats as they made their journey up and down the river to Wilmington or Southport. Unlike the creek, which was as wide and deep as some rivers and filled with rocks and all sorts of trees and vegetation, the lower Cape Fear River was a vast, muddy body of water surrounded by swampy grassland.

Cadie suppressed a smile as she remembered peering into the distance and waving at a male passenger who leaned over the side rails of a two-storied riverboat gliding past. To her excitement, he had waved back. "One of these days you're gonna see me on that ship, Tessie Hamilton," she had proudly announced. "And headed for somewhere far off. Maybe I'll go all the way to New York City myself, like that man."

"You don't know whether he's going to New York City. Besides, how're you gonna go all the way up there? The idea's about as silly can be."

Cadie had sighed, just like she sighed now, having heard the same objections time and again. She kicked at another stone, dreading the heavy feeling that accompanied thoughts of what the future held. Gazing into the forest that surrounded their farm, she imagined she was looking out onto the Cape Fear. "I've gotta do somethin' with my life," she said, not realizing she had spoken out loud. "I can't just milk cows forever."

"If you keep stealing these apples, you're gonna end up in jail," Tessie said as she hopped over a deep rut in the road. "Either that or Mama's gonna tan your hide, or Daddy for that matter." She grabbed an apple from Cadie's dress pocket and bit off a healthy chunk with a loud snap.

"I'm not afraid of them. I'm not afraid of nobody," Cadie said. "I'm gonna do what I want."

"Well, I know you're not gonna go sneakin' in on that church again," Tessie mumbled through a half-chewed hunk of apple. "He's seen you now."

"No thanks to you and your fidgetin'."

"I wasn't fidgetin'. I just got tired's all. But you're so stubborn. You'd sit there all day if you could, or in that apple orchard. You don't belong in either one of those worlds, Cadie, and the sooner you learn that, the better."

"It's a free country, ain't it? There's no law says I can't go to church on Sundee."

"Then why'd you go sneakin' around, peekin' through windows?" Tessie raised an eyebrow Cadie's way and took another bite out of her apple.

Cadie exhaled deeply and gazed at the moving clouds that peeked through the tops of the trees. "I might just sit on the front pew next time," she said with a drawl. "Might even get saved."

"No, you won't, 'cause you know what Mama and Daddy would do if they found out. You hear what people say about that church, and about *him."*

"That's all a buncha lies."

"Is not," Tessie said. "What about that shoe store owner who went out of business for not sellin' the reverend a pair of shoes? Or that newspaper editor who got sick for writin' that nasty article about him and the Gospel Church?"

"Served that shoe store owner right. The reverend's gotta have shoes, don't he? How's a preacher supposed to preach with no shoes? And as for that editor, well it serves her right, too, for writin' such filth 'bout somethin' and somebody she don't even know nothin' about."

"Cadie! She almost died!"

"And how's that supposed to be the reverend's fault?"

Tessie stared at her with a shocked expression. "You tellin' me you forgot about that time we ate nothin' but oatmeal and beans for supper?"

"Oh, hush!" Cadie wanted to grab Tessie's braid and yank it good, but she restrained herself. No one in Pleasant Oaks had forgotten about those beetles being all over the place, eating up everything in sight. It had been a horrible year for the Hamilton family, with no tobacco and corn to harvest, and had almost cost them their farm. Some families lost everything and eventually packed up and left town. Whether any of it was coincidence or not, no one was quite sure. But because all of it happened shortly after a bunch of men from town went hunting with Daddy and Mama's good bed sheets, the reverend was to blame.

"I don't believe any of it," Cadie said, trying not to think about what she had seen peeking over the reverend's collar. But she couldn't get the image out of her mind. A sick feeling oozed into her belly as she envisioned the white men in Pleasant Oaks, rich and poor alike, stepping aside and tipping their hats to him out of respect. It was true that after "that night," as Cadie liked to call it, everyone had left the Reverend Averill Thomas, Jr.

and his church alone.

"Cadie! Tessie! Where've you two been?" their daddy called from over the old split-railed fence that separated the house from the dirt road. "Those cows are goin' crazy wantin' to be milked!"

"Be right there!" Tessie said, ignoring his angry scowl. He shook his head in his typical Joe Hamilton fashion and adjusted his sweat-stained hat before returning to his work. Cadie shoved Tessie toward the farmhouse, scurrying as fast as she could down the path that led to the kitchen door.

The Hamilton farm was about three hundred acres of flat, coastal land that was just right for raising tobacco, a little corn, and a handful of milking cows. It was a pretty piece of property that had been in the family for many generations and provided them with a living, but not much more. There was a weathered barn near the tobacco shed where the crops were hung to dry, a two story white farm-house under a shady live oak tree, and row after row of tobacco plants.

Cadie never understood why people made such a to-do over tobacco. It tasted nasty, like a strong piece of black licorice, and could turn one's stomach green in the blink of an eye. Years ago, she had made the mistake of sneaking a bit of Daddy's chewing tobacco, and within a matter of seconds, was heaving by the side of the barn. Mama thought it was due to a batch of old potatoes she had cooked for supper, but Tessie knew the truth and never revealed the secret. Mama would've had a fit if she'd known Cadie had tasted "the chaw," as it was fondly called. It wasn't proper for a woman to use tobacco products, perhaps because of the spitting that was required, although Cadie had seen her mama spit into a tin cup while sewing in her bedroom, thinking no one else was looking. When Cadie asked if she was sick, she was told to "hush up" and "get ready for supper." Cadie soon figured out Mama wasn't sick at all, because the spit cup produced itself every night, especially on Sunday evening when she and

Daddy sat on the porch and rocked the night away, each spitting after three or four creaks of the porch boards.

Cadie slunk inside the house with Tessie close behind. She tiptoed through the kitchen, trying her best not to step on that squeaky place near the stove, but sure enough, the old floorboards announced their arrival with a loud, agonizing creak. "Girls?" They halted in their tracks until the sound of footsteps and rustling skirts from the front room sent Cadie clamoring for the staircase. "Where've you two been?" her mama snapped as she breezed into the room.

"Just out by the river," Tessie said.

"The river?" Mama shooed a strand of hair out of her eyes and shoved a needle into a pair of ripped trousers, her latest sewing project. "Child, look at you—" She grabbed Cadie by the arm and pulled her from the bottom step, giving her a cold glare. "What's in your pockets?" Without a word, Cadie hung her head and dumped the pile of fresh apples onto the wooden table. "Don't tell me you've been over there again! How many times've I told you? What am I gonna do with all these?"

Even with her angry countenance and her old-fashioned apron filled with pins and thread and other sewing paraphernalia, Cadie thought her mama was the most beautiful woman around, even prettier than the ladies at Magnolia Hill. The name, Irene Mills Hamilton, was known all over the county, and it wasn't just for her cooking and sewing abilities. Her thick blonde hair, full lips, and creamy complexion made her look years younger than most women her age—as well as the fact that she could still wear the dresses she owned before Tessie was born, so Daddy said.

"I think I can get a nickel a pie from Mr. McLain this time," Cadie said. "A whole nickel."

"And who's gonna cook all these pies?"

"Nobody cooks apple pie better than you, Mama." Cadie cast an innocent, wide-eyed look in her direction, which experience had proven to melt the hardest of hearts, especially her mama's.

"Cadie Inez Hamilton—I don't know what I'm gonna do with you."

Cadie breathed a sigh of relief, realizing she was out of trouble, at least for the time being. With a smile and a quick peck on her mama's cheek, she scurried up the stairs out of harm's way, scooted into her bedroom, and flopped across the patchwork quilt that covered her bed.

Cadie closed her eyes and basked in the afternoon breeze that blew through the open window, following her thoughts back to the man on the riverboat. *When I get to New York, I'll meet a rich and powerful and handsome businessman*, she said, the words tumbling through her mind. *And he'll fall madly in love with me and want to marry me and we'll get married and live in a grand house like the Stephenses and I'll wear fine clothes and we'll have wonderful parties that'll be the talk of the town . . .*

You and your dreams. That familiar voice came from somewhere deep inside, accusing and passing judgment. It was the cold, sharp voice of Tessie and her mama and every single person in Pleasant Oaks who had ever known her. *You know your daddy'd have a fit if you went off and married a Yankee*, she could hear them say. *And anyway, whatcha gonna do with Norman when you go runnin' off?*

"I don't want Norman. I never have," Cadie had answered a thousand times it seemed, but no one ever believed her. "I want someone who'll do something with his life. Someone who wants to see the world."

"Even if he's a Yankee?" Tessie always asked.

"Yep, even so."

"Guess what you want is a real man."

Cadie gazed out the window and watched her daddy busy in the fields, fixing a fence post that had come loose. Her eyes drifted upward toward a moving cloud that vaguely resembled a horse galloping its way into the heavens. *Yes*, she said to herself, sensing a newfound determination ignite within her. *A real man.*

Chapter 4

Robert Morgan hurled himself from a storage car of a train as it neared the station, tumbling and rolling until he came to rest under a prickly holly bush. He had jumped from trains many times before, and every time the landing was different. Once he almost hit an oak tree, another time he landed face down in a shallow pond, but worst of all was the time he disrupted a pack of wild dogs fighting over a dead raccoon. Luckily, his instincts had kicked in, and he was able to defend himself with a fallen tree limb and an exaggerated bear growl that would've made all of his friends at school howl with laughter. But as always, things seemed to work out just fine, like this holly bush. Compared to a pack of wild dogs, prickly leaves in the backside was nothing.

With a loud yelp, he hopped to his feet and picked the briars from his disheveled gray suit which was accented by a dark blue, silk brocade waistcoat. He noticed an old couple standing on the distant platform staring at him as if he were plagued with a horrific disease. "Afternoon, folks," he said, shaking the dirt and leaves from his blond mane and flashing a smile that he knew could light up a dark room for hours on end. But this time, the charm didn't work. They continued to stare, judging his bizarre behavior as unsuitable for one, who by all appearances, was a member of the Southern elite. With a nervous chuckle, he dug into the holly bush, retrieved his fedora, and placed it on his head.

Even though his name was Robert, everyone knew him as "Boy," an unlikely nickname for a young man who looked like he was well into manhood. But it fit, and he liked it. It kept him wild and free and prevented others from expecting too much from him, especially the young ladies. While the opposite gender had a fondness for the name, others thought it silly and made special effort to let him know how foolish it was. But he didn't care. To Robert Morgan, there couldn't be a better thing in the world to be called than *Boy*.

Boy whistled and hummed under his breath as he made his way toward the Cape Fear River, jumping over fallen trees and mud holes and scurrying through tunnels of gnarly thickets. The riverbank was his old stomping ground, one he enjoyed as a child when he had tagged along behind his grandpa, mimicking his every move. Finally, he approached the mouth of Jackson's Creek and slopped his way through the apple orchard until, there on the other side, sat Magnolia Hill Plantation.

He lingered under an apple tree for a long moment, taking in the sights and smells of the house and its stable and kitchen, the azalea gardens, lattice-covered gazebos, and flowering, vine-covered arboretums—not to mention the enormous magnolia trees that flanked either side of the house, giving it its name. All of that, along with the hustle and bustle of activity on the lawn, reminded him of days gone by, of happier times when his mama was alive. The pleasure of the senses filled him with such joy that he couldn't help but make his way toward the party. The fact that he hadn't taken a bath in days and his clothes and shoes were now covered in mud and dirt, and who knows what else, weren't given a second thought. He was home.

"Henry, stop your lollygaggin', you hear? And button your jacket quick 'fore Miz Stephens has 'nother one o' her fits."

Zena rolled her eyes as Ruby, an old Negro servant, emerged from the kitchen, barking orders at Henry, a young Negro man, who steadied a silver tray laden with delectable finger foods that would rival anything a French chef could conjure. Ruby waved her hand over the tray, shooing a fly off a pair of apple tarts. "I declare, everybody gonna be gittin' dysentery and the typhoid—" She stopped in midsentence, turning her attention to Zena, who quickly resumed pouring cups of lemon-sweet ice tea from the punch bowl. "Girl, you gonna put ice in those glasses 'fore that tea starts to stewin' in this heat?"

"Ruby, you best not start anything, now," her mama scolded, cutting her eyes over to Zena. She grabbed the tray from Henry and set it on a long, buffet table covered in white, Irish linen. "We don't wanna upset Miz Stephens."

"She's already mad as can be 'bout you bein' late 'cause of church, and that chicken not havin' time to fry up like she likes," Ruby said. "Says it ain't crispy 'nough and too salty to boot. Humph! White folks don't know nuthin' 'bout taste and seasonin'. Just sugar, sugar, sweet's all." Ruby rubbed her hip and adjusted her ill-fitting uniform. "Ought not be servin' on a Sundee anyway, an old woman like me. Oughta be home, prayin' . . ."

Zena bit her lip, trying not to giggle. They had all heard this same tirade from Ruby one too many times, and it was their common practice to ignore it like a bad itch that couldn't be "got to" as Mama often said. And besides, she and her mama had already gotten a good scolding from Mrs. Stephens about not having the food ready in time for the guests, particularly Mr. Lloyd Wallace, who was rich as could be and had come all the way from Wilmington to court Miss Molly. "You were late," Mrs. Stephens had said, scowling over Mamma's pot of sausage and spinach dumplings. "I don't know why you had to go to that church today, of all days, when you know how important this party is."

"It's Sundee, ma'am," Mama had explained, like she always did.

"The Good Lord doesn't mind skipping a Sunday every now and again. He knows Sundays are always the best days for a party."

"Yes, ma'am," was the answer her mama had given, because it was the only answer expected and the only answer that would be received. Zena thought about Mrs. Stephens's complaints about church, feeling a sense of pity for her employer. No matter how much time and preparation went into these garden parties, she was never satisfied. It was always, "Ruby, I thought you polished this silver. It's all dark along the edges, this won't do. And Zena, how many times must I tell you not to dribble water on the linens? Look at these spots. Henry, don't just stand there, go tend to our guests!"

Zena poured another glass of tea, pondering the reverend's sermon and how it applied to a woman like Mrs. Adelaide Stephens. But then suddenly, a sound made her pause—it was a familiar whistle coming from the trees. Squinting her eyes, she looked across the lawn and recognized Boy's confident, lanky stride coming their way. "Look, Mama," she said, smiling from ear to ear. "It's Mr. Robert!"

"Lord 've mercy," Ruby muttered under her breath. "The nerve of that boy, traipsin' 'cross the yard, lookin' like that. Actin' like white trash's all," she said, giving her head a good shake. "Like white trash."

A pang of shame washed over Zena, forcing her to look away. Ruby was right. Zena didn't know how he had the gall to show up like this on a Sunday when he knew a party would be in full swing. Why, he acted like he had every right in the world to be here in all his grit and grime. Hadn't he been told time and again?

"Leave him be," Mama said. "I'll tend to him." A hard scowl worked its way across her face. "I've a good mind to turn him over my knee."

Her words hung in the air like a dangling tree limb ready to fall to the ground, but Zena knew she didn't mean a word of it. Boy was like one of her own, because of her love for his mother, Miss Mabel, who had been Mr. Stephen's only sister and the apple of Old Mr. Stephens's eye. Zena remembered her as the sweetest and prettiest Southern lady one could ever meet, with a heart that matched all the finery she displayed on the outside.

"Mattie." Boy tipped his hat to her mama and then gave Zena a quick wink. "Ladies."

"Hey there, Mr. Robert," Zena beamed, knowing he preferred to be called Boy. "You come home for good this time?"

"Maybe. We'll just have to see." He smiled and said, "Thought you'd be in church on a fine Sundee like today—not throwin' me another one of your fancy parties."

"We already come and gone," Ruby replied with a snort. "It's you who oughta be goin' to church—"

Mama stepped in front of Ruby and glared at him, pointing her finger in his face. "You get on outta sight 'fore I take a strap to you. You hear?"

These words would have scared the daylights out of Zena, but not Boy. Judging from his expression, the notion of a strap coming down on him didn't scare him at all. "Now, you know that's just an idle threat," he said with a twinkle in his eye and a smile that had increased to twice its size.

"Idle, my foot. It wouldn't hurt you one bit to get a whoopin' after what I been hearin' from Mr. Stephens—how you been up to no good at that school of yours."

"Don't be listenin' to him. You know he's full of lies. I've been just as good as I've ever been."

He reached his hand out for a miniature biscuit, but she slapped it away. "I'll bring you somethin' later. Now, go on—git." He laughed and plopped a big fat kiss on her cheek, a common habit of his. She shoved him aside and cast her eyes to the ground, knowing full well there were guests with mouths hanging wide open at a white boy kissing a middle-aged Negro woman.

Before Mama could say another word, he popped a biscuit into his mouth and grinned. She gave him a scolding look, but he ignored it and ambled off toward the barn, more than likely to see his old black gelding, Holiday. Zena giggled at seeing him tip his hat toward a group of white ladies and bow with a cocky swagger.

"Mattie, is that that Robert Morgan, Greer's nephew?" Mrs. Williamson's sharp voice made Zena's heart race and her palms grow sweaty as that horrible swishing sound worked its way toward them. Zena pretended not to listen while she dumped the remainder of the sliced lemons into the punch bowl.

"Yes, ma'am," Mama replied.

"Well, I've never seen anything so vile and dirty in all my born days—walking and talking like a common field hand. I don't know why Greer puts up with such nonsense."

"He's a good boy, down deep. Just hasn't had time to grow up and mature's all."

"I'm afraid time is no longer the issue," Mrs. Williamson said, casting a curious glance in his direction. "It appears to me the damage has already been done." Zena knew what Mrs. Williamson meant, and Mama did, too, judging by the hard set in her jaw. "Well, it's no surprise, given that father of his," Mrs. Williamson continued. "It's downright criminal when you see a good, Southern boy with Yankee blood flowing through his veins. That Mabel should've known better. I tried to tell her not to marry that sorry man, but she wouldn't listen. Some things around here are meant to be, and stay the way they are. It always works out better that way, don't you agree?"

"I wouldn't know, ma'am."

"No, you wouldn't!" Mrs. Williamson hissed under her breath. Her expression became a cold look that brought a chill into the air. "It about turns my stomach at the way he treats you, like you were his own mama. I don't know why you people can't learn your place and keep it! You hear me?"

Zena stopped her work and watched Mama turn and meet Mrs. Williamson's steely gaze head on while these words thickened the air with their full strength of meaning. This wasn't a question where an answer was expected, but something far different, something dangerous that frightened Zena.

After a few blinks of the eye, Mrs. Williamson looked away as though nothing out of the ordinary had transpired. But the words were still there, forming an invisible line that none of them were to cross. "Well, I guess it couldn't be helped this time," she said with a sigh. "He lost his mama so young, and you've been the only one to raise him after that daddy of his died. It's a shame he never had a proper lady around to set him straight. A real tragedy . . ."

Mama nodded her head as Mrs. Williamson continued with her insults, but the tight clench of her jaw told a different story. It pained Zena to see her mama in this predicament, and after a while, she had to turn away and pretend not to listen. But the words kept coming in full force. Zena closed her eyes and said a quick prayer, asking and hoping that the Lord would help them make it through this ordeal the way the reverend would have them do.

Boy hid behind a live oak, watching his aunt Adelaide drag Molly down the front porch steps toward a group of guests sitting under a cluster of trees. Boy noticed how his aunt discreetly fluffed the back of Molly's skirt and brushed it clean with her hand like she was dusting a table top. It was obvious Molly had been dolled up for someone special. She wore a pale yellow, silk dress which brought out the green in her eyes and the golden strands intermingled in her brown, bobbed hair. Diamond studs with pearl drops glistened at each ear, and nestled against her throat was a thick stand of matching pearls.

"Ah, Miss Molly!" Lloyd Wallace rose from his seat at a beautifully appointed table, like a spider perched in an elegant web of fine linen and silver. One look at his oily hair and trimmed, black mustache made Boy's stomach lurch. How could his aunt think Molly could ever love a man like this? Sure he may be rich and from a prominent Wilmington family, but his face and neck were as bloated as a blowfish, and when he smiled, his lips curled over his teeth and hid beneath his moustache like a rodent digging for cover.

Boy turned away, repulsed by it all. He surveyed the spacious lawn and set his attentions on a table where his uncle Greer puffed on a cigar among a group of hand-selected guests. A young lady, who Boy recognized as Darlene Bradshaw from Southport, laughed at something Uncle Greer said and tipped her head back to flash a set of pearly teeth perfectly lined up under a bough of rosy lips. She was younger than the other girls he had seen his uncle seduce at these parties, and prettier, too. Boy couldn't help but smirk at how she propped her elbow on the edge of the table and leaned in a little too close, batting her eyelashes over a pair of deep blue eyes and an ample cleavage. He smiled to himself and adjusted his hat over his brow. *Guess I oughta pay my respects.*

The boisterous laughter reduced to an uncomfortable silence as Boy approached. "Hello, Uncle," he said. Without waiting for a response, he grabbed a chicken leg off a porcelain platter and sunk his teeth in deep, ripping a hunk of meat off the bone. He chomped down like an untamed animal, ignoring the shocked stares of puffed up gentlemen in ascots and suits and attractive ladies who wanted to sneak a peek from under their hat brims, but did not dare. Finally, his eyes locked with Darlene's. "Mmm," he said, licking the grease off his lips.

"I have guests," Uncle Greer said, blowing a stream of smoke into Boy's face.

"I can see that." He winked at Darlene and then ripped into the chicken again, smacking hard as he chewed. "A little young for you, don't you think?"

Uncle Greer slowly rose to his feet and glared with that familiar hatred etched on his face. Boy's eye wandered over him, noting the slight change in his appearance, despite his typical attire of dark wool suit, brocade waistcoat, blue silk tie, and old-fashioned bowler. Perhaps it was the shortened watch fob that hung against his midsection, which looked more rotund than he remembered. But then there was the pronounced puffiness to the eyes and the dark circles underneath, as well as the inflamed cartilage on the nose—probably from too many dips in the moonshine. As Boy's eyes drifted further down, he saw what was out of place—his uncle's right hand wasn't gloved as usual, revealing the scars on the back of the palm that looked like mangled plaster.

A queasy feeling swirled through Boy's stomach, causing him to look away. "Folks," he said with a nod, tossing the stripped chicken bone onto an empty plate Then tipping his hat, he moseyed his way toward the kitchen.

Boy counted to himself, waiting for that familiar voice to invade his ear. Sure enough, by the time he got to "five," Uncle Greer was hot on his heels. "How dare you show your shameless face in my presence looking and smelling like that!"

With a casual lift of his arm, Boy took in a whiff that filled the air with a musty odor. "I guess I could use a bath. Tell Mattie to run my water."

"You are a disgrace!"

Boy made his way toward the kitchen door just as Henry came bounding out with plates of coconut cake drizzled in chocolate sauce. "And tell her to make it hot."

The scowl on his uncle's face made Henry stop in midstride. All the help knew "that look" from Mr. Stephens meant one thing—to skedaddle and fast, and keep your mouth shut in the process. In no time at all, the lively kitchen became as still as death.

"Oh, and tell her to fix up my old room this time," Boy said, clomping up the steps. "I may be stayin' awhile."

"You are not stepping one foot into this house until you give me a good explanation. School's been out for a week now. You were supposed to be on that train two days ago. Why weren't you on that train?"

"I had a little business to conduct."

"What, whorehouses? Gambling halls? You call that business?"

"Whadda you call it?" Boy said, allowing his gaze to drift over to where Darlene sat. "Little dinners, soirees, tea parties on the lawn?"

"You watch your mouth. I won't have you sullying this family's good name with your antics, you hear?"

"You don't need my help in that department, Uncle."

Uncle Greer's eyes darted to and fro, checking to make sure there were no guests to overhear. "Get back here when I'm talking to you," he said, having slipped into his cowardly drawl. "I won't have this, I won't. I'll call the sheriff. I'll have you kicked out."

Boy slung the screen door wide open, feeling his skin prickle at the victory he was about to claim. "Would that be *before* or *after* I show him the deed to the property?"

Uncle Greer stared hard with those pitch-black eyes which warned Boy he had gone too far. "I've had enough, you hear?" he said, his voice rising to a low growl. "Magnolia Hill belongs to me and my family, the

Stephenses. Now, you name your price and let's get this thing over and done with."

"I ain't sellin'," Boy said.

"You holding out for more, is that it?"

"I told you, I don't want your stinkin' money."

"You sure could have fooled me the way you go through it like it grows on trees. I'm not gonna keep this charade up forever, paying for your schooling and who knows what else—"

"Just till I get myself set up," Boy said. "That was our arrangement, and I expect you to honor it. I've got my own plans for this place."

"That's just talk, plain and simple. You'd never be able to keep it up. I know, 'cause you've never worked a day in your life. Even the school master wrote, said you haven't been to class in weeks." Boy winced at this bit of truth, but he wasn't about to give his uncle the upper hand. "You're just a no good, rotten thief, trying to take what doesn't belong to you. Just like that father of yours."

The darkness grew in Uncle Greer's expression, sending a shiver up Boy's spine. For a moment, he was nine-years-old again, experiencing that familiar oppressiveness bearing down, threatening to suffocate him until every bit of life was gone. "You think you've got some hold over me?" Uncle Greer said. Beads of sweat covered his creased brow as he faced Boy again, toe to toe, almost nose to nose. "Well, I'll tell you, I will break you."

"The way you broke her?" Boy allowed the anger to rise up from a deep, long-forgotten place in his heart. "This was my mama's house, and you took it from her. That's why I ain't sellin'. I ain't ever sellin'."

"I never did such a thing, and you know it—"

But Boy wasn't listening anymore. "I'm gonna be needin' some cash. I think you owe me some rent money."

Uncle Greer's jaw flexed and popped like he was softening a piece of stiff rawhide. "After all I've done for you—why, if your mama could see you now, it'd break her heart, it would. It'd kill her." The screen door banged shut as Boy stormed through the hot kitchen, ignoring the final words that resonated off the backs of the copper pots. "You good-for-nothing, lazy, stupid—BOY!"

CHAPTER 5

Zena stood at the back counter of McLain's Mercantile while her mama placed their order with the owner and proprietor, Anson McLain. She enjoyed these trips to town every Monday morning, mainly because they got to wear their pretty clothes and second-hand coats fished from Mrs. Stephens's and Molly's reject pile. But there was one thing she didn't like about it at all, and that was having to wait for white folks to finish their shopping first. Sometimes she and her mama had to stand by the back counter for more than an hour when all they needed was one thing, like a couple of onions or a little package of salt. They had waited a good twenty minutes already this morning, but fortunately, the coast was now clear of white customers and Mr. McLain was free to serve them.

"And then, let's see," Mama read from a piece of folded paper that had been wadded up in her purse. "Miz Stephens, she says she needs a pound of butter, a quart of milk, some brown sugar, and a dozen eggs, too."

"Butter, milk, brown sugar, and a dozen eggs, comin' up."

While Mr. McLain moved around behind the counter, Zena's attention wandered over to Mr. Norman who worked at the front of the store, arranging tin cans on the store shelves. Suddenly, he dropped a handful of the metal containers and stormed outside. "What've I told you about hangin' around here like this?"

"I—I just wanna talk to Mr. McLain," came a shaky response that Zena recognized as coming from Jack Reynolds.

Zena peered through the window and caught a glimpse of a red ribbon, along with a curly, black pigtail of a little Negro girl. Immediately, she closed her eyes and said a quick prayer, hoping Mr. Norman wouldn't be so mean this time. She hated to see Nettie witness the evils of the world at such a young age.

"Mr. McLain don't wanna talk to you," Mr. Norman said, his voice echoing for all of Pleasant Oaks to hear.

"I heard he might be needin' some help—"

"He don't need your kinda help. Now, get on outta here, not unless you wanna buy somethin'! Now, git!" Mr. Norman yelled, pointing to the street. "And don't you come back!"

Boy paused outside the barber shop and watched Norman stomp back into the mercantile and slam the door. He gritted his teeth and flexed his right fist as the memory of their first encounter zipped through his mind—a fishing shack-turned-night club located on the outskirts of town. Even though that had been well over a year ago, Boy remembered it like it was yesterday.

Boy lowered his fedora on his brow and approached the mercantile. He smiled at Nettie, wincing at the tears rolling down her little cheeks. "Hey there, Mr. Morgan." Jack hung his head and stared at his worn, scruffy shoes while Nettie buried her head in his shoulder.

"Don't you listen to him, you hear?" Boy reached into his pocket and pulled out a wad of money.

"No, sir, I can't," Jack said with a shake of his head.

"Just take it."

"You know I can't pay you back."

"You don't need to pay me back." Boy folded the money and tried to wedge it in Jack's clamped fist, but he refused to budge. "Tell you what, I've got an old horse at the house—you remember Holiday? He needs lookin' after while I'm here. How's that sound?"

"But Mr. Stephens—he says he don't want me comin' 'round no more."

"Never you mind what he says." Boy squeezed Jack's shoulder and gave it a shake, trying to jostle the truth down deep. "Things are gonna be different one day, I promise you that." After a moment, Jack looked him in the eye and returned his smile. Boy slipped the money into his hand and then tipped his hat at Nettie, playfully pulling one of her pigtails. "I'll be seein' you, now."

Taking two steps at a time, Boy stomped up the mercantile steps and slammed through the front door, sending a good portion of Norman's stacked cans toppling into a clang of rolling metal. "Mr. Morgan, good mornin'!" Mr. McLain shot a look of warning at Norman's red face. "We'll get that all cleaned up—you back from school, I reckon?"

"Yes, sir, I am," Boy replied, glaring at Norman.

"Well, that's just fine," Mr. McLain said cheerfully. "I know your uncle's mighty proud of ya."

Boy locked eyes with Mattie, and her glower suddenly made Norman McLain and his shenanigans a remote concern. There was no doubt she was still hopping mad at his behavior at the garden party, and he could see she had her mind set on making him pay. Her punishment was sometimes subtle but brutal all the same. There were times she'd wake him up at the crack of dawn, knowing how much he liked to sleep, or speak sternly all day, threatening him with that invisible strap that never materialized in all the days he'd known her. But the worst was when she withheld her famous cooking and made him eat day old biscuits that hadn't been flavored with much of anything, knowing how he loved her fresh biscuits smothered in sausage gravy. His stomach growled at the very thought of one of her home cooked dinners.

"Can I help you with somethin' today?" Mr. McLain asked.

"Naw. You go on and finish up with the ladies. I'm just lookin' 'round." Boy winked at Zena and then nodded toward Mattie, tipping his fedora. "Mornin'."

The instant his hat left his head, Mattie fired off a look that hit him like a bullet from a revolver. "Tell him Mr. Stephens says we're not supposed to talk to him no more—"

"It's not that we don't wanna talk to ya," Zena said.

"Hush!" Mattie glared at Zena, who cowered under a row of thick eyelashes. Then squaring her shoulders, Mattie looked straight at Mr. McLain. "Maybe if he'd stop behavin' like a heathen every time he came home and acted more like a gentleman—the way I know he was raised—then maybe we could talk to him directly. You can tell him that for us."

Mr. McLain stared back at her, wearing a blank expression, and then looked at Boy. "Guess I'll just take a pack of chewin' gum," Boy said.

"That'll be a penny."

Boy took the gum and shoved his hand in one trouser pocket and then the other, but they both came out empty. "Put it on my uncle's account."

"Sure enough. Will there be anything else?"

"No, that'll do." Boy stepped toward Mattie, coming so close he could see the little pearl earrings in her earlobes, a gift from his mama many Christmases ago. He whistled a soft tune like a lilting butterfly, trying to get her attention, but she just readjusted her stance and stared straight ahead. He moved closer until he was all but breathing on her, but she held firm, never once returning his stare. This went on for what seemed like the longest time, and then suddenly, something happened—her look wavered, her eyelids fluttered, and then her eyes met his.

"You look a sight," she hissed. "Skin and bones's all. Git on home, now, and I'll fix you somethin' to eat." Boy grinned and let out a whoop as he lifted her off her feet and spun her around. "Put me down! I'm too old for that."

"You'll never be too old to me, Mama Mattie."

Zena giggled, and Boy gave her another quick wink.

"Go on, now," Mattie said, her emotions thickening in her throat, "'fore I give you that whippin'."

Boy's heart swelled with joy at hearing this familiar threat. He tipped his hat to Mr. McLain, who acted as though he hadn't heard or seen a thing, and then scooted out the door, mustering all of his will power not to knock over the remainder of Norman's pile of stacked cans in the process.

Cadie and Tessie made their way across Jackson's Creek, both with a fresh apple pie in each hand carefully wrapped in a clean tea towel. "Do we have to go this way?" Tessie asked as Cadie maneuvered the swirling water that tumbled across the exposed rocks and mounds of mud.

"Come on, it's quicker." Cadie took another step on a slippery stone, balancing the pies like a tightrope walker.

"Oh, I don't know about this," Tessie said, following behind. "These pies are gettin' heavy and my arms're already tuckered out."

"Don't you dare drop 'em, Tessie. I figure if Mr. McLain'll give us a dime for each and a sack of flour, we can give the flour to Mama and then split the rest—a dime for you and three for me. That's a whole forty cents."

"I don't think so! What about a nickel a pie? You'd be lucky to get that, and if anything, it should be me gettin' the three dimes and you the one."

"But I picked the darn things."

"And I helped Mama make 'em. So we should split it fifty-fifty."

"Oh, hush, Tessie."

"I won't. Besides, you're not the boss of me . . ."

They fought all the way to town until anger got the better of Cadie. "Well, I need the money more than you!" she blurted out.

"Says who?"

"Ohh—" A jealous rage flared up in Cadie's belly when she considered all the future plans set before her sister, including an upcoming scholarship to college. "You always get everything!" She almost gave in to the urge to slam one of those precious pies in Tessie's smug face, but instead, turned and marched toward Third Street with her arms outstretched and her head held high. As soon as she rounded the corner toward Main, a giant force came out of nowhere and knocked her flat on her backside, leaving her sprawled on the walkway covered with golden pie goop. The shock of the impact left her dazed for a moment, so that all she could see was a lock of matted hair hanging in her face and the bright, hazel eyes of a handsome, young man.

"You all right?" he asked as he grabbed his hat and slung a chunk of pie crust from his hands.

"Yeah."

"You oughta watch where you're goin'."

"You're the one who ran into me."

"Goodness gracious!" Tessie said, appearing with her pies in hand. She stared down at Cadie and gave her a scolding look. "Just look at you! Aren't you gonna get up off the street?"

"No," Cadie huffed.

Tessie turned to the young man and addressed him in a polite manner. "I'm Tessie Hamilton, and this is my sister, Cadie."

"Robert Morgan," he said. "But people call me Boy." He tipped his hat and licked a chunk of pie off the side of his mouth, smacking his lips. "That's mighty fine tastin', if I do say so."

Cadie stared at him and chuckled in a mocking tone. "Your name's Boy?"

"Cadie—" Tessie fired off a disapproving look, but the damage had been done, judging by the look on his face.

"Yes, ma'am," he said nervously, no longer smiling. "It's a nickname. Kinda unusual, I know. But you can call me Robert if you want. Robert'll do just fine."

Cadie surveyed Boy with a scornful eye, thinking she recognized him from somewhere. He couldn't be any older than eighteen, she figured, with a lanky build and a mop of hair that hung over his eyes like the mane of a horse set out to pasture for too long. She decided she didn't like what she saw, not one bit. Yet, when he swiped his hair back with his hand and tucked it behind his ear, there was something about him that was appealing. Maybe it was his eyes. Or maybe his smile.

She stood to her feet, noticing how his Adam's apple rose and fell in a hard swallow while his gaze flickered over her. "Well, Boy," she said, taking a pie from Tessie, "I think you're gonna owe us some money, here."

"Cadie!" Tessie turned to Boy and said, "Please ignore her."

"We were expectin' a whole dollar and a sack of flour—"

"A dollar?" Tessie squealed.

Cadie glared at Tessie, warning her to play along. "Yes, a dollar for four pies, and now we've only got two." She held the pie up in the air in a haughty pose, waiting for him to respond.

Boy adjusted his hat and scratched his chin for a moment. "Tell you what—I'll pay you, under one condition."

"And what's that?" Cadie asked.

"The two of you gotta have supper with me some time."

"Oh, that would be fine," Tessie said, her face beaming. "Wouldn't it, Cadie?"

Cadie's eyes narrowed as she studied him closer. "Why would we wanna have supper with the likes of you?"

The rumble of a motorcar drowned out her last words, turning their attention to a gleaming Duisenberg with white-walled tires that rolled to a stop. Mr. Stephens propped his elbow on the window opening and leered from behind the wheel with a smoldering cigar protruding from the side of his mouth. "What're you up to now, Boy?"

"Oh, just gettin' acquainted with these nice young ladies here," he said. "This is Tessie—"

Tessie nodded politely. "Mornin'."

"And Cadie Hamilton."

Cadie couldn't help but gawk at the Duisenberg and its beautiful, shiny exterior. She had seen it around town and on the neighboring dirt roads leading to and from Magnolia Hill, but never up this close. How sleek and lovely it was, and how clean and refined! What wouldn't she do to climb into the passenger seat and ride, with the wind flowing through her hair and the smell of wildflowers wafting into her face . . .

A puff of cigar smoke swirled in her direction, turning Cadie's focus toward the driver. Mr. Stephens's eyes fastened onto hers, and she realized he had read her thoughts just as sure as if they were written on paper in bold, dark ink. Shame crept around her heart, accusing her and passing judgment. "I know who they are," he said with a sneer.

Boy glared at Mr. Stephens and then gave Cadie an apologetic nod. "Please excuse this polite gentleman, my uncle Greer."

She stared back at Boy, sensing betrayal at what he had just revealed. Her gaze roamed over his mane of unruly hair and disheveled clothing as she racked her memory. *Yes*, she thought, as the recollection returned. He had been at one of the Stephens' parties a long time ago, maybe a year back. But he sure didn't look at all like this.

"You said you wanted a ride home. Well, get in," Mr. Stephens muttered.

Boy tipped his hat to Tessie. "Miss Hamilton."

"Mr. Morgan."

He tipped his hat to Cadie and then settled it on the top of his head. "Miss Hamilton." Cadie got a good look at his eyes and how they squinted when he smiled.

"Come on!" Mr. Stephens said, tooting the motorcar horn. "I don't have all day."

As soon as Boy hopped in and shut the door, the Duisenberg moved off, kicking up a cloud of dust in its wake. Cadie stood for the longest time and stared at the back window, watching the silhouette of Boy's fedora disappear into a haze. For a minute she thought she saw him turn his head and return her stare. But she couldn't be sure.

Chapter 6

By now, the mercantile was alive with the buzz of activity from a group of finely dressed white ladies, including fat Mrs. Williamson stuffed in one of her full-bodied girdles. A line had already formed at the back counter, and it was all Mr. McLain could do to attend to the white ladies' needs without shouting above the growing noise. Zena stood out of the way, still waiting with her mama for the last item on Mrs. Stephens's grocery list. Fear gripped her heart as Mrs. Williamson maneuvered to the front of the line with a swish, swish and a giant plop of her basket on the counter.

"A person shouldn't have to wait this long," her booming voice declared.

"I'm sorry Mrs. Williamson, ma'am. It just got busy on us all of a sudden," Mr. McLain said in a failed attempt to change her mood.

"Seems to me like you need to get some more help around here."

Zena eyed the clock on the wall and shifted from one foot to the other. They had been there over a half hour already and were way late for getting all of their cooking done before tonight's dinner party at Magnolia Hill. "Mama," she whispered, "Miz Stephens's gonna be wonderin' where we are."

Mama cast her eyes over toward the clock and spoke above the chatter of the other customers. "Mr. McLain, if I can just get those eggs—"

"You're gonna have to wait your turn!" he snapped.

Mama glanced over at Mrs. Williamson in a plea for favor, but Mrs. Williamson wasn't in a merciful frame of mind, as evidenced by the toss of her head and the cut of her eyes. Zena didn't know if it was this rude behavior or her hateful words at the garden party, but a strange look came over her mama's face that Zena didn't like at all. It spoke of frustration, anger, and being downright fed-up. "Miz Stephens's gonna be mighty mad when she don't have those eggs for her party tonight," her mama's voice rang out.

"Mama, don't," Zena pled. But it was too late. Suddenly, the noise level in the room dropped an octave as the ladies stopped their conversations and stared at them.

"She's havin' twenty-five people, real important people from the county government, over at the house," Mama said, "and I don't know how I'm gonna git all those soufflés cooked in time."

There was deadly silence now, a clear indication that no one in the mercantile could believe what their ears were hearing, most of all Zena. Oh, if only she could just dig a hole for herself, right there under the floorboards, and hide away! How could her mama stand there like this, knowing what could happen? Why, every Negro in the county knew even the sweetest, most genteel white lady could transform into something ugly and evil at the snap of the fingers, especially when black folks were the issue. Zena let her eyes travel around the store, seeing the looks on those pallid faces and knowing her worst fear had become a reality.

"When I tell her McLain's ain't sellin' eggs no more, well, she just might have me start doin' all her marketin' over at Whaley's," Mama said, extra loud. "They've got real good eggs over there, real fresh. I know she likes Whaley's 'cause I bought a big buncha collard greens from 'em just the other week, and she said they were the best greens she ever had. Just as tender, not the least bit bitter."

All eyes shifted toward Mr. McLain, wondering what he would say and do. After a long moment, he gave Mrs. Williamson a nod and mumbled, "Excuse me, ma'am," before glaring at Mama. "Come 'round back and I'll get your things."

"Now, wait a minute! I was here first, and I'm in a hurry!" Mrs. Williamson said, reminding Zena of a steaming teapot, spitting and popping and stomping her fat, swollen feet. "These people shouldn't even be in here anyway. What kind of an establishment are you running?" Soon bedlam erupted as the other ladies circled around them like a pack of wolves, pointing their fingers and shaking their heads.

"It'll be just a minute, folks!" Mr. McLain called out over the raging storm. Zena clutched the sleeve of her mama's coat and squeezed tight, hoping and praying to the Lord Jesus that it would all be over soon.

Cadie stood next to Tessie, not caring about her sticky clothes and gooey, matted hair, or what price Mr. McLain might offer for their two good pies—or the fact that Norman tried to make eyes at her over his tower of tin cans. Right now, she couldn't tear her attention away from Mattie and Zena, who remained quiet and still, in perfect control, despite the surrounding sea of angry, white faces. Their courage was something she had never seen in any boy or man she'd ever known, either black or white, all of which made the darkness of their skin take on a newfound luster in her eyes. It was like the rich, polished sheen of an ebony stone found in the river, its smooth texture luring one nearer to reach out and touch.

Zena's gaze latched onto Cadie's, registering a spark of recognition. Cadie felt her cheeks burn at the realization she and Tessie had been seen peeking in on the church service yesterday by more than just Reverend Thomas. The memory of it made Cadie blush even deeper, even though there appeared to be no look of condemnation from Zena. She simply lowered her head and flashed Cadie a timid smile.

"You think this is funny?" Mrs. Williamson said, staring at Zena with a contorted look. "Well, it is not. I don't care who you work for, you will not smirk at me, no you won't! And you wipe it right off your face this minute, you hear? Why, I've got a good mind to take you out back and give you a good hiding, that's what I oughtta do. Your mama, here, won't do it, I can see that, but that won't stop me from taking care of some uppity Nigra ninny that isn't fit to be seen in my presence!"

In a flash, Mattie stepped in front of Zena and snorted in Mrs. Williamson's face like a heaving stallion with miles to gallop before being put up for the night. Cadie could've sworn she grew two inches taller at that very moment. "You say one more word to my Zena, and so help me—"

"Don't you threaten me!" Mrs. Williamson said. "How dare you!"

Cadie watched in horror as the circle of angry white women pulled in closer to their victims, until someone—one of these supposed well-bred ladies raised by the best of families, educated at the finest schools and claiming to be conversant in Scripture and Bible history after years of attending church and Bible study—spit a vile glob of spittle on the side of Mattie's face. Again, the room grew quiet, except for the sound of Zena's gentle sobbing. Mattie didn't flinch or make eye contact with her assailants but simply retrieved an embroidered handkerchief from her coat pocket and wiped her face clean.

Anger welled up from deep inside the pit of Cadie's gut. This wasn't right, this wasn't fair! Zena and her mama shouldn't have to suffer because of Mrs. Williamson and her evil friends! Someone had to do something! Before she could stop herself, Cadie had marched forward, pushed her way through the crowd of ladies, and faced Mrs. Williamson eye to eye. "Leave her alone!" she screamed in a shaky voice. "You big—fat—smelly—COW!"

At that instant, the door to the mercantile swung open, and a powerful, baritone voice filled the room. "*Glory, glory. Glory, glory, glory, glory—*" Mrs. Williamson shut her gaping mouth and everyone else followed suit, including Cadie, whose eyes were fixed on the doorway. Reverend Thomas stood there like the most regal of kings, singing to his heart's content as though he was leading a choir of God's holy angels in song. "I said, *Glory, glory. Glory, glory, glory—Lord!*"

In unison, everyone stepped back a pace and cleared a narrow path for the reverend as he made his way to the back of the store like Moses parting the Red Sea. When he reached the back counter, he smiled and nodded. "Mr. McLain."

Mr. McLain looked around the room, searching for advice from one of the white customers as to how to respond, but no one said a word. "Hello there, Reverend," he answered in a nervous voice. "What can I do for you?"

"Just the newspaper, and a dozen of your freshest eggs."

Mrs. Williamson cast her eyes away and looked at the floor, as did the other customers. Cadie knew exactly what they were thinking—this was that bold, black minister of God, and no one was foolish enough to cross his path.

Mr. McLain grabbed a newspaper from the stack on the counter and, with trembling hands, delivered it to the reverend. "Here's your paper, and—I'll go get those eggs."

Reverend Thomas looked around at the quieted crowd while Mr. McLain rustled around in the back storeroom. "How is everyone today?"

No one was quite sure if the prevailing silence was any indication. For an instant, Cadie caught the reverend's eye and saw that *something* on him she'd seen on Sunday—not the scar around his neck, but that something special only the reverend possessed. It was a sweetness that soothed, a gentleness that calmed, and a power that could strike fear in one's heart.

Cadie felt it go deep into her soul and straight down into her being, causing a shudder to course up and down her spine.

"*Glory, glory,*" the reverend sung once more, his face broadening into an enormous grin. "It sure is a glorious day."

Mr. McLain returned and handed him a parcel. "Here're your eggs."

"You can just give 'em to this sweet lady right here," the reverend said, nodding toward Mattie. "She's been waitin' a mighty long time."

Mattie smiled. "I thank you, Reverend."

"Don't mention it," he said, setting his money on the counter. "Thank you, Mr. McLain." Then turning toward Mattie and Zena, he asked, "May I escort you ladies home?"

"That'll be just fine," Mattie replied, taking his arm.

The reverend tipped his hat to Zena. "Miss Zena." Zena grinned so big, it was as though the entire fiasco with Mrs. Williamson and the other white ladies had never even happened. The reverend lead them to the front of the store with their precious eggs in hand, nodding and smiling as he made his way through the narrow path of stacked sacks of flour, tables of fabric bolts, and Norman's tin cans. "I thank you kind folks for lettin' me jump in line. I'm much obliged. Much obliged."

All was silent as every ear waited for the door to close with a nice, soft—click. Cadie bolted toward the window with Tessie close on her heels and watched the reverend help Mattie and Zena into his shiny, black Model T like a perfect gentleman. He slid into the driver's seat, started the engine, and then looked at Cadie, dead on. They stared at each other for what seemed like the longest time, before he smiled in that glorious way of his and drove away.

Chapter 7

A cool breeze flowed through the open window of Cadie and Tessie's bedroom, fluttering the sheer white curtains like the robe of an angelic host. Cadie stretched up high from a stepstool to reach something hidden behind a row of books on the top shelf of the bookcase, keeping one eye on Tessie who lay on her bed reading. "Don't look," she said, retrieving a small, red coffee canister.

Tessie ignored her and turned another page in her novel. "Five dollars and fifteen cents, plus the extra in your pocket makes it five twenty-five."

"Tessie!"

"Sorry," Tessie said, casting a repentant look from behind her glasses.

"Now I'm gonna have to hide it somewhere else. I'm runnin' out of places." Cadie pulled a coin out of her dress pocket and shoved it into the red canister. They had sold the two pies for ten cents each, just as she predicted, plus an extra-large bag of flour and sugar for Mama. Cadie had the reverend to thank for that. After the incident in the mercantile, Mr. McLain had adopted an unusually generous spirit, which was a gross departure from his normal crotchety demeanor.

Cadie closed the lid of the canister and replaced it behind the books. "Well, don't tell anyone." Tessie twisted her fingers in front of her lips, imitating a button sealing her mouth closed. "Good. And keep it that way." Cadie jumped down from the stool and plopped onto the window seat near the open window. She looked deep into the night and imagined being able to make out the bright lights of Magnolia Hill twinkling across Jackson's Creek. "I bet the Stephenses're havin' a party tonight."

"They have parties every night, it seems."

Cadie sat up straight with her back erect, imitating a lady's demeanor. She held out an imaginary cup and saucer and brought the cup to her lips, pinky extended. "How do I look?"

Tessie peeked from behind her book for a second and then went back to reading. "Ridiculous."

Cadie pooched her lips out a little more and sucked in her cheeks like a stuffy aristocrat. "How 'bout now?"

"You look deformed."

Cadie shrugged her shoulders and stared out the window. A dreamy look came over her as she gazed into the distance. "I wonder what it's like to be in there, wearin' fine clothes and listenin' to music."

"Don't you think of anything else?"

"Nope. There ain't nothin' else—"

"Isn't."

Cadie rolled her eyes at Tessie's insistence on proper grammar. "There isn't anything else, is there?"

Tessie tossed a book toward the end of the bed. "I've got a good book, here, but you won't read it."

"You don't know what I won't do. How do you know I won't read it?"

"Doesn't have any pictures, that's why."

Cadie smacked the book away and gazed out the window again. "I don't wanna waste my time in books anyway. I wanna go out and live my life."

"How're you gonna do that sittin' at a window starin' out into the moonlight?"

"You think you're so smart, Tessie Hamilton, just 'cause you're the one who gets to go off to school."

"It's not my fault I won that scholarship. Anyway—since when did you get a hankerin' to go to college?"

Cadie sighed, knowing Tessie was right. She had never studied a lick, not like Tessie, who couldn't stand to go for one hour without her nose in a book. Tessie was unusually smart and could shame all the boys—and the teacher for that matter—with her knowledge of math, science, literature, you name it. In fact, she was so far ahead in her studies, she planned to graduate early and attend college in January. Each year, the owner of Hancock Textile Mills in Wilmington, Mr. Vance Hancock, gave just enough money from his yearly profits to fund one college scholarship for the graduating class of his hometown, Pleasant Oaks. This year, the recipient was Tessie, who, hands down, was the only contender in her class of ten students. When God was giving out the smarts, He certainly gave Tessie more than her fair share.

Cadie thought about what God had given her. It was all nice, but not spectacular by any stretch of the imagination. She was pretty, she knew that, but not beautiful, and smart enough to get by, but not smart like Tessie. She really had no interest in school and probably wouldn't go back in the fall unless Daddy forced her to.

The distant sound of a riverboat horn sent her thoughts drifting into the night. "Maybe I'll get on one of those ships, after all, and head for somewhere far off."

"Humph!" Tessie snorted, falling back on the bed pillows. "Not that again."

"Why is everything about my life so funny to you, huh?" The thought of Tessie leaving home and abandoning her to a life in Pleasant Oaks sent a jab of pain through Cadie's heart. All of her girlhood friends were either well on their way to being married, like Emmie Jenkins who was madly in love with Curtis Johnson, the jeweler's son, and couldn't be pried away from his presence for one second. Cadie remembered the day Emmie showed off her new diamond ring, going on and on about "Curtis this" and "Curtis that." Cadie couldn't imagine anyone being in love with someone like Curtis Johnson. Then there was Mary Ruth Bedford, who had been Cadie's best friend since she was little, until her daddy was forced to sell everything and move up north to Baltimore with his Yankee relatives. Cadie still missed Mary Ruth terribly, especially at times like these when there was so much to share. She knew Mary Ruth would want to get on one of those riverboats with Cadie and sail to a place far away, even farther than Baltimore.

"Ohh—" Cadie stood to her feet and snapped her sweater off the end of the bedpost, flinging it over her shoulders.

"Where're you goin'?"

"For a walk, if it's any of your business."

Tessie swung her legs off the bed-covers so that her toes dangled above the floor. "Don't get any bright ideas, Cadie. Mama's told you not to go messin' 'round the Stephenses anymore."

"I'll get any bright idea I want."

"Oh, no, you won't."

"Who's gonna stop me?" Cadie stared Tessie down before adding, "You want me to tell Mama how you've been dippin' into her chaw?" Tessie's face drained white before flushing a deep red, indicating her mind was churning up a big, fat lie. "Don't even bother," Cadie scolded, as she climbed on to the window ledge and prepared to scamper down a neighboring live oak tree, "'cause I *know*, and you know that I do."

"You wouldn't dare!"

Cadie flashed a haughty look, indicating she was more than willing to play her ace. "I'm goin' for a walk, and if Mama or Daddy ask, you just tell 'em I went down to the creek." Before Tessie could protest, Cadie disappeared down the oak tree like so many evenings before.

Boy chewed on a blade of grass as he leaned against one of the white Corinthian columns supporting the massive front porch of Magnolia Hill. The noises from inside indicated another party was in full swing, complete with piano music, dancing, and idle chitchat. But for some reason, Boy was in no mood for all of that. He tucked his thumbs into his new brocade waistcoat and stared up at the twinkling stars, lost in thought. He wondered what sort of worlds were sparkling up there, shining down on him from high above. He could see the Big Dipper, the North Star, and so many other bright lights that lit up the sky. Sometimes he wondered why they were up there and he down here. And since he was thinking on the subject, what was his purpose for being down here anyways? Would life be wasted time on earth, grasping for a dream that may or may not come to pass? And once the dream was attained, what then?

"Dinner's 'bout to be served now, Mr. Robert," Mattie called, rustling onto the porch in a freshly pressed uniform.

"I guess you're speakin' to me, then?" he asked, still staring at the stars.

"You don't plan on actin' like a heathen tonight, do you?"

"No, ma'am." He tossed the blade of grass into the night and turned to face her.

"Well then, I guess I am." She gave him the once over and nodded with approval. "You look like a real gentleman in that suit. Nice and clean. If I didn't know better, I'd say you was tryin' to impress some nice, young lady." An eyebrow arched heavenward as she cast a glance toward the window where the guests could be seen gathering around the dining room table.

Boy caught Darlene peeking at him from behind a velvet drape. He returned her smile until Mattie gave him one of her knowing looks, like she had caught him with his hand in the cookie jar. "Don't call me that," he said, resuming his somber mood. "Mister—and Robert."

"You should be prouda your name," Mattie said, adjusting his shirt collar. "You're a man now, and that nickname is no name for a man."

"That was his name, not mine. You and I both know I'm not Grandpa."

"You remind me of him. More and more every day."

Boy saw the truth in her eyes—the knowledge of what he could be and what he *should* be. "Oh, Mattie, what am I doin' here?"

"Whadda you mean? This here's your home."

"No, it's not. Not really." He flopped down on the steps and gazed out onto the lawn. Memories invaded his thoughts, transporting him back to the past. "You remember what this place used to be like?"

"I do. Just like yesterday."

"It's not right, what he's done." Boy pointed into the distance. "Those fields were full of rice, corn, and tobacco, too. And the apple orchard, we'd pick truck loads every spring. Now everything's just left to grow over and rot. Farming's for white trash in their mind. It's all about his lumber mills in Wilmington, and business—"

"And parties."

"Money, that's what it is. I don't know how I'm ever gonna run this place the way it's supposed to be run, the way Grandpa would want it, without a cent to my name. I've gotta find some way to make it all work."

"Don't you fret none." Mattie eased herself down on the steps next to Boy and looked up at the stars and the partially hidden moon sitting in the sky. "The Lord's got it all figured out. Always has, always will."

That same nervous sensation gripped his stomach every time Mattie started talking about God. Boy had heard from her a thousand times how "God had it all figured out" and how "He always made everything work out for good in the end" and how you had to "keep believing in His Word," whatever that meant, since he hadn't a clue what God's Word was. If God would only help him out, just this once.

"You listenin' to me?"

"Yes, ma'am." Boy sensed her irritation, knowing it frustrated Mattie to no end when he struggled with these doubts.

"And don't you forget it."

"I won't."

"Good. He's got everything, the whole world, right in the palm of His hand." She held her palm out to reveal the hard, cracked skin from years of washing, ironing, and cleaning. Boy wanted to believe that there was purpose and order to this life they were living, but her hardened, callused hands were a reminder of the great disparity that existed between them— the evidence that all she believed was a falsehood, an utter lie. He caressed a deep groove in the pale flesh, remembering the soft skin from so many years ago when she helped bathe behind his ears and tuck him in for the night or doctor him with her tea leaf salve after a whipping from his uncle. Now its deep ridges reminded him of an empty, dried out riverbed whose source of moisture and nourishment had all but vanished.

"One of these days, things are gonna be different," Boy said. "You'll see."

"I know," she said with a sigh.

He shuddered at her skepticism. She was patronizing him and didn't believe a word he said, and why should she, since he'd only made that promise a thousand times before. "No, I mean it," Boy said. "I'm gonna make this place right, like what it used to be. Somethin' that'd make Grandpa and Mama proud. And you'll never have to wash or iron or cook another day in your life."

"Now, what am I gonna do with myself if I'm not in the kitchen cookin'?"

"You're gonna be sittin' at that table, right next to me, eatin' what somebody else has cooked up."

Mattie chuckled like in the old days, and normally Boy would have laughed along with her, but not tonight. Tonight, he was deadly serious. "What'm I gonna do with you?" she whispered, her eyes filled with emotion.

"Nuthin'."

She swept a loving gaze over him, letting her fingers run through his hair. "Nuthin's right."

Boy rested his head on the soft flesh of her arm, not caring who might be watching. He listened to the crickets chirp and the creek lap against the shore. "Does Zena know—'bout me ownin' the place?"

"No. No one knows 'cept me. I figure you'll tell her in your own good time."

She was right. All in good time, that's what he had to keep telling himself.

"Mattie!" Aunt Adelaide stomped onto the porch, scowling like an angry cat. "We're ready to serve!"

"Yes, ma'am." She returned Mattie's smile with a look that read "hurry-it-up," before disappearing back inside the house. Boy made a mocking face at her wake, feeling the same intense hatred toward her that he felt toward his uncle Greer. "Now, you ought not be actin' like that," Mattie said in a scolding tone.

"I don't care. You shouldn't let her talk to you that way."

"I just let it go in one ear then right on out the other. Always have, always will." She gave his hand a gentle pat and said, "Well, I guess we better go on in now." She rose to her feet and adjusted her apron and cap. "You comin'?"

"No, ma'am. You go on ahead. I think I'll just sit here."

"You can't just sit on the steps like that. We're fixin' to serve. Everybody's gonna see you through the window, just settin' there like an ole lump on a log!"

"Fine, then." Boy stood up and stretched his legs, gazing toward the apple orchard. A stiff breeze rustled through the leaves and caused the limbs to sway like a ballerina. "Maybe I'll just go for a walk."

Cadie sat up in the branches of an apple tree, trying to steal a glimpse of the party. The lilting echo of a woman's voice and the tinkling of a piano, followed by Mr. Stephens' loud, rumbling laugh, wafted through an open window and across the lawn. But then another sound floated toward her, forcing her to peer through the leaves. It was a whistling coming from a man who strolled through the orchard.

Cadie scurried further up the tree, cringing at the way the leaves rustled against the branches in an unnatural way. She held her breath, trying her best to remain hidden, when all of a sudden, a branch snapped, sending a shower of apples plunking on the man's head and Cadie along with them. The ground slammed against her face and chest, igniting a piercing pain that shot straight to her head and knocked the breath clean out of her.

The slight chill in the air forced Cadie's eyes open, alerting her to the throbbing in her head. She rubbed the top of her skull, half expecting it to be hanging open, but all was intact. She sat upright and grimaced as the sudden movement made the pain more violent.

"You all right?"

"I think so," she said, wincing slightly. She turned to see who was speaking to her and saw a pair of hazel eyes staring back. It was that Boy, looking clean and polished in a set of gentleman's clothes. Cadie studied his face, which was more than handsome, she decided. There was a manly determination in the chin, yet a boyish charm to his features, and his hair—he was breathtaking, after all. How could she have been so wrong about him?

Boy smiled, prompting Cadie to make a run for it. "Wait," he said, grabbing her by the wrist.

Instinct made her pull away, but his grip was firm. He stared into her eyes, and it was as if Dashing himself had come wandering into the muck and mire of the orchard to drag her out into the Stephenses' world. An unusual sensation hit the pit of Cadie's stomach—something very different from what she felt while watching the garden party, and certainly nothing like what she'd experienced with Norman, which was too embarrassing to even recall. It was a tingling, a flush all through her body, like the expectation of a prize too grand to describe. Cadie forced the words off the thickness of her tongue and said, "You hurt?"

Boy rubbed his head and then rolled his eyes and fell back to the ground. She shook his shoulder, trying to rouse him, but his eyes remained closed. A wave of panic broke over her, and she shook him hard. "Wake up—wake up!"

Suddenly, his eyes flew open and he grinned. Cadie stood to her feet, giving him a nasty frown. "You think you're real funny don't you? You nearly scared me to death."

"Why? You afraid of what you might've done to me, or are you afraid of gettin' caught sneakin' around where you don't belong?"

"I'm not sneakin' around."

"Oh, you're not?"

Cadie looked behind her shoulder and whispered, "No."

"Well, you're trespassin', aren't you? Unless your last name happens to be Stephens, and I know for a fact it isn't. Now, ain't that right, Miss Hamilton?"

"Isn't."

"Fine. Now, isn't that right, Miss Hamilton?" he asked, smiling in a way that made him even more appealing. His eyes latched on to hers, sending that tingling sensation back down into the depths of her tummy.

"I just like to take walks by the creek's all," Cadie said, hoping he wouldn't notice the tremor in her voice. "I was just passin' by, just moseyin' on through and thought y'all wouldn't mind if I had myself a taste of an apple. They're just hangin' there, not doin' anybody any good. Thought I might be doin' y'all a favor so the ground won't be so messy—"

"Does one little apple require you to go climbin' all the way up in the trees?" Boy stood up and easily picked two apples, one in each hand. He handed one to her as he bit into his with a solid crunch. "Mmm, just like I remember. Firm, juicy, tart. With just a faint taste of sugar."

Cadie noticed how the reflection of the moon glistened in his pupils, reminding her of a pool of wobbly pond water. He drew closer and gazed into her eyes for what seemed like the longest time until finally, the tips of his fingers gently caressed her cheek. She gasped and stepped back, feeling her face flush with heat, as though it had been burned by a scalding iron. Something had just gripped her heart, like the long tentacles of Mama's wisteria vine that twisted itself around the latticework along the back garden wall, and she couldn't shake it loose. The way he was staring at her, Cadie wished he would stop, that he would look away.

"Shh. It's all right." He reached for her again, but Cadie knew there was only one thing to do. She dropped her apple to the ground and ran like the wind all the way to Old Hargett's Bridge.

Chapter 8

The next few days were strange for Cadie. She couldn't seem to get her head out of the clouds, even though she tried awfully hard to concentrate on her chores and all the things that needed to be done around the farm. But nothing went the way she expected. Her mama had yelled up a storm after a whole griddle of cornbread was ruined, because Cadie didn't "have sense enough" to take it off the stove when the edges started to get the slightest bit brown. By the time Mama finished correcting the sewing mistake Cadie had made to Daddy's overalls, the cornbread was black and smoking, with Cadie "just standin' there, hummin' to herself, like she didn't see or smell a thing," as Tessie relayed. And then to top that off, Cadie left the door to the barn open all night so that Blossom, the favorite cow, wandered off a good two miles down the road and found her way to a neighboring farmer's pasture. Daddy was so mad, he threatened Cadie good with a whipping, but Mama wouldn't hear of it. Cadie was a woman now, and not a little girl, and she "best start actin' like it."

"Whatcha gonna do when you settle down and get your own cow and you leave the door to the barn wide open—the cow wanders off and then there's no milk for the babies, huh?" her mama had asked.

"Whose babies?" Cadie had replied.

"Why, yours and Norman's of course."

"Mama! I ain't never gonna have babies with Norman McLain."

"Don't say ain't. You speak proper, you hear?"

Cadie had taken a deep breath before correcting herself. "I'm never gonna have babies with him. I'd rather die."

"And what's wrong with Norman?"

Cadie had had this same conversation with her mother countless times, and they always ended up with her slamming the door to her bedroom and Mama yelling up the stairs, "You don't know what's good for you, that's what it is! Your daddy and I can't do a thing with you! You need a man like Norman, a good man, someone who'll set you straight, someone to take care of you. Goodness knows, you're gonna need it."

It was after these discussions that Cadie felt as though she had been yanked back down to a state of clear-headedness, followed by the biggest urge in the world to go running back to the apple orchard and see what was waiting for her there. But the thought of seeing Boy again, of having him look at her the way he did, was enough to send her head right back up into the clouds with her heart all aflutter. Sleep offered no reprive, as her dreams became violent and fitful, filled with swirling, ominous visions where Boy, Norman, and even fat Mrs. Williamson were the cast of characters. She'd awaken with a start, her hair and pillow drenched in sweat and her heart racing a mile.

It was only the quiet mornings with her daddy that brought Cadie any peace. She would steal away in the early hours, just as the sun filled the sky with streaks of red, orange, and yellow, all smeared together like an artist's pallet. Sometimes she'd help pull weeds or cover the holes dug up by the chipmunks and squirrels, or on occasion, drive the old tractor. Many times, the hours would fly by, and the two of them wouldn't speak unless it was an order or direction regarding the task at hand. Cadie cherished the stillness with him where she was free from her mama's constant nagging. There was a depth to him that hadn't been tapped, like an undiscovered well of pure, crystal-clear water. They were alike in that respect, even though he didn't know it.

"Daddy?" Cadie asked one morning as she stood by the tobacco shed, watching him hard at work. "You ever had a dream of doin' somethin' different than farmin'?"

"Farmin's all I know," he replied, impaling the earth with the point of his shovel blade.

"I mean, what if you knew somethin' different from farmin'?"

"Like what?"

"I don't know. Anything." The cool air prompted Cadie to pull her shawl around her shoulders and consider how she was going to gather up the nerve to ask a direct question.

He pushed the shovel blade down hard with the toe of his boot and lifted up a clod of dirt. "This kinda talk's what's got your mama all worried. What's got your head all in the clouds, huh?"

"It ain't nothin'," she said, twirling the edge of her shawl with her fingers.

"Don't look like nothin' to me. I wish you'd go on and figure it out, 'cause it's 'bout to drive your mama crazy, and me, too. She's been in a mood ever since you let that cow get away. Ain't nothin' seemed to snap her outta it."

"I'm sorry, Daddy. How many times do I have to say it?"

"Once, like you mean it oughtta do."

He gave her a scolding glare, which made her hang her head in response. She sauntered up close to him and whispered, "Sorry."

"How am I supposed to work with you standin' there like that?"

"Don't know," Cadie said with a shrug of the shoulders. She looked up under the brim of his hat, like when she was little, hoping to gain a little sympathy. "You still wish you'd given me that whippin'?"

His expression melted, making him look years younger. "Well, I sure wanted to at the time." He dropped the shovel and pulled her into the crook of his arm where the familiar scent of sweat, tobacco, and strong, black coffee brought a peace to Cadie's heart. She slid her arms around his middle and squeezed with all her might, hoping the hot, stinging tears wouldn't come and spoil everything. "But it wouldn't 've done no good, I expect. Probably woulda made things worse." He planted a soft peck on the top of her head. "Your mama's right, you're a lady and ladies don't get whippin's, even though they might need it from time to time. And that includes your mama." His eyes twinkled as a grin spread across his face. "Don't tell her I said so."

Cadie giggled like she had been tickled in the armpits. The well was tapped and a secret had been shared, giving her the courage she needed. "Daddy? You ever wanted to go someplace far off, like on one of those boats that go up river?"

"Nope. Can't say as I ever have."

"Haven't you ever wondered where those boats go?"

"Everybody knows they go up to Wilmington."

"But what's beyond Wilmington? That's what I'm wonderin'. What about all those big cities—like Boston, Philadelphia, New York? And all those people who live there?"

"People're the same everywhere you go, Twiddle, and don't be fooled into thinkin' otherwise. They may dress and talk different, eat different food, things like that, but they're the same as you and me. Men have to work and provide for their families, women have to care for their young-uns, same as right here."

"But how do you know 'til you've gone out there and seen for yourself?"

"I just know."

"But—"

"Now, that's enough talk." He gave her a pat on the back and picked up the handle of his shovel. "I've got work to do. And you've got things to do for your mama."

The hardness came back in his look, like water receding from the wet sand along the riverbank. He had dispensed his words of wisdom, and the well was now closed—the world of Joe Hamilton and his family would not extend beyond the borders of their little farm. "But Daddy, I'm tired of listenin' to her go on and on about Norman."

"Don't talk that way about your mama. She's only got your happiness in mind, both you and Tessie. What you need to do is get your head back down to earth. And if you don't, I might just think about that whippin', after all. Lady or no."

But as hard as she tried, Cadie couldn't get her head back down to earth, despite her daddy's warning. She couldn't get away from the memory of Boy's touch and the way he had looked at her that night in the apple orchard.

Today was a Friday, and the Stephenses always had dinner parties on Friday nights. Cadie wandered to the barn to milk Blossom while engaging in a back and forth of *Should I go? Yes, today after chores*, but then came, *No, wait until tomorrow*. The debate continued until the milking was finished. Making doubly sure she closed the door to the barn, Cadie carried the two full buckets into the small milk house where Mama kept an extra ice chest and her butter churn and cheese-making contraptions. As she dumped the last bit of the liquid into the milk barrels, she had a feeling she would see Boy again—tonight. She didn't care if her face was dirty and streaked with sweat and her hair clung to her forehead and temples. She would go back to Magnolia Hill and see what she could see, and that was that.

As soon as Cadie emerged from the milk house, she heard a faint whistling echoing from the direction of the road. She peered from behind the door and saw Boy strolling toward the house. His hands were shoved deep into his pockets, and his straw hat was slung low over his eyes—but not so low as to miss a purple wildflower growing in the field, just ripe for picking.

What on earth? Cadie thought. She pinned herself against the side of the milk house, trying her best to keep her wits about her. She glanced down at the front of her dress and noticed a large swipe of dirt that was too obvious to camouflage with an apron. He couldn't see her looking like this, he just couldn't! She calculated whether she could make it to the kitchen door in time, but the house seemed to be miles away, and Boy was almost to the front porch. Mustering the spark of courage she needed, Cadie sucked in two deep breaths and made a mad dash for it.

Tessie was hunched over the kitchen stove, elbow-deep in flour, with several pie pans sitting out on the butcher block ready for baking. "Don't answer that door!" Cadie yelled as she rumbled up the stairs.

"What?" Tessie called with that edge to her voice Cadie hated.

Cadie hurried into the bedroom and took a quick peek in the mirror. Oh, she was a sight to behold, to use Mama's words! She licked her fingers and scrubbed the dirt off her face, smoothed down her hair, and pinched her cheeks hard for color. "Ohh—" She grimaced at the sound of a loud knock coming from downstairs. Rushing to the window, she looked out and saw the edge of a brown shirt and worn boots standing near the edge of the porch. "I'm not home!" she hollered down to Tessie.

"Too late!" Tessie hollered back.

Cadie wanted to say something unladylike, but she held her tongue—she had to face him, that's all there was to it. Taking a deep breath, she swung the bedroom door open and descended the stairs toward the kitchen.

"You have a visitor," Tessie said, nodding toward Boy.

He toyed with his hat, turning the brim around and around in his hands till wildflower was almost crushed into a shriveled weed. He cleared his throat and said, "Hey." There was heavy silence as Cadie hung her head and kicked an exposed nail in the floorboards with the toe of her shoe.

"I told him Mama and Daddy'd gone into town." Tessie said. "Cadie? You gonna say somethin'?"

Instinctively, she bolted to the kitchen door and disappeared outside. Her heart raced, faster and faster, threatening to explode. This fear was something she had never known—it was far worse that what she had felt in the Gospel Church with the reverend or what she had experienced with Boy the other night in the apple orchard.

Cadie plopped against the split rail fence that ran alongside the corn patch and folded her arms across her chest, trying to still her heart so that she could speak to him without her teeth chattering. Before long, Boy made his way toward her with his hat resting low over his eyes. She had no way of knowing whether he was looking at her or the ground, but as he approached, he pushed the hat back on his head, and she could see he was staring at her, after all. A spark of energy coursed through her insides and lodged into her chest with a pang, forcing her to look away.

"How's your head?" he asked.

The sound of his voice was like heat simmering in her eardrums, but to Cadie's surprise, she was able to answer. "All right. Yours?"

"Oh, I'm all right."

A long pause enveloped them until she forced her head up and said, "I've decided, you don't have to pay me for the pies."

"Guess that means you won't be havin' that supper with me sometime."

"Guess not."

Boy leaned against the fence beside her and looked out on the field. The sleeve of his shirt brushed up against her exposed arm, sending a tingling sensation down to the end of her toes. "Doesn't matter, since I wasn't gonna pay you anyway."

Immediately, the tingling dissipated and the fear dried up as quickly as it had come. In fact, nothing Mama had said over the past several days could have yanked Cadie back down to a solid level of clear-headedness than such a comment coming from him. It was as though an instant cure for a severe case of love-sickness was given, restoring the old Cadie to her former state. She glared at him, hard, feeling her stature increase to its normal fullness. "Whadda you mean you weren't gonna pay me?"

"Well, the way I see it, it was you who bumped into me on the street. And then to top it off, you go and fall out of a tree, right smack dab on top of me. Why were you up in those trees anyway?"

"I already told you. I was passin' by—"

"No, Miss Hamilton," Boy said with a chuckle, "you're gonna have to do a lot better than that."

"Why do you care? It's not your house anyway, is it? I don't guess your last name's Stephens, neither."

"No, it's not."

"So why all the fuss, then? If you're not gonna pay me for the pies, then you must be here for some reason. And you might as well tell me now, 'cause I've got work to do."

"I guess I just wanted to talk to you." His eyes twinkled as he brushed a strand of hair away from her forehead. "Just wanted to see if you're as mean as you pretend to be."

Cadie cocked her head and scrunched up her nose in the nastiest way she knew how, not realizing how ridiculous it made her look. Boy threw his head back and laughed. "What's so funny?" she asked.

"You."

"Me?" Cadie didn't see how any of this was the least bit humorous.

He gazed at her with a look of expectation that brought another wave of the tingling sensation. "I'll take that as a yes."

"To what?"

"To supper—with me. Tonight, at the house."

Excitement rose within her, but she quickly reigned it back in. "I never said I'd have supper with you."

"Well, I thought you might change your mind. Thought my uncle'd like to get more acquainted with the girl who sits in his apple trees and watches his goin's on."

Cadie's eyes widened at the thought of Mr. Stephens learning about her trespassing on his property. "You're not really gonna tell him, are you?"

"Maybe."

"Oh, you wouldn't. You just can't! I'm in enough trouble as it is from Mama and Daddy."

Boy scratched his head, appearing to rack his brain. "All right. I'll keep your secret, under one condition."

"And what would that be?"

He beamed another smile and said, "Be ready. Tonight, six o'clock, and I'll show you."

"What? Supper?"

"Supper."

"At Magnolia Hill?"

"Where else? You wanna see what it looks like inside so badly, now's your chance."

Cadie tried to read his thoughts, but, doggone it, that smile of his kept getting in the way. "How do I know you aren't lyin'?" she asked.

"I never lie about a thing like supper." He tipped his hat and made his way toward the road, strutting away like a puffed-up rooster.

"Wait a minute!" Cadie called to him. "I've gotta ask my daddy first!"

"Ask him. See ya at six."

"Seven!"

Boy turned and bowed, removing his hat like a gentleman. "Six-thirty it is." He walked back down the dirt road, whistling the same tune with his hands shoved into his pockets like he hadn't a care in the world. A huge grin spread across Cadie's face as she watched him disappear into the distance. Then with a loud yelp, she ran like crazy back to the house.

Chapter 9

Noisy laughter echoed around the oak inlaid dining room table as Uncle Greer entertained his guests. Tonight, it was Williford and Eugenia Smith from Southport, Molly, Darlene Bradshaw, Lloyd Wallace from Wilmington, and of course, Cadie. Boy cringed at the sight of his uncle cutting off a slab of butter and slathered it on the roll Zena placed on his Royal Dalton bread plate. "I don't know what we're going to do about these Nigras," he said, licking the oily substance with the flick of his tongue as it oozed into the corner of his mouth. "Everywhere I go, one of them is begging me for a job at the mill. I've got enough of them working for me as it is, and half of them don't even have enough sense to tie their own shoelaces, much less take on a responsible position." He took a healthy bite of hot, glistening bread and mumbled, "Most of them are good-for-nothing, lazy—"

"And dirty," piped in Darlene Bradshaw.

"Well, that's because they're closer to the ape," stated Lloyd, who smoothed his waistcoat over his bulging middle as he combed his moustache over his pale lips.

"Gentlemen, please," Aunt Adelaide said, shifting in her seat and readjusting the linen napkin in her lap.

Boy stared at his soup bowl and kept his mouth shut, appalled that the "ape topic" had been brought up, especially so early in the evening. He knew Aunt Adelaide disliked this kind of talk as much as he did, but not because she disagreed—she just didn't want to risk offending the best cook in the county. Everyone knew Mattie could get a job in any kitchen she pleased, even the fanciest restaurants in Wilmington.

More laughter ensued, which made Boy flush with anger. He felt that familiar sense of shame in sitting at the Stephenses' table, claiming the heritage that embraced this kind of thinking. And yet, he had never once risen to Mattie or Zena's defense nor supported his aunt's desire to squelch such conversations. Mattie understood this was his chosen course, as did Zena, both knowing he hated the word Nigra, which was just a polite way of saying that other word he hated even more. They all knew Boy kept his mouth shut, because he desired peace and harmony, especially with his uncle Greer.

But tonight was different. An irreparable division had been created, and Boy was being taunted to come to the other side where the majority opinion stood, even if it was from the pit of Hell itself. How could he endure such behavior while, at the same time, profess his devotion to Mattie and Zena? The hypocrisy of this fact filled him with sorrow, especially with Cadie sitting beside him, holding him accountable in her quiet reserve. Her frozen stare was proof these comments stung her as much as they did him.

"Whadda you mean by that statement you just made?" Boy asked, glaring at Lloyd.

"Well it's obvious," Lloyd said, as though the question was a failed attempt at a joke. "Their hair, their lips—their noses? Don't look at me that way, Mr. Morgan. You know what I'm talking about, and you know it's true."

"The only thing I know is true is that you're the one who looks like the animal—"

"Williford," Aunt Adelaide interrupted, "Greer was just telling me the other day about that adorable little cottage you and Eugenia are building at Wrightsville Beach." Her pleading look to Uncle Greer was met with stone silence as she smiled at Williford and Eugenia Smith, her speech as smooth as silk. "I hear it's just lovely . . ."

Lloyd leaned on his elbow and addressed Boy, despite Aunt Adelaide's effort to move the conversation along. "And what animal would that be, hmm?" A pasty, manicured hand ran over his dark, greased hair, slicking it back even tighter to his scalp. "How about a wild stallion maybe, with a rich, shiny, black coat?" He brushed a soft kiss over Molly's bare shoulders until she bristled.

"I was thinking more of a gelding," Boy replied without a hitch.

"That's enough, Robert." The sweetness in Aunt Adelaide's voice had disappeared, bringing the conversation to an uncomfortable halt.

"No, I'd like to hear what the boy has to say," Lloyd mocked. His eyes narrowed like a predator moving in for the kill. "A gelding?" He raised his nose as if he had caught wind of a horrible stench. "I think you could ask any man at this table, or woman for that matter, there's no question that my hindquarters are still very much intact."

"Really, Lloyd!" Aunt Adelaide blushed two shades of red as her napkin fluttered to her mouth. "I insist!"

But Boy continued to hold Lloyd's cold stare, carefully weighing his next words. "It's not the hindquarters I'm referrin' to. It's what comes out of the hindquarters. Now, that's what bears a strong resemblance."

Aunt Adelaide coughed and sputtered on a bite of bread, Molly shoved her napkin to her mouth to suppress a giggle, and even Darlene diverted her look to keep from bursting with laughter. Within minutes, the entire table became as silent as the grave, unsure of how to react. Aunt Adelaide made a "do something, say something, now" face to Uncle Greer, but his only response was a long, drawn-out chuckle that seemed to go on forever.

"Well, now," he said, swallowing a bite of food, "you gentlemen may disagree on who looks like what and what looks like whom—but we all have to agree that the Nigra is the one who resembles an animal when he opens his mouth." He chuckled again, making Boy's skin crawl. "I can barely understand a word any of them say."

"The same could be said for you," Boy said. "How many times have I told you, it's not Nigra."

Uncle Greer lowered his water glass to reveal an expression which no longer showed the slightest trace of a smile. "Don't you tell me how to speak."

"Then say it correctly. It's Negro. Knee-grow. And the reason you don't understand them is because you don't listen."

"Why would I want to listen to that nonsense? Mumbling and jabbering and always talking about the Lord and Jesus, always singing. It isn't practical. In fact, it's enough to make me want to up-chuck. Especially what comes out of the mouth of that preacher of theirs, calling himself a reverend—"

"Greer, please don't say anything about the reverend, now," warned Aunt Adelaide.

"Yes, Stephens, listen to the lady of the house, or you might get struck down," Lloyd said, glaring at Boy.

"God's not gonna strike me down for telling the truth," Uncle Greer said. "I've seen and heard him and I know he's no man of God."

Boy raised an eyebrow his way. "And how would you, of all people, know a man of God?" A cold, frosty silence encircled the room once more as Uncle Greer's scarred hand became the focus of attention. He carefully slipped it into his lap and settled his gaze on Cadie.

"Miss Hamilton, you've been very quiet. What do you have to say about all of this?"

"Leave her out of it," Boy said.

"I'm just trying to be cordial to our guest." He looked at Cadie once more and said, "Come on, Miss Hamilton, don't be shy. We all know you must have some thought on the matter."

Every eye was on Cadie as she looked around the table. Boy noticed her gaze lock firmly with Zena's before she returned to the kitchen. "Well, sir, Mr. Stephens," Cadie said softly, "if the reverend isn't a man of God, then I don't know who is."

Uncle Greer's nostrils flared while his eyes roamed over Cadie's red, gingham dress. "Pretty—one of your mama's old tablecloths?"

"Uncle!" Boy roared, while the snickers circulated around them.

"The problem with the knee-grow, is the same problem with poor white trash," Uncle Greer said, ignoring this outburst. "No intelligence. Now, if they had half the brains of decent white folk—"

"That's enough!" Boy said, throwing his napkin on his plate.

"—then maybe they'd learn a little something. But the way I look at it, they're only good for one thing. Serving up food, working the fields. Milking cows. Isn't that right, Miss Hamilton?"

The room was enveloped with a stifling, paralyzing fear that had moved far beyond an uncomfortable silence. Cadie held his uncle's stare, despite the watery film collecting in her eyes. "You're wrong," she said.

"Am I?"

Boy rose from the table. "Cadie, let's go."

"Yes, sir," she said with more confidence than before. "Maybe not about me, but you are about the reverend. What he says isn't nonsense. It's beautiful. He speaks of God's love."

"Don't fool yourself. Those people don't know anything about God's love. They don't know anything about God, except what they've made up."

Boy's chair tumbled to the floor, bouncing on the polished wood as if a grand and mighty statement was about to be made. "STOP this kind of talk while you're in MY house!"

The moment Boy's words left his lips, Zena breezed back in through the swinging doors, loaded down with an armful of hot plates. She stopped dead in her tracks and stared at Boy, almost stumbling on the edge of the Oriental carpet. "Lord 've mercy!" she cried, her eyes as wide as saucers.

"Excuse me!" Aunt Adelaide scolded, snapping her fingers toward the marble-topped sideboard. Zena resumed her composure and set the plates down where directed, barely rescuing a stuffed tomato from sliding onto Lloyd's head. "Let's see here," Aunt Adelaide said, chattering away, "we have a wonderful chicken a l'orange—one of Mattie's specialties with seasoned rice, and you should see the chocolate cake she made, and Zena here iced it—looks like it came straight from a New York bakery. Robert, why don't you sit back down. And Greer, dear, should we pour some more tea? Who wants iced tea?"

Boy sunk into his seat, scraping his chair under the table. "Stephens?" Lloyd asked, breaking the suspense that dominated the room. "What's the meaning of all this?"

Uncle Greer attempted a muddled response about legal title or some such nonsense, but the secret had been unleashed, never to be tucked into obscurity again. Despite Aunt Adelaide making light of the matter and engaging everyone in pleasant small talk, the atmosphere remained stiff and cold for the remainder of the meal. But Boy didn't care in the least. On the contrary, he felt an enormous sense of satisfaction that Uncle Greer's attempts to humble him and make a fool of Cadie had extracted from the Stephens family a most embarrassing price.

The moon cast a soft glow on the glistening river flowing below it. Boy sat next Cadie on the far edge of the plantation grounds, watching the water move past them on its way to a destination downstream. Despite the noises of the surrounding nature, it was nothing compared to the noise raging in his heart and mind.

The laughter of a young woman spilled out onto the lawn, disturbing the quiet moment between them. They could see Darlene walking arm and arm with Williford Smith while his uncle observed from the porch, evidenced by the faint light of a lit cigar. "Come on," Cadie said, grabbing Boy's hand.

They ran through the woods until they reached Old Hargett's Bridge. Like an expert, she maneuvered the rickety contraption, balancing with her arms as the bridge moved and swayed under her weight. Once on the other side, she motioned for Boy to follow. He hesitated and then crossed. After a few precarious moments, he fell onto the soft grass next to her, laughing hard. "You're one crazy girl."

"Thought you said I was mean." She flashed a smile, but it wasn't enough to change his somber mood.

"You gotta real taste of meanness tonight."

"Nobody from this side of Pleasant Oaks has ever been good enough for the likes of Greer Stephens," she said with a tone of sadness in her voice. "It's always been that way, and I guess it'll stay that way, too."

"Well, it's not right, and I sure wish you hadn't seen it. Now you know what goes on behind the money, big house, and fancy clothes. And it isn't pretty."

"I guess it isn't, after all," she said.

They sat in silence for a few moments, listening to the sound of the water rushing downstream. "My grandpa never used to talk to people like that, black or white, no matter where they came from—except for Yankees.

He didn't like them too much. But he was always cordial, a real gentleman." Boy gazed toward the direction of Magnolia Hill. "That was his house. He gave it to Mama when he died. Mattie always said she was his favorite. Uncle Greer, he never got over it. He said wild horses couldn't tear him away from his boyhood home. I think it was more pride than anything. He never loved this place like my mama."

"Where's your mama now?"

"In heaven, I reckon. She and my daddy."

"I'm sorry," Cadie said, her voice sounding sad.

"It's been a long time, now. They've both been gone a long time."

"You must miss 'em somethin' awful."

"I try not to, but every time I look at that house, I think of her." Boy took a deep breath and said, "Sometimes I wonder if things would've been different if she'd have come back here after she got sick, where it's calm and all, with the peacefulness of the river. But my uncle Greer wouldn't hear of it. He didn't want me or my daddy here, which was fine with Daddy, since he hated even breathing the same air as my uncle. They never got along, from day one. To Uncle Greer, Daddy was just a 'two-bit Yankee gold digger trying to get a hold of Mama's money.' If I heard that once, I heard it a thousand times. About tore my mama up the way they'd fight. Truth is, Uncle Greer, he wanted this place all to himself, and he didn't care what it did to her. He tried to get her to sell. Daddy wanted her to wash her hands of it, but she wouldn't listen to reason. She always dreamed she'd come back here someday and make it her home."

Boy gazed far into the night, feeling the fire of anger burn within him. "So I decided, when it came to me, I was gonna be smart. He could live here for a while, but he'd have to pay. That was our agreement—my schoolin' and a little extra each month. Although sometimes I have to come back and collect. It's wrong of me, I know, takin' his filthy money like that, but I guess I need it right now. A lot more than I do that big ole place."

"Why is that wrong?" Cadie asked. "It's your house and he's living there, acting like it's his own. It's about time someone gave him a piece of his own medicine."

"And I plan on doing that one day—when I've made my fortune."

"I'd like to see that," she said, looking into his eyes.

"You will." For a fleeting moment, he pictured her standing on the plantation porch with him, looking out at the fields of corn that seemed to extend for miles on end. He had never pictured another girl with him in that way. Suddenly, a profound realization hit him like a swift bop on the head—after all this time, he had finally found what he had been searching for.

Boy couldn't help himself, but pulled Cadie toward him, claiming what was his. In a brief and flickering moment, they become lost in the depths of each other's eyes, their souls quickly latching together like a powerful magnet. Time seemed to stand still as his mouth found its way to hers in a soft and gentle kiss.

Chapter 10

"Don't you go breakin' that child's heart," Mattie said the next day while serving Boy lunch in the kitchen. The other help had eaten and washed up, but Boy was still working on his third plate of hot clam fritters and fresh cooked turnip greens.

"I'm not gonna do that," he mumbled through a full mouth of food.

Mattie sunk her hand into her hip and scowled as she stirred a pot of vegetable soup, another one of Boy's favorite dishes. "She's not like those other girls you've been known' at school and all. She's tender—"

"I know that. I know what I'm doin'."

"She may be white farm trash—"

"She is not trash, and I'd like you to keep your thoughts to yourself!" Boy stuffed another clam fritter into his mouth and muttered, "You're just as bad as he is."

"Don't you be talkin' to me like that." Mattie yanked the soup ladle out of the pot and pointed it in his face, sloshing diced carrots and celery onto the clean butcher block. Boy knew the notion of being compared to the likes of his uncle would make Mattie's pride puff up like the feathers of a ruffled hen. "You know what I mean," she said. From the corner of his eye, he saw the ladle drop down to her side and reenter the pot. "She don't know nothin' about this way of life."

"What's there to know?" he said, popping another fritter into his mouth. "Silk dresses and hats—eatin' your cookin'? That don't sound too hard to me."

By the time Boy polished off a bowl of the vegetable soup, Mattie was convinced he had the situation with Cadie well under control. But as for his uncle Greer and aunt Adelaide, it was a different issue altogether. He knew they were worried about where this relationship would ultimately lead. For the next several days, he overheard Aunt Adelaide reassure his uncle that the odds of him marrying "that urchin" and taking over the plantation were slim. "It'll take money to do that, and he hasn't a dime to his name, other than the plantation itself," were words Boy heard coming from her time and again. A grunt from his uncle was evidence that he believed she was right—it was only a matter of time before Boy sold, and they would be ready, since their right of first refusal prevented him from selling to anyone else without their permission.

Nevertheless, the possibility that he might bring a girl like Cadie there to live, no matter how remote, was enough to keep a comfortable level of uncertainty alive and well in the house. Boy found it humorous that, while his uncle Greer grumbled and moaned during the day, he slept soundly at night, while Aunt Adelaide was the just the opposite. She was as cool as a cucumber during daylight, but when bedtime came, she was up until the wee hours, slamming doors and pacing the floor, wanting the whole house to know she was in distress. Boy overheard things like, "How could you've let this happen? Why didn't you made sure he sold?" Uncle Greer's loud snort only made her complaints more shrill. "How can you sleep at a time like this? What if that girl does become mistress of house and finds her way in this very bedroom, in this very bed?"

Loud clomps pounded the floor, until one night, Boy overheard a conversation that set the tone for the remainder of the summer. "Well, he just needs to meet someone else," Aunt Adelaide said. "That's all there is to it."

It was no surprise to Boy when Darlene Bradshaw appeared at the Stephenses' dinner table the following evening looking as ravishing as ever and having turned her flirtatious looks in his direction. After all, she was the perfect specimen for Aunt Adelaide's plan. She was the only child of the Bradshaw family of Southport, who owned a house in the city almost as grand and fine as Magnolia Hill, even though they didn't have the wealth of the Stephenses. "A girl like Darlene won't remain single for long. Why, any man in the county would give their eye teeth to be with her," Aunt Adelaide had said to him, her voice dripping with honey. "She'd be an excellent match for any young man."

Boy could almost see the wheels in her mind churn with thoughts of how it made perfect sense for him to sell to his uncle and use the money to establish himself with Darlene and her family's estate—not to mention the added plus of alleviating a distraction from her husband's wandering eye. Darlene was undoubtedly a fine specimen of a lady, and under other circumstances, he might have been tempted to entertain the idea, especially with all of her new silk dresses and hats and elegant new bob. But not when there were girls like Cadie Hamilton around.

As for Cadie, all she could do was sashay about the farmhouse like a queen, practicing on an old blackboard slate how she might sign her new name—*Mrs. Robert Morgan, Mrs. Cadie H. Morgan, Mrs. Cadie Hamilton Morgan*. Some were written in plain print, some in curly cursive, and another in a sloppy, one-of-a-kind signature. The fact that Boy hadn't asked her to marry him didn't dissuade Cadie in the least. Since he had come to call the day after the dinner party and every afternoon since, Cadie felt certain they were destined to be together.

Despite the warnings from her mama to "play it safe" and "be careful with her heart," it was much too late to do anything about that now. Her entire being had been elevated into a state of thick euphoria which was beyond her control. For the first time in her life, she felt truly alive, bursting with a newfound energy that brought a smile to her lips and a rosy glow to her cheeks. And yet, it rendered her inept in completing a simple chore around the farm, leaving her sister with the burden of carrying most of the load. Even though Tessie played the dramatics, threatening to head for college sooner than she was supposed to, nothing changed.

In fact, by the end of two weeks, things had actually worsened. Every moment Cadie couldn't be with Boy was like torturing a wild animal bent on escaping from its cage. As soon as she was free from her chores, she bolted from the farm and rushed into his arms with such affection that both Mama and Daddy had to give her a good scolding. But that made little difference to Cadie, since she would take a whipping before she hid her true feelings for Boy. The looks she gave him and the touches—always a hand caressing the other, even a finger touching behind her skirts, or the tips of their shoes, leather to leather—were a natural reaction when she was with him.

It wasn't long before Cadie took Boy to the special grassy spot where she watched the boats travel up and down the Cape Fear. He, in turn, took her riding on Holiday to remote, out-of-the-way places, like an old, forgotten rope swing hanging from a live oak that could send the rider up and over the creek and back again. A small lean-to built under the tree was just perfect for providing shelter from the blazing sun, rain shower, or the prying eyes of onlookers. It was here she let him kiss her without permission on the hair, neck, and face, not caring if anyone were to peek through the cracks in the wood and get an eyeful.

"You ever heard the Reverend Thomas preach one of his sermons?"

Boy asked one afternoon as she lay in his arms staring up at the clouds through a large split in the roof of the lean-to.

The blood rushed through Cadie's temples as her body stiffened at the memory of the Stephenses' dinner party where she had defended the reverend. Boy had never mentioned the subject until now. "Why're you askin' me about that?"

He adjusted his head on his palm and shrugged his shoulders. "Just wonderin'."

Cadie debated whether she should carry this line of discussion any further. She had shared her deepest secrets and desires with Boy, other than the reverend and the Gospel Church, and of course, Norman. These topics were better left alone for now. Yet, she had to admit, she still had a fleeting thought every now and again of the reverend, even though she hadn't been back to the Gospel Church in ages. Everything she could ever want was wrapped up in her Boy, wasn't it?

She ran her fingers along the top of his brow and down the length of his nose. "Have you heard him preach?"

"Naw," he said, kissing the tip of her finger. "I don't have much use for church. Although, Mattie's always fussin' about me not bein' saved. Says I gotta accept the Lord or I'm gonna burn in Hell. But I guess that'll be all right with me. I may have Yankee blood runnin' through me, but I'm a Southerner at heart. I'm used to things bein' hot," he said, flashing a smile.

"You don't mean that." Cadie wasn't sure she liked his callous disregard for God. "Well, I sure don't plan on burnin' in Hell," she said.

"Guess you better accept the Lord, then."

Cadie looked up at the clouds peeking through the holes in the roof, pondering. "I've often wondered, what does that mean, "accept the Lord?" Is it just walkin' up to the front of the church and fallin' on your knees? How's that gonna do anything?"

"Beats me. I don't usually pay much mind when Mattie starts talkin' about the Lord and Jesus and all that. It's the same ole thing I've always heard. 'God loves me, He died for me,' some such nonsense."

"I sure would like someone to explain it to me, "Cadie said. "But I guess if it was so easy to explain, a lot more people would understand it."

"Guess so," he said, rolling over so he could stare into her eyes. Cadie laughed at the way he tried to dig deep into her soul with the looks he gave. "Whatcha doin' listenin' to the reverend anyway?"

"I never said I listened to the reverend. I just said your uncle was wrong about him."

"I hear Mattie and Zena talk," Boy said, giving her a teasing smile. "Heard 'em say you got caught peekin' in on the service. Just like you peeked in on us from the apple orchard."

"You won't say nothin', will you?" Cadie pleaded, her cheeks flushing red. "I haven't been back since, and I don't plan to."

"Why not? You must've liked what you heard if you climbed all the way up on the roof."

"Well, he's always talkin' about love and all that."

"You don't like hearin' talks on love?" he asked. Cadie shrugged her shoulders and didn't answer. "Wonder why?"

It was moments like these that Cadie found it difficult to return Boy's look, since it demanded so much from her, leaving her weak and vulnerable. "I dunno," she said. "Just 'cause."

"'Cause of this?" His mouth melted on to hers, making her entire body scream with delight.

Strangely, one of the reverend's sermons jolted through her mind. *Love is patient and kind. It isn't proud or rude and doesn't seek its own way of doin' things. It always believes, always hopes, always endures. Love never fails.*

Cadie thought to herself, *This just has to be the love the reverend was talking about, it just has to be!*

As Boy pulled away, Cadie noticed how his eyes swam in a blue she had never seen before. "Cadie—" He rolled onto his back and stared up at the clouds.

"What?" she whispered.

"It's just—you're too beautiful, that's all," he said, the brightness of his eyes settling into a stormy gray. "I can hardly stand it." He stroked the hollow of her neck with a long strand of her hair. "You're the most beautiful girl in the world."

And to Cadie, he was the handsomest boy alive.

Chapter 11

The wind blew through the open windows of the Duisenberg, tousling Boy's hair as he rode to the train depot with his uncle. Summer had come to a close, and it was time for him to return to school. He had dreaded this day's coming, having put it off for as long as possible, but classes at State College were due to start on the following Monday. His heart was in his throat at the thought of telling Cadie good-bye. The winter holiday was a good three and a half months away, but if he was careful with his money, he might be able to make a surprise visit in October.

As they entered Pleasant Oaks, Uncle Greer shifted his gloved hands on the steering wheel and cleared his throat, a signal the silence between them was about to be broken. "We need to talk before you get on that train."

"I think we've said all we need to say," Boy said. "But if you think of somethin' else, I'll be home before Christmas, and you can say it then."

"Don't be smart with me." Uncle Greer pulled into the depot and brought the motorcar to an abrupt stop. "I asked you last night, and I want an answer." Boy ignored him and bolted out of the passenger door, grabbing his trunk from the backseat. "Did you tell her?"

"Tell her what?"

"You know what." His uncle emerged from the driver's side with his pocket watch in one hand and cigar perched between his back teeth. His beady eyes drifted over to the platform to where Cadie waited. "That it's over between you two." Boy gave him a cool look before making his way toward the platform, fighting the urge to slam a fist in his uncle's face. "You gonna make me do it for you?"

Boy stopped dead in his tracks and marched back toward the Duisenberg, staring Uncle Greer down in another one of their standoffs. "If you say or do one thing—"

"That girl's got to be told the truth. You've strung her along for the summer, but now it's time to set her loose. It wouldn't be right otherwise."

"I'll tell her when I'm good and ready," Boy said. "That I love her and I wanna marry her, that she's the only girl for me."

He turned and strutted toward the platform, bounding up the depot steps, two at a time. Cadie flew into his arms, and he wrapped himself around her, lifting her high off her feet so that her mouth could meet his. He lingered there for some time, not caring that his uncle was watching. "I'll be back at the end of term, in time for Christmas," Boy whispered through her hair. "And I already know what I'm gonna get you."

"What?" Cadie asked, giggling with excitement.

"Not tellin'."

"Please, tell me—tell me," she said, pleading like a little girl.

"Well, it's small and round and made of gold, and might just fit around this finger right here," Boy said, caressing her ring finger. "I don't care what anyone says."

"Oh, Robert!" Cadie threw her arms around his neck and breathed into his cheek. "Don't go, please don't go." The tears flowed, causing her words to catch in her throat. She kissed him in a maddening, frantic way as though she was memorizing every detail about his clothes, his hair, and every square inch of his face.

After a half hour of saying good-bye, the conductor called everyone aboard. "I'll write every day," Boy said, seeing the train begin to move. "And I'll be thinking about you every minute of every day." He kissed her one last time and then pried himself from Cadie's grip and jumped on.

"I'll be waitin' for you!" she called.

Boy leaned out of an open window and waved to Cadie, slinging his hat back and forth over his head. She waved back, on tippy toe, with her fingers extended to the heavens. He envisioned her standing on the plantation porch, gazing out at fields of corn that seemed to go on for miles.

Up above, the majestic cry of an eagle sent his thoughts rushing back to just a short time ago when they had sat under a tall pine, watching it soar above Magnolia Hill. His words echoed in his mind, *After this school year's over, I'm gonna get away, make my own fortune. Then I'll come back and make this place right—what it used to be.*

As the train disappeared from Pleasant Oaks, Boy's eye caught the faint silhouette of his uncle fading into the distance. Surprisingly, the usual, oppressive feelings weren't there to haunt him like before. Now, a surge of hope flooded his being, signaling that life was about to change, that he was finally becoming the man his grandpa had been.

"Is it here?" Cadie stood at the post office counter on a Friday morning like she had countless times over the past month, waiting for Mrs. Dwyer, the post-mistress, to sort the mail.

"Hold your horses, young lady." Mrs. Dwyer snorted while rifling through a stack of letters and postcards. "Let's see, do I have a Cadie Hamilton today? Cadie Hamilton, Cadie Hamilton, well, whaddya know?" She squinted through a pair of dirty, wire-rimmed glasses and held up a fat, crumpled envelope addressed in small, neat handwriting. "A letter for a Miss Cadie Hamilton."

"Give it to me." Cadie made a swipe for it, but Mrs. Dwyer pulled it away.

"Eh, eh." She grinned, revealing a set of brown, tobacco-stained teeth. "I didn't hear the magic word."

"Please?" Cadie snatched the letter from her hand and ripped it open, devouring the words written in Boy's distinctive hand.

My dearest Cadie,

I'm not much of a writer, but I find my pen rushing to keep up with the words flowing from my mind and my heart. I don't know if I'll be able to wait until Christmas. Every time I close my eyes, I hear the roar of the river and think of you and our time together there . . .

The day was blustery, and despite the heat, the rustling of falling leaves served as a stark reminder that autumn had come. Cadie spotted Norman standing outside the mercantile, throwing stones at the store sign which creaked and moaned as it swayed back and forth on its rusty hinges—first one, two, and then three stones hit their intended mark. She didn't pay him any mind but kept her head bent while wandering the streets of town, savoring each word of Boy's letter. She finished the second page and had just flipped it over, fumbling with the loose pages, when an enormous gust of wind rushed down the street, blowing everything in its path. Like an invisible hand, it yanked the page from her grasp and sent it tumbling down the street, just outside arm's reach, until it swirled under the heel of Norman's shoe.

He picked it up and read what was written on the crumpled page. "The smell of your hair?" he said with a chuckle.

"Give me that!" she screamed. Cadie tried to snatch it from him, but he was too quick for her.

"The sweet—sweetness of your breath?"

"Norman McLain, you give me that!"

Suddenly, his eye drifted toward something behind her, giving Cadie the opportunity to pluck the letter out of his hand. He didn't flinch or react but stood frozen in his spot, looking like a forlorn man whose thoughts had traveled miles away. She turned around and saw what had captured his attention—a blue Rolls-Royce with Lloyd Wallace at the wheel and Molly Stephens in the passenger seat. Lloyd craned his neck and sneered at Cadie and Norman as though they were aging, diseased animals. As for Molly, she kept her head forward and straight, without so much as a glance.

Norman wandered into the street and watched the Rolls disappear into a haze of dust and fumes. Cadie had heard Molly was planning on marrying Mr. Wallace this fall but hadn't given it a second thought as to how this news would affect Norman. He was angry and bitter, judging by the cloudiness in his eyes and the dark look that worked its way across his brow. She couldn't help but feel a bit of sympathy for him. "Don't worry about it, Norman. You don't wanna girl who'd marry an old man just for his money."

"Ain't that what you're aimin' to do?"

Cadie put her hand on her hip and glared at him. "Robert is not old."

"Well, so it's Robert now, instead of that stupid nickname. What happened, you make a *man* outta him?"

"You are vile and uncouth, Norman McLain. No wonder Molly won't even look at you." Cadie knew those words were a mistake before they left her lips, judging by the contorted look on his face. She stepped back as he picked up a rock, thinking he would hurl it at her. Instead, he heaved it at the mercantile sign until it sung a loud, squeaky song—back and forth, back and forth.

"Stop lookin' at me, and get on outta here!" he yelled. Cadie backed further away, keeping a watchful eye. "Go on!"

"I'm goin'!" She ambled down the street and tried to get back to her letter, but the heat from Norman's glare seemed to bore holes into her back.

"Hey!" he yelled. "And another thing, that Boy of yours is a sissy!"

"Leave me alone!" Cadie yelled back.

"A real sissy!"

She stuck her tongue out at Norman, and as soon as she did, a shadow loomed over her as though the sun had gone behind a cloud. She gave a startled turn, and there was the Reverend Thomas in his black suit and hat, smiling down on her. "Love is patient, love is kind," he said in a gentle voice. "It isn't proud or rude and doesn't try to do things its own way. It isn't easily angered, and it keeps no record of wrong-doin'. Love always believes, always hopes, always endures. Love never fails."

The soft look in the reverend's eyes and the sweetness of his face left Cadie speechless. She had never seen him up this close, except that time at the mercantile, but those circumstances were different. He had appeared larger than life that day, as well as all the other times she had seen him in town and preaching in the Gospel Church. But now, he was just like a normal man, looking and talking directly at her as though she was the only one in the world who mattered. "Hello," she said, through a pair of quivering lips.

"Hello, yourself." When he tipped his hat, Cadie marveled at how handsome he was, with his smooth cap of hair and sparkle to his expression. "You remember what I said, now." His eyes fell on the letter for a moment, and his smile diminished. "You remember." She nodded timidly, pondering the meaning of these words and why he had spoken them to her in that way. He adjusted his hat and continued on down the street with his shoulders thrown back and his head held high. "Mornin'," he said, nodding to Norman as he strolled past the mercantile.

"Who do you think you are, preachin' to white folks like that?" Norman said.

The reverend stopped and turned toward him, sending a premonition through Cadie that something terrible was about to happen. Immediately, She shoved Boy's letter into her dress pocket and crossed over to where the two men stood. "Norman, you leave him alone, you hear?"

He ignored her, as did Reverend Thomas, who seemed to be in his own world. "I know exactly who I am," the reverend said in an eerie voice. "I'm the righteousness of God in Christ Jesus, possessed with all the power and glory and might of the Holy Spirit." He drew closer, and his eyes resembled two dark chasms as they peered into Norman's, without bearing the slightest bit of the softness from before. Cadie decided she would never say anything to give the reverend cause to look at her in that way, like he was seeing with the eyes of the Almighty. After a long pause, the reverend cocked his head at Norman and asked, "The more appropriate question is, who do you think you are?"

Norman's face drained of color as a strange power radiated from the reverend, invading the air like an electric current. *Why couldn't Norman just leave well enough alone?* Cadie thought. Everyone in Pleasant Oaks knew it best not to pick a fight with the reverend.

After a paralyzing silence, the soft, sweet look returned to the reverend's face, and he tipped his hat with a nod. Norman stared at him as he continued down the street, his jaw pulsating wildly. "An ole Nigra man in a preacher's suit is all you are!" he yelled. "You ain't nothin' else but that!"

Reverend Thomas looked back and smiled, giving another nod of the head. "May the Lord bless you."

Like an enraged child, Norman scooped up a handful of rocks and flung them in the reverend's direction. "Norman, stop!" Cadie cried, watching in horror as the rocks went every which way. But miraculously, none of them touched the reverend at all. He didn't even flinch or miss a single step as he continued to parade proudly down the street.

Chapter 12

Dear Robert,

I haven't heard from you in over a week, so I've read your last letter over and over. I'm missing you so terribly. I don't know if I'll be able to wait until Christmas, either. Every time I walk along the creek or the river, I think of you and wonder what you're doing . . .

Cadie lay across her bed with head in hand, scratching away with pen and ink on a sheet of writing paper. Her thoughts drifted away to earlier that afternoon when she had walked along the rocks of Jackson's Creek with her skirt hiked up, being careful not to drench the hem. With a plop of her chin in hand, she was there in her mind, walking along the smooth, wet stones submerged under the bubbling water. In the distance, Magnolia Hill sat back on the creek bank where it met up with the Cape Fear. Cadie recalled shielding her eyes from the glare of the sun and looking closer. There, under the veranda, had been Mr. Stephens, watching her as she moved along. She had given a slight wave, but he hadn't responded, other than to snap his pocket watch closed and carefully sip from his china tea cup.

The reminder of Mr. Stephens's sour expression brought Cadie back from her thoughts. She flopped onto her back and stared up at a crack in the ceiling that ran along the length of the room like a crooked stick found deep in the woods. She just couldn't write anymore. She had said everything she could think of saying and had repeated it a thousand times. What she needed was him, Robert, her Boy, to be there to hold her and whisper in her ear.

Her eyes followed the crack to the red canister hidden away on the top shelf. She had sold so many pies now, she was sure she had at least ten dollars stashed away. A flush of excitement rushed through her as she jumped up from the bed and retrieved the canister, dumping its contents onto the bed quilt. After counting the coins and paper money, she was astonished to realize she held over twelve whole dollars in her hand! That would be more than enough to take the train to Raleigh and see Boy for a quick visit.

Cadie's thoughts drifted away, sending her tumbling down into a dreamy state. In her mind, she saw herself at State College in Raleigh, wearing a beautiful hat and fine pink taffeta gown, with a delicately gloved hand that gently lifted the knocker on an old, weathered door. The door swung open, revealing Boy in a disheveled shirt and cigar hanging out of his mouth, standing in a room that swirled with smoke and the chatter and laughter of school boys playing cards. He grinned, taking in every ounce of her appeal in one full sweep of the eye. "Your uncle says hello," she said in an unfamiliar voice as she handed him a thick, fat envelope.

Cadie jolted awake, her heart racing and her hands and face cold and clammy. An ominous dread consumed her, even though she knew it was ridiculous to be so easily moved because of a dream. She wasn't a superstitious person, but what made these imaginings enter her mind? She could only speculate, which sent her further down the road of worry and depression. She just had to go to Raleigh, she just had to see Boy, to make sure things were still as they should be.

Cadie shoved the money back into the canister, secured the lid, and then flopped back over on to her stomach and picked up her pen. She finished the letter with a curly, cursive signature and a heart dotting the "I" and then placed it in an envelope, which she sealed with a long lick from her tongue. She was sure he would agree to meet her at the train depot. He loved her, and she loved him, too. He would certainly understand three months was much too long for her to wait.

Thankfully, the house was empty, which meant Cadie could scoot off to the post office without any disruption. She slid the letter into her dress pocket and bounded down the stairs, skipping out the door into the bright sun. The crisp, clean air lifted her spirits and brought back the hope and excitement she had known while being with Boy. But by the time she got to the end of the road, the memory of that unfamiliar voice resonated in her ears, *Your uncle says hello.*

Suddenly, Cadie felt sick to her stomach. She shook her head and squeezed her eyes shut, trying to sling the sights and sounds out of her mind, but they wouldn't go. She imagined Boy leaning against the doorframe of his room, smiling that smile she loved so much while smoke and loud voices swirled in the background. She imagined herself there, too, wearing the gloves, the hat, even the taffeta gown, tilting her head and emitting a long, velvety laugh that Cadie instinctively knew did not belong to her. It was the voice of another woman—a voice she recognized from all those garden parties at the Stephenses. It was the laughter of Pretty Lady, whose real name Cadie had come to know as Darlene Bradshaw.

Another two weeks had passed, and still there had been no word from Boy. Cadie came bounding in to the post office as she did every day, slamming the door up against the back wall. "Good gracious, girl!" Mrs. Dwyer said from behind the counter. "You 'bout scared me to death. You ever walk anywhere, huh?"

"No ma'am, I guess not," Cadie replied, carefully closing the door behind her.

"Well, you might wanna consider it." Mrs. Dwyer glared through her smudged eye glasses, which were shoved through a mangled hairnet.

"Yes, ma'am."

Cadie handed Mrs. Dwyer a freshly-written letter and took her normal spot in the corner while she waited for the mail to be organized. In the early days following Boy's departure, Mrs. Dwyer made painstaking efforts to sort the Hs first, but now, Cadie noticed the Hs were the last to be sorted.

The door opened, and Molly breezed in, looking elegant in a powder blue silk dress with matching cloche hat that offset her eyes. "Mrs. Wallace." Mrs. Dwyer beamed. "How's married life treatin' you?"

"Just fine." Molly fondled her double strand of pearls while giving Cadie's worn calico dress and scuffed shoes the once-over. Cadie looked away, fully aware of where Molly's thoughts had gone. Now that she was married to Lloyd Wallace, she obviously believed her stature had been raised from plantation princess to queen of the county, and people like Cadie were nothing more than common subjects. Cadie had caught a glimpse of the extravagant wedding reception at Magnolia Hill just a month ago while tucked away in the apple orchard. If Molly's white silk gown and all the pearls, beading, and lace were any indication of Southern royalty, it was no wonder she considered herself on the level of a monarch. Cadie had never imagined such attention to detail over a wedding, from the floral decorations, food, and the lawn and surrounding grounds. Everything was cleaned, groomed, trimmed and hedged, and as for the guests, everyone who was anyone on the Stephens's side of Jackson's Creek was there, except Darlene, who was suspiciously absent. Even Norman couldn't keep away. Cadie had caught a peek of him near Old Hargett's Bridge, watching from behind the bulrushes. Poor Norman. If he only knew how lucky he was not to be strapped together with such an arrogant person as Molly Stephens Wallace.

Mrs. Dwyer handed Molly her mail from the W pile and then looked at Cadie. "Sorry. There's nothin' today."

"You sure?"

"I checked it twice," she said, glancing at Molly. Cadie noted how Mrs. Dwyer made no effort to hide the pity in her expression.

Cadie shuffled out the door and plopped down on the steps where Tessie was waiting. "Nothin'?" Tessie asked.

Cadie shook her head and gazed at her sister through watery eyes. "It's been almost a month."

"You gonna run off to Raleigh?"

"How'd you know 'bout that?"

Tessie shrugged her shoulders. "I just figured that's what you'd do."

Cadie fought the urge to burst into tears. "I don't know. I don't know what to do. Why hasn't he written?"

"I'm sure there's a good reason."

Molly stepped onto the porch and tipped her head in a haughty manner before making her way toward a row of shops. A surge of revelation seeped through Cadie—Molly knew something, she was sure of it.

"Cadie, don't," Tessie said as Cadie rose to her feet. But she wasn't listening. She marched down the street, right on Molly's heels.

"Where's Robert? Where is he? Turn around and talk to me, you hear?" But Molly simply ignored her and walked on, acting as deaf as can be.

It didn't take Cadie long to muster up the courage to face the Stephenses, head on. The next afternoon she stood outside the massive mahogany door of Magnolia Hill, pressing the doorbell again and again. She wiped her eyes and nose with the back of her sleeve, waiting a moment while the scurrying of footsteps and the rustling of movement from inside grew in intensity. Her eyes floated up the massive Corinthian columns supporting the porch and took in the intricate carvings nestled high above. There, in stark contrast to the pristine white paint, was an enormous, black spider swinging back and forth in the breeze as it hung suspended from a long sticky thread of glistening spider webbing. For a fleeting moment, Cadie had an impulsive desire to knock it loose and squash it with her shoe, but then a surge of sympathy washed over her. She watched it scurry up the thread toward its hiding place as if it had just read her mind.

"It's that urchin . . .," she heard through the front window. The velvet drapery moved slightly as a hand fluttered across the glass pane. "Go tell Mr. Stephens . . .," came the voice again, clearly belonging to Mrs. Stephens. "GO!" she barked in a wild, irritated manner that sent Cadie back into the depths of this ominous doom that had overcome her, like a drowning victim gasping for the last breath of life. The uncertainty of everything clutched at her throat, suffocating her, and she couldn't fight it anymore. She had to end this relentless torture, even if the truth was unbearable.

Cadie waited another moment and knocked on the door. She then pounded with her fists until she was banging with her palms. Thoughts of all the horrific things that could've happened to Boy flooded her mind—tragedy, sickness, death, and the unthinkable. She squeezed her eyes tightly as Darlene's image and voice brushed up against her mind. *Your uncle says hello—*

Cadie banged harder until the latch turned with a click and another loud call echoed behind the door, "Greer?" The door swung open, and Mrs. Stephens glared at Cadie. "What is it?"

Cadie swallowed the sob that was lodged in her throat and sputtered, "Mrs. Stephens—I was just wondering—I just wanted to know—"

"GREER!?" Mrs. Stephens called into the depths of the house, her eyes wide with a mixture of fear and disgust.

Abruptly and unexpectedly, a sob worked its way from deep inside Cadie and exploded out of her mouth. "Where is he, what happened to HIM?" she screamed, as heart-wrenching, breathless spasms convulsed through her body.

Mr. Stephens appeared at the door, securing the final button to his waistcoat. "Miss Hamilton," he said, nudging Mrs. Stephens out of the way. "Get control of yourself." The contempt in his voice was sufficient to slow Cadie's spasms to a point where she could take a normal breath. "I don't know a thing about the boy. Now, if you'll excuse me, I'd like you to leave. And please don't come back again."

The door swung shut, but Cadie stopped it from closing with the heel of her shoe. Her eyes worked their way up to his paunch hidden underneath the brocade waistcoat and then up to his bloated cheeks and red, bulbous nose where the curled lips resided underneath. "But he hasn't written in so long," she sobbed, feeling her lips quiver. "Something must've happened."

"Yes, I'm sure you're right. Something must have." His eyes narrowed like a coiled snake ready to strike. "I'm afraid, Miss Hamilton, you've been—how should I say it—*replaced*."

Cadie stared back at him as an awful ache struck her hard in the stomach. She locked eyes with Mrs. Stephens and, for a brief moment, saw a flicker of this same gut-wrenching pain that seemed to erase the divide between them. But then as quickly as it came, the compassion from Mrs. Stephens' expression dissipated, and the haughty glare returned. Without the slightest bit of emotion, she stepped forward and slammed the door in Cadie's face.

Part II

Chapter 13

A delicious smell of sweet potato mingled with pecan pie wafted into Cadie's bedroom, bringing with it the realities of the world around her. Christmas had come and gone, and all of Pleasant Oaks was bubbling with excitement over the annual New Year's Eve dance—all except the Stephenses and their friends, and of course the Negroes, who weren't allowed to attend—and Cadie, who didn't care one thing about dancing or having fun or anything else exciting the new year might bring. It was all a sickening reminder that Boy had never returned home as promised.

After several months of weekly letters, sometimes three a week, all correspondence had stopped. She never received another word from him and couldn't glean a bit of information regarding his situation, despite her efforts. The Stephenses wouldn't even look at her now, and there was never a mention of him at the plantation. Cadie had spent many days and nights hidden away in the apple orchard, hoping to overhear a conversation, but his name was never spoken. It was as though Robert Morgan had never existed.

Cadie closed her eyes and remembered back to Christmas Eve when she had huddled in the shadows while the last train pulled into the depot. Her heart had lurched when a young man stepped onto the platform, looking tall and lean and very familiar, but it wasn't Boy. She waited while the train hissed and popped for what seemed like hours before the brakes released and it moved down the tracks with a breathless clickity-clack.

Cadie had wrapped her coat around her shoulders to fight off the biting wind and trudged through the deserted town toward home. She remembered walking past the Methodist Church and seeing the Stephens family in their Duisenberg, dressed in fur-trimmed coats and velvet hats. The image of Mr. Stephens sneering at her before he stepped inside to where the congregation had begun singing *Joy to the World* made Cadie sob into her pillow. At that moment, she had come to realize what she had always known deep inside—Boy was not coming home. He would never come for her. She would never see him again, touch him, or kiss him. It had all been a dream from which she had been cruelly awakened.

Voices resonated from the kitchen, including Daddy's laughter and Mama's humming as they cleaned a chicken for roasting and prepared a pot of ham hocks and black-eyed peas for a slow simmer on the stove. There was even a loud cheer from Tessie when it was announced she could wear one of Mama's old silk chiffon dresses to the dance instead of her regular calico. Cadie shut the sounds out of her mind and smashed her cheek further into her pillow, staring at an advertisement for a hair product tacked to the wall. The model sported a flapper bob and whimsical pose that epitomized the happiness, confidence, and freedom that eluded the rest of the world. Cadie imagined her hands in a similar pose with her leg kicked behind her in a carefree manner. *If only I could smile that way—*

"Cadie?" Tessie's footsteps bounded up the stairs and into their bedroom. "You asleep?" she asked.

"Yes."

"You hear what Mama said?"

"Yes, the silk chiffon."

"Isn't it excitin'?" Tessie squealed, peeking over Cadie's shoulder. "Come on, and get up. Mama told you to milk those cows if you wanna go to the dance with us tonight."

Cadie heaved a heavy sigh and mumbled, "Don't feel like dancin'."

"Cadie—it's been weeks now. You're not sick, after all. Doctor Patterson says you're just fine. Says you oughtta get out of bed and do somethin', that's what you oughtta do."

"I am doin' somethin'."

"What?"

"Layin' here, lookin' at this picture."

Tessie gave her shoulder a slight shove until Cadie rolled over to reveal a tear-stained face. "You can't just stay in bed all day. Come on. I'm leavin' for college in a week, and it's New Year's. Let's don't spend it like this. You'll feel lots better, I promise."

"I don't wanna feel better. I like the way I feel just fine."

Tessie shrugged her shoulders. "Suit yourself." She went back to her vanity and fiddled with her hair. "Mama said you can come visit me sometime. I'll introduce you to a nice college boy." Cadie rolled over toward the wall and stared at the advertisement again, listening to Tessie brush her hair with one long stroke after another. "You know, he never really asked you to marry him. Not really."

A salty tear rolled down Cadie's cheek as the truth of these words resonated deep inside her soul. Tessie was right. Boy hadn't made any promises to her, and he never would. He belonged to some other girl by now, some Darlene Bradshaw-type of the Southern elite world, who would make him a suitable wife, just as the Stephenses desired. All Cadie had of him was a memory and a dream and a little stack of letters, nothing more. And the model with the flapper bob was in total agreement.

A five-man fiddle band played in the corner of Trader's Hall, belting out a countrified rendition of *Glory Hallelujah*. Several couples danced a jig with an occasional "ye-haw" and the stomp of a boot on the floorboards as the ladies were slung around the room by their gentleman partners. Others, including a few wallflowers, looked on from chairs while sampling cakes, pies, and other home-cooked goodies. Suddenly, the front door flew open, bringing in another gust of cold air, and with it, one of the most beautiful girls ever seen in Pleasant Oaks. The dancers stopped their jigs, the onlookers suspended their forks in midair, and the wallflowers stared at this gorgeous young woman who accompanied Tessie, Irene, and Joe Hamilton. She looked like one of those ladies who traveled in the Stephenses' circles—delicate and refined in a silk chiffon dress, and flaunting a modern, bobbed hairdo seen only in the fashion magazines.

"Why, Cadie Hamilton!" Eunice Johnson exclaimed as she approached with Rebecca Richards, charter members of the Pleasant Oaks Sewing Club. "Just look at you!"

Cadie held her head up high even though the look in every one of these ladies' eyes was a clear, unmasked picture of shock and contempt. "Your hair—" A pinched look worked its way across Mrs. Johnson's face. "It looks just fine, don't you agree, Rebecca?"

"Oh, yes," Mrs. Richards said in feigned agreement.

"Thank you, I'm glad you like it," Cadie replied in a curt tone. "I would've cut it shorter, but Mama took the scissors away—"

"Cadie, come on, let's get some punch," Tessie interrupted. "I'm so thirsty, I think my throat's parched bone dry." She pulled Cadie toward the punch bowl while Daddy excused himself to talk with a group of men standing in the corner.

"Oh, I don't know what I'm gonna do with that girl," Cadie overheard her mama say while fighting back the tears. "She's just gone and ruined herself, just ruined everything! If I could get my hands on that Morgan boy, I'd give him a piece of my mind, I would. He's the one who's done all this. If it weren't for him—" She pulled a handkerchief from her sleeve and cried into the dainty embroidery.

"Don't you worry about a thing, Irene," Mrs. Johnson said. "It'll grow out in no time, you just watch and see. And she'll forget about that Boy, you mark my words. From what I hear he's no good, full of Yankee blood, and just a disgrace to his entire family."

"She's right," Mrs. Richards said. "And besides, Norman's here—by himself. And I've heard his pa say he likes girls with those newfangled hairdos."

Her mama sniffed hard and dried her cheeks. "You really think so?"

"Why, yes," Mrs. Johnson answered. "You know how Norman is. He likes things different—just like Cadie . . ."

Cadie snapped her head toward the refreshment table, refusing to listen to anymore of what those ole busybodies had to say. She whispered some benign, girlish comment to Tessie that let Mama and everyone else in the whole room know she didn't give a flip what they thought about Norman McLain or her new hair-do. Snickering to herself, Cadie remembered closing her eyes good and tight while she had whacked away at her blonde curls in front of the vanity mirror with four loud, shaky, swipes of the scissor blades. She and Tessie had stared at the long tresses around Cadie's feet as if they were a dismembered arm or leg, not knowing whether to laugh or cry. But when their mama had barged into the bedroom, there was no doubt tears were in order. It wasn't until Tessie had dressed Cadie in the silk chiffon dress and applied a homemade version of lipstick and rouge to her lips and cheeks that the sobbing had stopped.

"Have you seen what our daughter's done?" Cadie visualized Mama glaring at Daddy while thrusting a pointed index finger at her shorn locks.

A heaviness had invaded the room as he stared at her like she was a disfigured replica of his daughter. "Looks like she's gone and cut her hair."

"Joe Hamilton, that's statin' the obvious. I want your honest opinion—whadda you think? And be honest."

"Woman, you insinuatin' I ain't aimin' to tell the truth?"

"Well, are you?"

"I'm not even gonna answer that. You asked for an honest opinion, and I'll give it to you, if you'll just let me take a look." He had surveyed Cadie's appearance again, but this time, there was a distinct sparkle in his eye that let her know he was on her side, despite his opposition to those "heathen" flapper dos. "Well, I'd have to say, honestly, that she looks real pretty. Like that fashion model there in that advertisement." Mama had shaken her head and sobbed even louder as Cadie fell into Daddy's strong arms, comforted by the familiar scent of sweat and tobacco.

That had seemed like ages ago, as if it had happened to some other girl. Just thinking of Daddy's approval lifted the sadness and heartache, making Cadie feel light as a feather every time her hair bobbed against her cheeks with each toss of her head. She didn't care what anyone else thought, she did look like the model in the advertisement, just like Daddy said, from the top of her head to the soles of her feet. She could sense the aura she was spinning in the room, as every eye focused on her face, hair, dress, and figure. It was as though she belonged somewhere other than this dusty ole place with remnants of corn husks and tobacco leaves on the floor and a bunch of farmers and small town merchants gawking at her. Why, if she didn't know better, she could see herself smack dab in the middle of a grand, Southern garden party.

Norman slunk in through the back door, suddenly sending Cadie's spirits plummeting back down into the pit of her stomach. She watched him turn toward the wall, slip a flask from his jacket, and pour a splash of something into a punch cup before it was returned to its place. He took a long gulp, allowing his eyes to roam the room till they met Cadie's. She couldn't help but look away, feeling him devour every inch of her. She could sense him measuring the length of her legs now that the shape was more defined in the silk chiffon dress instead of the old calico he was used to seeing her wear. With a giggle and another girlish whisper in Tessie's ear, she swirled her hands around her face so that he might see the faint outline of the delicate bones underneath the smooth skin. And with her thick, curly locks gone, the nape of her neck exposed the graceful lines flowing down into her shoulders and back.

Just as she expected, the heat from Norman's voice was there on her skin in a matter of seconds, like a scorching wind that somehow sent cold shivers down her spine. "Care to dance?"

She cut him a sly look. "Maybe."

"Go on, Cadie," Tessie said in a sarcastic tone. "He looks a little sad and lonely."

Norman smirked at Tessie and then grabbed Cadie's hand, pulling her onto the dance floor. Even though the band was banging out a fast jig, he swept her into his arms, holding her so close she could practically feel the blood pumping through his veins.

"Don't hold me like that." She struggled to get free, but his grip remained firm. Her cheeks flushed at the hard stares coming in their direction.

"You look real pretty tonight." He shook the hair from his eyes as his gaze swept over her face and neck. As soon as his lopsided grin appeared, she was reminded of Boy, and a pang hit her in the lungs. Norman pulled her closer, and then she smelled it—a strong whiff of moonshine.

"You've been drinkin'."

"A man's gotta have a little somethin' every now and again to help him relax."

"From what I hear, you've been doin' plenty of relaxin'."

"Why don't you stop talkin' and relax yourself."

"Don't tell me what to do."

"Why? It's what you need."

"You don't know what I need."

"I know you need a real man. One who'll take care of you, won't leave you high and dry, like some boy—"

Cadie pushed him away with all the force she had in her. "You are cruel and mean, Norman McLain. Just plain evil, that's what you are."

"Well, I guess that makes us two peas in a pod, then, don't it?" Norman's eyes narrowed into slits, as if he was claiming what belonged to him.

By now, the whole room was staring at them—Tessie and Mama and the entire sewing club—all with their mouths hanging wide open, and Daddy with his angry scowl. Well, she didn't care. *Let 'em look.* If they wanted something to talk about, she'd give it to them.

Cadie pushed past Norman, barreled through the crowd, and slammed through the front door of Trader's Hall with her head held high. She disappeared into the woods, freezing from the cold and not knowing where she was running to or what she was running from. All she knew was that she had to get away, to a place where there was no Pleasant Oaks, no Norman, and no reminders of Boy.

She ran all the way to Old Hargett's Bridge and crossed to the other side, racing all the way to the Gospel Church. She hid in the bushes, shivering from the chill in the air, and waited for the New Year's Eve service to end. She caught a word or two that seeped through the windowpanes, and then before long, the congregation streamed outside to shake Reverend Thomas's hand before heading home. As the last couple exited the church, Cadie heard the roar of the reverend's laughter. Oh, to laugh like that! His voice was rich and deep, like a vat of melted chocolate, just waiting for a finger to scoop down and take a swipe. If only she could talk to him, she was sure he could help her ease this pain within her. Her heart pounded as she fought the fear that seeped through her entire body. She willed herself to call out to him before he got into his car—just once, just one cry—but no sound would come. The fear took hold, and the moment was gone. The headlights came on, the engine started, and the reverend drove off into the night.

The light from the moon guided Cadie past the blackened oak tree and through the forest, where she stumbled over roots and logs near Old Hargett's Bridge. She walked across the wobbly contraption and sat down in the center where the creek flowed below. *Maybe the whole thing'll fall in. Maybe I'll just end this whole thing.* She grabbed hold of the railing and shook it back and forth, making the bridge sway in an agonizing dance, but it held firm, as it had for a hundred years.

Suddenly, a pop and a cracking noise made her turn. The trees rustled a moment and then Norman appeared from out of the darkness, standing in the glow of the moon. "What're you doin' here?" she said.

"Came to talk to you."

"If you've come to apologize, then forget it. It's too late for that."

"I don't see why I need to apologize for tellin' the truth."

A mental picture of her hitting him smack-dab in the middle of his nose came to Cadie's mind, making her glare at him with bright, glistening eyes. "Go away, Norman! Just go away!"

"Come on, now, and get off that bridge. It's freezin' cold and you don't have a coat. And besides, it ain't safe."

"Isn't."

"It isn't safe. Now, come on."

"Don't tell me what to do. You're not my daddy."

His look hardened, and Cadie sensed the blood rise to his cheeks. "You gonna come off that bridge, or am I gonna have to come get you?"

"You won't come out here," she said. "You're too scared."

"I ain't scared. I just ain't stupid, that's all."

"It seems to me you've been stupid about a lot of things lately." Cadie cocked her head in a seductive manner and employed another one of her best impressions of Molly Stephens in the throes of romance. "Wait for me, Norman—promise you'll wait—"

In a flash, he stomped across the rickety bridge, as if it were rock solid and a mile wide, and lifted her into his arms, ignoring her kicks and screams. "Stop it, Cadie! I said, stop!" He carried her to the other side and dumped her onto the ground like a sack of potatoes, pointing his finger in her face. "Now, you hush your mouth and listen to what I've got to say!" She started to protest, but his angry stare made her reconsider. Sweat covered his brow, despite the cold, and his chest heaved with every breath he took. "You think you're the only one upset with the way things've turned out? You think I wanna be stuck workin' in that store all my life? Stuck in this ole town? It was never meant to be—for either of us. Can't you see that? This is where we were born, on *this* side of Pleasant Oaks, and it's where we'll die, you and me both. Might as well accept it."

"I'll never accept that, Norman. Not ever." Cadie looked away from his piercing gaze, shivering more from his words than from the freezing temperature. She wrapped her arms around her legs and rocked back and forth, trying to stay warm.

"Here," Norman said, fumbling with his jacket for a moment. "Put this on." He draped it around her shoulders and sat down next to her, facing the creek that rumbled beyond them. He unscrewed the lid off of his flask and shoved it toward her. "You wanna little somethin' to warm you up?" She hesitated a moment and then took a swig, grimacing as the liquid burned her insides.

"Don't know how you drink this stuff." She took another healthy swig and wiped her mouth with the back of her hand.

"Careful, now. Don't wanna take you home crawlin' on the ground like an ole June bug. Your daddy's spittin' mad at me as it is."

"He never has liked you and for good reason," she said, passing him the flask. He took a long swallow for himself, sealed it up, and then shoved it in his back trouser pocket.

"Guess you could say the feelin's mutual."

The burning sensation subsided and filled Cadie with a warmth that softened her mood. She looked at Norman long and hard and noticed the thick, brown hair hanging over his forehead and the strong, muscular lines of his profile, all of which made him look innocent, almost angelic. She leaned back a little and found herself settling into the crook of his arm. "I probably shouldn't have yelled at you like that," he said, resting his chin on top of her head. "It's just—well, you make me so dadburn mad."

"You know you deserved it."

"Maybe I did," he murmured.

Cadie sighed and looked up at the stars. "What're we gonna do, Norman?"

He gripped the back of her arm and pulled her close to his chest. "We'll make do. Somehow."

"I don't wanna just make do."

"I know." Cadie heard his heart beat with a steady, rhythmic thump, realizing he was deep in thought. She nestled deeper into the folds of his shirt and decided she liked it here. His body was solid and strong, and the clean, soapy smell from his shaving lotion made her feel safe—but from what, she wasn't sure.

A bird called somewhere in the distance, destroying the solitude of the moment. "I always knew she'd never tell her ma and pa 'bout us," Norman said. "But Boy, he seemed different. He was willin' to fight for you."

But not hard enough, she wanted to say. Grief welled up inside of her like a mighty wall of water pushing against the makeshift dam of her new hair-do, dress, and make-up.

"Cadie—" Norman lifted her chin and wiped the streams of hot tears with his thumb. "Don't cry, now." The gentleness of his touch gave way to the familiar electric shock that shot through her entire body, setting it aflame, and this time, she didn't pull away. Her eyes latched hold of his and held firm, like a rope tied tight and taunt.

"I hate you, Norman McLain," she whispered.

"No, you don't." He pulled her toward him and pressed his lips against hers. Her heart raced, and she struggled to breathe, as if she were drowning in a pool of wondrous, glorious delight that paralyzed her body with its power. "You know you're the only one for me."

And with these words, she felt her chest being pried open like a resistant clamshell until the power took over and bathed her with it presence. Her arms lifted into the air and surrounded him, pulling him close as she gave in to what was destined for her.

Chapter 14

"Hush, now, I'm comin'." Cadie made her way through the gloomy morning to where Blossom and their newest addition, Dawn, mooed in unison, waiting to have their udders relieved. Winter was coming to a close and the first signs of spring were just beginning to sprout on the Hamilton farm. Everywhere Cadie looked, there was a smattering of green, especially in the tobacco and corn fields, where the hope of new life was most evident. But in her heart, there was a deadness, accompanied by a sharp feeling of loneliness and despair.

Tessie was off to Women's College, referred to as "WC", in Greensboro, thanks to Mr. Vance Hancock's generous scholarship. This left no one for Cadie to talk to, really, except Daddy, who indulged her at times with a little conversation when her spirits were low. Apart from that, the additional chores she had to complete in Tessie's absence kept her otherwise idle mind occupied with baking, sewing, and milking. It was as if she lived in a constant state of numbness where the mornings began early and the nights ended late in a never-ending cycle. Gone was the desire to sneak in on the Stephenses or the goings on at the Gospel Church. Like a seasoned prisoner content with her confinement, Cadie accepted her life as a Hamilton on her side of Jackson's Creek, just as Norman had done.

As she pulled the heavy barn door open, a wave of nausea washed over her, sending the empty milk buckets into the dirt. She ran to the side and buckled over in pain, her stomach heaving and convulsing in violent turmoil. For the past month and a half, Cadie was unable to get a bite of breakfast past her nose. Like a miserable passenger aboard a storm-tossed boat, it seemed there was nothing she could do to battle this constant morning habit of running to the side of the barn. With each contortion of her body, her secret was one day, one hour, perhaps one minute, from being discovered by her mama's watchful and discerning eye.

Cadie wiped her mouth with the back of her sleeve and then swiped it dry on the back of her old calico dress. She bent down to pick up the buckets and couldn't help but notice the gathering on the waist of her dress no longer laid flat against her stomach. "Please God, no," she whispered. Her throat constricted as the awful truth stared her in the face. She had never been much for prayer, but the past month and a half had looked as good a time as any to start. Every day she begged the Lord to stop this, but here she was at the side of the barn again. Perhaps He hadn't heard her and she needed to pray longer and louder. "Please God, please—," she wailed quietly. What if He never answered her prayer? What then? How could she go on like this?

Thoughts of running away fluttered in her mind, but like a bird trapped in a glass dome, her reasoning kept hitting the reality of unanswered questions. *Where would I go? How would I survive on my own? Who would ever love me if the truth was discovered?* She shook her head, trying to keep the tears at bay, but they rolled like waves down her cheeks and dripped off her chin.

Cadie shuffled into the dark barn and spoke to Blossom as she sat on the milking stool and massaged the cow's swollen teats. The rhythmic squirt of milk into the empty pails dulled her mind long enough to complete the task without erupting into hysterics. She just couldn't have a baby, she just couldn't! She squeezed the teats even harder, trying to chase the panic away, until the cow signaled her displeasure with a "moo" and a swish of her tail.

After tending to Dawn, Cadie disposed of the milk in the milk house and wandered back to the kitchen where her mama was busy preparing breakfast. The aroma of frying bacon and brewing coffee hit Cadie in the gut, sending another wave of nausea rolling through her.

"You're up early again," Mama said, shooing a strand of hair from her brow before wiping her hands on a dishrag. "You want some breakfast?"

"No, ma'am."

"Since when've you ever turned down a strip of my honey-cured bacon?"

Cadie shrugged her shoulders. "I'm not hungry."

"You need to eat, honey." Her mama cupped Cadie's chin in her hand and lifted her face so they could look each other in the eye. "Cadie, you've gotta snap out of this. It's gone on long enough." She ran her fingers through Cadie's curls that had re-grown to the top of her shoulders. "What's Norman gonna think seein' you mope around like this?"

At the mention of Norman's name, Cadie pulled away and stared at the knots in the pine floorboards. Since the night of the New Year's dance, he had given her bolts of fabric, bags of fruit from Wilmington, European chocolates, and had showered her with affectionate words and soft, stolen kisses which sometimes evolved into a shameful, animal aggressiveness—but it wasn't enough. Cadie could not bring her heart to love him.

"I got a letter from Tessie," Mama said. She reached into her apron pocket and pulled out an envelope. "Wanna read it?"

"Naw. Maybe later." Cadie trudged up the stairs, one step at a time, like a tired, old woman, so unlike her usual way of scurrying up and down the staircase in two or three bounds.

"Where're you goin'? We haven't finished talkin' yet. Cadie—," Mama called up the staircase. "You better start actin' right, or I'm gonna have your daddy go fetch the doctor."

Cadie shut the door to her bedroom and stared at herself in the mirror. She was gaunt and pale, and dark rings shaded her blue eyes like one of those war victims she had seen in pictures in some of Tessie's books. Even her hair, which had begun to grow out, was tangled and dull, having lost its natural luster. She turned away from the reflection and flopped down on the bed, staring at the ceiling. There was no reason to look out the window anymore, where the distant thoughts of a large white house perched on the creek bank haunted her. Instead, she let her eyes follow the crooked flow of the crack in the ceiling plaster, all the way to the bookshelf, where the red coffee canister was tucked away.

With a bout of eagerness, she hopped off the bed and retrieved the canister, hugging it to her chest as she drifted off to sleep. In her mind, she floated high above the apple orchard where Boy, Mr. and Mrs. Stephens, and Molly and Lloyd roamed through the trees while a grand garden progressed on the pristine lawn. Cadie peered closer and spotted Mattie and Zena, as well as Tessie and Norman, in the midst of the festivities, all attired in brocade, taffeta, and tulle and eating delectable food served on silver platters.

Like an angel from heaven, Cadie descended into the party and was received with smiles, nods, and words of approval, as if she were the most important guest there. Suddenly, the crowd parted, revealing a tall gentleman in a worsted wool suit and top hat who stood on the edge of the riverbank, facing the expanse of the Cape Fear. Cadie couldn't see his face but felt drawn to him in an inexplicable way, like a moth to a flame. She pushed through the throng of guests with her arms extended and fingers outstretched until she stood within inches of him. A gentle tap to the shoulder made him turn to reveal the handsome, smiling face of Reverend Thomas. Without taking his eyes off her, he snapped his gold pocket watch closed and tucked it into a fold of a magnificent brocade waistcoat, all in one smooth motion. His white teeth gleamed in the sunlight as he tipped his hat and nodded, releasing a bout of his deep, bellowing laughter.

"It's early. About two months would be my guess."

The mumbled discussion between Doctor Patterson and Daddy seeped upstairs, along with Mama's strangled sobs. Cadie turned her face toward the image of the flapper model tacked on the wall and squeezed her eyes closed, trying to clear her mind. As soon as the doctor's motorcar rolled away, she knew the moment had come when she was truly on her own—there was no one to rescue her now. Any minute, Daddy would be in this very room, demanding an explanation from her, and she had none to give. She was no longer his innocent little girl, nor would he ever consider her a lady like her mama. She figured she was sure to get that whipping from him, after all.

Heavy footsteps fell on the stairs, followed by Mama's frantic call, "Joe, don't go up there! Joe—" Cadie rolled over onto her back and stared at the crack in the ceiling, preparing herself for the inevitable. "Joe, stop it!" The door burst open, and Daddy jerked Cadie up by the arm. "Stop it!" Mama screamed, but her pleas fell on deaf ears. He yanked Cadie downstairs like a limp rag doll so that her feet lost their bearings and she almost fell headlong onto the hard kitchen floor. "Joe, please! She's pregnant! My baby—"

Cadie had never heard her mother wail in such frantic hysterics nor seen this pale, hardened look on Daddy's face since *that night*. The memory of it all came flooding back as Cadie was flung across the sofa on top of Mama's needlepoint pillows. In a flash, the image of an angry scar slithering around the reverend's neck jolted through her mind.

"Now, I want you to tell me who he is," her daddy said in a calm tone while straddling a kitchen chair with his shotgun across his lap. Cadie's eyes glanced above the fireplace to the empty place on the wall where the weapon usually rested. She knew she should answer, but her mouth refused to cooperate. Ironically, the surrealism of the moment sent a peace and calm over her, as if she had risen out of her body and was watching from above. She wanted to close her eyes and sleep to the rhythm of the words bubbling up inside of her—*Love is patient and kind. It isn't proud or rude and doesn't seek its own way of doin' things, it isn't easily angered—*

"Girl, you're gonna tell me who he is, and then I'm gonna go bring him here, and we're gonna have ourselves a weddin'—tonight!" They both knew who the "he" was but dared not say the name, since it had now become a vile, unclean thing that might foul the air if spoken. Her daddy's eyes darkened, and the angles of his features became more pronounced. "I hear folks talkin'—seein' the two of you down at the river, at his daddy's store, actin' like heathens. And don't think I don't know, 'cause I do. I know everything that goes on."

"I'm not gonna marry him, Daddy."

"Don't you call me Daddy." He rose from his chair and towered over her with the shotgun gripped in his hands. "I don't have no harlot for a daughter."

For the first time in her life, Cadie was afraid of her father, and the fear made him appear taller than ever, terrifying her with a power that seemed to squeeze the very air out of her lungs. She wanted to speak, to say something, anything, to explain herself, but the only thing she was able to extract was a hoarse whisper. "I'm not gonna marry him."

The last thing she remembered was seeing his hand leave the barrel of the shotgun and fly back toward the ceiling. A sharp, shrill scream pierced her eardrums as a thud stunned the side of her cheek, sending her down and down, into the darkness.

Chapter 15

The barn door creaked open on its rusty hinges, and a stream of sunlight shot through the darkness. "Cadie, honey?" her mama said. "Norman's here to see you."

Cadie hid in the back of the barn near a hay pile with her face tucked into the fold of her arms. She hadn't talked to a soul for days and didn't plan on starting today. "Please go away," she mumbled.

After a few moments, a choked sob came from Mama. "Try to talk some sense into her."

The door creaked closed, and Norman cleared his throat before making his way to the back of the barn. He patted Blossom on the hindquarters and sat down on the hay pile, a good distance from where Cadie hid. "Hey," he said, nervously clearing his throat again. The cow mooed as it bit into a mound of straw and began another round of endless chewing. "Just thought I'd come talk to ya," he said. Cadie turned her head slightly to reveal a large, pastel-marbled bruise on her cheek which sent a ripple of shock through his expression. "I guess your pa's pretty mad, huh?" An agonizing silence passed before he spoke again. "I think you know why I'm here."

"No, Norman—"

"You didn't even let me say it."

"The answer's no."

Norman dug deep into his pocket and pulled out a little jewelry box, popping the lid open. "I got you a ring." He scooted over a bit and held it out toward her, but its sparkle didn't entice Cadie at all. "It's a diamond. Kinda small, but it's real. Pa says it belonged to Ma. I know she'd want you to have it. Supposedly came all the way from New York City." He waited for her to look, but she didn't, prompting him to close the box with a snap. "Why won't you give me a chance?"

"'Cause."

"'Cause why?"

"'Cause I don't love you, and you don't love me."

"Cadie, you know I've always loved you."

"Not like that—" Her emotions caught in her throat, ushering in another long silence.

He stroked the back of her hand and said, "You and me, we've always had a special somethin' for each other. Maybe not what you'd call real, romantic love, but—well, people don't have to love each other that way to get married. Your ma says—well, she says that kinda love'll come later."

"But it won't. I know it."

"We don't have a choice, Cadie. We've gotten ourselves in a predicament, and I'm prepared to own up to my responsibility."

"I'm not your responsibility, Norman."

"You're carryin' my baby, aren't you?"

Cadie's throat tightened again at the truth blurted out into the open. Why did he have to be so crude and vulgar? He knew she couldn't answer him. She wouldn't, because of where it would lead. "Shoot, the whole town's talkin' 'bout us," he said, gripping her hand until it hurt. "Business's dropped way off 'cause of all this. Now, Pa and I wanna know—you gonna marry me or not?"

She clenched her teeth and forced her tongue to the roof of her mouth, refusing to answer. Before long, he left in a huff, gunning the motor of his truck before roaring off in a cloud of swirling dust. Mama ran after him, but he was long gone by now, and besides, it didn't really matter anyway. Cadie had already decided nothing would ever persuade her to become Mrs. Norman McLain. Not even his mother's diamond ring all the way from New York City.

Several hours had passed, and a powerful hunger gnawed at Cadie's insides. The constant nausea had ceased as of a week ago, leaving her ravenous every second of the day, yet her pride refused to allow her to ask for a bite. In the quiet darkness of the barn, Cadie's mind went wild, savoring some of her favorite foods, like smoked ham, salted pinto beans, and fresh cheese biscuits. Her mouth watered and her stomach howled to the point where she thought she might faint—and she almost did—but then her mama knocked on the barn door with a piping hot plate of food in her hands. "Brought you somethin' to eat."

The smell wafted through the barn, making Cadie's tummy rumble. "I'm not hungry," she lied.

"You need to eat somethin'. You've got your daddy and me worried sick, and Norman, too. It's not right to sit out here all day and night without proper food and rest. For goodness' sake, you're gonna have a baby—"

"Mama, don't say it! Don't say that word!" The strength Cadie exhibited around Norman no longer held firm when it came to her mother. She sunk her face into her mama's skirts and shook with sobs.

"Cadie—" Mama set the plate down and stroked her tangled hair. "This isn't make-believe anymore. You're a woman now, and this is life—real life." She pulled Cadie into her bosom and rocked back and forth. "Shh. There, now. You marry Norman like your daddy says, and everything's gonna work out fine, you'll see. Just fine."

Cadie blubbered into her mama's chest. "You might as well tell him to shoot me in the head with that shotgun of his, 'cause there ain't no way—"

"Now, you know Norman's a good man and there's many a girl in town who'd love to catch his eye. But he's never looked at any of 'em the way he does you. I've always seen it, and if truth be told, so has your daddy, even though he won't admit to it. He's never been wild about Norman, that's true, but I don't think any man'd be good enough for Joe Hamilton's little girl." Cadie sobbed even louder at the loss of what she and Daddy once had. Mama rocked her for a while, stroking her hair and wiping the tears from her cheeks with the hem of her skirt. "You know your daddy didn't mean any of those things he said. You've been his little Twiddle ever since the day you were born. Never seen a man look at a baby like she hung the moon till he saw you. 'Course, he did the same for Tessie, but you were different. Said you reminded him of his ma, and I reckon you do."

Cadie thought about Daddy being a little boy with a mama who rocked him when he was hurt, just like her mama was doing for her now. He never spoke much about his mother, probably because she died long before Cadie was born. She wondered if his ma ever sat in a barn for two days and cried her eyes out to nobody but an old milk cow.

"Daddy and Norman, they've had a good talk, and he's promised to take real good care of you, Cadie." Mama held her close and swayed back and forth to the rhythm of Blossom's chewing with an occasional "shh" and a soft kiss on the top of the head. "You think about that. A man like Norman's not gonna wait forever. He's got his pride."

"Mama, you're not listenin' to me," Cadie wailed.

"I know you're still broken-hearted over Robert. But a woman's heart can heal, you'll see. Just give it time, and it'll be as good as new. Before you know it, you'll be ready to love again."

Cadie wrapped her arms around Mama's waist and clasped her hands like she'd never let go. She wished this were true, honestly she did. But somehow, Cadie didn't think even her mother, deep down, believed a single, solitary word of it.

Cadie refused to change her mind regarding Norman, despite Daddy's threats and Mama's efforts to appeal to her growing appetite. Daily visits from the prospective groom became disasters that ended in ravings and screams and Cadie locking herself away in the barn with the cows. When she overheard Mama say things like, "Joe, just let her go. Give her time. She's just bein' stubborn," Cadie covered her ears with her hands, vowing to never give in to their demands, no matter what happened.

Finally, Daddy announced that he had "had enough" and put the deciding pressure on her. If she wanted to run off to the barn every time Norman was mentioned, then to the barn she would stay, day and night, whether she liked it or not. "It's winter and the barn's freezin' cold, for heaven's sakes, and it just isn't right, Joe," Mama objected. "What kind of father puts his own daughter out into the barn, especially in her condition?" But the discussion had come to a quick end, and Cadie found herself living in the barn with two ole milk cows, like a fugitive hiding from the long arm of the law. She saw the worry on Mama's face and overheard confessions to the sewing club like, "Surely, she'll come to her senses and marry Norman, won't she? How much harder'll Joe have to come down on his own little girl?" And then of course there were the prayers made to the "Good Lord," all within Cadie's hearing, asking Him to do something, anything, to break her daughter's will without shattering her spirit. Cadie thought this a terrible thing for a mother to pray and was bound and determined it would never, ever be answered.

The nights in the barn were cold and windy. The bitter air blew off the creek and whooshed through the gaps in the roof where the roofing tiles had blown away long ago, forcing Cadie to snuggle up in the hay with a pile of wool blankets and Mama's cotton quilts. But no amount of clothing or coverings could stop the cold from seeping through the deep crevices in the walls or stop the icy chill from slicing to the bone.

Cadie stared at the holes in the roof where the flap of wings and the shadowed movement of a bird shifted on its perch, back and forth, until it settled into the warmth of its feathers. It was the golden eagle that had haunted the banks of the Cape Fear for many years. Everyone who lived in Pleasant Oaks had seen it at one time or another, flying high above the riverbanks in sunny and stormy weather, displaying its wide wingspan. No one knew where it nested or whether it had mated, nor seen it swoop down to capture a rabbit or squirrel or other helpless animal in its deadly talons. It was only seen in the air or resting in a tree or on the rooftop of Magnolia Hill, watching and observing the world from its lofty perch and calling out with a piercing cry that, for some unexplained reason, could cut to a man's very soul. Cadie wondered why it had come here, of all places.

The wind blew harder and the extra blast of cold took her breath away, causing an uncomfortable twinge in her belly. Her fingers stretched over the top of her swollen stomach and pressed against the hard mound. Was there really a baby inside of her, a part of what she and Norman had made together? A person who would come forth from her womb and be a constant reminder of what she had lost, of what should have been?

The twinge increased to a dull throb, making her grimace. She rolled to her side, and the feeling gravitated to a sharp and excruciating pain, causing her to buckle into a fetal position. Panic gripped her as Cadie realized something was horribly wrong. Before long, a stream of red seeped out from underneath her skirt, snaking its way through the hay until it came to where her hand rested against her belly. She tried to sit up but fell back onto the hay, watching the eagle shift frantically on its perch. She couldn't move, couldn't cry out, but was paralyzed with a pain that had taken her breath away. An oppressive evil moved into the barn, like a thick, heaviness that could be felt, grabbed and swallowed, leaving a rank stench to the senses.

The eagle flapped its long wings and called into the wind with an eerie screech, until suddenly, a small light shone through the hole in the roof and began to glow in a strange way as though the moon had doubled in size. Before long, a bolt of light shot through the hole with such force that Cadie thought for sure she was dreaming. The brightness engulfed her, lifting the blanket of evil and causing the pain to subside until she was able to take a breath. She shut her eyes and opened her mouth, gulping down the light that filled her throat and lungs. A song gushed out of her in a soft, breathy whisper—a tune that was vaguely familiar.

Glory, glory—Glory, glory, glory, glory! Glory, glory—Glory, glory, glory, Lord.

Where had she heard that before? Cadie's vision blurred as she continued to stare up at the eagle while humming this tune under her breath. She watched its long wings flutter in slow motion, back and forth, back and forth, in the glorious, angelic brightness.

Time drifted along, like a dark void through the night sky. Cadie awoke to the sounds of people mumbling words that couldn't be deciphered. The sun streamed through her bedroom window, reviving her senses—she was in bed wearing a white, cotton nightgown with her hair fanned around her pillow in loose curls, dotted with white dogwood blooms, and her hands folded over her chest like a corpse in a coffin. Days had obviously passed, but she had no memory of what had transpired. She lay very still and stared at the crack in the ceiling.

"Dearly beloved, we are gathered here today to join this woman and this man in holy matrimony . . ." Father Helms, the minister from the Episcopal Church, read from his prayer book while her mama stood nearby with her arm looped through her daddy's. Norman and Mr. McLain stood on the other side with their eyes cast to the floor. "Norman McLain, will you have this woman to be your wife, to love her, comfort her, honor and keep her, in sickness and in health, and forsaking all others, be faithful to her as long as you both shall live?"

Father Helms smiled at Norman, but there was no sign of joy in Norman's expression. He shifted a bouquet of hand-picked flowers from one hand to the other and gave a shaky response, "I will."

"And you Cadie Hamilton, will you have this man to be your husband, to love him, comfort him, honor and keep him, in sickness and in health, and forsaking all others, be faithful to him as long as you both shall live?"

It was deathly quiet as all ears waited for her to respond. Her eyes shifted down the crack in the ceiling to where the red coffee canister was hidden away. It seemed to cry out, *No! Don't! Don't do it!*

Daddy cleared his throat and shuffled his feet, not saying a word. Cadie could feel his glare beating down on her despite his obvious guilt for forcing her hand in this cruel way. Finally, her mama's pathetic voice came to the rescue. "Cadie, honey?"

She blinked hard once, and then twice, as the canister continued to plead with her—but she knew its contents couldn't save her now. There was a baby inside of her who needed a mother and a father, even if that father was Norman McLain. It belonged to him, and there was no escaping that fact. She could be happy in this new life, couldn't she? Surely, a baby would fill the void in her heart right now, even if Norman couldn't.

The words stuck in her throat, but somehow, they eventually warbled their way out. "I will," she whispered, her voice barely audible. Daddy bowed his head and left the room, closing the door behind him, while Norman forced his mother's diamond ring onto her swollen finger.

"And now I pronounce you husband and wife in the name of the Father, and of the Son, and of the Holy Spirit. You may kiss the bride."

Norman leaned forward to kiss Cadie's lips, but she turned her head and offered her cheek instead. The moment his lips touched her face, she grimaced as though he had impaled her with a long, jagged knife.

Mama dabbed her eyes with her handkerchief and sobbed, "It's gonna be fine, honey. Just fine. Like the doctor said, you and the baby, you're all gonna be just fine. You just wait and see. Just wait and see . . ."

Cadie lay motionless, feeling what was left of her life drain away like water through a sieve while her mama carried on. As for Norman, he didn't say a word, but stood quietly by and glared at the floor.

Chapter 16

Molly glided through the door of the mercantile at one o'clock sharp, just like she had done every day since learning of Norman's marriage to that "Hamilton urchin." The memory of his arms around her waist and scorching kisses on her mouth and neck came flowing back to her mind with a vengeance so that she could think of nothing else.

In contrast, Lloyd's touch became more repulsive than ever, making her pull away, night after night. He disgusted her, but not enough to regret becoming his wife. Part of her reward was a large, Greek revival home on Main Street with an unlimited budget to decorate as she saw fit, which included six months of careful selections from French and English antiques, Oriental rugs, rich fabric coverings and draperies, as well as original art and wall hangings. Now that the decorations were complete, reality had quickly set in, and with it, a new repulsion that made the sight of her husband's slicked-back hair, paunch, and prickly moustache unbearable. But of course, in the darkness of the night, she could close her eyes good and tight and see whatever she liked, which lately consisted of a strong muscular chest, lock of brown hair falling over the eye, and lopsided grin.

As she wandered the aisles, Molly turned up her nose at the cheap fabrics and inexpensive bric-a-brac until she stopped at a full-length mirror in the men's haberdashery section. How pretty she looked in her peach taffeta dress and matching cloche with silk rosettes and netting! Norman wouldn't be able to take his sights off her today, of that she was sure. Her cheeks flushed and her skin prickled with excitement as more thoughts of him ran through her mind, making her giggle. A slight movement from behind a tower of tin cans quieted her for a moment, until suddenly, several cans fell to the floor and rolled down the aisle, bumping against her foot.

"Norman!" Mr. McLain's head popped up from behind the counter where he was counting apples from a large basket into wooden containers. "Don't be so clumsy!" Molly gently cleared her throat, and immediately, his demeanor changed. "Oh—Mrs. Wallace. I didn't hear you come in." He readjusted his spectacles and smoothed his hands on his apron. "How can we help you today?"

"I'm just looking."

"Well, all right. You just let me know if you need anything."

"Yes, sir." She waited until he went back to his work and then picked up a dusty can of peas parked near her bone-colored shoe and carried it over to Norman. "You dropped this." She extended the can toward him, being careful not to mar her white, cotton gloves.

"Thank you," he said, caressing her finger with his.

She hesitated, carefully choosing her words. "I haven't had a chance to formally congratulate you on your wedding." Her eyes connected with his, holding firm. "And I understand there's a baby coming. Congratulations." Molly felt her face flush and quickly turned toward a stack of men's dress shirts, pretending to take interest.

Suddenly, Norman grabbed her, digging his fingers into the soft flesh of her arm. He pulled her behind the curtain of the corner stock room where she fell into his strong embrace, clinging to him, desperate for what he had to offer. Her hat fell to the floor as his fingers clawed through her hair. "Molly," he growled, "when I think of that old man touchin' you—" He kissed her violently, until she could stand it no longer.

"I love you, Norman. I love you, I do." And for those few, precious moments behind the stockroom curtain, she believed it.

A bell jingled, sounding the entry of another customer into the store. Molly pulled away and retrieved her hat, securing it to her head. "Meet me at the bridge. Tonight," Norman said, pulling her close.

"Shh. Keep your voice down." In a hasty motion, Molly smoothed her hair under her hat and adjusted her dress. She scooted out from behind the stockroom curtain, and to her surprise, faced her husband, dead on. "Lloyd!" she exclaimed in a shrill tone. Her cheeks burned at seeing Norman emerge from behind the curtain as well. "What are you doing here?"

An eternity seemed to pass as a dark look clouded Lloyd's expression, making his moustache twitch in a revolting way. "I had to come into town and was wondering if I might take you to lunch." His eyes darkened even more as he glared at Norman. "But it looks as though you're busy—shopping."

"Oh—well, Norman was just showing me the special they're having on tinned peas," Molly said, catching her breath as her heart raced. "Two cans for a nickel, isn't that right, Norman?"

"That's right," Norman answered, holding Lloyd's gaze.

Lloyd shifted his eyes back to Molly. "Since when have you been known to eat tinned peas?"

"I—I don't know," she stammered.

"No, you don't know, do you?" He lifted her chin with the tip of his fingers and forced her to look at him. She cringed at the small beads of sweat pearling up on his brow and his thick neck, which appeared more bloated than usual. Instinct took over, and she tried to pull away, but he held firm, wiping away a smudge of lipstick with his thumb. "Tinned peas will never do for my sweet, hmm?" Her eyes met his once more, and she nodded in agreement. "Now, how about I take you to The Pelican where you can get some of those fresh, lump-meat crab cakes you like so much?"

"The Pelican?" she asked, not sure if she was in the mood for crab cakes.

"And then afterward, I thought we could stop in La Boutique and see what just came in from New York."

He eyed her with a raised eyebrow that sent a rush of excitement fluttering through her belly—she couldn't help but think about that full-length mink coat he had been promising her for some time now. "Why, yes," Molly said, feeling a smile slide across her face. "I think that's a fine idea."

"Well, then, shall we?"

Without giving Norman another thought, she took her husband's arm and allowed him to guide her toward the front of the store, as though nothing out of the ordinary had transpired. "Molly," Norman said, his voice sounding pathetic.

"It's Mrs. Wallace to you from now on, Mr. McLain," Lloyd snapped, flashing a look of contempt in Norman's direction. And then like a gentleman, he opened the mercantile door extra-wide and led her outside to where the blue Rolls-Royce was waiting.

Cadie stood at the train depot, twirling her diamond ring around on her finger and pulling it on and off her knuckle. Her hair had grown out, thick and full of curls, and the healthy glow of a mother-to-be was evident on her cheeks and complexion, not to mention her swollen abdomen. She instinctively caressed her full belly, mindful that a baby was well on its way to revealing itself to the world.

In the distance, a whistle blew, followed by a faint rumbling, indicating the train was beginning its arrival into the depot. As it came to a hissing stop, the doors opened and a young woman dressed in a smart suit and hat with short, bobbed hair and glasses, stepped onto the platform.

"Tessie!" Cadie squealed, standing on tip-toe as she waved at her sister. Pushing her way through the crowd, she fell into Tessie's arms. "Oh, Tessie—I'm so glad you're home."

"It's good to be here—finally," Tessie said, her face bursting into an enormous smile. "Let me take a look at you." She held Cadie at arm's length and surveyed her new size. "Goodness! There's definitely a baby in there."

"There definitely is," Cadie said.

Tessie grabbed Cadie's hand and surveyed the diamond ring. "Hmm—not bad. Even for Norman."

"Stop it, now. It was his mama's. Says it's worth a bundle."

"Oh, he does?" Tessie eyed her with a side-glance. "So—how is life as Mrs. Norman McLain?"

Cadie's expression soured for a moment. "I don't wanna talk 'bout that." She linked her arm into Tessie's and smiled, feeling her spirits lift again. "I wanna hear 'bout you and all those college boys."

After a long walk home, Cadie had heard all she wanted to hear about Tessie's new life at WC. Besides classes and homework, there were bridge parties, teas, dinners, and dances with the boys from Davidson. Cadie noted how out of place her sister looked with her modern hair and stylish clothes. The college scholarship had provided extra money for Tessie's living expenses and necessities, as evidenced by her stylish appearance, but Cadie refused to be jealous of all that. She squared her shoulders and listened to Tessie talk, not saying a word until they reached the little place she and Norman called home.

Live oaks, pines, and dogwoods bordered the property, which was off a dirt road near the creek. As pretty as the surroundings were, the same could not be said for the house. Cadie hated for anyone, especially her family, to see the depths to which she had sunk. The front porch sagged to one side, the exterior siding needed painting and repair, and the yard was overgrown with weeds and crabgrass.

"Well, come on in," Cadie said, ignoring Tessie's shocked expression. "I hate to tell ya, but it isn't much better inside."

Tessie followed her through the front door to a kitchen with a wooden table and a large room with a fireplace decorated with a threadbare sofa and two matching wingback chairs. A bedroom was off the kitchen and a staircase led to a small, empty loft that overlooked the living area. "Oh, my—"

"Don't say it," Cadie said, cringing at Tessie's ashen face. "I know it's awful." Cadie fired up the tea kettle on the stove and then climbed a small step-stool where she dug into an iron pot hidden among some glass jelly jars on the top kitchen shelf. "But I've got somethin' here that'll change everything." She retrieved the red coffee canister and pried the lid off, dumping its contents onto the old kitchen table.

"Gracious!" Tessie gasped, staring at the paper money and coins heaped in a pile. "How much is there?"

"Over sixty dollars," Cadie said, proudly. "Mostly from Mama's extra sewin' jobs. Mr. McLain won't let me sell pies anymore since I'm his daughter-in-law now. He says it ain't right—"

"Isn't."

"Gotten all big-headed from that college of yours," Cadie said, smirking at Tessie. Tessie smiled back in way that said it was good to be home, despite standing in Cadie's abysmal kitchen. "Isn't," Cadie said, correcting herself. " He says it isn't right, that we ought not compete with the other ladies in town, since we're the owners of the mercantile. 'Cept I don't see Norman bringin' any extra money home besides what we need to get by."

"Surely, his pa pays him well for workin' in the store."

"Oh, he pays him. It's just what comes home's the problem. Most of it he drinks away."

"Cadie, you're not serious, are you? I know Norman liked a bit of the nip here and there, but—that much?"

"It's every night. Sometimes all day." Anger crept into Cadie's voice as she continued. "Sometimes he doesn't even show up at the store. His pa has to come down here and drag him outta bed, but it doesn't do any good. He just goes right back to drinkin'. Neither one of us can do a thing with him."

Tessie sunk into the wooden chair and looked around the room, making Cadie blush with shame. "You could fix this place up a bit," Tessie said dreamily, surveying the empty windows and walls. "Make it a home. Then maybe he won't drink so much."

"You takin' his side?"

"No."

"Sure sounds like it."

"It's just—well, you've got a baby comin', and you're gonna need him."

Cadie twirled her diamond ring around on her finger and pulled it on and off her knuckle. "I don't need him," she said, caressing her swollen abdomen. "What good's he gonna do me? I've got sixty dollars here, plus this ring, which could fetch me another sixty, maybe more."

"You're gonna sell his mama's ring?"

"She's dead now. She don't need it."

"Cadie! You are evil." Tessie looked away, casting another glance toward her heavy midsection. "Well, where you gonna go lookin' like that?"

"I'll wait till after the baby's born, and then I'll take the train back with you."

"With me?"

"I'm sure I can find a job sewin' or bakin' pies, or somethin'."

"What about the baby?"

"It'll work out, somehow. I'll make it work."

"Cadie, you don't know what you're sayin'. You can't just up and leave."

"I can and I will!" she said, feeling the fire leap from her eyes.

The roar of an engine resonated in the distance, punctuating Cadie's words with warning. She moved toward the window to see Norman's truck lumbering down the dirt road. "Quick!" she said, grabbing the money and shoving it into the coffee canister.

As soon as Cadie tucked the canister back in its hiding place, the front door opened and Norman stumbled in, looking like he'd been twirled around all night on a carnival ride. His eyes were glassy and glazed and his hair stood on end as if he'd been struck by lightning. Dirt and mud covered the front of his shirt, and there was a rip in the knee of his worn trousers. He took one look at Tessie and grinned, slurring his words. "Well, now—if it ain't the sister—back from school."

Tessie took a step back and smiled. "Hello, Norman."

He leered at Tessie the way he did almost every young woman under the age of thirty, regardless of their appearance. "You sure've changed. Never knew you was this pretty. Take off your glasses and lemme take a look—"

"Norman—" Cadie grabbed his arm, but he slung it away.

"I wasn't talkin' to you!" Venom seethed from him as he swayed on his feet, trying to maintain control, but it was no use. He was a leaning tower, ready to topple over at any second.

"Go to bed," Cadie said, plopping her hands on her hips and setting her head at an angle like a mama scolding an impudent child. "You're drunk."

"What'd you say?" Norman breathed in her direction, making her grimace from the smell of moonshine.

"I said, 'You're drunk!' Now, go to bed."

"Don't you tell me what to do—" He stumbled toward Cadie and tripped over the leg of a kitchen chair, falling flat on his face so that the whole house shook. His head lifted off the floor and then fell back down with a heavy thud.

"Is he all right?" Tessie whispered.

Cadie nudged him with her foot. "Norman?" She grabbed the kettle off the stove and held it over him. "Norman?"

"What're you doin? Don't—" Tessie squealed as Cadie dribbled the hot liquid over his back.

"It won't hurt him none." They waited for a reaction of some kind, but he didn't move a muscle. "See? Told ya. He'll just think he fell into a briar patch or somethin' like that or maybe a nest of yellow jackets."

"Cadie Hamilton McLain! You are evil," Tessie said, suppressing a smile.

Cadie snickered at Tessie trying to play the genteel lady. Norman responded with a loud snort that made her laugh, and before long, Tessie joined in with her, howling like a hyena.

Chapter 17

Cadie couldn't sleep at all that night. She kept tossing and turning on the old, lumpy mattress, trying to get comfortable as the baby kicked and fluttered inside her belly, pushing its heel up against her ribs. When moments of sleep finally came, she dreamt of Magnolia Hill. Again, she floated high above the apple orchard where Mr. and Mrs. Stephens, Molly, and Lloyd roamed through the trees while another garden party was being held on the lawn. This time, Boy sat up high on a tree limb in the middle of the orchard, beckoning her to come and sit with him, but the wind blew her in the opposite direction until she descended into the party, well out of his reach. Norman waited for her among a throng of guests, looking handsome and well-groomed—the complete opposite of his normal appearance. He stood with Reverend Thomas, who snapped his gold pocket watch closed and smiled a brilliant smile.

Above their heads, the golden eagle dipped and soared in the sky as a dark storm cloud gathered in the background. The wind blew with a great intensity, causing all the ladies to secure their hats with a quick glove to the top of the head. Even the men held their hat brims as the wind picked up and a torrential rain began to fall. Suddenly, an enormous gust of wind ripped across the lawn and sent the reverend's top hat sailing into the sky. Cadie followed it, floating up and away with the wind until she landed in her bed at the Hamilton farmhouse. The crack in the ceiling was a familiar sight, leading her eye down its crooked, winding path, all the way to the row of books on the top shelf where the red coffee canister normally had its home. She got up to retrieve it, but nothing was there, other than a dirty, plaster wall.

The heavy slam of a motorcar door woke Cadie with a jolt, leaving her with just one thing on her mind—the red coffee canister. She tore the bedcovers off her legs and raced into the kitchen, her heart pounding. The floor was covered in broken glass, and on the kitchen table, pried open and laying on its side, was the canister—empty.

A scream gurgled up from deep inside Cadie and worked its way into her throat. "NorMAN!" She ran to the canister, oblivious to the shattered glass covering the floor. A broken shard sliced her bare foot, but her scream was muffled by the cough of a truck engine and a blinding pair of headlights. "NORMAN!" She rushed out into the wind and storm, leaving a trail of blood behind her.

Norman stared through the windshield, looking like a demented corpse. "Give me my money!" Cadie screamed. With a jerk of his shoulder, Norman threw the truck into reverse and sped backward down the dirt driveway toward the main road. Cadie chased after him, despite the wind and rain and the pressure from her swollen belly.

Finally, the truck bumped up to a tall pine and came to a stop. Cadie stood in front of it, glaring at Norman with every bit of meanness she had in her. By now, her hair hung in her face in wet, matted clumps, and her soaked nightdress clung to her breasts and abdomen, leaving very little to the imagination. "Give it back!" she yelled. Norman revved the motor, and the truck inched forward a bit. Cadie pounded her palms on the hood and shot daggers through her eyes. "Give it back, you low-down, dirty, rotten thief!" He revved the motor once more and gunned the accelerator, forcing her out of the way. The tires spun in the mud for a moment and then the truck headed for the main road. "Norman!" Cadie chased after him, running with all of her might until her sides began to cramp up. She buckled over, trying to catch her breath. "Norman, Norman!" she screamed, as the taillights disappeared around the bend.

Cadie stood for the longest time and looked down the dark road, willing him to come back and hand over what was rightfully hers. She shivered from the cold rain, as well as the anger that set every fiber of her being aflame. She could kill him, she could. She could take a hammer and smash his head in, she could take a knife and stab him in the throat, she could take her daddy's shotgun and shoot him in places too vulgar to tell. She could do a million things to him right now.

The rain subsided, allowing her eyes to adjust even more to the darkness. She took a deep breath and willed herself not to cry. She wouldn't let Norman McLain make her cry! The sparkle from the ring on her finger caught her eye, reminding her there was still a glimmer of hope. She could still sell it, couldn't she? But where in Pleasant Oaks? Not to Mr. Johnson at Johnson's Jewelry Store, because of him being friends with Mr. McLain. Somehow she'd have to find her way to Wilmington or Southport to sell it there. But how in the world was she going to get anywhere with no money of her own?

Cadie leaned over and gasped as her abdomen tightened into a cramp. A stream of water trickled down her leg, washing away some of the blood that oozed from the laceration in her foot. She wiped it clean, but the trickle soon turned into a gush, dumping a douse of warm liquid onto the road.

Groaning, Cadie managed to stand upright and hobble back toward the house, but her sore foot hit a deep mud puddle, sending her down onto the wet, muddy road with a skinned knee. What was she going to do? The baby was early and she wasn't ready. And besides, she couldn't have a baby in the middle of the road! Cadie resisted the urge to scream, and instead, took several deep gulps of air to calm her nerves. A moment of relief passed, and then a wave of severe cramping hit her hard, causing her to buckle into the fetal position again. How was she going to get word to Mama in time? How could she do this on her own? Oh, why had she sent Tessie back to the farm tonight?

Cadie willed herself back onto her feet and continued hobbling to the house. *If I can just lie down in the bed, if I can get there before the next pain comes...* This time the contraction sliced through her like a dull knife so that her very thoughts were suspended. Screaming, she fell to the road as the pain took control. She tried to speak, but the only sound she could make was a whisper, "Norman, Norman—"

The headlights of a motorcar penetrated the night, heading straight for Cadie's slumped form. Like two bright eyes, they moved closer in growing intensity until she could think of nothing but the night Blossom's hay was covered with her blood. As the headlights descended upon her, she thought she heard the eagle's long wings flapping in her ear like they had the night that strange, majestic light had shone through the hole in the barn roof. The brightness from the headlights gave her the same sense of comfort that everything would be all right. She closed her eyes and heard a soft, breathy tune come from her lips. *"Glory, glory—Glory, glory, glory—"*

The vehicle screeched to a stop within inches of Cadie, bathing her in an intense light. A door opened and voices came forth. "Lord 've mercy... sweet Jesus. Get her to the house... no, put her in the car, hurry, no, not that way..."

But then a deep, clear voice rose up amid the commotion and declared, "Move out of the way and let me get to her. Move, now." Strong, muscular arms lifted her up while the other voices resounded in frantic confusion. The pain ripped through her again, and she moaned. "Shh, it's gonna be all right. We gonna get you to your mama. It's gonna be all right. Henry, go on and fetch the doctor. Tell him to meet us at the Hamilton's. You know, the farm down yonder, past Old Hargett's Bridge. Go on, and hurry. Lord Jesus, give him feet like eagle's wings." Cadie pried her eyes opened and peeked into the face of her rescuer who continued to speak soothing words. "Jesus, Lord Jesus, protect this sweet child, protect her, in Jesus' name, protect her...."

As her eyes closed again and she bore into the pain, an image came to her mind that matched the voice she now heard—one of a tall, dark figure of a man with close cropped hair and a set of gleaming, white teeth.

Cadie dreamt the same dream every night. She was safe in the arms of Reverend Thomas, feeling a peace flood her heart despite the pain ripping through her body. "Mr. Hamilton. Mr. Hamilton, sir!" he bellowed at the top of his lungs while a young Negro man beat on the front door of the farmhouse until it threatened to burst off its hinges. He and Jack Reynolds stood outside with the reverend, banging hard with wild, terrified eyes.

Finally, there was the sound of scurrying, like the feet of squirrels or mice, and then came Mama's frantic cry, "Joe, open that door! Open it—" Before Cadie knew what was happening, the reverend reared back like a wild stallion and kicked the door in. The last image in Cadie's mind was of Mama covering her mouth with her shawl and Daddy standing by the bedroom door with his shotgun in hand while the reverend prayed over her belly. She could feel the reverend's hands on her skin and hear his prayers echoing through her mind, *Jesus, Lord Jesus, protect this sweet child and her little one. Protect them, in Jesus' name, protect them...*"

A breeze fluttered through the bedroom window, pulling Cadie out of a heavy sleep. The reverend's voice swirled away with the remnants of the dream while her body quickened at the gentle tug on her breast. A smile came to Cadie lips as she heard the rhythmic sound of swallowing after each frantic suckle—the pain and discomfort from her sliced foot, as well as the other past days' events, were momentarily forgotten. Forcing her eyes open, she broke the crusty band of sleep that glued her eyelashes together and squinted into the sunlight.

"Cadie?"

She blinked heavily and saw Norman sitting next to the bed with his head in his hands. Judging by his appearance, he had slept all night in the stiff, old kitchen chair Tessie and Cadie used as a vanity seat. He smelled musty and soiled and his hair was greasy and stood on end from repeatedly running his fingers through it. Tremendous, deep circles surrounded his eyes, and his grisly face was marred with red splotches that made him almost unrecognizable.

Cadie had overheard her mama describe how it had taken days for her daddy and Mr. McLain to hunt Norman down. They had searched high and low in every backwoods bar and cathouse until they caught wind of a secret moonshine shack hidden deep in the squalor where drinking, cards, and other unmentionable activities were the standard of the day. Sure enough, there he was, sprawled out on an old, dirty straw mattress with his arms and legs spread eagle and his mouth yawning wide open. At first blush, Mr. McLain thought he was dead, judging by the pallor of his cheeks and the contortion of his face, but as her daddy had begrudgingly acknowledged, he was just "drunk as a skunk."

But now there was a change in him that was clearly visible. The normal smirk and humorous glimmer to his expression had been replaced by a sadness that was dark and painful, as if he had undergone some horrible torture. He hung his head low, like he had done on that afternoon when his daddy informed him "that Nigra preacher" had rescued his wife and baby in the dead of night from certain death.

"You awake?" Norman asked in a hoarse, groggy voice.

"My eyes are open, aren't they?"

He looked away, obviously stung by her tone. Cadie's skin crawled at the sound of the calluses on his fingers and palms swiping against each other like coarse sandpaper. "I guess you're feelin' better, then?" She shrugged her shoulders while he remained silent. Then craning his head forward, he tried to sneak a peek at the baby. "Would it be all right if I got a good look at her? Your ma, she won't even let me get near—"

"I reckon so," Cadie said, pulling the blanket away from the baby's face. "She's yours, too."

Norman's eyes welled up as he gazed at the infant, forcing Cadie to look away so that her heart would harden back to a state far more to her liking. "She's beautiful. So little." He caressed the tiny fingers and lay his thick hands on the baby's downy head. "I think she's got your eyes."

"How can you tell that? She's barely a week old."

"I can tell. A daddy can see things in his little girl others can't."

"You gonna be a daddy to her, Norman? How you gonna do that, doin' all you've been up to?"

"That's in the past now. I'm gonna do right by you two from now on. I promise."

"Your promises don't mean nothin', Norman. Only thing you know how to do is drink and who knows what else. And steal." Cadie spewed the words out as if she was spitting a wad of chaw right into his face.

His head hung low before he was able to look at her again. "It was wrong of me to take that money, I know. It was yours and I had no right. But I'm gonna work hard and get it back."

Cadie turned toward the baby while the tears steamed up behind her eyelids. She thought of all the pies she and Tessie had baked and the sewing jobs she had finished into the wee hours of the night—all gone now—wasted. "You don't know how long it took," she sobbed.

"I'll get it back, I swear I will," he said, stroking her arm.

"It'll be too late by then," she said, recoiling from his touch. "I need that money now. I need it, you hear? I need it—" Cadie had promised herself she would never let Norman see her cry again, but here she was, sick and in bed with a baby, crying like a baby herself. Oh, how she did hate Norman McLain!

"Cadie, why do you need that money?" he asked. "I'll take care of you. Why won't you let me do that?" His lips brushed against her forehead as his prickly cheek meshed into hers. "Pa says he'll help us out for a while till we get things settled at home and get the house fixed up for the baby. And I thought I could get a second job with Mr. Stephens at one of his lumber mills and work more hours at the store. I've got some ideas on how to make the mercantile bigger and maybe sell some fancier stuff, and you can help me." He kissed her lightly on the brow. "Whadda you think?"

The silence echoed off the walls, throbbing in her ears. "I think you're a fool," she hissed. "Drink yourself to death, see if I care. Spend all your time with that Molly Stephens Wallace. Maybe she'll listen to your lies."

"I've told you already, I'm done with her. All she is is a fancy, spruced-up harlot."

"Seems like that woulda made you like her even more."

Norman grabbed Cadie by the arm until she met his gaze. The circles under his eyes appeared deeper and more pronounced, making him look sadder and more tormented. "What can I say to make you believe me?" His gaze swept over her face as his lips came close to hers. "You know you're the only one for me."

"You have a fine way of showin' it."

"You've never let me show it, that's the problem. But I wanna change all that now—Cadie, what can I do? What can I say to make it right?"

The desperation in his voice repulsed her, and she had to turn away. "Nothin'. Just leave me be."

The minutes ticked by as he stared at her, his hot gaze bearing down hard. Cadie debated whether she should scream at him to "leave and never come back," when he spoke with a thickness in his throat. "Is that the way you're gonna be, not even willin' to try? 'Cause I won't fight you on this, Cadie. Not anymore."

She blinked the tears away, focusing on the sleeping baby. "You don't know how to fight," she muttered to herself. Although barely audible, these words were sharp and lethal, and she knew it.

"One day you're gonna be proud of me," he said, pushing the wooden chair back from the bed. "One day. You'll see." And in a moment, he was gone.

Good, thought Cadie. *Leave!* She rolled over and looked at the door, but the room was empty, just as she expected. Rolling back on her side, she stared at the baby. Norman was right—she did have Cadie's eyes. She stroked the infant's hair and silky cheek. "One day," she whispered. "One day you're gonna live a real life far away from this place. I promise." She kissed the baby's soft head and marveled at her squirming motions as she began to awaken. How sweet and innocent, with so much possibility, so much of life to experience!

A name whispered off Cadie's tongue from somewhere down deep. "Zow-ee." She thought she had seen it in a fashion magazine, spelled Zoe, although she couldn't really remember. Perhaps it was the name of a beautiful model, sporting a chin-length bob and a drop-waist dress, or perhaps she had heard it at one of the Magnolia Hill garden parties from long ago. Even though Cadie didn't know what it meant, it had a nice sound to it.

She smiled at the baby as if they were being introduced for the very first time. "That's what I'll call you—Zoe. My sweet, little Zoe."

Chapter 18

Norman didn't show his face around the Hamilton Farm again, which was just fine with Cadie. Word leaked back that he had been showing up at the mercantile every morning, working hard and doing much more than stack tin cans into useless, toppling towers. Her daddy sang a different tune when the subject of Norman came up, commenting on "how well he's doing," that "he sure didn't know he had it in him," and how "he's full of more surprises than Christmas mornin'." Cadie knew this was said with an eye toward getting a response from her, but she refused to take the bait. She would never forgive Norman for what he had done to her and their baby. He may be her husband and Zoe's father, but it was all in name only. For Cadie, there was no redemption whatsoever for the likes of Norman McLain.

Her new life was completely absorbed in little Zoe now. The days were busy with feedings, bathings, cooking, cleaning and sewing, not to mention, milking Blossom and Dawn every morning and afternoon. The doctor came and went for regular visits and even the reverend showed up several times to offer prayer and words of encouragement, but only while her daddy was out of the house, since he couldn't stand the sight of the reverend. Neither he nor her mama seemed to mind Cadie and Zoe living under their roof. The farm was filled with a newfound joy that hadn't existed since the days before Tessie went off to college. Many evenings were spent laughing till their sides split over something her daddy did, or her mama said, or the baby gurgled out of her mouth or bottom. It was times like these that Cadie stared at Zoe's little face and wondered why on earth she ever wanted to run away from this. But then the image of a grand white house sitting high on the creek bank fluttered into her head, invading her memory with images that threatened to make her sad again.

"Land sakes, that child's startin' to look just like her daddy," Mama exclaimed one morning while changing the baby's diaper. Cadie hated hearing this kind of talk, especially after she had tried for weeks to shake all thoughts of Norman from her mind.

"She most certainly does not!" Cadie said, scowling at her mama. "She don't look nothin' like him." She grinned at Zoe and made a scrunchy face as the baby wiggled and squirmed on the bed. "I think she looks like me in the eyes, and I see a little of Daddy in her, especially in the mouth."

"Whadda you mean? She don't look nothin' like your daddy," Mama said, examining Zoe. "She looks just like Norman when she smiles like that." She pointed at the baby, who grinned, big and wide. "Looka there."

"I'm not gonna look. I know what I know." Cadie picked Zoe up in a quick, jerky motion, causing the baby's mouth to turn down in a frown before an enormous howl erupted.

"Cadie! There's no need to act like that."

"Then stop tellin' her she looks like him. She's never gonna be like him, never! You wanna curse her with that kinda talk?"

Cadie stomped down the stairs with Zoe in her arms, hearing Mama's bedroom door slam closed behind her. She bolted outside into the cool air, not even thinking about putting on a wrap or covering the baby with an extra blanket—but it didn't matter anyway, since she couldn't feel a thing other than the heat rushing through her veins. How could Mama say such things about Zoe?

"It's okay, sweetie. Shh. It's all right," she cooed, jostling the baby up and down on her hip in hopes that the movement would be enough to quiet the frantic crying. Finally, she unbuttoned her blouse, feeling her breasts tingle with the sensation of fullness. As soon as the baby was placed in the nursing position, her little mouth latched on, and the rhythmic gulping began.

With Zoe firmly tucked in her arms, Cadie made her way through the woods toward the creek bank and down to Old Hargett's Bridge. She carefully tip toed to the edge of the embankment and looked down at the swirling water, remembering all the countless times she had crossed over the rickety contraption without a bat of the eye. Now, with a babe in her arms, she wouldn't consider taking a single step. Instead, she wandered back toward the woods and sat on the stump of a large tree where she could relax and clear her mind.

Cadie smiled at Zoe and smoothed down the pink flowered dress that barely covered her little legs now. She thought about how Mama had made the dress and matching blanket from left over sewing scraps and several yards of delicate baby cloth given as a gift from Mr. McLain. The cloth had been accepted, even though it should have been a gift from Norman, but he wasn't man enough to do such a thing. Cadie shook her head in disbelief, fully convinced her decision to hate him was fully warranted. What father would go for weeks without seeing his own newborn daughter? "You're nothin' like him, you hear?" Cadie said softly, shifting the baby in her arms. "Not one little bit."

Zoe pulled away from the breast and rocked her head back, having fallen asleep in mid-swallow. Cadie stroked the soft cheek as the full, pink mouth stretched out into a little bow. With each new day, she marveled at how beautiful Zoe had become and how she seemed to flourish more and more, being a ravenous eater who slept soundly all night without the slightest whimper. Cadie usually fluffed her short, curly hair and adorned it with a pink ribbon or, if they ventured outside for a bit, she tied a white, lacey bonnet around Zoe's tiny chin, one that had been Cadie's when she was a child. The cool air sent a wave of guilt through Cadie, reminding her of the bonnet hanging from the end of her bedpost at home.

A horn sounded from the other side of the bridge, indicating a boat was moving along the river. Immediately, a breeze blew off the water, lifting Cadie into a suspension of time as the memories of what lay on the other side of the creek taunted her—apple orchards, garden parties, boats like that one moving along the river to unknown destinations. Her eyes fell on the pilings of the bridge. They were old and weathered, yet still held firm. Why shouldn't she be able to cross with a baby in her arms? She'd done it countless times with a hot, fresh-baked pie in each hand. Shouldn't Zoe see a glimpse of what that world had to offer?

Cadie shifted the baby to her shoulder, adjusted her blouse, and carefully stood to her feet. "Come on, now," she cooed under her breath, not sure who she was trying to convince, either herself or Zoe. She walked toward the bridge, getting as close to it as she could, and stopped, staring at it like it was a foe to be conquered. Then with a deep breath and a firm squeeze of the baby to her bosom, she strode across. "One, two, three, four, five . . ." She kept on counting until, before she knew it, she had crossed to the other side. "See," she said, smiling at the sleeping Zoe, "that wasn't so bad."

Cadie tromped through the thick woods, using the soft blanket to shield the baby from any wayward briars and thorns. Despite the jostling, Zoe never batted an eye, still intoxicated from her last feeding. After a few minutes, they reached the grassy clearing by the bank of the Cape Fear where the ships could be seen. Cadie strained her eyes and just barely made out the form of a boat heading in their direction. "Look, Zoe, look! There it is." A gust of wind rushed off the water and over the riverbank, sending a chill through Cadie. "It's goin' someplace far off. Just like where you're gonna go. Someplace far away and excitin'." She turned the sleeping baby around so that her face was turned toward the river. "Look, now. That's gonna be you one day," she said, gently kissing the top of Zoe's head and waving her hand bye-bye. "One day."

The wind began to pick up as another gust of cool air rushed all around them, whipping Cadie's skirt around her legs. High above, a dark storm cloud brewed, and several thick drops of rain hit Cadie's back and the baby's leg. Zoe stirred in her sleep and let out a whimper, but Cadie hardly noticed. She hadn't experienced this sense of joy in such a long time. She waved at the boat, not caring that they couldn't see her from such a distance. She was going to wave for herself and for Zoe.

Another splat of rain hit the baby on the forehead, causing her to squirm and whine. Cadie shifted her over to the other breast and rocked her back and forth in her arms with a gentle sway as she watched the boat continue on its course. "Everything's gonna be all right, Zoe. I promise you. It's all gonna be fine."

By the time Cadie got back to the farm, rain was coming down in torrents. She ran all the way home with the baby folded tightly to her breast and covered with a blanket, but it wasn't enough to protect them from the effects of the downpour or the chill in the air. Both of them were soaked to the bone and shivering from the cold. Mama, being the mother she was, had a warm bath ready for the baby and a pot of hot soaking water for Cadie's feet. She stood at the door, dry-eyed and hopping mad, with her hand on her hip and her head cocked.

"Don't know why you had to go runnin' off like that. Your poor daddy and I've been worried sick. He went tearin' off in the truck and with his shotgun to boot, lookin' for this sweet baby." She pried Zoe from Cadie's stiff arms and fussed, "Come here, little one. We'll get you all warmed up." Then glaring at Cadie, she added, "Not even four months old, and out in this kinda weather."

"Mama—" Cadie whined, trying her best not to cry.

She looked away and nodded toward the soaking pot sitting by the kitchen chair. "It's a wonder the two of you don't catch your death of cold."

"I said I was sorry."

"Sometimes sorry isn't good enough. You should know that by now, Cadie. You're not a little girl anymore. When're you gonna realize that?"

"Is it my fault rain started fallin' from the sky? How was I supposed to know it was gonna rain?"

Somehow, Cadie should've known, Mama argued. And indeed she should have. Within a day, Doctor Patterson was called to tend to Zoe, whose nose and lungs became so congested, she couldn't breathe to nurse. Each suck was accompanied by a guttural rattling sound and a weak, pathetic cry that was like a dagger to Cadie's heart. Mama filled every room in the house with hot steam, as the doctor ordered, and sent Daddy on a mission to find the ingredients for her special mustard plaster concoction. When the burning salve hit the baby's chest, Cadie cried more than Zoe did. "Mama, you're hurtin' her!" she wailed. After several minutes of Zoe's agonizing screams and Cadie's persistent pleas, the plaster was removed, and it was back to steamy rooms and gentle whacks to the back until the doctor could return.

But it was too late. A fever set in and there was nothing to be done. Ice and cold compresses couldn't break the heat coming from Zoe's little body, and no amount of jostling or soothing talk could rouse the baby to feed.

Cadie rocked her all night in the old, wooden rocker in her bedroom, and spooned Blossom's warm milk into Zoe's mouth. "Come on, sweetie, you need to eat for Mama," she said, watching the milk run back out as quickly as it was spooned in. "Here." Another spoonful was given, and out it ran again. Fear gripped Cadie's throat until the tears clouded her vision. "We're not gonna cry, are we? No, we're not." Then placing the baby over her shoulder, Cadie gazed out the window to where the lights from Magnolia Hill burned in her mind, just as brightly as ever.

The funeral was a private affair on a cold, winter Sunday, a few minutes after noon. Mama dressed Zoe in a long, pink dress and matching bonnet, an outfit she had sewn and embroidered for months, not knowing it would be the child's burial clothes. Daddy had stayed up until the wee hours of the morning building a small, pine box and sanding down the sides to remove any splinters and sharp pieces. By sun up, he had brought it upstairs and placed it on top of the hope chest at the end of Cadie's bed. Cadie shooed him away and wouldn't let anyone else in the room while she lined the coffin with the baby's favorite blanket and lace pillow. She lifted the stiff body from the bed and laid it inside like a doll in a cradle. The bonnet and dress were adjusted and an attempt was made to fold the little hands together, but they remained clenched into tight balls as if in the throes of a temper tantrum. Cadie tried to at least flatten out the fingers, but they wouldn't budge.

"Oh, Zoe," she whimpered. Cadie bit her lip until the coppery flavor of blood flooded her tongue. She wouldn't cry, she couldn't, because she'd never be able to stop—not this time. The familiar dagger in her heart had been plunged deep by her own hand, crumpling it like an old, rotten tomato. The word "no" repeated itself in her mind, but Cadie wouldn't say it aloud or she'd collapse like the mental image of that mushy vegetable with rank, red juice spilling out all over the place. She closed her eyes and tried to think of something else, but the ache in her chest made it impossible.

"Cadie?" Daddy knocked on the door and entered. "The minister's here."

A memory of Zoe soared through her vision, along with the sound of a coo and a baby's laughter from a pink, toothless smile. Suddenly, the pain took control, and there was nothing to stop it from rising like a wall of water rushing toward an unsuspecting beach, ready to annihilate everything in its path. Daddy caught Cadie in his arms, cradling her as the word "no" erupted from her like vomit. She shoved her mouth into the sleeve of his jacket where the smells of tobacco and coffee could no longer comfort. He squeezed her tightly while his body shook along with hers. "Twiddle," he whispered, "Twiddle—"

Cadie howled at the sound of his strangled voice. All her life, she wondered why he called her that name. When she had asked, he shrugged his shoulders as he often did, and said that it "just fit," and for a long time it did. But today it seemed silly and out of place. "Twiddle" was a name for a little girl who looked to her daddy to make things right when problems came her way, even if she disagreed with his solution. But there was no solution to this. No one could ever make this right. Not even Daddy.

After a long while, the wave of pain subsided, and Cadie was able to catch her breath again. They stared at Zoe's little body, now a mottled, purple-tinged color. "Everyone's waitin' downstairs. Lemme take you down there so I can tend to her."

"No, I can't leave her, Daddy. I can't."

"Cadie—" He wrapped both arms around her and gave one of his bear hugs.

"I wanna stay."

"You sure?"

Cadie nodded and pulled away from his embrace. She stood over the coffin and stared at the baby, hoping her little eyes would open or her fists would wiggle. "I'm sorry, my sweet darling," she murmured through a trembling frown, caressing Zoe's curls. "Mama's sorry she took you out in the rain." She kissed Zoe on the cheek, trying not to cry again. Then nodding toward her daddy, she gave him permission to slide the lid on the coffin. It made a loud, rough sound as it popped into place.

Daddy opened his jacket and pulled out a hammer and a box of nails. His hands shook as he took his time to settle the first nail in its hole before slamming down on it with a powerful bang. Cadie turned away as she felt the sharp point of metal pierce through the wood and straight into her heart.

Time seemed to slip away, until Cadie became aware of her surroundings. Father Helms stood in the Hamilton graveyard under a shady live oak that grew over a freshly dug grave, droning on about life, death, and the hereafter. Cadie's tried to listen, but her thoughts wandered to benign concerns, such as the sewing jobs piled up in her bedroom, or the washing that needed doing, and then, *Where on earth was Tessie?* Her eyes skated the small gathering, searching for her sister. There was Norman with his head hung low, Mama dabbing her eyes with a kerchief while Daddy bit his lip with that stony, far-away look on his face, and Mr. McLain holding his hat over his heart. The minister flipped the page of his prayer book, and the sound of crinkled paper refreshed Cadie's memory like a pop to the head. Ah, yes, Tessie was still in school and wasn't able to catch yesterday's train, but promised to be home by tomorrow evening. *Oh, well, it doesn't really matter. Nothin' really matters now.*

Cadie shifted her gaze to the little pine coffin with the lid now securely shut. The wood was fresh and smooth and emitted the pungent scent of pine, a reminder that a tree had been sacrificed for this very occasion. Her eyes followed its length—so small but too large for the earth to consume. It was perfectly fashioned by Daddy's strong, capable hands, and yet, there was a flaw they had both overlooked, something mocking her now—the tiniest point of a wayward nail protruding from the side panel. Cadie wanted a hammer so she could slam it down where it belonged, but then it might splinter the wood and hurt Zoe inside. Suddenly, a surge of panic flooded her being. *Zoe was inside! She was inside that box!* Even though her milk had dried up days before, Cadie's breasts twinged with grief. She squeezed her eyes closed, unable to look any longer. How could they put her baby girl in the ground where it was so cold and damp and dark?

As the prayer came to a close, Cadie swayed on her feet, dreading the utterance of the final "Amen." Norman put an arm around her shoulders and held her steady as she folded into his chest. "Norman!" A lone, pathetic sob muffled through his plaid shirt, piercing the solemnity of the occasion.

"It's all right. It's gonna be all right," he whispered.

Anger shot through her like a lightning bolt. How could he say that? It wasn't all right and it never would be! Wrenching away from his embrace, she took off toward the creek, running as fast as her legs could carry her. She had to get far away from everything she'd ever known—she'd run all the way to Wilmington if she had to. She'd keep running and running until she reached a place where this pain could never catch up with her.

A tree limb slapped against her chest, breaking the skin, a twig caught her on the cheek, leaving a deep scratch, and a fallen log made her stumble. She thought of those stories about the shadowy figures in the forest who could exhale fire hot enough to burn a tree, wishing one of them would come out of hiding and breathe on her until she disintegrated into smoking ashes. But the notion of burning made her run even faster, sending her deeper into the tangled forest.

Finally, she fell to the ground, and Norman was there, leaning over her, his chest heaving. A mixture of anger and grief swirled in his eyes, terrifying Cadie as he stared deep into her soul. "Norman—" His mouth descended on hers, covering her with power and strength and a sensation that was so different from the suffering that consumed her. Her arms wrapped around his back, clinging to him, tighter and tighter until she was clawing at him, feeding off the sensation he had stirred. She needed him, and yet, she wanted to hurt him the way she had been hurt.

"Norman, no," she said as he unbuttoned his jacket and yanked it free.

"Hush, now." He folded the garment into a pillow and guided her back down onto the mossy ground, tucking it underneath her head.

"It was my fault," she moaned, looking away from his intense gaze. She stared toward the direction of the river, straining her ears just enough to hear the sound of the current rushing downstream. "I took her out to see the river. I didn't know it was gonna rain. I was mad at Mama for somethin' she said, somethin' about you. And I just ran out."

"You stop your runnin', now, you hear? Don't run away anymore, Cadie. Don't." His voice broke as he gathered her into his arms, forcing her to look at him. Cadie had never seen such depth in his eyes, like she could drown in them, right then and there. Her lungs constricted at the way he held her close, almost nose to nose. "You come home with me. We'll start over and make things right. You'll see. Come home with me."

"I can't. I can't, Norman."

"I said, hush." And he kissed her again and again until her mind reeled with faraway thoughts that made her lose all sense of time and place.

Chapter 19

Cadie did go home with Norman, but not because she wanted to. Despite Mama's efforts to bargain for more time, Daddy made it clear she couldn't live at the farm any longer, hiding away from the realities of life. Mama argued that Cadie's heart needed to heal from the loss of Zoe, but he wouldn't hear of it. "She's a married woman now, and her place's with her husband. They can heal together, and besides, what better way to heal than to start havin' more babies? They certainly can't do that if she's livin' under our roof."

This kind of talk made her mama blush and Cadie wince with shame, but perhaps it was for the best, she reasoned. Her presence around the farm was a raw reminder to Daddy of what had been lost. His hard demeanor had returned, as solid as petrified stone, rendering him unwilling to show any mercy whatsoever, even for the smallest thing. He had become mean and hateful and could inflict a major beating with his tongue, frequently sending Mama to her room in tears. Cadie knew he was grieving in his own way, as they all were, but his method only made the pain worse.

And so, on a cold, winter day, Cadie packed up her meager belongings in an old tapestry satchel and waved good-bye as Norman's truck took her down the dusty, unpaved road to their little house. Daddy couldn't even be persuaded to come out of the barn where he was chopping wood. He had said all he needed to say, and besides, he'd see her Sundee wouldn't he?

The days crawled past at a snail's pace, putting the fear of God in Cadie that she would never, ever experience another ounce of joy in this life. She spent many a night sitting in the middle of Old Hargett's Bridge, listening to Jackson's Creek rush below her feet. Tonight was no different from the others, except that a full moon shone on the glistening water. Somehow, she had survived another dismal day of being Mrs. Norman McLain. She tried cooking him a meal, even baking one of her apple pies, but for some reason the oven overheated and the crust was burnt to a black, flaky crisp. Next, she cut up her old gingham dress and sewed a pair of curtains for the kitchen, but once they were hung, decided they made the house look ugly and old. Finally, she tried taking a nap, hoping to sleep the drudgery away, but the mattress was lumpy and smelly and the house itself was so damp, dusty, and drafty, it was like living outdoors. Cadie wouldn't be surprised if they both caught their death of cold or worse before the winter was out.

Then, there was the problem of Norman himself. Cadie had never known a person more full of faults than this man she had married. His snoring kept her awake at night, he couldn't keep a set of clothes clean for one hour, and his nasty chaw habit was enough to make her lose her stomach. How did he expect her to touch him with that tobacco juice in his mouth? But he did. "I want a buncha little ones 'round and lots of 'em," he would often say with his bulging lower lip and a look in his eye that filled Cadie with a stifling oppression. The thought of what this would entail sent her on many of these walks along the creek bank that extended long past his bedtime.

Staring past her dangling legs, she studied the reflection of the old, weathered pilings that wobbled with the steady movement of the creek. How could this ole bridge stand month after month, year after year? Why didn't it just cave in and quit? "Seems like it'd be a lot easier," she said out loud. She could quit, too, couldn't she? She could lean over a bit and fall in. Cadie closed her eyes good and tight, imagining her body hitting the water, her head smashing against a rock, and then instantly, being with Zoe forever. She could do it, she could. She scooted her bottom closer to the edge of the bridge, feeling a splinter cut through her stockings. *I can lean forward, just a little. Just a little more—*

Suddenly, a soft moan drifted over from the pines nearby and caressed Cadie's ear, sending a chill up and down her spine. She drew her shawl around her shoulders and listened, fighting the fear that gripped her. Before long, the moaning became a cry and then a bout of undecipherable words that erupted into a roar of rumbling laughter. Cadie hopped to her feet and made her way through the dense forest until she came across a small clearing. A Negro man lay prostrate on the ground with his face hidden in his hands and his white shirt illuminated by the moonlight. "Reverend?" she cried. "Reverend Thomas—you hurt?"

"I'm all right, child," he answered, not moving.

"Why're you on the ground like this? You want me to fetch someone?"

"Shh. I'm prayin' to the Lord."

Cadie reduced her voice to a whisper to match his. "Prayin'?"

"Talkin' to Him." He turned his face toward hers and gazed into her eyes. "Mostly 'bout you."

"Me?"

"Shh!" The reverend put his finger to his lips and placed his head back down into the praying position. Cadie waited for his mumbling to cease before uttering another word. At last, a "Jesus" and an "Amen" was said, prompting him to rise to his feet and dust off each trouser knee.

"Why're you prayin' about me?"

"Why wouldn't I pray for you? Aren't you in sore need of prayer?"

Cadie tried to look at him, but his eyes were like fire, boring holes into her very soul. She turned away and kicked the dirt with the toe of her shoe. "I think it's too late for that."

"Oh, child, it's never too late for prayer. Never." He took a step toward her, and it was as if an electric charge filled the air, forcing her backward. His presence was overpowering, and it wasn't just because of his stature and muscular frame but how he filled the space around him, with such confidence and authority—it made Cadie shiver from head to toe. "I know what you've been through—I heard about the little one. Your heart's hurtin', I can see that, but the Lord's a master at healin' up wounded places, especially here," he said, tapping his chest with his long, dark index finger.

Cadie lifted her head and stared. He seemed taller than usual and his shoulders broader than what she remembered. His white shirt was open at the throat and chest, revealing the outline of the dark muscles underneath and the mangled mass of a thick scar that wound around his neck like a piece of twisted jewelry. Most white girls would be terrified to be standing in the middle of the woods looking at a strong, strapping black man like this, but Cadie wasn't the slightest bit scared.

A grin spread across his face, revealing the gleam of his smile. She couldn't understand why in the world he would be smiling at a time like this. "You laughin' at God, Reverend?"

He threw his head back and laughed so loud, Cadie thought for sure the Stephenses would be able to hear it all the way to Magnolia Hill. "No, child, no," he said, his laughter subsiding. "Only a fool would do that." He shook his head in mock dismay. "I've discovered a wise man fares much better if he laughs with God."

"You sayin' God's laughin'?" Cadie gave him a skeptical scowl. "At me?"

"Nope. I'd say it's the other way around. He's mighty grieved. Yep, mighty grieved, He is."

"Grieved? At what? What'd I do?"

"It's not what you've done. It's what you haven't done."

Cadie's eyes narrowed. "Whadda you mean?"

The smile left his face, and the fire in his eyes flickered for a second. "I think you know." The nausea hit Cadie's stomach, and the sweat beaded on her brow, despite the night air. "You remember what I told you? Love is patient and kind. It doesn't envy or boast. It isn't proud. It isn't rude, or self-seeking, or easily angered. It keeps no record of wrongs?"

His words were like a slap in the face, forcing Cadie several steps backward. "I don't wanna hear all that love talk right now."

"That's 'cause your heart's so filled with anger and unforgiveness."

"You don't know nothin' about me," Cadie said.

"Maybe not. But God does. He knows everything."

Her eyes brimmed with tears at the reverend's kind look that smoldered with that special *something* he possessed, that something no one could quite put their finger on. Surely, he understood her heart, didn't he? Maybe she could tell him, of all people, about the agony that raged within her.

Before she realized it, the words were tumbling out of her mouth and falling from her lips in an uncontrolled, disjointed manner. "It wasn't fair, Reverend. I just went for a walk to the river, and it started rainin'—it wasn't her fault. It should've been me who got sick, not her. It shoulda been me. You tell Him that. Tell Him it shoulda been me!"

"Why don't you talk to Him about it yourself?"

Her eyes widened at what he was suggesting. "I can't talk to God!"

"Why not, child?"

"I just can't—I won't."

"But you must."

Cadie's heart sank as that familiar knot of pain lodged itself in the base of her throat. "You sayin' you won't talk to Him for me?"

"You must talk to Him yourself. I can't do it for you."

His eyes darkened as she tried to read his expression. He really expected her to talk to God Almighty in heaven! How could she do that? Not after all that had happened. Surely, God was mad at her, furious even, at something—everything she'd done. She must not be good enough. She was too wild and rebellious and thought too deeply about dark things. She was evil like Tessie and Norman said. How could the reverend ask her, of all people, to talk to God?

The reverend reached out and gently touched her arm. "Let Jesus set you free from all this—"

Cadie jerked away, feeling the anger flush over her like hot water on a washboard. "I don't want nothin' to do with God or your Jesus neither, you hear? He's not real. If He was, He wouldn't 've let my Zoe die, not unless He was evil and mean, and in that case, I double don't wanna have nothin' to do with Him! And stop lookin' at me like that or—or—I'll tell my husband, I will."

"Tell him. Tell him Jesus wants to talk to him, too. There's nothin' that'd please Him more than for the two of you to come to Him, together."

"Well, that ain't never gonna happen!" Cadie felt her face contort in an angry scowl as she jabbed her finger in the air for good measure. "Not ever!"

Reverend Thomas stood still, giving no reaction, just like one of the live oaks surrounding them with roots fixed into the ground—a stalwart with every intention of remaining in his appointed place. After a long hesitation, he opened his mouth and said, "Love is patient, love is kind—"

"Stop it. You be quiet!"

"It doesn't envy or boast or delight in evil doin'—but rejoices with the truth."

Cadie stepped back and stumbled over a dried-out log. As soon as her bottom hit the wood, the split of rotten bark echoed into the night air, ushering in a fear that seeped over her like the trickling from a cracked dam. "I said stop it!" She stood up and glared at the reverend. "Mr. Stephens was right—you people don't know nothin' about God, except what you've made up!"

But the reverend wasn't listening. "It bears up in all things, believes in all things, hopes in all things, endures in all things. Love never fails." He smiled at her and shook his head. "Never, child. Never. His love never fails."

These words fell on her like soft balls of cotton, penetrating her chest and lungs and paralyzing her with a warmth that cascaded from her ears all the way down to the soles of her feet. She was glued to her spot, unable to move or think. "Come," he coaxed, motioning his hand toward her and extending his fingers with a soft, beckoning invitation. "Come pray with me, child."

Oh, how she wanted to! Cadie wanted more than anything to give in to this sensation, to fall into the reverend's arms and weep a great river of tears—but she couldn't. The adrenaline coursing through her veins won over, and instead, she did what came naturally to her.

Cadie turned on her heel and ran with all her might, tearing through the dense forest until her lungs burned and her heart raced more rapidly than her feet could go. At last, she came to the river's edge and splashed through the mud and grass until the cold water slowed her pace to a steady trudge. Why had it taken her so long to come to this place? Hadn't it been calling to her all this time? She didn't need to jump off that ole bridge. She could just come here, to the river, and be a part of the never-ending flow that kept going and going.

The cold water sliced her cheek like a knife, making her gasp. Submerged under the surface, she opened her eyes and saw something floating in the water just below her—a little bonnet and matching pink dress with arms outstretched and little clenched fists, just within reach. Cadie's heart pounded as she swam toward the baby and tried to grab hold, but her arms wouldn't move. Panic fell upon her in waves, causing her mind to thrash around in her head like a caged animal.

No! Cadie wanted to scream, while she watched Zoe float downstream with the current, becoming a faint blob of pink and white. But no sound would come. Instead, her hair and skirt wrapped around her like a collapsed sail, taking her down and down, to a place where the heart slowed and the thoughts grew quiet—to a place where life drained softly and gently away.

Part III

Chapter 20

"Mr. McLain, I just wanted to tell you those eggs Mattie brought home the other day were the freshest I've ever tasted," Mrs. Stephens teased with a flirtatious tilt to her head. "Much fresher than Whaley's."

Zena blushed at the way her employer batted her eyelashes at the crusty ole merchant, and all for a quarter's worth of free eggs. Sometimes rich people didn't make any sense to her at all. It was only because the store was empty that someone like Mrs. Greer Stephens could get away with such behavior, and surely Mr. McLain knew that.

"Well thank you," he said with a wink. "Since you're such a good customer, I'll throw in a few extra for you this time."

Mrs. Stephens laughed and twittered on at something Mr. McLain said, something about collard greens and flour, but Zena continued to blind her eyes and numb her ears. She bowed her head and prayed extra hard that someone would walk in and bring this transaction to a swift close.

At that moment, the front door opened with a soft creak, and a person scooted behind a standing shelf of canned goods. Zena waited for either Mrs. Stephens or Mr. McLain to say something, but neither of them took any notice. Then stepping backward, she leaned on her heels to see who was hiding there. Just as she lifted her head to catch a glimpse under the brim of her hat, her eyes locked with those of a thin, dirty white girl who looked slightly familiar. The shock must have been written on Zena's expression, because the girl cowered from sight as a can of peas slid into her dress pocket.

Lord in heaven! Zena almost said out loud. Wasn't that Miss Cadie Hamilton who Mr. Robert had loved that summer before he went off to school—the same one who had peeked in on the reverend's service that Sunday? Zena remembered the day she had shown up at Magnolia Hill, crying and carrying on, wanting to know what had happened to Mr. Robert. Zena still shuddered at the memory of what transpired between her mama and Mrs. Stephens after Miss Cadie was told to leave. "Don't answer the door for that girl again, you hear?" Mrs. Stephens had said. "She needs to learn her place."

"That ain't right, ma'am," her mama had replied.

"Don't you tell me what's right."

"It ain't right." Mama's angry tone had alarmed Zena, causing her to fear what the Stephenses might do. "It ain't ever gonna be right what you done to him—"

"What do you mean, what we've done to him? He's a grown man now, not a little boy. He makes his own decisions."

"You make it so hard. He ain't never had a chance to learn what it means to be a man."

"Mattie—" Zena remembered Mrs. Stephens reaching out to touch Mama on the arm, but then stopping before her fingers made contact.

"I don't know what you done," her mama had said in a choked voice, frightening the wits out of Zena. "But you done somethin', I know it. He wouldn't just stop writin' like that, not 'less there's some reason. You want this here house, and you won't stop at nothin' till you get it, till you do to him what you done to his mama—"

"We had nothing to do with Mabel and the decisions she made!"

"That's right. You won't have nothin' to do with real love, will you Miz

Stephens? You'd rather sell your soul to the devil himself 'fore you do that."

Mrs. Stephens had tried to hold Mama's gaze, to retain the decorum expected of the mistress of a grand plantation house, but the way Mama had looked at her, with those piercing eyes clouded with anger and hurt, it was clear she had taken the upper hand. A paralyzing fear descended on Zena when she thought of her mama staring at a white lady like that, even if no one else was around to see. But praise God, all Mrs. Stephens did was stiffen up like a dried-out board, narrow her eyes to slits, and thrust her chin upward, disconnecting any power Mama had over her. "I suggest you get back to work before we upset Mr. Stephens," were her final words, and that's exactly what Mama had done. From then on, the subject of Mr. Robert was never mentioned again.

Zena turned away from Miss Cadie, trying to forget about that day, and trying to forget what she had just seen hiding behind the canned food aisle—a cold, sad stare from eyes ringed with dark circles, a gaunt frame, and sallow, pale skin. Locks of dirty, unkempt hair lay against Miss Cadie's head in long, matted clumps and her clothes were so filthy and worn that Zena could smell her all the way to where she was standing. Without realizing it, she closed her eyes and began to pray again, starting with a whisper which slowly grew to a loud mumble. "Lord, bring someone to heal that girl's heart even if it is Mr. McLain's son who stays half drunk all the time. And Lord, give her another sweet baby who she can cuddle and love. And most of all, Lord, send Mr. Robert home so as he can see what he's helped do, if he's done it, and seek forgiveness—"

"Zena?"

Zena opened her eyes to find Mrs. Stephens staring at her with a shocked expression. "Yes, ma'am?"

"What are you mumbling about, girl? I can't take you out shopping for one day without you embarrassing me. Now, you stay close and keep quiet, you hear?"

"Yes, ma'am."

Mrs. Stephens's glance shifted away from Zena to the back wall of the store, as though a great confusion had come over her. "Oh, my—" She took a deep breath and scrunched her nose up into a ball. "Mr. McLain, what is that awful smell?"

"I don't know." He came from behind the counter, sniffing the air with flared nostrils like a hound dog heavy on the scent of trapped prey.

Thinking of a quick excuse, Zena said, "Maybe it's just a rat crawled up under the floorboards, Mr. McLain, sir."

"Hush up!" Mrs. Stephens snapped. "Mr. McLain does not have rats in his store! You think I'd shop here if that were the case?"

He gave Zena an equally cold look and then made his way to the shelves where Miss Cadie was hiding. "Don't touch me with your filthy hands!" he exclaimed, shooing her out the front door. "And don't touch anything! Just go 'round back like I told you, and I'll get what you want. Go on!" The door banged shut, and Mr. McLain huffed and puffed toward the back of the store, muttering under his breath, "Isn't fit to be seen!" He nodded toward Mrs. Stephens said in a subservient manner, "If you'd excuse me for just a moment—"

"I'm in a hurry and need to get my things, now."

He hesitated for a moment and said, "How about I add a sack of extra fine sugar to your order, at no charge?"

Instantly, her harsh demeanor changed, and the coo returned to her voice. "Well, I guess I could wait just a few minutes. If you don't plan on being too long?"

"I'll be back as quick as a flash."

Zena waited beside Mrs. Stephens, who clucked her tongue against her teeth like an old barn-yard chicken. "Poor Mr. McLain, having to be saddled with that urchin."

A screen door creaked open from the recesses of the back storeroom where Mr. McLain's biting voice filled the air. "Here. And tell Norman if he wants to get paid he might consider showing up for work. The two of you are a disgrace!"

Zena gazed out the side window of the mercantile and watched Miss Cadie walk past, clutching a brown paper bag. As their eyes met, Zena thought she noticed a lone tear roll down the side of her dirty cheek.

Cadie held the crumpled grocery bag tightly in her fist as she munched on a stale roll and a piece of cold, fried bacon. The tin cans clanged around in her dress pockets, making a disjointed sound while she moved along the dusty road. She tried to convince herself she didn't care if Norman's pa yelled at her and called her names in front of Mrs. Stephens and one of her help, but the image of Zena's sad expression argued otherwise. She knew what Zena and Mrs. Stephens thought of her, and the whole town for that matter. She was "that Hamilton urchin" who was acting stubborn and rebellious, refusing to accept what life had sent her way and "get on with things," just like the rest of them had done. *Who hadn't suffered a broken heart, or lost a child, or had a dream shattered into smithereens?* she could hear them say. She was a product of her own doing, a down-right disgrace that made everyone, including Mama and Daddy, and even the sewing club ladies, shake their heads and look away. "Pathetic, weak, simple-minded," were words thrown in her direction. "White trash" as Mr. Greer Stephens had once said, and "worse off than a common Nigra."

With a stomp of her foot, Cadie tried to extract all of this from her mind, but it wouldn't budge, just like a nasty bug stuck in her hair with its legs tangled in the dirty strands. She watched the oily locks swing back and forth across her chest, catching a whiff of their scent with each movement. "One, two, three—" She counted her steps as her worn, scuffed shoes pounded the earth.

The tears blurred her vision, causing her to stumble along the road. Without any clear direction or sense of purpose, she found her way back to Magnolia Hill and climbed her favorite apple tree. Like a little child crawling into her father's lap, she nestled into its strong boughs and looked out onto the Stephenses' world, staring at the clouds. She tried to use her imagination to form shapes like she and Tessie used to do, but there was nothing she could see other than a stream of puffy blobs of white.

Soon her mind drifted away to a dreamy place where she tried to picture Dashing's lips on her hand, but the fantasy soon transformed into visions of Boy and then Zoe floating away in the river. The image of a little pink dress and tightly clenched fists disappearing with the swift current melted into a picture of the reverend standing in the middle of the Cape Fear. He was wearing his minister's collar and robe and held a Bible in hand, preaching up a storm while the river rose over Zoe's sputtering lips, threatening to wash her away.

In her dream, Cadie swam toward the baby, but the waters rushed harder, sending her tumbling and turning with the flow until she landed in the mercantile. There was the reverend again, looking handsome and strong in his white shirt open to the chest with scar prominently revealed. He threw his head back and laughed out loud while stuffing small morsels of apple pie in Zoe's stiff, dead mouth until the golden muck oozed out of her nostrils like squiggling earthworms. Suddenly, a gush of muddy river water rushed through the store, taking Cadie with it. She flailed her arms back and forth, but her lungs filled, causing her to sink further into the deep. Her heart slowed and her mind grew quiet, and then something or someone plunged into the cold water, grabbed her by the hand, and lifted her up and up toward a marvelous and glorious light—

Cadie awoke with a start as the echo of the reverend's plea to "come and pray," resonated in her mind. Her heart rammed against her chest and her skin dripped with sweat as on a hot, summer's day. She scampered down the tree and headed back toward the road, stumbling along the way. Cadie couldn't remember a thing about what happened after she confronted the reverend in the woods, but somehow, she had ended up in her bed, dressed in dry clothes, and wrapped in a warm blanket. The slightest reminder of that evening ushered in dark thoughts that plagued her like never before, and they weren't of death or dying or losing Boy or Zoe but, curiously, of the Reverend Thomas praying on the forest ground. Sleep offered no reprieve, since her dreams were equally plagued by these strange images of the joyful, smiling reverend refusing to save little Zoe from one calamity after another while Cadie helplessly looked on.

Lately, the images had grown so invasive that she refused to lay her head on the pillow, instead resuming her long walks along the riverbank that would sometimes last until sun up. Norman's patience had worn out long ago, so that most mornings Cadie found the stove cold and the bed still made. She figured he had found comfort elsewhere, probably in one of his flophouses or bars in the squalor. The smell of liquor had been on his breath for a long while now, a clear sign he had started drinking again. But could she really expect any more from a man like Norman? Just as predicted, his promises and words of love weren't real, and they never would be. *So be it*, Cadie thought. As long as he stayed away from home, she didn't have to cook or clean or reduce herself to the humiliation associated with being a wife. She could be on her own, alone with her thoughts and images and her memories of the past.

Suddenly, a motorcar horn sounded, startling her out of her depression. Cadie fell onto the shoulder of the road, skinning her hands and knees on a bed of sharp rock as a convertible whizzed past, leaving a whirlwind of grime and debris in its wake. She peered into the dust and saw that it was the Duisenberg. The driver sounded the horn once more and turned his head ever so slightly to reveal the outline of a bowler hat and a long, brown cigar wedged tightly in his teeth.

Chapter 21

Zena walked up the long, dirt walkway to the McLain house, with every fiber of her being screaming to turn back and head home where it was safe. This was her one day off a week from working at Magnolia Hill, and no one, not even her mama, knew she was paying a visit to that "dirty, white trash urchin," as Mrs. Stephens referred to Miss Cadie these days. But Zena couldn't help herself. Every time she closed her eyes in prayer, she got a vision of that pretty girl in all of her filth and despair. She just had to do something to help. Somehow, she knew Mr. Robert would want her to love Miss Cadie.

As soon as the house came into view, Zena stopped in her tracks and whistled through her teeth. "Lord in heaven!" she muttered. She had never seen anything like the mess this little dwelling was in. The yard was littered with old newspapers, opened tin cans, half-gnawed corncobs, and broken glass bottles, and a swarm of ants had started building an enormous colony in a mountain of food scraps piled next to the porch steps. As for the house itself, the paint was peeling off every square inch of the wood siding and the porch was sagging to one side in its slow separation from the front wall.

The wind whipped around Zena's legs and over the yard, blowing the screen door open on its squeaky hinges. Suddenly, a horrible stench came from inside the house, wafting toward her so that she choked and coughed for a good minute. She retrieved a handkerchief from her dress pocket, covered her mouth, and made her way up the porch steps.

"Hello?" Zena called, gently knocking on the door. She squinted through the dirty window and pulled the flimsy door open with a creak. "Miz McLain?" There was no sound other than a pop of the porch boards. Zena took a deep breath and stepped inside.

The front yard hadn't prepared her for what she would find on the other side of the peeling, clapboard exterior. The kitchen was an atrocious mess like she had never seen, with dirty dishes piled up in the sink, the table covered with stained waxed paper and greasy, saturated dish towels, and the entire wood floor covered in a film of white, dusty flour. "Gracious sakes!" Zena let out another soft whistle through her teeth. She'd known black folk who lived like this, but never anyone white.

The screen door banged shut behind her, hitting her on the backside like a swift kick in the caboose. She took a step and felt something soggy underneath her shoe—a wad of brown tobacco chaw oozing from the side of her heel. With a grimace, she scraped it against the wooden floor several times and took another look around the place, letting her eyes fall on a pair of red gingham curtains at the kitchen window.

"Anybody home?" she called. There was complete silence, indicating she was all alone. Letting out a sigh of relief, she plopped her knapsack into one of the kitchen chairs and took off her sweater. Normally, she didn't like cooking and cleaning on her day off, but her instincts couldn't tolerate this disarray for long. Something inside of her said, *Get busy and get to work!* And so, rolling up her sleeves, Zena picked up a bucket by the door and did just that.

"*Amazing Grace, how sweet the sound, that saved a wretch like me—*" The sweet, soft lilt of a soprano voice drifted toward Cadie as she shuffled through the junk littering her front yard. It had been several days since she'd been back to the house, and even the time away was not enough to shock her senses into noticing the appalling nature of things. Mama used to come by often enough, armed with a mop and bucket and a tasty casserole, but Cadie purposely stayed away for days at a time rather than face her mama's condescending look. Finally, Daddy put a halt to Mama's efforts and the cooking and cleaning stopped. Even Tessie was ordered not to communicate with her any longer until she and Norman could start "actin' right," as he would say.

Cadie listened as the singing continued—something about being "lost" and then "found," or something of that nature. She kicked a broken bottle aside and pushed the ant hill down with a stomp before making her way up the porch steps where she peered through the screen door. The sight of Zena on her hands and knees scrubbing the sitting room floor while she hummed away filled Cadie with an inexplicable rage. She slammed the front door open and yelled, "Whadda you think you're doin'?!"

Zena froze in mid-scrub as if a loaded shotgun had been shoved to the back of her head. She turned toward Cadie with eyes downcast and a shaky, tottering voice. "Mr. McLain, down at the store, he hired me to help you and Mr. Norman out a little bit 'round here durin' my spare time."

"He didn't tell me 'bout it."

"Guess he didn't want you to know." Zena looked away, her voice wavering even more. "I didn't think you'd mind me cleanin' the floor. It's real dirty."

"I like it dirty."

Zena stood and dropped her scrub brush into the wash bucket. "I'm Zena, by the way." She wiped her hand on her apron and extended it toward Cadie in a cautious manner.

"I remember you." Cadie glared at Zena, refusing to shake her hand. "I don't need nobody cleanin' my house, you hear?"

Zena hung her head and shifted her weight from one foot to another. "Well, ma'am, you see, Mr. McLain, he's already paid me, and if I don't clean, I'll have to give the money back, and I really need the money. So if you don't mind, ma'am, I think I'll go on ahead."

Her downcast look made Cadie cringe with guilt for having spoken so harshly. As her eyes drifted around the room, she saw that things did look a whole lot better. The sink was empty and the counters were clean, the floor had been swept and mopped and the clean pots returned to the pot rack. "Suit yourself," Cadie said, shrugging her shoulders. Then turning away, she marched to the bedroom and slammed the door.

A strange reflection stared back at her from the smudged dresser mirror. Cadie hardly recognized herself now—her face was so thin that the hollows in her cheeks made her look much older than sixteen. She shut her eyes, not letting herself look any longer. She jerked the top drawer open and pulled out a small burlap sack that held a stack of letters tied up with a length of dirty twine. Carefully, she slid one from the stack and plopped onto the bed to open it. Her eyes scanned the words, soaking in their full meaning like a starving animal devouring a long awaited meal. Before long, the tears spilled over her lashes and onto her cheeks, blurring her vision. She then sunk deep into the pillows with the letter crumpled to her chest, giving way to the comforts of sleep.

Cadie awoke to the heat of the afternoon sun shining through a slit in the window curtains, mingled with the sound of humming outside. She pushed herself off the bed pillows and looked out the window to where Zena was hanging laundry on the line. A pair of Norman's wet underdrawers was spread out, long and wide, making Cadie laugh good and loud at the way Zena cast her eyes away before securing them to the line. *Just let 'em fall in the dirt*, she thought. *That's where his underdrawers end up most of the time anyway.*

Cadie swung her legs off the bed and edged the bedroom door open. A whiff of a delectable aroma made her stomach lurch as a raw hunger pang gnawed against her insides. She tiptoed into the kitchen and saw the culprit sitting on the stove—a pot simmering with a thick, brown liquid bubbling around lumps of seasoned meat, carrots, and potatoes, just ripe for the tasting. Cadie hadn't smelled or seen anything this good to eat in so long, it was a wonder she didn't pick up the whole pot, hot handle and all, and drink the contents down with one big gulp. She grabbed the wooden spoon off the counter and stirred the stew, making sure she scraped the bottom of the pot, and then brought a spoonful to her lips. Her eyes closed in anticipation as the warm liquid coated her tongue and dribbled down her throat.

"Is it good?"

Cadie whirled around to find Zena staring at her with a pair of wide eyes. Her smooth, dark skin looked as soft as velvet, and her shy, gentle smile alleviated some of Cadie's guilt for being caught red-handed with the wooden spoon in her mouth. She swallowed awkwardly and said, "It is."

"I figured a pot of beef stew'd keep you and Mr. Norman fed for a while. It's my mama's recipe. People come from miles 'round just to take a bite."

"I can see why."

An uncomfortable silence hovered over them as Cadie tried to think of something more to say. She licked her lips and took a good look around. The kitchen sparkled like she'd never seen, even down to the gingham curtains, which looked as though they had been freshly pressed. "Sure looks clean 'round here."

"Yes, ma'am. I didn't mind cleanin' up one bit."

"I guess not, since Mr. McLain's payin' you."

Zena bowed her head slightly and said, "Yes, ma'am."

"How much's he payin' you anyway?"

"Well, ma'am—" Zena continued to stare at her feet. "I'd rather not say."

"Probably not much. He's 'bout as stingy as they come." Cadie studied Zena's downcast expression, trying to figure out why this was a source of embarrassment. "Well, just don't let him cheat you."

"Yes, ma'am."

A black, leather-bound book sat open on the kitchen table with gold edged paper, small writing, and even some parts that were printed in red, which seemed strange to Cadie. She lifted the front cover and looked at the title, which read *The Holy Bible* in bright, gold-embossed lettering. "This yours?"

"Yes, ma'am."

Cadie was impressed with how pretty it was, even nicer than the one Reverend Thomas preached from on Sundays. "Sure is fancy lookin'."

"Yes, ma'am, it is. It was a gift from the reverend."

"Oh." Cadie noticed how Zena's face lit up at the mention of the reverend's name. She couldn't help but remember their last encounter in the woods, and immediately, shame engulfed her. How could she have said those horrible things to him that night, especially after all he'd done for her and Zoe? The thought of little Zoe sent the sadness rushing back, followed by a wave of nausea. Cadie tried to steady her emotions as she gazed at the Bible. "He gives these out to everyone?"

"Nope. Just when he has one extra."

"Huh." Cadie flipped through the crisp pages, feeling the puff of breeze against her hand as her thumb skimmed through the crisp paper. She had never read the Bible, and didn't even know what one looked like until the day she was putting laundry away and found one hidden in Mama's linen drawer, covered by a lace handkerchief. That had been years ago, but to her knowledge, her parents had never read it or talked about Jesus or God too much, other than the "Good Lord this" and the "Good Lord that" or the obligatory church outing at Christmas and Easter. On the rare occasion, when Mama was in a righteous mood, Cadie heard, "God helps those who help themselves, and that's straight from the Good Book, missy." Cadie pictured her now with hand on hip, wagging a judgmental finger as she quoted from the *Good Book*. She often wondered why Mama called it "good," yet kept it tucked away in her vanity drawer.

"You read it?" Cadie asked, flipping through the pages again.

Zena's smile spread across her face, and her eyes widened even more. "Oh, yes, ma'am."

"All of it?"

"Yes, ma'am."

"What's it say?"

Zena gave her a curious look. "You never read it?"

"Nope. We only had one Bible, but Mama wouldn't let us touch it. Guess she was afraid we'd mess it up."

"Lord, I don't know what I'd do without my Bible." Zena fanned herself with her palm as if she was suffocating from the heat. "I'd probably die. Yep, I'd probably just shrivel up into nothin' and float away with the wind."

"Is that why you go 'round singin' all the time?"

"Guess so," Zena said, toying with the edge of her apron. "You don't mind, do you ma'am? I mean about me singin'. Reverend Thomas says that's how you can tell when someone's really happy—when they have a song in their heart, and it just has to burst its way out."

The sound of Norman's old truck pulling up the dirt driveway made Cadie frown. She brushed Zena aside and peeked around the gingham curtains, watching him kick the driver's door open and tumble out. *Yep, drunk again*, she thought as he stumbled up the path toward the porch. But what did she expect? He was no good, a bad seed who'd never change. Not in a million years.

The door burst open and Norman shuffled inside, reeking of liquor and tobacco and other smells too vile to name. He fought to maintain his balance while staring at Cadie through a pair of bloodshot eyes. "You home?"

She propped her hand on her hip and glared at him. "I'm standin' here, ain't I?"

He ignored her and shifted his focus to Zena, who cowered behind Cadie. "What's she doin' here?"

"If you showed up for work every now and again, you'd know your daddy hired her."

"Hired her for what?"

"To clean up all your mess. Whadda you think?"

His expression exploded with a short blast of fury. "Ain't that what a wife's supposed to do?!"

"I wouldn't know," Cadie said, narrowing her eyes. "I ain't never had a husband. A real one, that is."

He took a step toward her with his hands formed into tight fists, and for a split second, she thought he might hit her. In fact, she wouldn't have minded if he did—it would just give her another good reason to hate him even more. "I don't want no Nigra in my house for long," he hissed like an old, leathery snake. His eyes glistened like two shiny marbles as his look bounced over Cadie to where Zena continued to cower. "Get her outta here once she's done, you hear?" Then pushing past the two, he made his way toward the bedroom.

"She's gone and cooked you a meal!" Cadie called to him. "Ain't you gonna eat it?" But all she got was a slammed door in response. "Stupid man!" she said, glaring at Zena, whose eyes were wide with fear. "I don't understand how anybody could be happy livin' 'round here!" Then with a loud stomp and a slam of the screen door, she stormed out of the house in the same manner Norman had come in.

Chapter 22

The fresh scent of cherry and dogwood blossoms filled the morning air with the promise of winter's end. Even the azaleas were starting to bud and the oleander and wild honeysuckles emitted a strong scent every time Cadie ventured near the outhouse, which was a blessing, indeed. She sat on the front porch, rocking back and forth in an old, broken-down rocker Norman had retrieved from the junk pile, letting her wet hair dry in the sun. She had taken a bath this morning, washed her hair, dressed in clean clothes, and had even done a fair amount of housework. The bed was made for the first time in weeks, the furniture dusted and floors swept, and the kitchen had been made good and ready to cook up another one of Zena's delicious creations. Cadie knew Norman's pa wasn't paying the girl a nickel to help out around the house, him being so mean and selfish, so she couldn't let Zena do all of that work, week after week, on her own. Why Zena kept coming over to help free of charge was a mystery, but Cadie didn't dare ask, as her visits were the one thing she had to look forward to.

Cadie flung her hair over the back of the rocker and rested her eyes until Zena came swaying down the dirt path in rhythm to the tune she hummed to herself. *My goodness, that girl's always singin' about somethin'!* Cadie couldn't help but smile as she listened to Zena's sweet voice, wishing she could be more like her. Before she knew it, she was humming along, not even aware of what she was singing. Something she had heard before, something about grace. Wonder what this grace was anyway, and what was so amazing about it?

"Hey there, Miss Cadie!" Zena said with a grin, waving a long, lean arm back and forth in the air. She held up a brown paper sack and shook it a bit. "I've got the fixin's for my crispy fried chicken!"

"Good, 'cause I sure am hungry!"

Zena jogged up the path and bounded up the creaky, old steps to the porch, her face beaming with excitement. "You sure look pretty today, Miss Cadie." She gently sniffed Cadie's neck and smiled extra big. "Mmm—and you smell good, too."

Cadie smiled back, wanting to hug Zena hard and plant an enormous kiss on her cheek. "Oh, Zena, you look pretty, too. But then, you always do." She opened the screen door extra wide and stepped aside for Zena to pass. "Come on, and let's get that chicken to fryin'."

Over the next several weeks, Zena shared all of her best recipes with Cadie, including country fried steak with onion gravy, collard greens cooked in ham hocks, squash and cheddar cheese casserole, and extra flaky buttermilk biscuits, while Cadie, in turn, showed Zena how to make one of her famous double-crust apple pies. After the food was in the oven baking or on the stove simmering, Zena often pulled her Bible out of her knapsack and read stories to Cadie, starting with Adam and Eve, Noah and the ark, Abraham and Isaac, and all sorts of other crazy characters she found between its pages. Zena acted out all the parts with great drama, keeping Cadie on the edge of her seat as she listened intently. Cadie was amazed at what she heard, especially when it came to the story of Joseph and his brothers.

"You mean his brothers threw him in a pit and tried to kill him? And then sold him as a slave? Just 'cause he had a dream and his daddy gave him a pretty coat? What kinda brothers do that?" Cadie couldn't help but ask the obvious.

"Mean ones, I guess," Zena said with a shrug of her shoulders.

"I'd say so."

"But wait till you hear what happened." Zena scooted to the edge of her seat and leaned in toward Cadie as if she was about to divulge a wonderful, mysterious secret. "Joseph becomes a very important slave but gets put in prison for somethin' he didn't do. Then 'cause he's good at dreamin' and all, he deciphers a dream the king has about a famine comin', and the king makes him prince over the whole land. And then one day his brothers come to see him to get food, 'cause they're starvin' and all—"

"They oughtta starve for what they've done," Cadie said.

"Course they don't know it's Joseph, 'cause he's dressed like an Egyptian. See?" Zena flipped to a page in the front of the Bible where an artist's rendering of Joseph in full Egyptian attire gleamed at Cadie from a glossy, gold-trimmed page.

"Hmm." Cadie eyed the picture with suspicion. "Looks kinda funny."

"That's how men in Egypt dressed back then. Skirts and makeup."

"That don't sound right, Zena."

"I know, but just listen, now, and lemme finish the story." She set the Bible down and resumed her wide-eyed look. "So his brothers come askin' for food, and they don't know it's Joseph they're talkin' to, and so he tricks 'em into bringin' his little brother to Egypt. And when they do, guess what happens?"

"He kills 'em all, except for the little brother."

"Naw!" howled Zena in protest.

"Well, he throws 'em in prison for the rest of their lives."

"No. He shows 'em who he is, that he's really Joseph, and then he forgives 'em and gives 'em food and money and the best land in Egypt to live on."

"Huh?" Cadie placed her hand on her hip and stared at Zena like she had grown an extra head. "After they lied and stole and tried to kill him, he's just gonna forgive 'em? Just like that?"

Zena beamed another one of her enormous smiles. "Yep. Just like that."

"But how he can do that?" Cadie glared at Zena as if she had lied to her outright. "Why would he do that?"

Zena swished her arms up into the air like she was casting fairy dusty over their heads. "'Cause of grace."

"Grace?" Cadie said it like she'd just been slapped in the face. It always came back to this talk of grace. Zena had taught her a number of songs, including all the verses of her favorite, the one she was always humming—*Amazing Grace*. Cadie had memorized all the words and could sing it along with Zena, loud and with conviction. The trouble was, she hadn't the foggiest idea what it all meant, and she hated to ask, for fear of looking foolish. "Zena, I just don't get it. I've racked my brain tryin' to understand what this grace is. We keep singin' about it and all, and now you're tellin' these stories about it, but for the life of me I can't seem to figure it out." Cadie looked Zena dead in the eye and asked the question that had plagued her for months. "What on earth is grace?"

Zena looked like her tongue had been tied up with rope and her mouth glued shut with cement. In all the time Cadie had known her, she'd never seen her this quiet, like a mouse hiding under the kitchen floorboards. Her face remained dark and contemplative until Cadie was forced to ask, "Well, don't you know?"

"I do. I'm just tryin' to put it into words." Zena tilted her head and batted her long, dark eyelashes. "Well, it's kinda like this—it's like when you discover you've done somethin' horribly wrong and bad—"

"Like lyin'," Cadie added.

"Yeah, like that," Zena said, looking away and batting her eyelashes even more, as if a secret had just been uncovered. "And a terrible beatin' is waitin' for you, maybe even death itself, and you know there's no way out, you have to take it—pay the penalty for what you've done, and then someone, someone special, comes along and says, 'I took that beatin' for you, Zena girl, and I even died for you so you can escape all that out there. You've just gotta believe I did it's all, just believe it and say it's true, and it'll be like you never did that horrible thing to begin with, and you can go on with your life and live it, happy and free.'" Zena stared at her with wide, innocent eyes. "Does that make sense to you, Miss Cadie?"

"No, Zena," she said, shaking her head. "That don't make no sense at all. Who's gonna do a thing like that?"

"Someone who loves you, that's who."

Cadie thought long and hard. "Someone like my mama I guess? She'd take a beatin' for me, I think. She'd probably even die for me." Cadie's gaze wandered off to the trees just outside the kitchen window and beyond. "I sure woulda done it for Zoe if I'd had the chance."

Zena pulled the gingham curtains over a bit so she could gaze out the window as well. "Problem is, your mama's got her own bad stuff she's done. How she gonna take your beatin' or your death if she's gotta pay for her own wrongs?"

"Don't know. Guess I'd have to find somebody who loved me, who hadn't done nothin' wrong."

"Yep, that's true."

"Guess that's where this grace comes in, huh?"

Zena nodded as her eyes met Cadie's, glistening like two pools of deep, sparkling water. "There's only one person who ever lived who ain't done nothin' wrong."

Cadie knew who she was talking about, but did she have to say that name? What was it about this Jesus that brought fear to her heart? Why was she so afraid? An image came to her mind of a bloody, beaten corpse suspended in midair, making her shudder. "You're sayin' He did it for me?" she asked with a nervous catch to her voice. "And I wasn't even born yet—thousands of years ago? He died there on that cross for me and all my evilness?"

"Why not? He's God's son, ain't He? You think He can't do it?"

"No, I didn't say that, I just don't believe it. He'd have to love me an awful lot, and He doesn't even know me, or at least I feel like He doesn't know me, 'cause I sure don't know Him." Cadie gazed out the window again at the swaying of an oak tree in the wind. "I believe He died and all, and He rose up like you said. I just don't believe He did it for me. I can't believe that."

Zena touched Cadie's back with a gentle pat, sending a rush of warmth across her chest and arms. "What else you gonna believe in, hmm?" Her words were like a surge of electricity penetrating Cadie's eardrum "Yourself? Mr. Norman?"

"No."

"Mr. Robert, maybe?"

"Don't mention him, you hear?"

"Yes, ma'am."

Zena removed her hand and the warmth dissipated. "I won't believe it," Cadie said. A single tear flowed down her cheek and dripped onto the porcelain sink where a pile of potato skins formed a little mountain. "Ain't nobody loved me that much—nobody." She sniffed back another tear and thought of all those people in her life who claimed to have loved her—Mama, Daddy, Tessie, Norman. Even Boy. Cadie slammed her eyes shut at the thought of him. Nope, she was right, not a single one loved her in that way. Not a single one. Not even little Zoe.

After their discussion on grace, Cadie noticed a quiet, unspoken division fell on her friendship with Zena. Things just weren't the same as before, no matter how hard Cadie tried to resurrect the connection they once had. It wasn't Zena's fault, as she continued to laugh and smile, sing and tell stories while she cooked, cleaned, and did the laundry. Cadie knew the problem lay within herself and her unresolved fears over so many things. She wanted to talk about them more than anything, but something was holding her back from everything Zena represented.

The problem was only exacerbated by Norman's return home. Somehow, he had figured out the days Zena showed up and made sure he got his fair share of her good cooking. Of course, he was always filthy and stinking drunk, but it didn't stop him from finding his way back to the house and gorging himself like a swine being prepared for Easter dinner. Cadie couldn't stand the sound of his slurping and smacking. It was disgusting to her and made her detest him all the more. Not only had he intruded on her time with Zena, but he left a colossal mess in his wake that she and Zena had to clean up.

It was a warm spring afternoon—almost hot—and the opened windows carried in the fresh smell of pollen which mingled with the aroma of Zena's chicken and pork stuffed dumplings simmering on the stove. Before sitting down to eat and hearing another Bible story, Cadie decided to scrub the muddy boot prints Norman had left on the sitting room floor while Zena swept the loft and the bedroom. Cadie was looking forward to hearing about Ruth, one of Jesus' ancestors, and her love for Boaz, a strange name to her mind. But as usual, Norman had flopped down at the kitchen table, and now everything would be delayed.

It was his habit to glut himself without looking Cadie's way or saying a word, other than grunting a command, like "fetch me the salt," or "pour me some tea," before disappearing in his truck, all in about an hour's time. But lately, he was staying longer, sometimes napping in the bedroom afterwards and making idle chitchat, including downright mean and nasty comments directed toward Zena that made Cadie's blood boil. She had put up with his mouth for some time now, but her patience had run its course. Zena told her to ignore him and show the love of Jesus, but that "turnin' the other cheek" business was ludicrous to Cadie. She had her own interpretation of the words of Jesus—she wouldn't mind slugging Norman across one cheek and turning to slug the other so he could get a taste of his own medicine. And today happened to be one of those days.

A horrible coughing from the kitchen table stopped Cadie from her scrubbing and Zena from her sweeping, as the sound of Norman choking on something brought an eeriness into the house. He coughed again, violently, and then retched a wad of fatback on the kitchen floor as if he was spitting on the ground outside. "Norman McLain!" Cadie dropped her brush into the soapy bucket and stood to her feet. "I just scrubbed those floors, and you go and spit on 'em like that?!" He didn't respond but shoveled another spoonful of dumplings into his mouth and kept chewing as though her voice didn't carry an ounce of sound in it. "Norman? Did you hear me?" she said, grabbing a wet dish towel from her apron and whacking him on the back. No sooner had she struck him, than his hand swooped out like an animal claw and grabbed the end of the towel, pulling her close. Darkness filled his expression, causing fear to gather in her throat.

"You're lookin' real pretty these days, Cadie." His eyes scathed her body and rested on her face.

"Get your hands off me. You're dirty." She tried to pull away, but his arm latched around her backside, pulling her even closer. He motioned with a nod toward Zena, who was now cleaning on the far side of the room. "Tell that Nigra to go on outside for a little while, so you and me can talk."

Cadie stared at him in shock—the fact that he kept calling Zena that terrible name sent a hot rage coursing through her veins. She grabbed a handful of whiskers on either side of his face and yanked his head back, glaring at him with deep hatred. "Don't call her that! Don't you call her that!"

He pushed her away and stumbled to his feet, his eyes ablaze. "Woman! Whad you go and do that for? I'm just tryin' to talk sweet to you, act a little tender!"

"Well, you might as well save it for one of your hussies down in the squalor, 'cause I ain't never gonna touch you again in that way, you hear? Especially after you go and talk 'bout Zena like she was some animal or somethin'. She's not an animal, she's a person, full of love and kindness. Not like you! You're just a sick, fat ole pig, that's what you are, eatin' your slop like you were headin' straight to the slaughter. If anyone here's the Nigra, it's you, Norman McLain! You're just an old, beaten-down, worn-out Nigra—"

Like a bullet from a shotgun, Norman's bowl slammed against Cadie's chest, knocking her backward. She looked down at her dress, half expecting to find blood, but instead saw a giant blob of a ruptured dumpling with its innards running down the front of her apron. Before her thoughts could register, the kitchen table flipped wrong side up with one mighty heave, sending the dishes, silverware, and full pot of supper splashing all over the kitchen wall and gingham curtains.

Cadie backed up against the stove as he came toward her, but there was no escape. He pulled her toward him, his fingers cutting the back of her arm. "You're gonna shut your mouth and shut it good!" His shoulders were thrown back in the fighting position, and his jaw worked back and forth like a deranged cow about to chew its tongue in half. "Now, I ain't never hit you, not ever before. But right now—right now, you tell that *nigger* to wait outside."

Zena stood wide-eyed with her mouth hanging open like she'd seen a specter in the forest, just like all those tall tales Cadie had heard over the years. She stumbled over her words, stuttering, "I'll jjjust go ssstep on— sstep on out, Miss Cadie."

"No, you stay right where you are." Cadie cringed at the shakiness in her voice, yet she refused to look away from Norman's stare. The seconds ticked by as his eyes remained latched to hers. Finally, he spit a nasty wad of spittle on the floor, right at Cadie's feet, which was all Zena needed to high tail it out of there. She dropped the broom to the floor and scooted out of the house as quick as a jack rabbit.

A grin slid across Norman's face, revealing the remnants of pork stuffing stuck in his teeth. "I hate you Norman McLain," Cadie said. He laughed, and the smell that came from inside him was revolting, like oily shoe leather with a hint of Indian spice that had sat in the cupboard for far too long.

"You know that ain't true."

"It is. It is true!" He moved in on her, backing her into a corner like a pursued animal. In the shadow of the afternoon sun, Cadie saw how mangy and bristly he had become, and she turned away, appalled at the very thought of him. Slamming her fists against his chest, she pushed him back with all of her might, but he was too strong. The stench of him grew in power until his mouth descended on hers, sweeping her back toward the wall. "I hate you!" she cried. And with each successive gulp of air she repeated over and over, "I hate you, I hate you!"

Chapter 23

"Sweet Jesus, please protect Miss Cadie, protect her!" was all that went through Zena's mind as she tore out of the house like she was being chased by a pack of starving wild dogs. Down the banks of the river she ran, hiding among the live oaks for what seemed like hours. Her hands trembled and her whole body shook while the pangs of guilt for having left Miss Cadie in such a predicament interrupted her prayers. What if he hurt her? What if she was laid out on the bed like a beaten animal or strung up in a tree or worse? Zena shuddered at the images these thoughts conjured. Surely, Mr. Norman wouldn't do such a thing, would he?

Zena hadn't seen a white man that mad since the time Mr. Stephens got so angry at Mrs. Stephens for reading his private mail. She remembered the screaming and crying and carrying on that had taken place between the two, and then the crash of one of Mrs. Stephens' special ceramic vases against the marble fireplace. What a mess that had been! Zena and her mama had spent an hour picking up the little pieces of glass off the burgundy Oriental rug so Miss Molly wouldn't cut her precious, bare feet. Then there were the tales about the mean white men who had come for the reverend that night so long ago. Zena breathed in deeply and took control of her thoughts. Hadn't Mama told her time and again not to think about that, not to ever breathe a word of it?

Zena exhaled, trying to concentrate on the matter at hand. Mr. Norman was Miss Cadie's husband, and what they had was just a lover's quarrel like Mama had explained to her was common in marriage, wasn't that right? *No,* she thought, *that couldn't be right.* Everyone in town knew Miss Cadie and Mr. Norman had never loved each other, not even from the start. *Oh, Lord, what if he did do something terrible? What if—what if Miss Cadie's dead?*

Zena knew she had to get back to the house and quick. She emerged from the trees and backtracked through the woods with her knees still knocking and her teeth chattering. She'd rather face ten fat Mrs. Williamsons and a pack of angry white women in the mercantile than Mr. Norman when he was in one of his drunken, foul moods. But her conscience wouldn't let her cower in the trees like an ole yellow belly any longer. "Lord Jesus, you're just gonna have to give me the strength to stand up to him, that's all. Miss Cadie don't have no one else, and she needs me." Zena looked up at the sky and pointed a shaky finger heavenwards. "Spirit of fear, you go on your way and leave me be. I ain't afraid of no mean white man, even if he does talk about us black folk lookin' like animals and calling us that nasty name and looking at me in that dirty way. He's just a heathen, that's what he is, holdin' a one-way ticket to that place down below that I don't wanna even mention right now. He's gonna be burning' up somethin' awful if he's done anything to Miss Cadie. And Mr. Devil, you best not be messin' with Miss Cadie no more. She don't belong to you, and you don't have no right workin' through that sorry husband of hers and messin' up her house after we've gone and cleaned it all up . . ."

Courage returned to Zena as she talked to herself, the Lord, and the devil all the way back to the house. When she got close enough to see through the trees, she stilled her prayers and tiptoed to the back porch, hovering close to the peeling sideboards. She peeked around the side yard and noticed Mr. Norman's truck wasn't there. *Good, he's gone—for now.* She couldn't help but recall the look on his face when he flipped over the kitchen table. Lord, he sure was a mean one. Wonder what made him that way? Was he always so hateful, or was there a side to him that Miss Cadie had taken a liking to long ago? She did have a baby with him, after all. There must've been something there, something buried way down deep.

Zena inched her way to the front porch and entered the house. Dumpling stew was slopped all over the walls and floor and had stained the curtains, but she pushed these concerns aside and made her way toward the bedroom. "Miss Cadie?" A muffled cry came from behind the door, like the meowing of an injured kitten. "You all right?" She pushed on the doorknob and a long, agonizing creak of rusty hinges permeated the house.

Miss Cadie was curled up on the bed in the fetal position with her feet tucked up tightly under her skirts, sobbing. "Miss Cadie!" Zena hurried to the bed and touched her shoulder. Her eyes were open, but they had a strange look about them, focusing on something Zena couldn't see. "What'd he do?"

"Nuthin'," she murmured through her tears.

"Miss Cadie. I'm here for you. I'm here," Zena said as she smoothed Miss Cadie's hair away from her face. Her white porcelain skin, blue eyes, and blonde hair reminded Zena of a beautiful china doll bearing a giant crack right down the middle of its face, like the twisted leg of a granddaddy long-legged spider. Zena had never owned a pretty doll, except for one of Miss Molly's hand-me-downs that had suffered a smashed foot and hand and had all of its eyelashes and hair pulled out of its head long ago. Yet, Zena had loved it and treated it with the most tender care. She remembered the grief she experienced the day its head broke away from its body and no amount of glue or twine could hold it together. She and Mama had performed a quiet funeral for "Martha," as the doll was fondly called, and buried her in an old shoe box under one of the live oaks in the back yard. For days, she cried and cried until Mrs. Stephens put an end to the mourning over what was described as a piece of "useless trash that should've been tossed out years ago."

Hot tears pricked the corner of Zena's eyes, threatening to spill over onto her cheeks. "I'm sorry I ran away like that," she said, "but I was scared. I know I shouldn't 've been, but I couldn't help it. You understand, don't you, Miss Cadie?" She sniffled and waited for a response, but there was none. "Oh, Miss Cadie!" Zena couldn't help but sob at the injustice of it all. It broke her heart to see her friend lying there on the bed with her spirit fractured in this way. Maybe Mr. Norman was her husband, but what right did he have to hurt her like this? Why couldn't he leave well enough alone?

"Zena?"

"Yes, ma'am," Zena said through her tears.

"Zena—" Miss Cadie rose up off the bed and threw her arms around Zena's neck. "Don't cry, Zena. Don't."

Zena shook with grief as she sobbed even harder. "I'm so ashamed, Miss Cadie. I'm ashamed for leavin' you all alone."

"Hush now," she said, patting Zena's back with her palm like she was rocking a baby to sleep.

Love swelled in Zena's chest like an inflated balloon, threatening to burst at any moment. Now she knew how her mama felt every time she had fallen and skinned her knee when she was little, or gotten a bad scolding from Mrs. Stephens, or been threatened by Mrs. Williamson and those white ladies in the mercantile that day. Mama had always been there to care for her, just like any mother would do, and at this moment, Zena felt the same way about Miss Cadie. She was special and precious and in dire need of saving.

"I ain't never gonna leave you again, Miss Cadie. I don't care what he says or does. You hear?" Zena said, kissing her tangled curls. "I ain't never gonna leave you." She wrapped her arms around Miss Cadie and squeezed hard, just like her mama would've done if she was the one crying and in need of comforting. Soft words of encouragement were whispered, and she even hummed a little tune under her breath while Miss Cadie sat as silent as the grave. They remained there in the dim light with their arms around each other until the sun went down over the horizon.

It was no surprise to Zena that her mama had caught wind that she was up to something, since she was good at finding out things, as most mamas are. "Girl, where you been all this time?" she asked, yanking Zena into the plantation kitchen the next afternoon.

Zena had been late from her noon day break for four days in a row now, and Mrs. Stephens had started asking questions, wanting to know "why her good money was being wasted on help who didn't even bother showing up!" Zena did show up, but was a good half hour late and as sweaty and out-of-breath as a just-broken horse after running all the way from Miss Cadie's house. She was full of excuses, from breaking a shoelace to falling asleep by the river, but today, Mama wasn't listening.

"Miz Stephens's been snoopin' 'round here like a fox in a hen house wantin' to know where you are. I've held her off for long enough, but now you're just gonna have to tell me. Whatcha been up to? And where you been goin' night and day when I got my back turned?"

Zena couldn't look at her for long, for fear her eyes would give away the truth. "Well, I don't rightly know—"

Mama shoved a hand on her hip and tapped her toe like she was pumping an old sewing machine. "Now, Zena Goodwin, you know that's a lie, and lyin's a sin before the Lord!" She shoved an index finger in Zena's downcast face. "I've a good mind to turn you over my knee this minute and give you a whippin'. Now, what would the reverend say if he knew what you'd just done?"

"You're not gonna tell him are you, Mama? Please don't tell him! Please!" Zena wailed. She flung herself at her mama's skirts and sobbed into the starched apron, imagining what the reverend would say or do if he could hear their conversation just now. "I'll take the whippin' Mama, just don't tell the reverend! Promise me, please!"

"Goodness gracious, child! Ain't no use carryin' on so. Come here." She drew Zena into her lap and rocked her in her arms. "I won't tell him, but you've gotta let me know the truth. What is it, now? Come on and hush," she cooed.

"Mama, I'm afraid. I'm afraid to tell you."

"Zena, since when've you been afraid of your own mama?" She tipped Zena's chin up and wiped her tears away with the edge of her apron. "Does it have somethin' to do with that missin' ham from the smokehouse and those chickens?" Zena nodded without looking into her eyes. "You took 'em?" Zena's eyelashes fluttered in a way that gave no doubt what the answer was. "You know that's stealin' don't you? What's Miz Stephens gonna say when she finds out we're stealin' from her? You know she's gonna figure it out, she always does. Ain't nothin' gets past her."

"I know, Mama. I know."

"Well, you better have a good explanation, a good one yes, ma'am, you better. 'Cause if you don't, you might just get that whippin', after all."

"You're not really gonna whip me—are you?"

Mama raised an eyebrow and tipped her head in a decisive way. "It may not be me doin' the whippin'."

Zena searched her expression for some sign of exaggeration but could see Mama was just relaying the facts. A picture soared through her mind that sent a chill down to the very bones—an image of Mrs. Stephens taking a strap to her like she'd done to one of the housekeepers who had gotten caught red-handed stealing from the silver chest several years ago. The girl had been given the choice between a beating and a trip to the sheriff's office, and of course, the beating won the day. Zena could still remember the howls of pain coming from the back of the barn with each slap of the strap.

Zena bit her lip and sputtered, "I cooked up that food for someone who needs it, someone who's hurtin' real bad."

"Who?"

"That girl Mr. Robert took a likin' to that summer."

Mama's shocked expression made Zena cringe. "You mean Mr. Norman's wife—that white trash settin' in the apple trees and up in the church steeple?"

"She's not trash, Mama."

"Zena! You know what Miz Stephens thinks 'bout her. Whatcha doin' helpin' her out anyways? Don't you know how much trouble she could make for us?"

"She needs me. She don't have nobody else, and she needs me. I don't care if Miz Stephens does find out, I can't just turn a blind eye when I see hurt in the world. I'll pay for the ham and those chickens outta my own money, I will! But I won't turn my back on Miss Cadie, I can't!"

Thankfully, Zena's tears were enough to convince her mama that Miss Cadie was worth the risk of being caught by Mrs. Stephens. And the decision was confirmed when Reverend Thomas preached another sermon that Sunday on the power of God's love. As he worked himself into a wild frenzy like he was known to do, pointing his finger at someone over here and waving his arms at this person over there, he zoomed in on them and spoke right in Mama's face as if he could read her thoughts. "*Do* for that white girl, no matter what she done, you hear? *Do* for her!"

Zena sat there with a thick lump stuck in her throat. How on earth did he know? He didn't—but God did. It was because of the reverend's amazing connection with the Almighty that allowed him to talk this way to other folks like no one else could. She relaxed into a smile, marveling that, after all the needless worry, fear, and concern, her instincts to help Miss Cadie had been right in line with what the reverend thought and believed.

Chapter 24

Zena begged Cadie to come home with her, but she wouldn't hear of it. Norman's actions had brought her to a new low, but not low enough for her to leave the house she and Zena had cleaned and scrubbed and fixed up to its presentable condition. They tidied up the mess in the kitchen, putting the curtains to soak in the wash tub, and righted the table to its proper place. Then sitting down to a pot of hot coffee and a piece of Zena's pecan pie with whipped cream, they devised a plan—there would be no more elaborate cooking to entice Norman to return home, and Cadie would spend as little time as possible alone in the house, even resorting to sleeping in the woodshed out back if she feared his return for some reason. Zena would check on her every day, and if things got really bad, Cadie promised to reconsider staying with the Goodwins. But Cadie had no intention of doing that—she had been enough of a burden on Zena and her mama as it was.

Once they finished discussing the details, Zena slid her pie and coffee to the side and grabbed Cadie's hands. "Now, Miss Cadie, the last thing we're gonna do is pray, and it shoulda been the first. We're gonna pray for you and me, but mostly, we're gonna pray for Mr. Norman."

Cadie shook her head as if a vile taste had entered her mouth. "I can't, Zena. You pray if you want to, and I'll just listen. But I can't pray for him."

"All right, then." Zena squeezed Cadie's hands before closing her eyes and bowing her head. "Dear, Lord Jesus . . ."

Cadie immediately shut her mind off from what Zena was saying. Not that she would've understood anyway. It all sounded good and righteous, like what Reverend Thomas would've prayed, but it just didn't seem to matter to Cadie. What good were a bunch of words gonna do to help out her situation with Norman?

Nevertheless, Cadie closed her eyes and bowed her head out of respect for Zena. She tried to think of positive things, but the negative images of Norman and the sweatiness of his skin swirled around in her mind like an afternoon windstorm. Her memory took her back several weeks ago, to a day when Cadie was helping Zena hang the laundry on the line. Norman had shown up around lunch time for a plate of cornbread, honey smoked ham, and turnip greens, and afterward, lay sacked out on an old, knotted hammock he had strung up between two pine trees. He had stayed there for hours it seemed, just swinging and snoring and disrupting all of nature around him. It didn't seem to bother Zena, but for some reason, it absolutely drove Cadie crazy. She had thought about stuffing his mouth with an old sock, sticking acorns up his nostrils, or cutting the hammock ropes with a sharp knife, but none of that was practical and would just make matters worse.

Suddenly, Norman had let out a particularly loud snort that made Cadie and Zena jump about a mile and even caused the birds to stop chirping in the trees. "That's it!" Cadie had said, scooping up a handful of pinecones on the ground.

"Miss Cadie, what's you gonna do?"

"I'm gonna shut that man up, once and for all!"

"Now, Miss Cadie—"

Before Zena had time to secure the clothespin to the line, Cadie had hauled her arm back and thrown one, two, and three pinecones right at

Norman's forehead, while muttering under her breath, "Stupid, stupid—man!" The last pinecone had whacked him right between the eyes, causing him to sit upright and flip out of the hammock onto his behind. Even now, Cadie couldn't help but giggle at the memory of Norman sprawled on all fours in the dirt.

"It isn't right the way you treat Mr. Norman," Zena had said later, her eyes glistening with emotion. "I don't care what he's done—he's your husband."

"He ain't my husband," Cadie had lashed back. "Not in my heart he's not."

"In the Lord's eyes, he is."

"What does the Lord know about it?"

"Everything."

The Lord knows all about it. He knows everything. Cadie shook the memory of that day from her mind as Zena finished up her prayer with a "Jesus' name, Amen." She studied Zena a moment, pondering what she meant by those words, *The Lord knows everything.* "Zena, how's the Lord gonna know everything about me and Norman?" Cadie asked. "Does that mean He sees us all the time, you know, even when we're alone together?"

Zena pulled her hands away and smiled in a shy manner. "Goodness, Miss Cadie. I don't know 'bout stuff like that."

"But you do—you must. You're the only one I can talk to who'll answer these questions in my head." Cadie grabbed Zena's hands again and held them firmly in her own. "If the Lord knows all about me and Norman, and you say He even picked Norman out for me, then why don't I feel differently about him? Why do I hate him so much? It ain't right for a girl to hate her husband, to be sickened by him, is it?" Tears came to Cadie's eyes as she contemplated her next words. "I know what it feels like to love a man, and it don't feel like this. It's wonderful and good, and this—this is shameful and dirty."

Zena was quiet for the longest time, her mind obviously busy at work, trying to come up with an answer. "I don't know, honest I don't, Miss Cadie. All I can think to say is, even though Mr. Norman's mean and sorry and all, he shouldn't be forcin' things on you and makin' you feel that way."

Cadie looked at Zena for more, but all she saw was a blank stare in her dark eyes. Her gaze wandered over to Zena's knapsack hanging on the back of the chair. "Wonder if the answer's in that Bible of yours?"

Zena shrugged her shoulders. "I guess we outta take a look." She pulled the black, leather book from her knapsack and opened up its gold-lined pages. "The reverend says if you ever need an answer to a question about God things, you should go to the book of Psalms, right in the middle." She flipped a few pages backwards and then forwards. "Let's see—" Her eyes fell on something and Cadie could tell she was reading intently. "Oh, Lord—"

"What? What is it?"

"Oh, this is Isaiah. I need to go back to Psalms like the reverend said."

"No, you don't Zena!" Cadie smacked her hand down on the page, almost ripping it from the binding. "You're gonna tell me what it says."

Zena sucked in a deep breath and blew out. "All right." She cleared her throat and began to read in a loud, authoritative voice as if she was standing at the pulpit. "'Do not be afraid, for you will not suffer shame.'" Zena looked over the edge of the Bible, but Cadie encouraged her on with a nod. "'Do not fear disgrace for you will not be humiliated. You will forget the shame of your youth and remember no more the reproach of your widowhood—'"

"Widowhood?" Cadie asked.

"That's what it says."

"What else does it say?"

"'For your Maker is your husband—'" Zena cast another quizzical look Cadie's way and then slid the Bible over toward Cadie. "Don't you wanna read it on your own?"

"No, you're doin' fine. Keep goin'."

Zena took the Bible back and continued reading, slowly and carefully. "'The Lord Almighty is his name—the Holy One of Israel is your Redeemer; He is called the God of all the earth. The Lord will call you back as if you were a wife deserted and distressed in spirit—a wife who married young, only to be rejected, says your God.'" Zena stopped once more and then bowed her head and read the final lines. "'For a brief moment I abandoned you, but with deep compassion I will bring you back. In a surge of anger I hid my face from you for a moment, but with everlasting kindness I will have compassion on you, says the Lord your Redeemer.'"

Zena closed the book and stared at Cadie. "Guess the reverend's right. The Bible's full of answers, even if they do seem strange and a little jumbled up."

"Jumbled up is right," Cadie said. She thought for a moment, rolling the words she had just heard over in her mind, trying to figure out their meaning, but it was just too difficult to understand. Was God saying He was her husband? Surely not! Surely, those words didn't apply to her at all, did they? "Well, you're just gonna have to read more, Zena. Go on, open it back up and keep on reading."

And so Zena spent the rest of the night reading the Bible to Miss Cadie. One passage led to two questions, which led to two more passages, which led to four questions, and on and on until Zena thought her head would spin with all the flipping of pages and reading and answering questions Miss Cadie asked. She reminded Zena of a hound dog intent on finding some old, forgotten bone it had buried in the back yard. *How on earth did the reverend keep all of this Scripture straight in his head?* Zena wondered. *And how was he able to find the answers to all these questions?*

Never in Zena's wildest dreams would she have thought she could teach anyone about the Bible, much less a white woman, but every moment the two of them were together, there seemed to be nothing else Miss Cadie desired to talk about than God and His Word. And the studies were taught in the most unusual places. Sometimes they snuck away to the grassy place by the river where Miss Cadie used to watch the riverboats going to and from Wilmington, except she didn't seem to be as interested in the destination of boats as she once was. When that became too conspicuous, they studied by the old rope swing Boy had shared with Miss Cadie deep in the woods, or tucked away in the little lean-to when the weather demanded it. Occasionally, they put the Bible down and took turns on the swing, flying high and wide over Jackson's Creek, and on other occasions, when a streak of boldness hit them, they stripped down to their skivvies and cooled off in the water.

Despite their discretion, word got back to Mrs. Hamilton's sewing club that Miss Cadie had been playing in the woods with some "uppity" Nigra girl. Zena warned her to tell the truth, but when confronted with an unexpected visit from her mama, Miss Cadie lied and promised never to see Zena again if it was kept a secret from her daddy and Mr. Norman. "I'll do the best I can, honey," Zena overheard Mrs. Hamilton say, "but you know I can't guarantee anything like that with Eunice Johnson lovin' gossip the way she does."

"But Mama," Miss Cadie wailed, "you can't let her tell anyone, especially Norman—you just can't! If he finds out, I'll run away, I swear I will! I'll run away and you'll never see me again!"

"Hush, now. You won't do any such thing. You come on home for a while, eat some of my cookin' and get some meat back on your bones.

You're too skinny. Haven't I been tellin' ya? A man can't love a girl with her ribs stickin' out like that." She fluffed Miss Cadie's hair around her shoulders and adjusted the waist on her dress. "Give 'em a couple a weeks and they'll have somethin' new to gossip about. I hear tell Emmie's pregnant and gonna have Curtis's baby and Mrs. Johnson's plannin' a big ole party to celebrate . . ."

Zena knew Miss Cadie had stopped listening by now. But she did just as her mama suggested, even agreeing to sleep in her old bedroom, where the picture of that flapper model tacked to the wall and the crack in the ceiling taunted her with their lies.

After two days of eating her fill of her mama's apple-fried pork chops, squash dumplings, cheese biscuits, and hot rhubarb pie, Cadie announced she was heading back home. She didn't care what Mama or those sewing ladies had to say, she couldn't stay in that house another minute. Daddy drove her back on a cold winter morning without saying a single word. The silence between them was deafening, and the air in the vehicle was so thick only a freshly sharpened meat cleaver could cut its way through. Finally, the truck came to a stop by the front porch of Cadie and Norman's little home. She was relieved to find the outside looking neat and tidy, which meant either Norman hadn't been around or Zena had come by to clean up.

Cadie got out of the truck, closed the door, and stared at her daddy. How she wished he would look at her, just once, but she figured the sadness and shame of all they'd been through wouldn't let him. "Bye," she said in a soft voice.

He put the truck in gear and slightly pressed on the accelerator, never turning his head away from the wheel. "Come see your mama on Sundee. She's been missin' you and needs to see you every now and again."

"I know. But it's so hard for me—"

"Well, you do what you have to. You're a grown woman now."

Cadie grabbed the side of the truck and pulled herself up to the window, hoping he would turn and look at her. "But I'm not, Daddy. I'm just barely seventeen."

"That's old enough." And off he drove, leaving her standing there in a cloud of dust.

His rebuff hurt, but not enough to stop her from being with Zena. Before a full day passed, they were back to their normal routine of reading the Bible, just as Cadie planned, but they had to be more careful now, since people were watching from every side. A secret nook in the wood shed was a great place to hide away from the eyes and ears of others, as well as a hidden closet under the loft stairs camouflaged by an old coat rack. The inside was musty and damp smelling inside, but that was soon forgotten once Zena began to read from the light of a lone candle held securely in Cadie's hands.

Cadie had never been much for reading, especially books with small print and hardly any pictures, but this book was different. Everything about it was mysterious and alluring, as if beckoning one to come closer and discover the truths that lay behind the compilation of words and formation of letters. Cadie learned about all Jesus did healing the sick, giving sight to the blind, and even raising people up who'd been dead in the grave for four days. At the thought of Jesus raising the dead, especially that little Jewish girl, Cadie felt that familiar pang to her heart. What if Jesus had been there when Zoe was sick? Would He have straightened out those balled up fists and raised her up out of that wooden coffin in her little pink dress and matching bonnet?

As predicted, Zena couldn't answer these questions, which left Cadie empty and frustrated, yet strangely comforted. Perhaps Cadie didn't understand, but she knew in her heart the answer had to be in those fancy pages, like buried treasure begging to be unearthed by anyone tenacious enough to dig it up. Cadie knew she wasn't as smart as the reverend when it came to God matters, or Tessie when it came to school work, or even Zena with her sweet, child-like acceptance of everything she was reading, but she vowed she wouldn't rest a day until she understood it all for herself. She'd keep digging and digging until she found exactly what she was looking for.

Chapter 25

For the next several weeks, Miss Cadie tried her best to keep Mr. Norman away from home, but nothing seemed to work, especially around suppertime when he was on one of his nightly prowls. Like a rabid, mangy raccoon scavenging through an abandoned campsite, he was always looking for something to eat, and tonight was no exception. Zena had spotted his truck coming down the road a good ten minutes ago and had quickly helped Miss Cadie gather their things before skedaddling into the woodshed.

"Cadie! Cadie, you home?" he called at the top of his lungs as he swayed back and forth on his feet. "I know you are! Cadie! Come on out, now. I miss you, I jus' wanna talk to you—"

"Shut up you ole coot," Miss Cadie muttered under her breath, which was far better than telling him to "just dig a hole and die, why don't you?" or the worst to Zena's ears, "go straight to Hell, straight to Hell!" Zena always shut her eyes and said a prayer when she heard this, and she wasn't just praying for Mr. Norman. Usually, her prayers were directed toward Miss Cadie, who didn't have an inkling as to what she was saying when those words came out of her mouth. No one who knew even the slightest thing about Hell would wish that on anyone, not even their worst enemy.

Mr. Norman's tirades always ended with him falling flat on his face in the dirt, often lying there all night long. After a several minutes of whispering and waiting, Miss Cadie would pull Zena out from the woodshed, and they would approach his drunken carcass like a dead animal by the side of the road. She would do mean things like scuff dust in his face, sometimes kicking him hard in the backside. Zena would beg her to stop, but it wasn't until she started quoting Scripture and praying out loud to the Lord that Miss Cadie would leave him alone.

Sure enough, after a bit more ranting and raving, Mr. Norman passed out cold near the oak tree in the front yard, like he always did, with Miss Cadie giving him a swift kick to the bottom. But this time, he moaned as if he was in great pain. "Miss Cadie, I think you've gone and hurt him bad!" Zena exclaimed. "Maybe we need to call the doctor." But Miss Cadie didn't say a word. She just hauled off and kicked him again, making him writhe on the ground like a snake with its head chopped off.

Zena had a hard time getting that image out of her mind as she and Miss Cadie read the Bible later that night in the closet nook under the loft stairs. They had eaten a quick supper of cold fried chicken, day-old angel drop biscuits with a slab of smoked cheese, topped off with a wedge of a Granny Smith apple, and a mug of hot coffee laced with melted chocolate Miss Cadie had saved from her last birthday celebration. The kitchen was clean and tidy, and the fire had been stoked to take the chill out of the air, but still, Zena couldn't stop thinking about Mr. Norman lying outside in the dirt, kicking around in his agony. Goodness knows, that man needed saving more than anyone! She hated to admit it, but he terrified her, like some fireside, ghost-story boogey man who supposedly stalked the woods around these parts. "What if he wakes up," she asked with a tremor in her voice, "and finds us in here?"

"He's passed out by now, Zena—dead to the world," Miss Cadie said. "You know he won't rouse till the sun's way up in the sky tomorrow. We're safe as can be in here. Now, go on and read." Miss Cadie pushed the Bible into Zena's hands while she held the little candle high above her head to illuminate the darkness.

"Well, all right." Zena pulled her shawl closer around her shoulders and read from the Gospel of John in a careful, dramatic whisper. "'In the beginning was the Word, and the Word was with God, and the Word was God. The same was in the beginning with God. All things were made by Him, and without Him was not anything made that was made. In Him was life, and the life was the light of men—'" Suddenly, the sound of a loud thump outside gave her pause. "What's that?"

"I didn't hear nuthin'."

"Yes, you did."

"It's probably just some animal that's got in the kitchen."

"We haven't cooked nothin'. And anyway, how's an animal gonna get in the house?"

"Shh." Miss Cadie put her finger to her lips and held the candle steady with her other hand. They waited a moment, but all was quiet. "See—it's nuthin'. Go on, and read."

"I'm not. I'm scared, Miss Cadie. What if it is Mr. Norman? What if he's woke up?"

Miss Cadie looked at Zena in the strangest way, as if she knew what was about to happen and welcomed it like a warrior eager to meet her opponent. Her eyes burned like flames of fire as she extended her hand toward the Bible. "Give it to me."

Zena handed the Bible to Miss Cadie and took the candle from her hand. She'd never known Miss Cadie to read from the Bible—she always insisted Zena do the honors, as though she wasn't worthy to recite the Word of God. But for some reason, tonight was different. Miss Cadie's fingers stroked the pages like they were priceless jewels while her eyes scanned the words. The thump moved inside the room, and a loud clump of heavy footsteps echoed just outside the door.

"Miss Cadie!" Zena whispered frantically.

"Hush, now, Zena. We're gonna read this Bible, aren't we?" Miss Cadie gripped the leather binding and swallowed hard, like she was trying to shove an unchewed lump of food down her throat. She read in a low, steady murmur, "'In the beginning was the Word, and the Word was with God, and the Word was God. The same was in the beginning with God. All things were made by Him, and without Him was not anything made that was made. In Him was life, and the life was the light of men.'" The coat rack slid away from behind the door, making Zena gulp involuntarily, but Miss Cadie continued on, "'And the light shines in the darkness—'"

The adrenaline took over, paralyzing Zena with fear so great that she was unable to move. The only thing she was conscious of was her heart pounding in her chest. For a moment, she thought she wasn't breathing, but she must have been, because the candle blew out with a firm gust of her exhale. The next words from Miss Cadie's mouth chilled Zena to the very bone. "'But the darkness has not comprehended it—'"

The next thing she remembered was the closet door opening with a crash and Mr. Norman grabbing Miss Cadie by the hair and dragging her into the light. Her feet flailed across the floor as she tried to kick him. "Let go of me!" she screeched. "Let go, you pig!"

"You shut your mouth!"

Zena had never seen Mr. Norman possess a countenance that was this evil. He seemed to have grown five inches in height and about fifty pounds of solid muscle in his chest and arms, and his face was a dappled purple color with flushes of red around his neck. And the eyes— Zena couldn't look at them for long. They were bulging wide and shiny, yet flat as a dark, black abyss, giving her the unshrinking sensation that she could be sucked into those two gaping holes like dirty water down a sink drain. If there really was a boogey man who roamed the woods outside, he surely couldn't look any scarier than this! "You're gonna answer me when I call you!" He grabbed the Bible from Miss Cadie's hand and flipped through it. "What's this?"

"Give it back." Miss Cadie lunged for it, but he held it high above her head.

"You're readin' the Bible—in the closet?"

"Give it back! It's Zena's."

Mr. Norman hesitated, staring into the darkness where Zena huddled. His expression was so terrifying, she had to close her eyes and pray. "You're readin' the Bible—with a daggone *nigger*?" Miss Cadie lunged at him and swung her fists, but he grabbed her hands and held them back. "Don't you hit me, you hear? Don't you hit me 'less you wanna git hit." He smacked her hard in the face with the Bible, and she went down to the floor like a fighter in the ring.

All fear drained away from Zena, and she bolted to her feet. "Please, Mr. Norman, it was my fault. I won't do it again. Just don't hurt Miss Cadie."

"Miss Cadie?" he asked, glaring at her with hatred in his eyes. "She ain't Miss Cadie to you. She's Mrs. McLain, you got that?" He came within inches of Zena's face and it was like she was looking into the eyes of the devil himself. "I don't want this kinda trash goin' on in my house," he said, holding the Bible by the back cover so that its pages dangled by his leg. "And I don't wanna see your black face round here ever again, you hear me? You don't work for my daddy. I asked him. So I'm wonderin' where you get the money to cook up all of this food and keep hangin' 'round."

"I don't wanna get paid, I'm just doin' it 'cause I want to. I've used my own money and some things I had at home."

Mr. Norman laughed and shook his head. "You expect me to believe that?"

"No, sir, but it's true."

"You better hightail yourself on outta here, or you're gonna be sorry! I mean it. Now, go!"

Zena wanted to run more than anything in the world, but something inside of her said otherwise. Sweat rolled down her brow as her heart raced. "No, sir. I ain't leavin' Miss Cadie."

"Why, you uppity, no good—" He unbuckled his belt and pulled it out of his trouser loops like he was cracking a whip. "I said git!"

All she could see before her was raw evil, but her feet still wouldn't run. *Oh, Lord, Lord, Lord, sweet Jesus,* kept running over and over in her mind as he slung his arm back and came down hard on her arm. The shock of the first lash on her bare skin stilled her thoughts to a mindless hum—her breath evaporated from her lungs and her eyes swam with tears as everything around her became distorted and out of focus.

Before the second strike made contact, Miss Cadie had risen off the floor as if she'd been resurrected from the dead. The side of her face was swollen and blood laced her lip, but that didn't stop her from leaping on Mr. Norman's back like a flea on a dog, kicking, screaming, and slapping him around the face and arms. "Leave her alone! Leave her alone!" Zena looked on in shock as the two of them stumbled around the room in an all-out struggle, rattling the pictures and the figurines on the mantle. Miss Cadie fell off his back and lay sprawled on the floor, kicking and screaming. "Run, Zena, run! Get outta here!"

Zena shook her head. "I ain't goin'."

"Zena—"

"No, I ain't goin'! I ain't never gonna leave you, Miss Cadie! Not ever!"

Cadie knew Zena was true to her word—she wasn't about to go and leave her there with Norman in his fit of rage. That left her with one option—let her body go limp so there was nothing for him to struggle against. "You gonna stop fightin' me?" he asked, out of breath. She lay still in his arms for what seemed like the longest time while they both gasped for air. His lips brushed up against her hair, and she caught a whiff of liquor. "You gonna let me be nice to ya?" He put his hands on her face and forced her to look at him. His eyes softened at the sight of her swollen cheek, and for a second, his countenance looked almost gentle. "Cadie, why do you have to make me so mad? I don't wanna hurt you, I don't. All I've ever wanted to do is love you." She pulled against him, trying to get free, but he held her tightly in his arms, drawing her close. "Did you hear what I said?"

"I heard you, and it's a lie."

"It ain't a lie, Cadie." His eyes sparkled briefly, reminding her of the old Norman from the Stephenses' apple orchard long ago, thinking he could possess her like a piece of chattel. But Norman McLain would never possess her. Never.

He moved close for a kiss, and she spit in his face. The dark look in his eye returned, and he pushed her away, wiping his cheek with the back of his hand. "You think you're so high and mighty—" He picked up the Bible and waved it in her face. "'Cause of you readin' this—this piece of trash?!"

"It's not trash. You wouldn't know anyway. The only thing you know how to read is the back label of a tin of sweet peas!"

"You think that's right? I'll show you who can read." He slapped the pages open and read the first thing his eyes fell on. "'Blessed are the peacemakers for they shall be called the children of God!'" All was silent as these words fell over them like a clean, white sheet being snapped across a blank bed mattress. He slammed his eyes back down and read some more.

"'Blessed are they which are persecuted for righteousness' sake, for theirs is the kingdom of heaven.'" Cadie met his gaze and held it. They both knew these words didn't mean a hill of beans to him. "See, it's just trash," he said, as another cloud of anger moved across his face. "And I'm not gonna have it in my house!" He stomped toward the fireplace, dangling the Bible close to the flames.

"Don't you do it, Norman! That's Zena's and it don't belong to you." She lunged for him, but with a casual flip of the wrist, he tossed it into the fire. "No!" she screamed, watching in horror as it crackled in the heat. Instinctively, she made a grab for it, but Zena was there, pulling her back to safety.

"Don't, Miss Cadie. Just leave it."

"But it's burnin', it's burnin'!"

"Let it burn. It'll be all right."

"No, no it won't," Cadie moaned, as the fire engulfed the beautiful black leather binding and gold edged pages.

"We'll get another one. We'll talk to the reverend—"

"No! No—" Cadie shoved Zena aside and stood tall and erect, facing Norman. Anger filled her limbs with a superhuman strength that was frightening. She wanted to kill him now, more than ever before. She had a deep desire to pound on him until he was knocked six feet under the earth, or punch him in the jaw and watch his head fly off his body straight to the moon, or better yet, strike him with a sword and break him in half so that the life gushed out of him in a never-ending flow.

"You!" she said, backing him into the bedroom. "You burned it! You burned it!" She pushed him hard, and he fell against the wall as if he'd been hit by a violent force. Rage flushed through her, sending her arm across the dresser with one long swoop so that everything—her comb, hairbrush, and lamp—crashed down on his head like a terrific hailstorm. Just as expected, he covered his face with his arms like the stinking coward she knew he was. "You've taken everything from me! Everything!" She yanked the diamond wedding ring off her finger and threw it so that it hit the floor beside him with a pronounced "ping," landing somewhere under the dresser. "It was mine! Mine!" Her voice wavered as she jabbed a wobbly finger in his face. "That was *my* money!"

Cadie made her way toward the kitchen, unable to share the same space or breathe the same air with the likes of Norman McLain. "She better not show her face 'round here no more. I mean it!" he called from the bedroom in a weak, pathetic voice. "You hear me? You get back here!" As Cadie and Zena scurried away into the night, the last words they heard were, "You're my wife!"

Chapter 26

The moon shone through the window of Zena's bedroom, casting long shadows on the blue ceiling laced with painted, white stars. Cadie lay next to Zena and gazed at the creation above her. She tried to count all the little celestial objects in an effort to keep her mind off what had transpired earlier that evening, but her eyes got tangled up in the dim light, forcing her to start over for the umpteenth time. Now she was more awake than ever.

Cadie pulled the blankets away, crept out of the squeaky bed, and tiptoed to the window. It slid open with a gentle push, allowing her to lean out past the sheer curtains to breathe in the crisp air. Above her, the night sky appeared more alive than anything she had ever seen, with its myriad of stars twinkling down at her in a way Zena's painted creations never could. The moon was its main attraction, displayed in three-quarter brightness and enthroned by an array of spectacular courtiers who seemed to cry out words of hope and better things to come to those who dared to believe. Hope rose up in Cadie as she beheld this glory that could only be from God. Was there a better life for her out there? Did God have a plan for her?

"Miss Cadie?" Zena whispered. She sat up in bed and rubbed her eyes.

"Did I wake you?" Cadie asked.

"No." Zena slipped out from under the bed-covers and joined her at the window.

"You sure?"

"Sure." They gazed up at the sky and stared at the moon and stars. "Looks different from what's on my ceilin', don't it?"

"It does."

A long hesitation passed before Zena spoke up. "I'm sorry I lied to you, Miss Cadie—'bout workin' for Mr. McLain. It's just—well, you needed someone to help you, and I knew you wouldn't take help from me—not 'less I lied."

"It's all right, Zena. I knew it the whole time."

"You did?"

Cadie looked at her tenderly and smiled. "Yeah."

"It was wrong, I know," Zena said. "I've asked the Lord to forgive me every day."

"You don't need forgivin'. It's me—and Norman—who need the forgivin'. I owe you my life, I do. Don't know what I woulda done if you hadn't come along." Cadie rested her arm around Zena's shoulder and nestled her head in the crook of her neck like she used to do with Tessie sometimes. "Zena, why do you stay 'round here? You don't have a husband to tie you down or anything like that. Why don't you go off somewhere excitin'—go see the world?"

"Goodness, Miss Cadie. Where would I go?"

"I don't know. Somewhere far off."

"But I like it here. It's my home and my friends and family are all 'round me. I can't imagine a better place on this earth to be, except maybe Heaven."

Cadie traced the edge of the moon's crescent with her eye, trying to follow where it disappeared into the night. "I envy you, Zena Goodwin."

"You, a white woman? Envy me?"

"I do. You work your fingers to the bone and make barely enough to live on, but I never hear you complain. I'd give anything to have what you've got."

"Just be patient, Miss Cadie. The Lord'll do the same for you one day, you'll see."

"Maybe," Cadie said, with a deep sigh. "All I know is, I can't ever go back there to him, Zena. And I can't go home, either. It's hard on Mama and Daddy, and it all reminds me of things. Things I'd rather forget."

"You'll know what to do when the time's right." Zena's palm was a soothing touch against the small of Cadie's back. "In the meantime, you stay here as long as you want."

"You sure your mama don't mind?"

"Naw! She thinks it's fine. But she's gonna put you to work."

"Oh, is she, now?"

"Yep, but if you behave yourself, maybe she'll share some more of her recipes. Like maybe—" Zena tapped her index finger on her chin and looked to the ceiling as she contemplated, "apple fritters with cinnamon sugar, and hot gingerbread with melted white frosting, and oh, let's see—maybe her lemon custard pie with whipped cream on a buttery, shortbread crust..."

Cadie giggled at Zena's wide-eyed excitement while she talked on, describing the food they'd be cooking while she stayed there--food fit for a king. Her spirits soared up to the moon, and for a brief while, she forgot all that had happened just hours before. Finally, when Zena exhausted her recollection of Mattie's scrumptious recipes, it was time to head back to bed. Cadie tried to close her eyes and snuggle down under the covers, but there was no way she could sleep. After some time, she rolled over to her side and gazed at Zena, watching her chest rise and fall in a slow rhythm, indicating sleep had come her way. Her velvety, smooth skin shone in the light like an ebony jewel that made Cadie smile, the way one does when observing a wondrous thing of beauty. And Zena was beautiful in every way. Her eyelashes curled up to her eyebrows, giving an innocent appearance, but the rest of her features were refined, yet thick in the areas in keeping with her race. "Regal elegance" was the term that came to mind when Cadie looked at Zena, especially when she wore her hair wound in a neat braid tucked at the nape of her long, slender neck.

Her eyes traveled down Zena's arm until they stopped at the white bandage tied around a lean, muscular bicep. Nausea rolled through her belly, choking her with grief. "Zena, you asleep?" she whispered. Zena didn't stir, and Cadie was glad. "I'm so sorry he hurt you. I won't rest a wink until I've made it up to you, I promise. He won't ever touch you again. And I'll get you another Bible, a real fancy one with gold trim and maybe some extra pictures, too." She leaned over and kissed Zena's wound, planting her lips on the bandage. "You sleep tight."

The floorboards creaked under Cadie's weight as she made her way down the narrow hallway to the kitchen and opened the screen door to the covered porch. A swing moved back and forth, making a ghostly sound as the breeze rustled through the trees.

"Come sit down, child," Mattie's voice called in the darkness.

She approached the swing and wedged herself in the seat, feeling the soft side of Mattie's flesh against her leg. Mattie swung her arm around Cadie's shoulder and pulled her close like Cadie had done with Zena just minutes before. "Can't sleep?"

"No, ma'am." Cadie didn't know Mattie at all, other than what she'd observed at Magnolia Hill and what Zena had told her, yet she was comfortable sitting here next to Zena's mama with her arm draped around her like this. Cadie imagined Zena sitting in this same space countless times before.

Mattie pushed the swing with the edge of her toe, sending it back and forth in a rhythmic creak as the crickets chirped in the background. Cadie relaxed like a piece of old, softened tanner's hide, sensing a cloud of sleep fill the air like a dense fog. Before long, the crickets and the creak of the porch swing drifted further and further away. "You ever wonder what happened to him, what he's doin'?" Mattie asked. Suddenly, the cloud lifted, turning the volume of the world back to its full level. Cadie remained quiet, acting like she hadn't heard the question. "Well?" Mattie asked again, staring hard at Cadie. "You gonna answer me?"

Cadie looked away, her voice barely audible. "I don't know who you're talkin' about."

"Oh, yes, you do. And it's not your Mr. McLain, neither."

The silence continued as Mattie waited for her answer. "I try not to think about that," Cadie said.

"I expect not." Mattie pushed the swing harder this time, so that the breeze flowed through Cadie's hair. "He promised he'd come back, didn't he? Promised to marry you, too, I reckon." Cadie's silence was answer enough. "I told him not to do it, not to break your heart."

"He didn't break my heart—" As soon as the words left her mouth, Cadie cringed like a thief caught red-handed. They were a lie and she knew it.

"He wouldn't listen," Mattie said, shaking her head. "Never has listened to me. Not ever. Just like his mama, he is—Miss Mabel was her name. Sweetest child you ever saw and pretty, too, but with a mind of her own. Old Mr. Stephens couldn't do a thing with her."

By now, tears streamed from Cadie's eyes and rolled down her cheeks like giant, salty boulders. These feelings had been pushed down so deep and locked away, never to resurface, hadn't they? But there, in her mind, was a reminder of something—a flash of a smile, the strength of a confident swagger under an old straw hat, and a head full of tousled blond hair.

"He never said a word," Cadie whimpered. "Not a letter, nothin'."

"That ole fox got to him, that's why—Mr. Stephens. Lord knows how he did it, but somehow, he got to him, but good. Everybody knows that boy can't last a day without his pockets loaded with money. Oh, he talks 'bout comin' back and settin' up house here, makin' that plantation some grand farm and all, but it's just talk. Those days've long gone. It's a dream to him, somethin' he don't know how to take hold of." Mattie resumed a slow, steady rock of the swing with the heel of her foot. "He don't know how to be a man, that's the problem. He wants to be somethin' bad, but it'll cost him, and I guess he figures the price is just too high. He hates Mr. Stephens somethin' awful, but he can't break away from that money hold they've got on him." Her voice trailed off into the night. "I reckon the Lord knows what's been done."

Cadie hid her eyes in Mattie's dress as her shoulders shook uncontrollably. Mattie plopped her foot on the porch floor and brought the swing to a wobbly stop. "You've gotta forgive him, you know that, don't you?" She cupped Cadie's chin in her hand and wiped a fresh stream of tears away before it flowed into the crevices of her lips. Her voice was soft now, with a gentle inflection that was warm and soothing. "Lord knows, I've forgiven that boy 'bout a thousand times for all the things he's done to me, and even when he kept on doin' 'em, too. But you—you gotta do the same if you want your heart to heal." She pulled a crisp handkerchief from her pocket and dabbed Cadie's face. "There, there, you just cry on Miss Mattie's shoulder. Come on, child." Cadie did as she was told and sunk her cheek into Mattie's soft bosom, letting her emotions have free reign. "Start with Mr. Robert, and before you know it, you'll be able to forgive that ole sorry husband of yours, too. Lord, he is a sorry one," she said. "Mean as an ole rattlesnake, he is."

"It's 'cause of me, not Zena." Cadie blubbered. "He hates me, that's why he hit her. Probably 'cause I hate him."

"Hate's a strong word, child. Why you hate him so? Just 'cause he's mean and sorry?"

"No, I don't know. I just do."

"And it's gotten you into a fine mess, hasn't it? Yes'am, hate in a marriage can be a mess not worth cleanin' up. But, when you love the man, like I loved Zena's daddy, that mess seems—well, it seems a lot less messy—'cause you know he's the man God made for you, if you can imagine that. May not seem like it at times, but you know it to be true, way down deep in your heart. That's how I felt about Mr. Goodwin. He was my man, you know, and everybody else knew it, too. He was a good, solid man."

Cadie sniffled and looked into Mattie's face. "Has Mr. Goodwin been dead a long time?"

"Alive with Jesus, that's how I call it. Yes'am, it's been a long time now, more than twelve years 'bout. Zena was just a bitty child when he went on to Heaven. He was workin' out in the field early one mornin', and his heart just gave out. I remember 'cause he wanted hotcakes with his eggs, but I had to go on to the Stephenses' and didn't have the time to fix 'em up right the way he liked 'em, with honey and melted butter and a few roasted, sugar pecans on top. They're mighty good that way." Cadie thought she saw a tear teetering on the edge of Mattie's eyelashes. "Guess it wouldn't 've hurt Miz Stephens none if I'd been a little late that day."

There was a change in Mattie's tone, a deepness that matched the shift in her expression. "I'm sorry to make you sad, Mattie."

"Oh, child, don't be," she said, pulling Cadie close and pushing back on her heel for a firm swing. "The Lord's been my husband, and a daddy to Zena, all these years. He's got a mighty way of fixin' messed up, broken things. He fixed us up good, and I know He's gonna fix you up, too, if you let Him."

"How's He gonna do that, I wonder?"

"Don't know. But He will. You do like I told ya. Forgive and He'll take care of the rest. Yes'am, He will. He surely will."

Zena was right when she said Mattie would put Cadie to work. All that talk from the white community about how Negroes were lazy and dirty and just "good for nothin'" couldn't have been any less true at the Goodwin home, based on what Cadie observed. The days started early, sometimes long before sun-up, where prayer time preceded a typical breakfast of fried eggs, bacon, and biscuits with fresh blackberry preserves washed down by a cup of dark coffee caramelized with a dash of heavy cream. Then the real work began. First, there were pots and dishes to wash and put away, the stove and butcher block to wipe down, and the floor to sweep. Next came the laundry that had to be either scrubbed, rinsed, and hung on the line, or pressed with a hot iron and a spritz of starch and lemon water, depending on the day of the week. By that time, Mattie and Zena were just preparing to leave for a full day of work at Magnolia Hill, and Cadie was ready for a nap.

But there would be no sleep for Cadie. Mattie always left a long, detailed list of things to be accomplished before she and Zena returned in the evening, and today was no exception. Cadie looked at the list and cringed. The cow, Georgia, had to be milked, the tomatoes picked from the garden, the flower beds weeded, and the windows washed, inside and out. And that didn't even include preparing supper.

It was late in the afternoon before Cadie had finished everything on the list, including wiping the last window pane clean. "Glory be!" she said, realizing she hadn't even had time to think about cooking the evening meal. The beans hadn't been snapped and put to soak or the squash diced and set to boil on the stove. And what about that apple pie she was going to bake as a surprise dessert? Swiping a lock of sweaty hair behind her ear, she scurried around the kitchen like a chicken with its head cut off, slamming pots and bowls, lighting the stove, chopping the apples and squash, and snapping the beans, four or five at a time. But by the time Mattie and Zena were due to arrive home, everything was well on its way to being ready, including a chicken and squash casserole in creamy butter sauce, snap beans cooked down in ham hocks, fresh sliced tomatoes, buttermilk biscuits and a hot, steamy apple pie which had just been pulled from the oven and was sitting on the window-sill to cool.

Cadie flopped down in the porch swing and fanned her face from the heat while she waited for the two ladies to appear. For the first time, she took a good look around the house Mattie and Zena called home. It was the loveliest place Cadie had ever seen, besides Magnolia Hill. The front path was lined with dogwoods, interspersed with two live oaks on either side of the house, and the front porch was surrounded by azalea bushes and matching flower beds that were home for pansies and snapdragons in the winter and impatiens and candy tuff in the spring. The outside of the house was painted white with a red door and black shutters, and Cadie noticed there wasn't a place that didn't look like it had a fresh coat of paint. *How was that possible?* she wondered. *Why, Norman McLain never lived this good, even on his soberest day!*

And she hadn't even considered the inside of the house. Everything, from the kitchen to the sitting room, to the two bedrooms, were bright and clean with yellow flowered curtains at the windows over sheer netting to protect against the mosquitoes in the summer. The sitting room furniture was old and worn but decorated with quilts and homemade pillows sewed from scraps of old fringe and material. Flower vases of old, colored milk bottles were arranged in small groupings on a pine end table, a magnificent rock collection adorned the fireplace mantle, and the walls were decorated with colorful, old stained glass windows framed in painted plywood that hung in families of three. In the center of the room was a make-shift coffee table consisting of an old oak door sitting on four pillars of stacked bricks—just perfect for serving a pitcher of juniper and mint tea from a pretty, painted, wooden tray.

But the most stunning décor in the house was a portrait of Jesus that hung over the mantle, above the rock collection. It was strange to Cadie, since it didn't look anything like the Jesus she'd seen in pictures, even the ones in the back of Zena's Bible. This Jesus wasn't thin and pale with hollowed, blue eyes but was dark-skinned and ferocious-looking with an expression that reminded her of Reverend Thomas. And his features were sharp and angular, like the shoe store owner who went out of business some years ago after refusing to sell the reverend a pair of shoes. The artist had made the hair long and wild with matted clumps of red paint that oozed from a wreath of thorny vines wound around the head. What a picture that was! Why Mattie and Zena would want a thing like that hanging on their wall, especially in such a prominent place, was beyond Cadie's imaginings. She tried not to look at it but couldn't help being drawn to the swirling, abstract colors.

From a distance, she saw other figures imbedded in the portrait, like a horse rearing up on its hind legs with a faceless rider pulling on the reigns, or from another angle, a small, unidentifiable animal that lay on the ground looking sweet and gentle. But when she drew closer, the imbedded pictures disappeared and became blobs of paint again—all except something in the bottom right corner that piqued her interest. Cadie remembered how her nose almost touched the canvas the first time she saw letters scrawled there in white paint, just barely visible, yet plain and clear all the same—"Zena" was what it read.

Cadie smiled to herself and closed her eyes, picturing Zena's tall, lean frame painting the portrait of Jesus on a hot summer afternoon under a live oak. Before long, the slow, steady movement of the porch swing lulled her into a dreamy state where the strange portrait took on three-dimensions. The wild, matted hair grew out of the paint, looking thick and wooly, as did the dry, brittle thorns, which resembled the brambles that often snagged Cadie's stockings when she tromped through the woods near Jackson's Creek. The entire picture expanded until the facial features were as real as if Jesus Himself were bending over her right now, looking into her eyes with a fire that burned so intensely.

"Hey there, Miss Cadie!" Zena called, waking Cadie from her slumber. She waved from the road, acting like an exuberant child. "Sure hope you've got supper ready!"

Cadie smiled and waved back until Mattie appeared behind her, clutching the elbow of a tall, strapping black man wearing a dark suit. The blood drained from Cadie's face and a lump rose up in her throat when she heard his distinctive laugh and saw his close-cropped hair and white, gleaming smile.

Chapter 27

It was some time before Cadie was able to still her racing heart after laying eyes on the reverend walking arm-in-arm with Mattie. Her first impulse was to jerk a knot in Zena for not telling her all that window washing and cooking was for Reverend Thomas, of all people. Zena knew good and well Cadie didn't want to talk to him!

Cadie nodded at him in a cordial way, never once making eye contact, and still, a nervous sweat began to saturate the under parts of her dress sleeves. With each breath, her chest tightened like a drum until she wondered whether she would make it through the evening without fainting. At last, when the initial small talk had worked its way through the group, such as the weather, the conditions of the flowers and vegetables in the garden, and the price of eggs at the mercantile, it was time for supper to be served. Cadie grabbed Zena by the arm and drug her into the kitchen while Mattie stayed in the sitting room, entertaining the reverend.

"What do you mean bringin' him here like this?"

"Don't fuss at me," Zena said. "It wasn't my idea, but Mama's. She's the one who invited him." Cadie's skeptical look didn't sway Zena one bit. "Honest, Miss Cadie. I wouldn't lie to you 'bout that."

"Well, what am I supposed to do?"

"Jus' talk to him—"

"I've told you a million times, Zena—I don't wanna talk to the reverend!"

"Why? Lord knows you won't meet a nicer person on earth—and who better to answer all those Bible questions you've been wearin' me out with?"

Cadie shot Zena the evil eye she had wanted to unleash since the evening began. "I haven't been wearin' you out with Bible questions!"

"Says who?"

A loud, bellowing laugh from the sitting room punctuated Zena's reply like an exclamation mark. Her eyes narrowed, and for a minute, Cadie sensed anger in her expression. "What're you afraid of, huh?" Zena asked.

"I ain't afraid—"

"Don't say ain't."

"I'm not afraid!" Cadie stared into Zena's gaze until she saw something that resembled the painting over the mantle.

"Good," Zena said, her eyes softening a moment, "then you can help me serve this delicious chicken casserole." Grabbing up two kitchen towels, she pulled the hot dish out of the oven and set it on the pine kitchen table, giving Cadie a sassy look. "'Cause I'm starved."

The meal was a resounding success, especially Cadie's apple pie. The reverend ate two pieces, back to back, smacking his lips and groaning with pleasure at each bite. "Miz McLain, you sure do know how to cook up an apple pie, don't you? Mmm—I do believe this is the best one ever crossed my lips!"

"Thank you," Cadie said, refusing to return his look.

"Miss Cadie's learnin' lots about cookin' while she stayin' here with us, isn't that right, Miss Cadie?" Mattie beamed at her like a proud mama. "We've showed her how to fry chicken and stew tomatoes, and cook up a batch of butter beans—"

"Fried chicken and butter beans, umm umm," the reverend said, smacking his lips with pleasure.

"And don't forget about the blackberry preserves," Zena said.

"Blackberry preserves? With hot biscuits?" he asked, feigning astonishment.

"Buttermilk and angel drop," Zena said with widened eyes.

"Oh, now, Miss Zena, you know the only kinda biscuits I ever eat is angel drop." The reverend threw back his head and laughed in his typical raucous style, and Mattie joined in, too. But Zena just smiled in a shy way, with bright, glassy eyes that had latched on to his like a flea on a dog's hind leg.

My, my, Cadie thought to herself. *There sure is something going on between Zena and the reverend.* Cadie watched him hold his gaze on Zena a little too long and laugh at her schoolgirl comments that weren't really that funny. Zena, in turn, batted her eyes and fiddled with her apron in a nervous way while she giggled and smiled. Cadie looked away, not wanting to intrude, even though she was convinced Zena and the reverend would've never noticed.

Like many in Pleasant Oaks, Cadie often wondered why he had never settled down and started a family. It wasn't due to lack of opportunity, since it was plainly obvious that all the Negro women in town, young and old alike, had a keen eye on his comings and goings. There were several ladies in particular who insisted on vying for his affections, making a spectacle of themselves every Sunday at the Gospel Church—so Cadie had heard Zena say.

First, there was Bernice Turner, who was a rival to Mrs. Williamson for taking the title of fattest woman in the county. Every Sunday she came to church with a basket draped in a decorative napkin and loaded with cookies, breads, and cakes, all made especially for the reverend. He accepted them graciously, even though he never took a bite, since everyone knew Bernice was often known to confuse the salt with the sugar. Then there was Celie Samford, who was even more pathetic than Bernice. She had the awful habit of weeping and wailing and calling out praises during the service so that no one could hear what the reverend was saying. On several occasions, he had to rebuke her in front of the whole congregation, but that didn't stop Celie. The next week she'd be back on the front row, weeping and wailing, "Amen, Reverend! Preach it, brother, preach! Oh, Lord in heaven, preach!" until she had to be carried out the front door due to sheer exhaustion. Everyone knew Celie was just as crazy as she could be and hadn't a clue as to what she was "amening" to.

Then there was Arnetta Mattocks, a name that always turned Zena's chuckle into a deep gulp every time it was mentioned. She was the most beautiful girl in the church, by far, with smooth, dark hair and a creamy, caramel complexion like a white woman with a golden tan. Her refined features made her look like a film star, and she dressed like one, too. Somehow, she was able to take an old house dress and sew it up with ribbons and buttons until it looked just like something out of a fashion magazine. And the way she carried herself was the envy of even the Darlene Bradshaws of the world. Whenever Arnetta breezed into a room, every head turned and looked, both black and white, alike. Cadie had no doubt that half the young men who attended the Gospel Church every Sunday weren't there just to listen to the reverend's sermon.

But despite Arnetta batting her eyes and cocking her head seductively while the reverend preached, or even flawlessly quoting chapters of Scripture in his presence, he never looked at her or any of the other ladies like he was looking at Zena right now. Cadie smiled to herself as another round of his boisterous laughter filled the room, all directed toward something Zena had said. Finally, Mattie stood up and wiped her hands on her apron. "How 'bout I put a pot of coffee on the stove and we head on out to the porch?"

"That sounds mighty fine to me," he said with a nod Zena's way.

"And Reverend, maybe you could tell us one of your stories. I'm sure Miss Cadie'd love to hear somethin', wouldn't you, now, Miss Cadie?" Mattie gave her a wink as she placed her dirty dish in the sink.

"I don't know."

"Sure you do." Zena moved toward the edge of her chair and muttered to Cadie under her breath. "And maybe you can ask him some of those God questions you been askin'."

"Zena, hush."

"What? The reverend knows everything 'bout the Bible."

"Well, now," he said with a twinkle in his eye directed toward Zena, "I don't know about knowin' everything about the Bible, but I reckon I could come up with somethin' tonight that even Miz McLain would appreciate." He looked straight at Cadie, and instantly, the heat from his expression seared her like it did that night in the woods. He then pushed his chair back and stood up, straight and tall. "Ladies, may I escort you two out to the porch?" Zena smiled and took his arm, but Cadie wouldn't budge.

"Come on, now, Miss Cadie," Mattie said while placing another dish in the sink. "You've worked hard today. Why don't you head on out to the porch and get some fresh air?"

"Yes," the reverend said, "fresh air'll do you a world of good."

A stillness descended on them, demanding her reply. Reluctantly, Cadie pushed her chair back in like manner and stood up with her eyes toward the floor, not wanting to budge, yet not wanting to offend. She figured she had to go out to the porch, whether she wanted to or not.

The reverend and Zena followed her outside, where she and Zena settled into the swing. Zena pushed against the porch boards with the heel of her foot so that the slow, steady creak of the metal chain above their heads harmonized with the call of a distant bird and the flash of lightning bugs. The reverend stood opposite them and propped his leg on top of the porch railing so he could look out into the dusk. He leaned the back of his head against the porch post and took a deep breath, waiting for what seemed like forever. Cadie felt his eyes on her, tempting her to look his way. Her heart pounded in her ears—she hoped and prayed he wouldn't say anything about that night in the woods.

"Let's see, now," he said in a faraway voice. "I think I've got just the thing. This is an old, old story that starts out with a beautiful princess who lived deep in the woods in a snug little, cozy cottage. Which seemed fine and all, except there was a mighty big problem—she didn't know she was a princess. No, sir. How she got there, nobody really knew, and how come she didn't know she was a princess was another mystery, too. She spent her days cookin' and cleanin', milkin' cows, and hoein' the land, but deep down in her soul she was sad and unhappy, 'cause she knew this wasn't where she really belonged."

The reverend waited a moment and then continued. "Meantime, there was a prince from a faraway kingdom who looked high and low for the princess for years and years, 'cause you see, she belonged to him and he loved her so. In fact, the word was, she up and left the day of their weddin', just left him high and dry without a trace. Folks said they could hear the hooves of his mighty stallion poundin' the dirt paths as he rode from town to town lookin' for his bride, callin' her name in the night wind like the screechin' of an ole barn owl. But he never found her. He even went ridin' by the little cottage one night, but since she didn't remember her name or know who she really was, she didn't recognize his voice."

"Oh, the prince was mighty sad, mighty sad indeed, and all the people in the palace knew it. He wouldn't eat, wouldn't sleep. The king heard about it and got real worried. 'Son,' he said, 'there are lots of pretty girls in the kingdom, lots of 'em who could be your bride. Go find another, marry her, and live happily ever after.'"

"'No,' said the prince. 'No, sir. There's only one fair maiden for me—my beloved, who's stolen my heart.'"

"When the king saw that the prince couldn't be persuaded, he sent out his soldiers to discover what had happened to the princess. They scattered throughout the countryside, questionin' every man, woman, child, and beast, until a giant eagle with strange powers told them where she was. This eagle roamed the skies, right above where the princess lived, and knew everything about her. They learned that on the day of her weddin', she was gatherin' roses to wear in her hair, when the king's enemy—a former general of his army—cast a powerful delusion over her and made her believe she was a lowly peasant girl livin' in the woods. From time to time, he'd ride by and tell her how dirty and low-down rotten she was until she could barely look at herself." The reverend shook his head as though he couldn't believe such a thing.

"Now, the king's soldiers found the cottage," he said, "just as the eagle had said, but the princess wasn't there. They listened real hard and heard her cryin', so they followed the sound of her tears. And there she was—deep in the woods mournin' over her unhappiness. One of the soldiers told her who she truly was and that he would take her to the prince, but she wouldn't believe him—it just couldn't be true to her mind. So she ran away, deeper and deeper into the woods. Sometimes she thought about what the soldier had told her, and when she did, her heart was filled with hope, 'cause her heart knew the truth, even if her mind couldn't believe it. *No,* she thought, *There's no way, no way in the world I can be a princess loved by a prince, no, sir!' Not my scraggly ole self?*'

The reverend shifted his weight against the porch railing and continued,

"When the soldiers returned to the palace and told all to the king, the prince was filled up with joy and rose from his bed to go to her. But the king warned him, 'You can't go dressed as a prince, 'cause she's gonna run further and further away 'til you'll never be able to find her.' No, he was gonna have to go dressed like a peasant—just like her. Then maybe, just maybe, he could get her to believe the truth."

"So, the prince did just that. He took off his robe and crown and laid 'em next to the king and said, 'I'm gonna go get my bride and then I'm gonna be back.' And the king said that was 'just fine,' so off the prince went lookin' just like a peasant. Sure enough, he found the princess by the edge of the river just as sad and forlorn as could be. She was tired, thin, and sickly by now, and her clothes were all worn out. 'Course to the prince, she was just as lovely to him as she'd ever been. He'd sit on a big rock by the river, just out of eyesight of the princess, and watch her, day and night. Many times he'd sing a soft love song—one only the two of 'em would've known. He could see that she heard it and that it was speakin' to her soul, 'cause remember, her soul never forgot who she truly was."

"And wouldn't you know it," the reverend said with excitement, "before long, she began to eat berries from the forest and roast fish she'd caught by the river, until her skin became rosy and pink and her hair thick and wavy. She began to hum the song the prince sang, even though she had no idea it was bein' sung. She stood straight and tall and took long walks by the riverbank, thinkin' 'bout all that the king's soldier had told her. *Maybe I am a princess from a faraway kingdom! Maybe there is a prince who loves me and who's comin' for me!*"

"Now, the prince could see the hope risin' inside of her and convincin' her of the truth, so he came out of his hidin' place and showed himself to her. 'Course, he looked like a peasant to the princess, but there was somethin' in his eyes that told her he was more than that, much more, indeed. And when he opened his mouth, he sang the song she'd been hummin' all this time." The reverend cast his eyes into the night and took a deep breath. "Let's see, what'd he sing? I guess it was somethin' like this,"

Come with me, my love, my bride, come with me once more.

With a glance from your eyes, you stole my heart, my love, my bride, my love, my bride. Come with me once more.

Come with me, my love, my bride, come with me once more.

How delightful your love fills my heart, my love, my bride, my love, my bride.

Come with me once more.

The reverend's voice was rich and deep like a vat of dark molasses on a warm, summer's day. Cadie snuck a peek at Zena and saw goose bumps on her arms, and it wasn't due to the chill in the air, of that she was sure.

He drew another long, deep breath and said, "Oh, how the princess's heart soared with gladness, 'cause she knew this man, she did! She didn't even need to ask his name, 'cause she knew this could only be the prince who her soul had testified about. She could tell by the way he was looking at her and the way his hand was outstretched toward her as he sang. The next thing she knew, she was wadin' across the river, reachin' out to grab hold of him, when somethin' terrible, somethin' just awful happened."

The swing continued its slow, gentle rock as the thickness of expectancy surrounded them, making it difficult for Cadie to breathe. She hated to admit it, but she didn't want the reverend to stop for a single minute. The story captivated her imagination in a way she hadn't experienced since her days hidden away in the apple orchard, and it took all her will power not to ask him to continue. Zena stopped the swing with her foot and leaned forward. "Well?"

The reverend looked at Zena in a way that reminded Cadie of a sly fox. "Well, what?"

"Well, aren't you gonna tell us what happened?"

"You wanna know?"

"Yes, sir, you know I do."

He focused on Cadie and smiled. "What about you, Miz McLain?"

She hesitated, feeling Zena's eyes on her. "Miss Cadie?"

"Go ahead. You might as well finish," Cadie said, keeping her eyes cast down as if she wasn't the least bit interested.

The reverent chuckled, flashing that radiant smile of his. "Yes, ma'am, might as well." He rested his head against the porch post once more and gazed into the night. "Let's see, where was I?"

Zena stopped the swing and leaned forward with more of her wide-eyed enthusiasm. "She's about to grab the prince's hand and kiss him and tell him she'll love him forever—"

"Zena," Cadie muttered under her breath.

"What?" Zena said, with a hint of irritation in her voice. "That's what's gonna happen, isn't it, Reverend?"

"That's right, Miss Zena. That's exactly right."

She settled back into the swing with that "I told you so attitude," which reminded Cadie of Tessie when she was in one of her moods.

"'Cept at that moment, the king's enemy came ridin' up on his black horse," the reverend said. "By now, he'd grown disfigured and terrible lookin', covered with all kinds of disease and pox sores 'cause of all the evil that had come out of his heart. The princess was frozen with fear, but not the prince, 'cause he knew this enemy had no power over him. He asked, 'What is it you want, Deceiver?' He called him Deceiver, 'cause he knew how he'd tricked the princess. He called out, 'Go away from this place and take your deception elsewhere!'"

"But the deceiver replied, 'You can't have this girl as your bride, 'cause while she was betrothed to you, she turned away from your promises and believed my words. She can never be yours, never, 'cause she belongs to me!'" The reverend sighed deeply and looked far into the night. "Oh, but the prince's heart was cut to the core, 'cause he knew it was true."

"But he tricked her, he did!" Zena said. "She didn't know she belonged to the prince!"

"You think so?" the reverend asked. "What about on her weddin' day when she was gatherin' roses for her hair? How was the deceiver able to trick her into believin' she was really a peasant girl? She didn't have to believe that, did she? Why, she was betrothed to the prince who would rule the kingdom one day." The reverend shook his head again, contemplating. "No, I figure there must've been somethin' that ole deceiver said that enticed her and made her question who she truly was—and so the deception took on power."

"That don't seem right, does it, Reverend?" Zena pushed the swing extra hard with her toe so that it soared, back and forth.

"Well, maybe it does, I don't know," he replied, crossing his arms over his chest like a teacher in front of a classroom. "She coulda ignored him when he told her those lies, I reckon. I figure she coulda just gone about her business without another thought." He exhaled, long and deep, adjusting his leg along the porch railing. "But I guess it doesn't really matter now, does it?"

"Why do you say that?" Cadie couldn't believe it was her voice that had spoken. It sounded hostile and angry, as if she was defending some horrible accusation.

The reverend didn't bat an eye but responded calmly. "'Cause she'd already done it." His eyes latched on to hers, revealing that *something* that raged inside of him. "She gave her heart away to someone else, someone who had no right to it."

The heat rushed from Cadie's chest up to her neck, igniting her cheeks like the whoosh of a flame, as if he'd called her by name and pointed a long, judgmental finger her way. Truth hovered over them, swirling around in the air with each creak of the metal chain securing the swing to the porch ceiling.

"So, what's he gonna do now, Reverend?" Zena asked, breaking the silence with her soft, girlish voice. "How's he gonna get her back?"

"Well, the only way you can get back somethin' that's been taken away and belongs to another now. He's gonna have to buy her back. Problem is, that ole deceiver doesn't want money or land or gold or anything like that. So the prince asked him, 'What is it you want for my bride? Let me pay it so she can be set free.'"

"Oh, don't you know that deceiver was just as evil as he could be! You know what he said?" Zena shook her head at the reverend, her eyes wide with expectation. "He said, 'There's only one price I'll accept and that's you! Give me your life, and I'll let her go!'" The reverend's voice rang out into the night, silencing the crickets and the other forest sounds for a brief moment. "The prince didn't hesitate," the reverend said, "'cause he knew it was the only way, even though the princess cried, beggin' him not to. So, he climbed up to that big rock where he'd been hidin', singin' that special song just as loud as he could,"

Come with me, my love, my bride, come with me once more.

With a glance from your eyes, you stole my heart, my love, my bride, my love, my bride. Come with me once more.

"As he stood straight and tall on the edge of that rock, he sang the next verse."

Come with me, my love, my bride, come with me once more.

How delightful your love fills my heart, my love, my bride, my love, my bride

I'll come for you—once more.

"Now, the deceiver didn't hear the last line and how it was different from before, but the princess did. The princess looked deep into the prince's eyes as he sang it one more time, *'I'll come for you—once more.'* And with that, he stretched out his arms like so and fell headlong into the river with a giant splash." The reverend held his arms out to his sides and pretended to fall face down into the river into a watery grave. "There he floated, dead and broken, until the river grass reached up and pulled his body deeper and deeper into the depth of the water—until he was seen no more."

Reverend Thomas' voice sounded sorrowful as he continued. "The princess wept and wept for the prince, even though she knew somehow he'd come back to her. She wasn't sure how, but knew it to be true, probably 'cause she was free from the deceiver, and her soul wasn't bound up by lies anymore, I don't know. But she knew. She waited and waited by the shores of the river for the river grass to release the prince. For three whole days she waited, but nothin' happened, or so she thought. What she didn't know was that the eagle had flown long and far to tell the king what had happened."

"Oh, the king was mighty proud of what his son had done, so he gave the eagle a secret message that only the prince could hear and understand. The eagle flew back to the river, and with a loud screech, dove down into the water, past the rocks and river grass, and down and down to where the prince lay wrapped up in death. It released the message the king had given, and here's what it said, 'You will not die, but will live, my son—because you gave your life for another—out of love.'"

"Even under water, the words sounded just like that, but really they were like little pellets of life that seeped into the prince's ears and eyes and nostrils, fillin' him with a light that couldn't stay down where he was. It was a light that had to come up to the surface so it could shine for all the world to see. The prince felt it—it was this great power from high above that descended toward him and then grabbed hold and pulled him up and up and up . . ."

Cadie closed her eyes and tried to stop her ears from hearing any more, but the image of her wet hair and skirt wrapped around her body was lodged deep in her mind, dragging her down into a place where life drained away, to a place that had claimed Zoe. But then something or someone had come for her—someone had grabbed her by the hand and pulled her back up to the surface.

She stood to her feet with a jolt, letting the swing whack her on the back of the legs. "I don't think I wanna hear any more of this made up, silly story! It doesn't even make any sense!"

Before her foot hit the edge of the top porch step, the reverend said, "Death couldn't hold him down. Just like it couldn't hold you down—that night in the river."

Cadie stood stone still and stared into the distance. She could sense it in his expression—he knew. He had been there and seen her try to give her life away like some, weak, pathetic offering to assuage the pain in her heart. She hung her head, keeping her eyes glued to his black, leather shoes that were clean and polished with just the slightest bit of sheen. Slowly, Cadie raised her eyes to meet his, expecting to see judgment and condemnation, but there was only a flood of peace that gushed over her like a spring of bubbling water. Was he the one who had pulled her up? Was it the hand of the reverend that had reached down into the depths of the river and pulled her up to the light? She gulped hard and said, "I'm gonna go take a walk now."

"The Lord's sent me to tell you something, Miz McLain. You've been runnin' from Him a long time now, a long time. When're you gonna stop and let Him catch you?" His eyes glistened, piercing her heart all the way to the soul. "When're you gonna stop?"

Cadie looked into his soft gaze, past his dark skin and the mangled scar creeping over his collar, to where the real reverend resided. Except this time, she didn't see a preacher or a righteous man of God but a lover singing to her in a way she had wanted Boy to sing—and perhaps someone else, someone with a lopsided grin and a lock of dark hair falling over his eye. *No, not him, not him!* she thought.

The reverend's deep, smooth voice echoed in Cadie's mind, *Come with me, my love, my bride, come with me once more. How delightful your love fills my heart, my love, my bride, my love, my bride. I'll come for you once more. I'll come for you once more. I'll come for you once more.* Someone was singing to her, but it wasn't Boy or Norman or even the reverend. It was someone else, someone who had been singing this song all her life, yet she didn't know it, not until now. *I'll come for you once more. I'll come for you once more.* The words resonated in her mind, over and over. She knew that voice, she did! Closing her eyes, she saw a face that was dark and wild with eyes of fire, just like the portrait hanging over the fireplace inside the house. His hand was outstretched, beckoning her to come. *Come with me, my love my bride . . .*

A sob caught in Cadie's throat as something inside of her broke, like a crack in a porcelain cup where a swallow of hot tea was waiting to leak out. She stumbled for a moment, but the reverend's hand steadied her, preparing for what was about to happen. "Just stay still, stay still, now," he whispered. But Cadie couldn't hold the sob back any longer. She opened her mouth to inhale, and a lone, bitter, bone-chilling wail came out that almost turned Zena's face deathly white, if that were possible. Instantly, the reverend's arms went around Cadie and scooped her into his embrace before she fell to the porch floor.

"Miss Cadie! Miss Cadie!" Zena screamed. The screen door slammed, and Mattie barked out a slew of guttural commands while she scurried about—or was that her own voice she heard? Cadie couldn't be sure.

"Go fetch that coffee quick, Miss Zena. Go on and help your mama, now. She's gonna be all right." The reverend's calm voice was like a soothing balm to Cadie's soul that had been sliced open like a lanced boil, and yet, the wailing continued louder and louder until she could hardly breathe. "That's right, child. Just let it out, let it all out. Oh, sweet Jesus, Lord in heaven, clean up this child's heart real good, now. Clean it up, clean it up."

The last thing Cadie remembered was being rocked back and forth in the reverend's strong arms like Mama used to do. She clung to him until her fingernails practically ripped holes in his suit jacket. "Don't leave me, don't leave me!" repeated itself over and over while her body wracked with sobs.

"He ain't never gonna leave you now. No, sir, huh uh. He's right here. He's right here."

The familiar smells of lemony soap, peppermint, and apple pie began to fade away, as did the reverend's voice, which became less distinctive, like the sound of the river rushing downhill. Its power was washing over her, cleansing things deep inside the way the furious flow of water cleansed the debris caught between the rocks and crevices of the riverbed. All of it was being taken away—the hatred, anger, bitterness and sadness of life, but more importantly, the grief over the loss of little Zoe and the dream of living in Magnolia Hill or going on a riverboat to a place far away from Pleasant Oaks. Like a passenger on one of those ships, her old self was being taken far away, to an appointed destination, of which only the river knew.

Chapter 28

The reverend's black Model T lumbered down the dirt road that led to Cadie and Norman's little house. Cadie sat in the passenger seat with the window rolled down, letting the wind whip her hair around her face and neck like a curtain in the wind. She didn't care if her eyes stung from the dust in the air or her hair tangled in the breeze, she was going home after four joyous weeks of living with Mattie and Zena, and there was nothing to stop her from being happy. Not that old, drafty house that waited for her, nor the sloping porch about to pull away from the foundation, nor her husband, himself.

Cadie marveled that the thought of Norman didn't conjure up feelings of hatred like they once had. He had become anonymous to her, like a stranger who needed introduction in order for a relationship to take root. Her fingers touched the place under her eye where he had hit her with the Bible. It was still tender, even though the bruise had long since gone. A slight sense of fear rustled deep in her belly when she considered his reaction upon her return.

The motorcar hit a bump, jolting Cadie's thoughts back to her newfound place of happiness. So much of life had changed since coming to live with the Goodwins, especially because of the reverend. She peered at him through the strands of wind-blown hair that swept across her face. He was as handsome as ever in his black suit and hat, sitting straight, tall, and proud as he drove his shiny car. Cadie felt like a queen riding with him, statelier than Molly Stephens Wallace in the front seat of her husband's blue Rolls-Royce.

The reverend glanced her way and asked, "You all right, Miz McLain?"

"Yes, sir, I'm fine."

"Well, whatcha got on your mind?" He grinned and gave her a sly look. "You so excited 'bout seein' that husband of yours?"

Cadie smiled back and turned her face into the wind. "I was just thinkin' 'bout all the times you've saved me. Startin' with me sittin' up on the roof of the church. You never called me down when you knew it was me. And then the night Zoe was born. But mostly—mostly, for pullin' me out of the river. I do thank you."

"You oughtta thank the Lord for that, 'specially since I never learned to swim too good." He chuckled hard and beamed a white smile.

"I don't remember any of it, really. Guess I tried to block it from my mind."

"As it should be."

She hesitated and then asked, "How come you did all that, Reverend?"

"'Cause the Lord told me to. Told me to fight off that nasty devil tryin' to snatch you up and make all kinds a mischief."

A chill slithered up Cadie's arms at such a wild notion. "You fought off the devil for me?" she asked in a skeptical tone. "How'd you do that?"

"Just told him to go, in the name of Jesus's all. Same way I deal with an ole, stray tomcat. Just tell him to scat."

"Sounds like another one of your stories," she said, looking out at the trees as they rushed past.

"No, ma'am. Not this time." The hard set to his jaw and that dark, faraway look made Cadie wonder where his mind had gone. "You may not understand now, but you will—one day."

The motorcar pulled up to the house, and the tightness rose in her throat again. The porch was more lopsided than before, and the screen door dangled by the top hinge from being banged shut a thousand times. The rocker was on its side with a broken armrest, and the yard was worse than ever with all of the empty bottles and trash strewn all over the place. She didn't know how in the world she was going to get all of this cleaned up by herself.

The reverend put the motorcar in park and stared straight ahead. "Well, looks like you and me gonna have to roll up our sleeves and get to work, huh?"

"No, sir. We've already decided. This is somethin' I gotta do on my own."

"You sure? 'Cause I can tidy up real good."

"I thank you anyway." For a moment, the scar protruded from the top of his collar in a ragged fashion and then disappeared back into its designated place. He smiled in a way that let her know permission was given to discuss what had become forefront in her mind. "How'd you keep the devil from snatchin' you up—*that night?*"

"Same as I did when he led you off to the river." He leaned forward and spoke with that fiery blaze in his eyes. "Told him to scat."

Cadie pondered the simplicity of this, trying her best to understand. "And you forgave those white men for what they did to you?"

"I did."

"Includin' my daddy?"

He nodded. "Includin' him."

"And you love 'em? All of 'em?"

"I do."

"Guess I can love Norman then, can't I?"

"Through the Lord's strength, you most certainly can. Greater is He who is in you," he said, pointing his long, dark finger toward her heart, "than that rotten devil and all that's out there in the world. Don't ever let his lies deceive you again. You just keep on believin' God's Word when times get tough. Keep believin' and tell him to "scat" in Jesus' name when he gets too close. You do that, and he'll run. 'Cause to his ears, it sounds just like the voice of God."

Cadie leaned over and kissed the reverend on the cheek, feeling the silky smoothness of his skin with just a touch of bristle. She had never kissed a black man before, but by now, Reverend Thomas wasn't black to her anymore. He was just a man, like any other, a person with hopes, dreams and desires, just like her, possessing that *something* from God burrowed just beneath the surface of the person. It muted the pigmentation of skin and the thickness of features, as well as the texture of hair, so that a Negro man and a girl with blue eyes and fair complexion could claim to be from the same peculiar race of people. "Oh, Reverend," Cadie gushed, "I don't know how I'll ever repay you—and Mattie and Zena—for all you've done."

"I can't speak for the Goodwin ladies, but as for me, there's no repayment required. Everything I said and did was because the Lord told me to say and do it, it's that plain and simple." He kissed her on the forehead and gave her a pat on the arm like her daddy would have done. "You were the one who was willin' to listen and obey."

Cadie rested her head on his shoulder, taking in the scent of lavender on his collar. She could sit here forever without moving a muscle, safe and secure in his strong arms. "You better go on, now, Miz McLain," he said, nudging her away. "You got a husband inside waitin' for you."

She nodded and opened the door. "I'll be seein' you on Sundee, I reckon."

"You might be seein' me before then, 'specially if you be needin' me.

I've got ways of knowin' things, you know," he said with a twinkle in his eye.

"All right," she replied, smiling at the truth of this statement. "That'll be fine."

"And you remember what I said, now."

"Yes, sir. Love never fails." Cadie hoped her response sounded convincing to him, even if it sounded like a half-truth to her.

"I'll be prayin' for you, night and day," he called through the open window. "All of us, we'll be prayin'." And with that, he drove away, whistling a tune—a hymn Cadie had heard some time before. She watched the dust from his motorcar billow up like a dingy cloud and then settle back down into a haze. How she longed to be back in the front seat, driving away with him, but something inside of her said, *This is the life God has called you to.* Cadie turned and looked at what the Lord had given her—a broken-down shack of a house with peeling paint and lopsided porch. And a husband whose name was Norman McLain.

Cadie shuffled into the kitchen like she was a visitor in someone else's home. The mess was typical for Norman, so it was no surprise to find half-eaten food on the table, the sink piled high with dirty dishes, and wads of tobacco spittle lining the floor like murky, brown polka dots. She sighed to herself and then wandered into the sitting room where the fireplace yawned before her. In the ashes was a broken liquor bottle but no evidence of Zena's burned Bible. Cadie closed her eyes and fought back a sob. "What's done is done," she whispered. Like she had heard the reverend say, 'a man can burn down a church house or toss a Bible in the fire, but God's Word can never be destroyed.'

Cadie made her way into the bedroom and set her tapestry bag on the unmade bed, surveying her surroundings. Things weren't too bad, really.

The sheets needed washing and the floor swept, but other than that, a floral picture on the wall required adjusting and the dresser needed a dust rag wiped across the top. Her eye caught the glimmer of a sparkle in the crystal dish her mama had given her as a wedding gift used for storing pins and sewing needles. But there was something else in there now. Cadie lifted the lid and saw her diamond ring.

A pang of guilt hit her heart at having thrown it across the room, as well as harboring plans to sell it. She picked it up and slipped it on her finger. It was snug but fit just fine, and she could see no harm had been done to it. It was a pretty little solitaire on a platinum band that sparkled as she rotated her hand in the sunlight. And to think, it had come all the way from New York City—

The rumbling of a truck motor stilled her thoughts for a moment, and before long, the screen door creaked open and slammed shut with a bang. Cadie stiffened as Norman's footsteps neared the bedroom and shuffled to a stop by the doorway. "You're not livin' with those coloreds anymore?" he asked.

Her blood boiled up, but she decided to keep quiet and silently pray. *Love is patient and full of kindness . . .* Cadie's mind ventured back to last Sunday when she had attended the Gospel Church with Mattie and Zena for the first time. The reverend had looked her dead in the eye while giving one of his impassioned sermons and asked flat out, "Won't you love him? Won't you do it?" Cadie had known the "him" referred to was someone other than the Lord.

"I'm talkin' to you."

"I hear you," she snapped. "I've got two good ears." Cadie hated sounding so mean and unchristian, but she couldn't help herself.

"Well, answer me, then. You're not livin' with those coloreds?"

"Do you have to call 'em that?"

"At least I didn't call 'em that other word you don't like."

Cadie cringed from head to toe, yet somehow, she was able to answer in a manner that sounded somewhat civil. "How about the Goodwins? They do have a name."

He didn't reply but shifted his weight and leaned against the doorframe, watching her every move. "Whatcha doin' unpackin'?"

She opened the top dresser drawer and caught a glimpse of the twine wrapped around the burlap sack that held Boy's letters. To her surprise, there was no emotion other than a benign recognition of something old and long forgotten. The clothes plopped on top of the burlap sack, and the drawer closed. "I'm home now, and I'm gonna stay."

In a flash, Norman was beside her with his fingers clamped tightly around her arm. "What if I don't want you here, huh?"

Cadie's eyes raged with fire, but her voice was calm and in control. "You can't hurt me anymore, Norman. I've been saved. I'm a Christian now." She latched on to the reflection in his right eye that swam in a sea of soft brown, as if it were a remnant from last winter's snow-storm. He stared back at her just as intently, but her hold was stronger. The reflection became larger and more pronounced, drawing her closer for inspection until she felt she could almost drop down into his soul and lay his thoughts and desires out on the bed for all to see. She didn't dare look away. She was almost there, so close to seeing the real Norman, when he blinked, and his gaze shifted. The reflection disappeared, and the moment was gone.

He released his hold and ground his teeth like he was in the habit of doing when things didn't proceed as planned. Cadie got a good look at him, and was shocked at what she saw. He was thin and drawn and looked as if he hadn't eaten a bite since the day she left, despite all the messy dishes in the sink. His hair was long and shaggy, but his clothes looked clean and presentable—a first since they'd been married. To her surprise, her heart melted a bit, and her anger turned into a sickening form of pity.

"Norman, you want me to fix you somethin' to eat?"

"I don't want nothin' from you, Cadie. I know what you think of me, I can see it in your eyes. You don't wanna be married to me. And the truth is, I don't wanna be married to you, neither. I don't see no sense in drawin' this out any longer."

"It doesn't matter what we want," she said, twisting the ring around on her finger. "We said our vows in front of the minister and our parents and God Himself. Even though we didn't mean it at the time, we still said it, and I plan on doin' what I said. I don't care what you've done to me or me to you, I'm gonna be a wife to you now." He stared at her like she was speaking a foreign language and then turned his attention to the ring on her finger. Cadie's cheeks flushed with heat, and immediately, she shoved her hands down by her sides. "I'll cook and clean and do all I can do—"

"But you can't really love me, can you?" His eyes had that look of ownership that always brought shame to her heart. "Not like you're supposed to."

She looked away, hoping these feelings would depart, but they refused. He was right. She didn't want any part of *that* in their marriage, but if she was going to be obedient, she couldn't deny him. She raised her head and looked him in the eye. "I said I'd be a wife to you."

"That's not what I'm talkin' about. A man can find a million different ways to get that kinda love."

"Oh, really?"

He didn't answer, but stared hard, and this time his eyes latched onto hers. She tried to stare back, to concentrate on the reflection that had returned, but his hold was stronger, pressing down on her will, until suddenly, something strange happened—a surge of warmth trickled through her chest and down into the veins of her arms and legs, almost like that electric current she had experienced so long ago. She couldn't help herself, but had to blink, knowing he had won this round.

"You think that's all there is to me? An animal wantin' his needs satisfied? I'm talkin' about your heart, Cadie. What happened to that?" His mouth was so close to hers, and yet, she wasn't repulsed.

"I—I don't know."

"I know I did you wrong, and after the baby was born, well—I said I'd make it right, but you never gave me a chance. You never would, even after I tried. Maybe if my last name had been Stephens—or Morgan."

"That's not true, Norman."

"You gave everything to him. He rode into town one summer with no intention of makin' good on his promises. And you shoulda known, Cadie. You shoulda known it wasn't real."

"I'm sorry, Norman. Truly I am."

Despite the tears pricking the corners of her eyes, the hardness in his expression didn't waver. "There ain't nothin' left now," he said, his eyes pooling with emotion to match her own. "'Cause what he didn't take, died with Zoe."

Cadie felt like he had hit her square in the face. It wasn't so much the pain of the blow, but the surprise of its delivery, and it made every bit of warmth toward him evaporate like spit in a scorching wind. "Norman McLain," she whispered, "you are—" She bit her tongue to stop the vile words from coming.

"Evil, huh? What about cruel and mean, full of lies?" The heat of his breath was on her cheek, burning her skin like the flames from a torch. "Well what about him? Ain't he evil, mean, a liar? You wasted it all, Cadie. Wasted it all on a boy claimin' to be a man."

"And I suppose you're a man now?"

"I'm still here, aren't I?" He grabbed his jacket off the end of the bedpost and headed for the kitchen door.

"Where're you goin'?"

"To work—at the store."

Cadie followed him out to the porch. "The store?"

"Yeah, the mercantile. Been back about two weeks now. Pa's gettin' up there in age and needs me to take over, and that's what I aim to do."

"Will you be home for supper?"

He opened the door of his truck and climbed inside. "I'll take my food at the diner. Don't wanna inconvenience you none."

"It's not an inconvenience, Norman. I've gotta cook anyways."

"Well, maybe you can invite that Goodwin girl over. I know you'd rather spend time with her."

"Norman—"

The door slammed, and he was gone. Cadie stood with hands on hips for what seemed like forever, watching his truck disappear down the road. Oh, what a difficult man he was! The Lord was gonna have to give her the strength of ten men to put up with the likes of him.

She stomped back into the house, feeling the sting from his words that had cut deep. Her impulse was to run back to Mattie and Zena and the comforts of their loving home, but she couldn't quit on the first day back. Even though she looked the same to Norman on the outside, she was different from who she was the last time they'd seen each other. She did have a heart, contrary to what he thought, because God had brought it back to life. She couldn't prove it to him today, but in time, he'd come to understand.

Chapter 29

For two whole weeks, Norman remained true to his word and insisted on taking all of his meals at the diner or the drugstore counter. *Oh, well, suit yourself*, Cadie thought, as she dumped another plate of Norman's uneaten supper into the trash. *Go on and eat that greasy steak and mushy chicken. See if I care.* She couldn't understand his stubbornness. What a waste of his hard earned money to be spending it on restaurant food when he could have a hot meal at home! She even made his favorites—creamy mashed potatoes with butter, crispy fried chicken, and green beans cooked in ham hocks, and still, he refused to take a bite.

In so many ways, Norman was the same ole ornery mule he had always been, and yet, strangely, something in him had changed. He had stopped drinking, of that Cadie was sure, and he was going to work every day, Monday through Saturday, from sunup to sundown. His truck pulled up to the woodshed every night, where he slept in a bed made of straw and hay, and every morning he departed without a single word. On most days, he left a little money on the kitchen counter for groceries and the like, but Cadie didn't dare set foot in the mercantile after the way Mr. McLain had treated them. She did all her shopping at Whaley's now, and Norman never uttered a syllable in protest.

Today was Sunday, the one day a week Norman didn't go to work, because the mercantile was closed. Cadie had awakened early, as was her habit, and fixed a good breakfast of fried eggs, honey smoked bacon, and skillet biscuits washed down with a mug of cream-laced coffee. After the kitchen was tidied and all the dishes washed, she opened the bedroom wardrobe and stared at her choices of church-going clothes—a beige calico dress, a pink, drop-waist jumper with white blouse, and her mother's old pale blue silk chiffon she had worn on New Year's Eve so long ago. Cadie fingered the delicate material, delighting in its light and airy feel. It was a bit fancy for church, but she didn't care. Who better to dress up for than the Lord?

She pulled the dress off the hanger and slipped it over her head, examining herself in the mirror. The dress had looked nice on her before, but now it fit perfectly. Her body had filled out in all the right places, and her cheeks and eyes were no longer hollowed and sunken but were full and plump with a rosy glow that spoke of health and vitality. The blue fabric made her eyes appear brighter and more vibrant, and when she brushed her hair, it shone like spun gold. Cadie swept it up to the base of her neck in a tight chignon and looked at herself this way and that, admiring the angles and shape of her face. *Very pretty*, she thought. *Elegant, even. Looks like I could be on my way to Magnolia Hill.*

Immediately, she released her hold, letting the locks tumble to her shoulders in soft curls. She couldn't think those thoughts anymore, especially on a Sunday when she was on her way to worship the Lord. They were long behind her, buried deep in the past.

Cadie grabbed her shawl and made her way down the porch steps, stopping for a moment to listen to a faint mumbling coming from the direction of the woodshed. It couldn't be Norman, since he would be sleeping at this early hour. Usually on a Sunday, he slept all day or sat out in the trees just staring off into space. Sometimes Cadie wondered if all that moonshine he'd drunk over the years had done something to that brain of his.

She took a few more steps toward the road and stopped once more. There it was again—a loud mumbling coming from inside the woodshed. Cadie crept toward the shed and listened closely, but she couldn't make out what was said. "Norman?" She tapped on the door and pushed it open.

He scampered to his feet like a skittish colt and bopped his head on a low-lying crossbeam. "Oww!" he yelped, holding the top of his head.

"Oh, I'm sorry. You all right?"

"Whadda you want?" he said, rubbing his head while his face contorted in pain.

"I heard you talkin' and was just wonderin'—who're you talkin' to?"

"I wasn't talkin'."

"Yes, you were, Norman. I've told you, I've got two good ears on my head."

"I know," he said. "You hear everything, 'cept the sound of my voice when I'm in need of somethin'."

Cadie reigned in her tongue with all the effort she could muster. She had a good mind to tell him what he was in need of, but she wasn't about to let him get the best of her. She noticed him staring at her dress but not in the sarcastic way that matched the edge in his voice. He was taking in her whole attire, from head to toe, causing her cheeks to flush with heat.

"What're you starin' at?" she asked.

"I'm not starin' at nothin'. I'm just lookin' at you. You tellin' me I can't even look at you now?"

"Norman, you're bein' ridiculous. Just go on back to mumblin' to yourself, then." As she turned to leave, she noticed a dark, rectangular object tucked behind his back. "And what've you got hidden behind there?"

"That ain't none of your business."

"It's not one of those girlie books, is it? 'Cause you know this is the Lord's day—"

"It ain't that."

"Then what is it?"

"Never you mind."

"I don't understand why you won't tell me, Norman. I see you sittin' there in the woods lookin' at somethin' all day long. Come on, and show me."

"Can't a man have some privacy? You wanted me to leave you be, and I've done that. Now, you do the same. Just get out and go to that ole colored church if you want, I know that's where you're off to."

"Okay, I will! And I don't care what anybody says about it, neither—includin' you!"

"Good, then go on!"

"Fine!" she yelled, slamming the shed door closed. "And I might just pray for you this time!" She turned away and then stopped. "If you're hungry, I put some breakfast on the stove!" She waited for a response, but of course, there was none. Wrapping her shawl around her shoulders, she stomped away, hoping and praying she'd have the power to forgive him before the reverend started the service.

"Praise be the Lord, Miss Cadie, somethin' sure is goin' on inside of Mr. Norman, that's for sure," Zena whispered from the front pew of the Gospel Church as they sang the first hymn, *A Mighty Fortress Is Our God*.

"Whadda you mean?" Cadie whispered back.

"Well, you oughta see how he's been actin' down at the mercantile. Dressin' all fancy with a white shirt and apron over his trousers and actin' like he's the boss and all. Why, he has Mr. McLain countin' those tin cans now. And you oughta see this special bakery counter he made with his own two hands and painted it up real pretty. He's sellin' fresh bread and pies, even some of Mama's cookin' and some of Bernice's sweets." Zena smiled and nodded at Bernice who held her basket of goodies for the reverend. "Some of the white ladies made comments 'bout how it wasn't right to be sellin' Negro cookin' to them, and wouldn't you know, but Mr. Norman, he said just as loud and clear, 'a blueberry pie's a blueberry pie, regardless of the color of hands that made it!'"

"He said that? I don't believe it. Not Norman McLain."

"I'm not lyin' to you, Miss Cadie."

Mattie shushed them and the conversation came to an end, but Cadie couldn't stop thinking about this change that had come over her husband. She tried to picture him talking back to a group of snobby white ladies, including fat ole Mrs. Williamson in her tight girdle, thinking she was too good to pay for the likes of Mattie's cooking. *Wonder what's gotten into him?* she thought.

By the time Cadie returned home from church that afternoon, Norman had her more confused than ever. Never in a million years could she have imagined he would take time out of his Sunday to do things around the house. In just a half day's time, he had propped up the sloping porch with a new grouping of bricks, fixed the bashed-in rocker, cleaned up the front yard, and stood perched on a ladder, painting the house a crisp shade of white. Cadie could barely disguise her shock at seeing all he had accomplished. "Norman McLain, what're you doin'?"

"This house's in need of a paint job, and I'm slappin' it on. It won't get on there any other way."

"Well, what possessed you to paint the house, and fix the porch and all this?" Cadie looked out over the lawn, amazed. "And it bein' the Sabbath?"

"About time I started bein' a husband to you bein' a wife. Sabbath or no. Anyways, it ain't right havin' our house lookin' worse than some poor colored's."

"Norman, you know I don't like that word. And besides, their houses look mighty fine, especially Mattie and Zena's. We'd be blessed, indeed, if our house was as pretty as theirs."

He plopped his paintbrush in the paint bucket and frowned. "I don't like you sayin' that."

"Well, it's true."

Norman picked up the paintbrush again and resumed painting. "What about that preacher of theirs? What kinda house does he have?"

"I haven't had the pleasure of seein' it, but I hear it's a fine place."

"He wears a nice, black suit and drives that shiny car. Where'd he get the money for all that and a fine house, too?"

"Where do you think?"

"That don't seem right to me, Cadie. Why does he have all that and some of those other people don't have nothin'?"

"Well, I guess God wanted him to have it, 'cause he needed it." Norman threw back his head and laughed as if she had told the funniest joke he'd ever heard. "What're you laughin' at?" she asked, feeling her mouth turn to a scowl.

"You. You're brain's been so jumbled up by those people, you don't even know what's right anymore."

"Don't the preacher of the Word have a right to a house and a suit and a motorcar to get around in? If some people I know who drink and spend all their days down in the squalor—up to no good—can have all that money and other people's, too," she said with an extra mean glare, "then surely the man of God's entitled!"

Norman dropped the paintbrush back in the bucket and climbed down from the ladder, drawing way too close to Cadie's liking. He squared his shoulders and puffed out his chest like a rooster in a chicken yard. "What'd you say?"

"You heard me." He drew even closer, and she pushed him away. "Don't get that paint on me!"

"I know you were never good at schoolin' like Tessie, but sometimes—sometimes, Cadie, I wonder if those coloreds haven't sucked out all your smarts."

Her temper raged like a steaming tea kettle sitting on a hot stove. "Norman McLain, I'm gonna tell you somethin'. You can use that kinda evil talk and be just as mean and nasty as you want," she said, wagging her finger in front of his face, "but I am not leavin' here, you understand me? As much as I may want to, I'm not leavin'!" Before she could blink, he grabbed her around the waist and slammed his lips onto hers so that she could taste him. This time there was no flavor of liquor or tobacco or anything sour, but a sweetness that sent that familiar tingle of warmth all through her chest. She felt herself melting into his arms as he ran his fingers through her hair and kissed her hard on the lips, face, and neck. "Then come be with me, Cadie," he whispered. "Be with me—"

Repulsion swept over her, forcing her to push him away. "You think I'm gonna be with you after you speak such filth, and call me stupid?"

"I didn't say you were stupid, I just said—well, you started it with that comment about the squalor."

"I didn't start nothin'!" Cadie pushed him hard, sloshing the paint over the top of his boots.

"Dadburn it!" He looked down at the mess she had made. "That wasn't very Christian-like!"

"I don't have to act Christian when I'm in the presence of a devil!"

Cadie stormed back into the house and threw herself on the bed, slamming her face into the pillows. Oh, how she hated him, she did! This love business would never work! Never, never, never! She pounded the mattress and fought back the reverend's words, *love is patient, love is kind, love holds no wrongs against anybody* . . . But she couldn't pray that today, she wouldn't! Instead, she closed her eyes and willed herself to sleep, where the land of dreams was a welcome respite from this life of hers.

Sure enough, within several minutes she had floated away to the river where the prince in the reverend's story was waiting for her, standing on a rock high above with his hand extended, beckoning her to come. She grabbed it, and instantly, a glorious light shone all around them. He pulled her up toward the rock and into his arms, and when she looked into his eyes, she saw the face of someone familiar, someone with a crooked smile and a lock of brown hair falling over his eyes.

"Norman?" Cadie bolted upright on the bed, drenched in sweat. The sun had just begun to set, filling the bedroom with shadows that shifted and moved with each flutter of the curtains. Her heart pounded and her head throbbed with pain as the echo of a horrible yell resonated in her mind. She jumped to her feet and hurried out to the porch "Norman?" Cadie ran to the woodshed as fast as her feet could fly. "Norman, what is it?" She rushed through the door, and there he was, hopping around like a jackrabbit snatched up by two ears. His white shirt was covered in blood where he held his left hand tightly to his chest. "Oh, Lord, what has happened? Here, let me see that." Cadie tugged his hand away and examined a deep gash between the thumb and index finger. "Norman, hush your cryin', and let me tend to it. Come on, now."

After binding up the wound with a strip of an old sheet, she dragged him into the house, ignoring his dramatic howls. She grabbed a needle from the crystal dish on her dresser, then retrieved her box of thread and twine from the cedar chest and squatted down in front of him. "You're not sewin' me up, if that's what you're thinkin'!" he cried. "I know for a fact you can't sew that good!"

"Oh, really?" Cadie said with a hint of sarcasm. "Well, I can call for the doctor, which might take another day, seein' as it's Sundee, or you can let me do it myself and get the healin' process started right now. I've seen Mama do it many a time, just like sewin' up two pieces of cowhide." He winced as she took another peek at the cut. "Oh, there's nothin' to that. It'll only take a minute, and you'll be as good as new. Come on, don't be such a baby."

This was one time Cadie wished Norman had a bit of moonshine on him to calm his nerves and dull the pain, but eventually, he settled down and let her sew him up. He whimpered a bit but, for the most part, bore it bravely. Cadie was right—it took no time at all. She cleaned the wound, sewed it up, and dressed it with a clean strip of sheet. She then fixed him a hot cup of coffee and a wedge of warm cherry pie topped with a slice of hard, tangy cheese. They sat at the table together, neither one of them saying a word as he silently chewed. "Norman?" Cadie asked. "You may think it's none of my business, but since you did bleed all over my blue chiffon, I think I have the right to know how you cut yourself."

He stared at his plate, chewing his last bite of pie. "I thought I'd make you somethin'."

"Me?"

"Yep."

"Well, what'd you make?"

"It ain't nothin'."

"No, you went and cut yourself over it, so I'd like to see."

He rose and shuffled outside, returning with a crude, wooden cross made from two pieces of foot-long split rail bound together with twine. He hung his head as he handed it to her. "Here."

Cadie took it and fingered the wood which had been sanded down until it was silky smooth. It was simple in its construction, yet the ends had been intricately carved with symmetrical notches resembling half-moons. "You made this?"

"Yeah," he said. "Just sorta whittled it together. I know how important it is to you now, bein' a Christian."

"Even though I don't always act like one."

"I've seen a change, even though you still can get as mad as a wet hornet. But there's somethin' different now. You're willin' to put up with me, I can see that."

"Like the reverend says, 'a seed in the ground takes time to grow before we know what kind of plant God has in mind.'" She smiled, rubbing her fingers along the grain of the wood. "Thought you didn't like anything about the Bible and all. Thought it was all trash to you."

He shrugged his shoulders and said, "Truth is, I don't really know what I think anymore."

"Then why'd you say those horrible things today?"

"I don't know. I didn't mean any of it, Cadie. Honest I didn't. I was just mad's all. And I shouldn't have kissed you like I did. I don't know what came over me. I guess seein' you in that dress again. I'm sorry—it was wrong. All of it."

Cadie reached over and touched the top of his bandaged hand. "I forgive you, Norman."

He lifted his eyes and looked at her with surprise in his expression. "You do?"

"Yes."

"Just like that? After all I've done?"

She cut him a sideways look and smiled. "Just don't do it again, you hear?"

He nodded and cracked a grin. "Guess you have changed."

Cadie gazed at the cross and said, "He's changed me, in ways I can't explain. Sometimes it don't seem like it, but at times like this, I know it's true." Her fingers skated over the smooth wood. "It's beautiful. I do love it, Norman."

"Thought maybe you could put it on the wall if you'd like. Except I don't know, seein' as I got blood on it."

"Crosses are supposed to have blood on 'em. You know that, don't you?"

"I've heard."

"Well, maybe you could come to church with me sometime and learn more."

"I'm not goin' to that church, Cadie."

"All right. But if you change your mind."

"I won't."

"But if you do—"

"I said I won't." His voice was loud and firm, signaling an end to the discussion.

Cadie bit her tongue, not wanting to get into an argument over the Lord. She let out a little sigh and stood to her feet. "Well, I better go get cleaned up."

"Cadie?" He grabbed her hand and a jolt of electricity surged up her arm and lodged in her heart, almost taking her breath away. His good thumb swept across the soft flesh of her palm and bumped up against the diamond ring. "I didn't mean to bleed on your blue chiffon."

She stared into his eyes, trying her best to reply, but her heart pounded and her throat constricted at these feelings that stirred within her. "I'll let it soak for a while," she managed to say with a shaky voice, "and it'll be as good as new."

Chapter 30

As soon as Norman hung the blood-stained cross over the fireplace mantel, the very air in the atmosphere of the house changed. Cadie knew it wasn't because of a piece of wood he had whittled with his carving knife but because of something God was doing, something unseen. From that point forward, Norman ate Cadie's cooking and slept every night on the sitting room sofa. He snored occasionally, but for some reason, it didn't bother her like it had before. And he was good about using his spit cup when chewin' tobacco, yet after about a week, Cadie noticed the spit cup disappeared, as did the chaw habit.

Norman had a ravenous appetite, and his body filled out, returning to a healthy ruggedness that was evident in his strength and complexion. He worked hard, spending every spare moment at the store or improving things around the house. The wood siding was painted a fresh coat of white, the shutters a glossy black, and the front door a deep red just like Mattie and Zena's place. And not only that, the screen door was repaired with new hinges, the porch secured with new floor joists and a fresh douse of wood stain, and trees were pruned and shrubbery trimmed so that Cadie could plant a vegetable garden and a flower bed. Lastly, Norman painted the inside walls a pale yellow, which matched the tiny yellow flowers in the calico material Cadie used to cover the sofa. He had found some leftover red striped cloth at the mercantile, enabling Cadie to cover the two chairs.

Now, with the gingham curtains, calico sofa, and wooden cross hanging over the mantle, the whole house was well on its way to becoming a lovely, comfortable home.

The subject of church was never mentioned again, and neither was the reverend nor Zena. Mostly, she and Norman talked about the store, the weather, how the vegetables were coming along in the garden, and what repairs needed to be done to the house. Even though there were smiles and the occasional bout of laughter, there was a sadness in Norman's eyes. He never looked at her in that way that made Cadie blush and never touched her unless it was an accidental brush of the hand when serving the supper plates or the bump of a knee under the table. But each time that happened, a jolt of electricity rushed through her that often took some time to subside. She often wondered if he felt the same sensation.

Cadie soon found herself dreaming about Norman, not in specifics or details, but in broad generalities. A few times, she dreamt of his lips on hers and his arms wrapped around her body, but these visions were fleeting and momentary, yet lingered for days on end. She began to watch his movements and noticed quirks in his habits, such as the way he held a glass with a thumb and only two fingers, the way he cleared his throat after a meal, and the ease of his laugh when she said something humorous. She also noticed things about his features she had not observed before. His cheekbones, for example, were high and defined, his lips full and always rosy, and his eyes held a glint of mischief. It was as if there was something just beneath the surface of the outward Norman McLain worthy of discovery, like a colorful river stone buried in the muck of sand and silt waiting to be pried loose and placed in a collection of valuables. Even the scent of him became enticing to her—a concoction of cinnamon, soap, and sweat that reminded Cadie of something delicious baking in the oven.

Norman was coming home early today to repair the fence behind the back vegetable garden to keep out the stray dogs and wild animals. Cadie had started her morning early so she could finish all of her chores before he returned. Normally, she dreaded washing and ironing, but today she was excited, for some reason, and didn't mind at all scrubbing the sheets, towels, and Norman's shirts and hanging them out to dry. The clothes from Thursday's wash were taken from the ironing pile and pressed with lilac and lemon water and then laid in the dresser drawers in organized stacks. Cadie opened and closed her lingerie drawer several times, taking things out and putting clean clothes back in, and each time, the burlap sack with Boy's letters lay at the bottom of a pile of nightclothes, untouched.

Next, she poured the washing water into a bucket and began scrubbing the sitting room floor. She noticed the glint of her ring and a song rose up within her, the one she and Zena always sang when they were busy at work. *Amazing grace how sweet the sound, that saved a wretch like me. I once was lost, but now am found, was blind but now I see.* Cadie hummed for the longest time and even sung another stanza or two, blending it into a rendition of *When the Saints Go Marching In*, and a few lines of *Give Me Jesus*. Norman's wooden cross hung over the mantle, substituting as a willing and eager audience. After a few vigorous scrubs, she stopped and stared at the dark smudge of blood smeared across its bottom. Who would've thought that she, Cadie Inez Hamilton McLain, would be singing with joy while cleaning the sitting room floor? The emotion got the better of her, and she belted out another line from *How Great Thou Art*, giving the floor another hearty scrub. "I think I'm startin' to see some things, Lord," she prayed out loud. *I think it's all comin' clear—*

The kitchen door creaked closed, and Norman stood staring at her, holding a bunch of wildflowers, including wisteria blooms and daisies. "Norman!" Cadie exclaimed. "I didn't hear you drive up."

"Probably 'cause of you singin'."

Her cheeks flushed at the way he stared at her. "Oh, well—" She wiped her hands on the back of her skirt and tucked a stray strand of hair behind her ear. "That's Zena's song. She taught it to me."

"You sing it real pretty."

Another rush of blood flooded Cadie's cheeks. "Thank you."

He shifted his weight from one foot to the other and fiddled with the flower stems. "I got you these. Don't know whether you like 'em."

"They're beautiful."

An awkward hesitation hovered over them, waiting to be cleared away by a few chosen words. "Guess I'll go put 'em in water," he said.

"There's an old milk jug there by the sink."

He placed the flowers in the jug, filled it with water, and carefully stepped around the wet spots on the floor to get to the fireplace. He set the jug on the mantle, directly underneath the cross.

"That looks real nice, Norman." Cadie dropped the brush in the bucket and stood to her feet, adjusting her skirt around her knees. But then something odd happened—she took one step, and it was as if both legs were knocked forward by a powerful force, sending her up in the air like a skater falling on a frozen pond in the dead of winter. She cried out with arms flailing, trying to grab hold of something, but before her backside hit the floor, Norman was there, slamming his knees onto the hard wood as he caught her in his arms.

Cadie clung to his shoulders like a frightened child and looked into his eyes. He was staring at her with that same fiery blaze that brought a tingling sensation to her stomach and familiar flood of warmth through her chest and arms. The air filled with an electric charge that made the hair on the back of her neck stand on end and the skin on her arms shrivel up like goose hide. She tried to look away, but she couldn't. Her eyes were locked onto his and drawn into the reflection in his irises, like a moth to the flame.

"You all right?"

Cadie nodded. "Yes—I think so."

"Guess you washed that floor so good, it's about as smooth as slippery glass," he said with his crooked smile. "I'm just glad I was here to catch you. And hear you sing that pretty song."

His fiery expression matched the heat from his touch, all of which had Cadie terribly confused. "Norman?" she whispered, not realizing what was about to happen. She leaned forward and slowly pressed her lips onto his.

His arms tightened around her waist as he returned her kiss—slowly at first, and then wildly, frantically, as though he could devour every inch of her. "Cadie, I love you, I do," he said, his words caressing her cheek. "Do you love me? Tell me you love me—tell me."

She caught her breath and stared into his eyes while her mind reeled. "Oh, Norman. I think so, but—I'm not sure." Immediately, he stiffened like an old, dried up plank left out in the sun for too long. Cadie realized her mistake and kissed him again, but he pushed her away.

"Norman—"

"I better get goin' on that fence." Then tracking wet shoeprints through the clean floor, he slammed the screen door and was gone.

Cadie stood by the kitchen window, stirring a pitcher of fresh-squeezed lemonade while she watched Norman split rails for the new fence. The heat was so intense that after several whacks from the axe, he would stop, adjust his hat and wipe his forehead with the back of his sleeve before resuming his work. After a few more swings, he dropped the axe to the ground and pulled his shirt over his head, flinging it onto a pile of bushes. She looked away briefly and then snuck a peak at his bare back, amazed at the thick muscles and how the veins and sinews in his shoulders and arms strained with each swing. *How long can he stay out there choppin' that wood without even one water break?* she wondered, fighting the constriction in her throat. Surely, he couldn't stay mad at her all day, could he?

Cadie gathered her courage and wandered out to the fence with a wooden tray holding the pitcher of lemonade, two jelly jar glasses, and a plate of oatmeal raisin cookies. "Norman, I brought you some fresh-squeezed lemonade."

"Not now." He still wouldn't look at her but hoisted the axe and released a powerful swing, popping a log in two.

"Norman, you need to drink somethin'. It's hot as blazes out here."

"I know that."

"Then drink some lemonade. Or I'll get you some water, if that's what you want."

"You know what I want."

"Norman, I'm tryin'—"

"Well, I am, too."

Cadie set the tray on a tree stump and prayed silently. *Love is patient, love is kind* . . . She reached out her hand to touch the sweat on his back, surprised at the coolness of his skin. "Norman?" He didn't move, but kept still as her palm flattened against his flesh so that she could feel the smooth muscles flowing underneath. A bead of sweat rolled from his neck down the ridge of his spine that formed a valley, giving her the irresistible urge to wipe it away. She extended her index finger to set it off course, when suddenly, he pulled away.

"No, Cadie. I don't want you lovin' me that way, not unless you really mean it."

"You want me to lie to you, is that it?"

"No."

"Then what? Whadda you want from me?"

He pushed back the brim of his hat and glared at her. "I want you to look me in the eye and tell me what I know you told him."

Instantly, her mouth sealed shut. Lying was a sin against the Lord, and no one had to tell her that or read it to her from the Bible. She just knew it to be true, way down deep in her heart.

Norman turned away and lifted the axe in the air, splitting another dry log in half with a powerful pop. He then dropped the axe head into the dirt and wiped his forehead with a bandana tucked into his back trouser pocket. "I'm willin' to wait, Cadie, even though I know I may never hear you say it, but I'm willin' to hold out. I don't know why. Part of me wants to just run away from you and all this. But I've tried everything else out there—liquor, what little money I could get my hands on. Women."

"Like Molly Stephens?"

His back stiffened at the sound of that name. "I guess I figured, if I couldn't have you—" He faced her again, coming so close that his shadow shielded her from the sun. "I always compared her to you, just like every girl I've ever been with." He lifted her chin and forced her to look at him through a pair of watery eyes. "There's only been you, Cadie. Ever since we were kids. I know that for sure now." He wiped away a stray tear with his thumb before it rolled down her cheek. "There ain't no one else."

Cadie threw her arms around his waist and pressed herself against his bare chest, not minding in the least that her whole front side was doused in his sweat. "One day, Norman," she said. "One day." She squeezed him with all the strength she had until his arms embraced her as well.

He kissed the top of her head, breathing in the scent of her hair. "I'll be here. Choppin' wood or tendin' to the vegetables or whatever else needs doin'."

"I do thank you for it."

There was a long pause as they stood with their arms around each other in the blazing sun. "Well—you better get on inside 'fore you melt in this heat."

She wiped the sweat and tears from her face and smoothed down the front of her dress. "It's hotter in the kitchen then it is out here, especially when the stove gets fired up," she said. A smile crept across her face as she looked into his eyes. "Thought I'd cook you one of my apple pies."

"It's not made from those Stephens apples is it?"

"No. I bought 'em at Whaley's."

"You know Pa's 'bout to have a fit 'cause of you shoppin' over there."

"Let him. I can shop where I want, can't I?"

"I reckon so." He gave her a smirk and then lowered his hat onto his forehead. "All right, fine, then. I'll have a piece when I'm done." Cadie turned and headed back to the house, when he yelled, "Hey! What about my lemonade?"

"You gotta whole pitcher there to yourself and two jelly jars."

"Aren't you gonna pour it for me, seein' as I'm fixin' this fence?"

"Norman McLain, I've got an apple pie to cook. You're just gonna have to pour it yourself." Then flashing a playful grin, she skipped into the kitchen. "Bye, now."

As the screen door closed behind her, she turned her head to see if he was looking. And he was.

Part IV

Chapter 31

The train rumbled past clumps of trees, houses, and farmland as it made its way toward Pleasant Oaks. Boy sat by the window and stared at an opening in the forest, hoping to catch a glimpse of the Cape Fear River that flowed just beyond a line of pine trees. As soon as a firmament of blue appeared in the horizon, he slunk back into his seat and dipped the brim of his fedora onto his forehead. He hated coming home under these circumstances, but decisions had been made, and there was no going back. Besides, Cadie was married now and hadn't been willing to wait like she had promised.

Thoughts of her always brought a surge of pain jolting through Boy's body, forcing him to suppressed a moan. It reminded him of the early days when his leg would awaken after a round of morphine had run its course. The pain would howl at a feverish, excruciating pitch, limiting his thoughts and speech to the bare necessities, such as "water," "pain," or "nurse." Hours were spent in suffering, staring out the hospital window at the mass of yellow, orange, and red that floated off the trees and onto the brittle ground. Occasionally, his focus would shift from the leaves to a pronounced streak of dirt on the windowpane, formerly a dribble of muddy rainwater from the roof gutters that had splashed onto the glass. At times, it resembled the trail of an earthworm that had lost its way from the comforts of a bed of warm compost, but at other times, when the sunlight shone through the glass just so, it looked like the crooked finger of an old woman, scolding him for having jumped that train when it was clearly moving too fast.

He had only been away to school for a couple of months when the money ran out due to gambling debts. There was no other choice but to go home to see about wrangling another advance from his uncle, an idea that didn't seemed so bad at the time because of the added bonus of seeing Cadie. As it turns out, his bad landings from years of train hopping paled in comparison to what had happened on that afternoon. He would've much preferred a pack of wild dogs fighting over a dead raccoon than being slammed up against the side of a tobacco shed.

"Boy, I'd say you've gone and done it now . . . ." The echo of his uncle's voice and the click of a pocket watch accompanied every wave of pain, like the ocean pounding the surf. Boy recalled Uncle Greer standing at the end of his hospital bed, wearing his typical attire of dark wool suit, brocade waistcoat, blue silk tie, and bowler. His hands were gloved, as usual, and his arms folded onto a black enameled walking cane with silver domed handle, which seemed to be more for affectation than necessity. "They say your leg's broke in three pieces, may not ever heal up properly." The memory of cigar smoke swirled through Boy's mind, violating his senses. "Say you might even lose it."

"I ain't sellin', if that's what you've come for."

"Well, I'd like to know how you plan on paying these hospital bills," Uncle Greer had said, staring at him with a pair of beady eyes that were more wild animal than human being. "'Cause if I remember correctly, hospital bills weren't part of our arrangement. They say it'll be months before you can leave. And then, if you lose it—" His eyes had swept over Boy's injured leg, revealing a look of pity, but certainly no mercy. "Well, it might take even longer."

"I'm gonna marry Cadie. I'm gonna marry her, and then I'm gonna come live in that house—"

"Word is she's sweet on Anson McLain's son." The sound of Uncle Greer's cane tapping against the floor haunted Boy, coating his tongue with the taste of rotting liquor and cigars. "He's a strong, strapping man, working in his daddy's store, not having to jump trains to get from one place to another. Not stupid enough to become a cripple and chop his leg up into mincemeat." Boy could still visualize his uncle's nostril hairs protruding like wayward, silvery vines and hear the whistling that came from inside his capillary-lined nose. "You can marry her if she'll have you, but she won't be living in my house, 'cause you're gonna sell. The doctor tells me there's an operation—cost a lot of money, but he guarantees it'll save your leg. You think about that, huh? But not too long. I can smell the stench of gangrene setting in as we speak . . ."

The train lurched, causing a bead of sweat to roll down Boy's forehead. He closed his eyes and went through the details again in his mind, living it afresh as though it had happened only moments before. Anger welled up from deep inside his heart, spurring on a plan of revenge. His uncle would be sorry one day—they all would, including Cadie, if she wasn't sorry already. He'd sign that purchase agreement the lawyers had drawn up, take the money, and set up a business in Raleigh somewhere, maybe his own lumber and building company, and then a manufacturer of something. He'd make so much profit that he'd come back and buy that ole plantation back at a price even Uncle Greer couldn't refuse. *One day*, he said to himself.

The train slowed as it neared the depot, hissing and popping in a jerky motion. Boy gripped the head of his walking cane and readjusted his leg, trying to keep it stable. The operation had been painful, but it had done the job and saved his leg, just as predicted. And as for the healing process, it had been long and arduous but had gone as well as could be expected, leaving the right leg a little bowed and shorter that the other. With exercise and time, the doctors assured him the muscles would become stronger and more agile, and he could resume life without the assistance of a decorative pole with a silver knob on the end. Boy cursed under his breath as he struggled to stand to his feet. He just wished that day was today.

"Hello, cousin." A sultry, feminine voice greeted Boy as he hobbled down to the platform. Molly was dressed in a rose-colored suit with matching shoes, hat, and gloves, and poised like a model who had just arrived from the fashion district of New York.

"Mrs. Wallace—I didn't expect such a grand welcome."

"Well, it's been almost two years, and you know your reputation traveling on trains," she said with a coy smile, emitting a hint of peppermint on her breath. "Daddy wanted to make sure you actually got off—clean and sober that is—and all in one piece." She eyed his bad leg with a twinge of revulsion and added, "And able to sign your name, of course."

"There's no concern about that."

The revulsion evaporated, and she smiled again, revealing a neat row of even, pearly teeth. "No, I can see that."

"Good." Boy gathered his fob chain in his palm and tucked it into his waistcoat pocket where a watch would normally rest. "I just need to make one stop, and then I'll be ready." He gripped a leather satchel in one hand and his cane with the other and led Molly down the street toward Johnson's Jewelers, which was just two stores down from McLain's Mercantile.

The train whistled loud and clear as Cadie walked toward the mercantile at a brisk pace, loaded down with Whaley's shopping bags. Just as she passed Johnson's Jewelers, she slowed her steps, debating whether she should peek through the window of the mercantile and see Norman at work. Her curiosity had nagged at her for weeks now, and she wanted more than anything to catch a glimpse of him as boss of the establishment.

Cadie shielded her eyes from the glare of the sun and peered into the glass. The store was full of people, including fat Mrs. Williamson and several of her Bible study friends, one of whom was Edna Brown from Mama's sewing club. Obviously, there was something going on, because Mrs. Williamson stood at the back counter and pointed her finger at Mr. McLain while stomping her foot and flapping and squawking like a wet hen.

"That woman! You'd think she owned the whole town!" Cadie exclaimed out loud, not caring who heard. She shook her head in dismay until she saw Zena standing by the wall, out of harm's way, looking so fresh and pretty in comparison to Mrs. Williamson's sweaty, red-faced self.

Temptation got the best of her, and Cadie decided she just had to go inside. She checked her appearance in the reflection of the glass and felt a sense of delight in how becoming she looked. She had coiffed her hair to resemble an elegant bob and topped it off with a straw hat lined with blue silk flowers she had made herself. It looked pretty with her blue linen drop-waist dress she had sewn from a bolt of leftover material, a surprise gift from Norman.

Cadie stepped inside and set her Whaley's bags by the door just as Mrs. Williamson pointed a pudgy finger at a fresh baked blueberry pie and said, "Goodness knows, Mr. McLain, is this how you let that son of yours run this store? Sellin' Negro cooking to us white people?" One look at the pie and its golden crust adorned with decorative pastry leaves, and Cadie knew there was only one person, black or white, who could've made such a mouth-watering dessert.

"Now, Mrs. Williamson," Mr. McLain said in a timid voice, "you know Mattie Goodwin bakes everything to the highest, freshest standard. Why, Mrs. Stephens wouldn't have her in her kitchen if that weren't the case."

"I don't care what Adelaide Stephens says and does . . ."

Cadie snuck up behind Zena and whispered in her ear, "What's she gripin' about today?"

"Miss Cadie!" Zena whispered back, taking in her new attire. "Look at you!" Cadie smiled and then nodded toward Mrs. Williamson, causing Zena's excitement to dissipate. "Oh, she don't want Mama sellin' her pies in here. Same old thing she's been sayin' for weeks now. He'll just give it to her free when no one's lookin', and she'll take it. Word is Mama's blueberry pie is her husband's favorite."

"You don't say."

"Yep. She even tried to finagle the recipe from Mama, can you believe that? Mama'd rather die than give that woman the recipe for her blueberry pie."

"You oughtta say something, Zena. Don't just stand there and listen to her lies."

"I'm not sayin' nothin', and neither are you, you hear? Don't be goin' and makin' trouble for me, Miss Cadie. You've caused me enough trouble as it is."

"Well, I didn't mean to. Besides, thought you'd forgiven me."

"I have, but you gotta remember sometimes—you and me—we're different."

"We're not different," Cadie said, almost too loudly. Immediately, her eyes honed in on an enormous sweat stain under Mrs. Williamson's arm pit. "You know that ain't true, Zena."

"Isn't."

"It isn't true, and you know it."

Zena stared straight ahead and said in a firm voice, "Not sayin' what's true. Just sayin' what *is*."

Cadie's mind reeled at these words. It stung to realize that a barrier existed between the two of them when women like Mrs. Williamson were around, despite all she and Zena had been through. "You think I'm like her," Cadie said, fighting back the tears, "'cause my skin's white? You think I'm full of the devil like that—that big, fat cow?"

"Naw!" Zena scowled. "And you ought not be talkin' about mean white folk that way, especially now you bein' a Christian."

"Well, I can't help it. Someone needs to shut her up, but good." A lone tear streamed down Zena's cheek, making a clear, pearl-like track along her velvety, black skin. Cadie brought her lips close to Zena's ear and whispered, "I'd paint my skin black, I would. I'd crawl back up in my mama's womb and beg God to change me in every way, to make me a Negro, the blackest of the bunch—"

"Hush, now, Miss Cadie." Zena said.

"I'd do it all if it'd take the difference between us away and put me over there with you and not with people like this." Cadie glared at Mrs. Williamson as she carried on with her vicious rant. She grimaced at how the flesh bulged off the woman's cheeks like hunks of boiled ham with rivers of fat swimming through that led down into the neck and bosom region. A string of white froth lined the corners of her mouth, and the edges of her dampened hair protruded from her sweaty neck like wiry whiskers on a cat. What a horrible, hideous thing she was, and that was the truth, regardless of whether Cadie was a Christian now or not. All of them, Mrs. Williamson and all her friends, they were animals. *Just big, fat, sweaty—animals!*

Mrs. Williamson spun around as though she had heard every thought flowing through Cadie's mind. "Did you just say something to me?"

Cadie gulped awkwardly. "If I did, it was private, not meant for your ears."

"How dare you! I asked you a question."

"And I answered it."

Mrs. Williamson's eyes widened, and her face turned bright pink. "Who do you think you are, speaking to me that way?"

Cadie thrust her nose up in the air, trying her best to look like a wealthy, prominent lady. "The fact of the matter is, my husband runs this establishment. He may not be here right now, but I know he won't appreciate you speakin' ill toward the goods he sells or the customers who baked 'em and frequent this store. Now, I think the thing you oughtta do is apologize."

"Apologize?" Mrs. Williamson emitted a deep, phlegmy laugh. "And just who am I supposed to apologize to?"

"Well, you can start with Miss Goodwin here, since it was her mama who made that blueberry pie. And you can apologize to me, since my husband runs the place, and Miss Goodwin here is a friend of mine."

"I'm not apologizing for a thing! What I said was the truth. I can't pay good money for that. What do you think my husband would say if I told him I paid for food baked in some mammy's filthy kitchen?"

"Her kitchen ain't filthy, and she ain't nobody's mammy!"

Mrs. Williamson stepped toward Cadie with her finger wagging and her head bobbing like a buoy in the river on a cold, stormy night. "Don't you be talking that Nigra-loving white trash talk around me, you hear? We all know who you are—that broken-down hussy who used to roam the riverbanks like some heathen tramp. Then living with Nigras, under the same roof and even going to that heathen church of theirs—just shameful, a disgrace! I remember you, you can't fool me. You and your insults. You may've cleaned yourself up, but deep down you're just as filthy as they are. Just filthy, black—"

"It's your mouth that's about as filthy as an old broken-down outhouse!" Cadie pointed at Mrs. Williamson, in a duel of sorts, where index fingers and words were the weapons. "Why, you aren't fit to lick the floor of a barnyard stable, although it looks like you'd be right at home there, wallowin' around with all the hogs!"

Mrs. Williamson reeled back, as if she had been smacked square in the face. Zena grabbed Cadie's arm and cowered behind her. "Miss Cadie," she whispered. But Cadie wasn't listening. It felt good to tell that woman off. She felt entitled and empowered, and yet, there was something inside of her that nudged a warning to stop before it was too late.

"Mr. McLain! I've never in all my born days! You're just gonna stand there and let this—this urchin speak to me this way?"

"Now, Mrs. Williamson—" He wiped his sweaty brow with a handkerchief and said, "You don't pay her any mind."

"No, Mr. McLain, something must be done about this. Yes, indeed." Mrs. Williamson tapped her toe and looked to her Bible study ladies for support, even though it was obvious she was the ring-leader of the bunch, and all decisions were made by her, and her alone. She glared at Cadie again, her eyes inflamed with something that could only be described as pure, unadulterated evil. "I see you and that Nigra ninny laughing and talking together, and it's not right. That's the whole problem, you putting ideas in their heads, that they're the same. Well, they're not. And they won't ever be, you understand?" She stepped closer, signaling the Bible study ladies to gather around like a pack of snarling dogs. Her eyes darkened as they shifted to Zena, who recoiled even further behind Cadie. "Mr. McLain, I know you keep a strap back there behind the counter, 'cause I've seen you use it to sharpen those butcher knives." She flung her arm back toward the counter while holding a steady gaze on Zena. "I suggest you give it to me now, so I can teach this uppity Negro how to talk right."

"She didn't say nothin'!" Cadie screeched.

"Now, Mrs. Williamson—"

"Mr. McLain, if you don't give me that strap, I'm gonna take my business over to Whaley's, and I'll make sure all my friends do the same."

Mrs. Williamson brought her eyes back over to Cadie and said, "Isn't that right, ladies?"

Cadie stood almost nose-to-nose with Mrs. Williamson—if that were possible given the size of her girth—smelling the stench of her exhale with each hard-labored breath. "You touch her, and I'll—I don't know what I'll do," Cadie seethed. "But you'll regret it, you will!"

There was a general grumble from all the ladies, even Mrs. Edna Brown, who acted like she had never even laid eyes on Cadie before in her life. Cadie cast a quick glance in Mr. McLain's direction and shook her head, feeling the grip of Zena's fingers digging into the back of her arm. But he just looked away and reached under the counter. "Make sure you go out back."

Without the slightest hesitation, Mrs. Williamson grabbed the strap with one hand and Zena's ear with the other and made a beeline to the back door, with Zena whooping and hollering and Cadie screaming at the top of her lungs. "You leave her alone! You can whip me if you want—whip me, just leave her alone! Leave her alone!" The Bible study ladies held her back, and no matter how hard she pushed and shoved, Cadie couldn't fight her way through.

Zena was swept into a whirlwind of angry, white flesh, gnashing teeth, and the swish of a cotton girdle rubbing one fat leg against the other—the sound of the fires of Hell itself. She closed her eyes and yelled, although she had no idea what she was saying, other than "Stop!" and "No!" and "Please don't, sweet Jesus!" Her ear hurt like the blazes, as though it was being ripped from the side of her head with a jagged knife. She fell once against a stack of flour sacks, but the incredible force pulling at her ear jerked her to her feet and drug her toward the back of the mercantile. Miss Cadie's screams echoed in the background while the only decipherable words heard were "I'm gonna teach you a thing or two!" and "You dirty Nigra!" Zena could take the names, she was used to those, and she wouldn't have even minded if one of those ladies had spit on her like they had her mama, but the throbbing in her ear and the anticipation of biting whips on her flesh left her terrified. *Oh, Lord, don't let 'em hit me in the face. I don't wanna go to church on Sunday and let the reverend see marks on my face.* "Oh, Lord! Lord!" Zena let out a blood-curling wail, but it didn't slow her attacker in the least. "Lord, forgive these people, forgive 'em, forgive 'em, oh Jesus, Jesus!"

"You be quiet, you hear?" Mrs. Williamson screamed as her arm came down with a mighty blow.

Suddenly, the bang of the back door to the mercantile and the whack of the leather strap brought the entire commotion to a standstill. To Zena's shock and dismay, Miss Cadie had somehow barreled her way through the Bible study ladies and stood before her with watery eyes and her palm clutching her cheek where the strap had made contact. And there, towering over them all, was Mr. Norman, with his arms full of firewood.

"Norman!" Miss Cadie cried. "Tell her to get her filthy hands off Zena! Tell her!"

Mrs. Williamson stood in horror with her mouth wide open, looking from him to Miss Cadie and then back to him. "I didn't mean to—she just—"

With one powerful move, he dropped the firewood on the floor with a kerplunk and yanked the strap from Mrs. Williamson's hand. "She stepped in front of me!" Mrs. Williamson exclaimed, pointing at Miss Cadie with a fat, stubby finger.

Mr. Norman's cold demeanor made Zena shudder. "This is my store, Mrs. Williamson, and anything that goes on in here concerns me. Now, you take your hands off this girl and tell her and my wife you're sorry for actin' like the devil, and maybe, just maybe they'll forgive you."

Mrs. Williamson clamped her fingers even tighter around Zena's ear, making her wince. "I won't," she said. "I apologize to you and Mrs. McLain, but this is a private matter."

"Mrs. Williamson, I ain't never hit a lady with a strap but one time." He looked at Zena for a moment and said, "And for that, I am deeply sorry. But today—I don't think I'd have any regrets whatsoever."

"You threatening me?"

"Call it what you like," Mr. Norman said. An awkward silence permeated the room before Mrs. Williamson cast her eyes down to the strap and released Zena's ear with a jerk. "Now, you gonna say you're sorry?"

"I said my apologies."

"Fine, then, if that's the best you can do." He kicked a piece of firewood out of the way and stepped toward her, lowering his voice in an authoritative manner. "How would you like to pay for that fresh baked blueberry pie? I know Herbert'll be most obliged at puttin' a morsel of that heavenly concoction in his mouth tonight after a good, tasty supper you've cooked up for him in that clean kitchen of yours. You can give cash to Miss Goodwin right here, or would you rather me put it on your account?"

Again, another long silence reigned as he stared hard at Mrs. Williamson, flexing his fists and clenching his teeth while she huffed and puffed until her sweaty face became as red as a beet. Finally, she turned on her heel and stomped back to the front of the store. "Pa, go on and charge Mrs. Williamson for that pie and box it up real nice for her!"

Mr. Norman followed her through the throng of customers, addressing all of them like a politician conducting a town hall meeting. "Anyone else here have a problem with Negro cookin' bein' sold in this store, well y'all're welcome to take your business elsewhere. We only sell the best here at McLain's, and this here blueberry pie baked by Miz Mattie Goodwin is the best there is, and y'all know it." He took the pie box from Mr. McLain's shaky hands and held it up over his head. "Mrs. Stephens serves the same thing on a silver platter with fresh flowers at one of her fancy garden parties, and y'all fight for the last crumb! Why, I have it on good authority the chefs at all the top restaurants in Wilmington've offered good money for the recipe, even offered Miz Goodwin a job to go up there and cook all their food for 'em!" He smiled as he faced Mrs. Williamson again. "Ain't that somethin'?" Then holding the box out to her, he plopped it into her fleshy arms, smiling even more. "Enjoy your dessert, ma'am."

The next thing he did almost made Zena faint. He strode to the back of the counter and slapped his palms on the surface. "Miss Goodwin, come on up here, and I'll get you what you need. The rest of you ladies are gonna have to wait over to the side, thank you. Come on, let's make room for Miss Goodwin to come up here."

Everyone stepped aside as Zena made her way to the counter with her head hung low. "Humph!" Mrs. Williamson said. She swished out of the store with the pie box in hand and her friends streaming behind her like a row of ducklings following a mama duck.

Zena waited until the front door shut before speaking up. "Mr. McLain, sir? I do thank you."

"No need for that. I did what any decent person oughtta do." Zena noticed that his gaze was different now—it went past the skin, lips, and hair and straight into her soul. "It's me who oughtta be thankin' you for what you've done for us after all my evil doin's," he added. "I'm not good at askin' forgiveness, Miss Goodwin, but I do ask—if you can somehow find it in your heart to give me another chance?"

She wiped her face with the back of her hand and smiled. Was this really the same man who had scared the daylights out of her several months ago? Surely, the Lord was up to somethin'! "Oh, yes, sir, Mr. McLain, sir.

That's long forgotten."

"You can call me Norman if you like."

"And you can call me Zena."

He grinned for a moment and then grew solemn as Miss Cadie approached with her left cheek bearing a red mark that had started to swell. Immediately, he bolted from behind the counter and gathered her in his arms. "You sure you're all right?" he asked.

"I'm sure."

He kissed her gently and then gave her another firm squeeze. "Nobody's gonna hit you again, Cadie," he said with tears in his eyes. "Nobody."

"That's all in the past, Norman," Miss Cadie said. She gave him another hug and then looked over at Zena. "How about you, Miss Zena? How's your ear?"

"Ringin' like church bells, but that's all right by me." Zena took in every ounce of Miss Cadie, from her polished shoes and new dress, all the way to her flowered hat and carefully coifed hair. Oh, she did look fine folded up in Mr. Norman's embrace! Zena smiled at Mr. Norman and said, "I declare, even with that mark on her face, Miss Cadie looks as pretty as a picture in your arms."

"Zena," Miss Cadie said, blushing.

"Just a little ice and vanilla-butter mixture'll make it as good as new."

"Yep, I'm sure it will," he said, gazing at Miss Cadie. "But even so, she looks prettier than any picture I've ever seen."

Zena beamed inside as Mr. Norman and Miss Cadie looked at each other, long and hard, like everything and everyone else in the mercantile had faded away. Never in all her life would she have thought the Lord could work such a change in two people's hearts, but He sure had done it. He surely had.

Chapter 32

Mr. Johnson stood behind the jewelry counter, dangling a shiny, silver pocket watch from its chain before dropping it into Boy's outstretched palm. "A fine selection, Mr. Morgan." Boy fingered it, feeling the grooves of the engraving on the cover and the weight of the metal. It was a solid, well-made piece that would last a lifetime and look fine hanging from a fob on any Southern gentleman's waistcoat. He popped the cover open and read the time. It was a half hour before his meeting with Uncle Greer.

"Nice," Molly said with an air of disinterest.

Boy snapped the cover closed and handed the watch back to Mr. Johnson. "Thank you, but I'd like to see what you have in gold."

"Certainly." Mr. Johnson put the watch away and locked up the merchandise in a drawer beneath the counter.

Molly eyed Boy with curiosity. "Gold? You must be expecting to negotiate favorable terms with Daddy."

Boy kept silent. He didn't trust Molly and never had. Despite her elegance and cultivated attire, she was as slippery as a serpent underneath, just like her mother—and just like his uncle.

Mr. Johnson pulled out a second tray filled with gold watches, causing Molly's callous comments to melt into a litany of "ohhs" and "ahhs." They were exquisite watches, all of them, yet none appealed to Boy. The gold was too yellow in some, too dull in others, and much too shiny in a few that caught his eye. Molly picked up a heavily engraved specimen with an emerald watch stem and dangled it in front of Boy. "How about this one?"

A motorcar door slammed in the distance, and a familiar voice made the hair on the back of Boy's neck stand on end. He turned and looked out the window, recognizing the loping gait and broad shoulders that had always reminded him of a lumberjack or a farmer who had spent years working in the fields. Yes, it was Norman McLain. Boy watched as he helped an elegant lady into the driver's side of his truck, when suddenly, the blood drained from Boy's face and arms and descended into his lower extremities. He knew who the lady had to be, but his mind couldn't register what he was seeing. She was beautiful and refined, lovelier than Darlene Bradshaw on her best day.

The lady looked Boy's way, but did she see him? He nodded and smiled through the window, noticing a slight change in her expression. Molly moved next to Boy, and they both watched in silence. Norman set the lady's packages into the flatbed of the truck and then leaned through the open window and kissed her long on the mouth. Boy thought he noticed Molly stiffen, but he couldn't be sure—he was only aware of a deep throbbing that had started in his injured leg and now resonated throughout his entire body.

"Mr. Morgan, sir?" Mr. Johnson looked like a barn owl with an eyeglass wedged in his eye. "I have several other nice selections here for you to look at."

"I'm late for a meetin' with my uncle," Boy said, fighting the constriction pressing against his throat. "I'll come back later." Then grabbing the handle of his walking cane, he pushed through the door of the jewelry store and stepped outside.

Boy waited until the truck drove off and Norman disappeared into the mercantile before making his way down the street, trying with all his might to minimize the limp in his bad leg.

"Robert?" Molly called to him, but he ignored her and followed the truck to the edge of town. He despised using a cane, hating the fact that he couldn't run like the wind and jump into the passenger side next to Cadie. After a few minutes, the truck picked up speed and disappeared into a cloud of dust. Boy stared into its wake, ignoring the hard looks from pedestrians and the tooting of horns from motorcars and trucks.

After a few moments, the blue Rolls-Royce pulled up next to him. Molly rested a silk-covered elbow on the edge of the driver's window and smiled in that teasing way of hers. "How about a ride?" she asked. Boy hesitated and then limped to the passenger side and slipped in. "Don't look so sad," she said, shifting the car in gear and driving off. "You know it wasn't meant to be." Boy gazed into the distance, not wanting to engage in any conversation, especially one that dealt with Cadie. "The world we live in doesn't allow for romance with just anyone, you know. If that weren't the case, you think I'd be driving this motorcar? What would someone like me be doing driving an old, beat up truck like that?" She shifted gears again and settled back into the plush seat. "It's unthinkable."

"A small price to pay for sellin' your soul."

"I haven't sold my soul."

"You're married to Lloyd Wallace aren't you?"

"Very funny," she said with a scowl. "Especially coming from you, dressed the way you are, looking at gold watches because silver just *won't do*. Everything's been maneuvered in the Stephens family so that money stays where money belongs, and you know it."

"I don't care about the money."

"Yes, you do," she said. For the first time, Boy felt a mixture of hatred and pity toward Molly that created a horrible combination, making her appear downright ugly, despite her creamy complexion, bobbed hair, and stylish outfit. "Let's not argue," she said, holding her chin that much higher as they listened to the steady whir of the motor. "I want us to be friends. I want to help you."

Boy gave her a skeptical look. "How're you gonna do that?"

"Well, you know how husbands are after the first year of marriage—they get bored with things. So, I've decided, if Lloyd can have other distractions to keep him busy, then I can, too."

"I don't see how that has anything to do with me."

"Silly," she said in a condescending tone. "All I have to do is say the word, and Norman'll be right back in my arms."

Boy chuckled to himself. "You flatter yourself."

"I know how Norman feels about me, and those feelings don't die easily."

"Norman McLain would never leave Cadie for you. He's not that much of a fool."

Molly's eyes flashed with anger. "I'm trying to help you, and you insult me?"

"No. You insult yourself."

Her leather gloves gripped the steering wheel even tighter as her foot pressed against the accelerator. "And what about your milkmaid?"

"She's not a milkmaid."

"One look from you would change everything."

Boy stared out the window again, trying not to think about the throbbing pain in his leg or the familiar tightening in his chest and throat that caused a band of sweat to form at the edge of his brow. He removed his hat and wiped his forehead with a handkerchief. "She had her chance, and she chose him."

"You think Cadie Hamilton chose Norman over you?" Molly lips slid upward in a smile. "Robert Morgan—I thought you were a lot smarter than that."

"Whadda you mean?" Boy asked, his eyes narrowing.

She glanced at the glove box under the dashboard and nodded in its direction. He stared at it for a moment and then turned the lever so that the door fell open, revealing a stamped envelope addressed in a familiar, cursive handwriting. He picked it up and read his name—*Mr. Robert Morgan, State College, Raleigh, N. C.* And the return address was from a *Cadie I. Hamilton, Pleasant Oaks.*

Cadie sucked in a deep breath as her thoughts ran wild. *It was him, it was!* The image of Boy standing in the middle of the road haunted her like a specter, bringing with it a wave of nausea. *Oh, God in heaven, Lord Jesus! Why had he come back? And why had he followed after her?*

After what seemed like miles of dirt road, she pulled up to the house and scrambled out of the truck, grabbing her Whaley's bags from the flatbed and dumping them on the kitchen table. Her hands trembled and her heart raced at what she had seen in the rear-view mirror as she drove out of town. With his obvious limp and cane, she would have never recognized him had she not seen his face through the jewelry store window. *Something had happened*, she thought. *Something terrible.*

Cadie knew she had to talk to someone, but Mattie and Zena were hard at work in Mrs. Stephens's kitchen by now, and she certainly couldn't talk to Mama or Daddy. That left only one person—the reverend. She threw her shawl over her shoulders and hurried outside, feeling the heat of the sun on her face. She could drive the truck but decided it would be better to walk.

Even though summer wasn't quite over, the smell of fall was in the air and the leaves were beginning to turn that wonderful burnt orange-red color that marked the change in the seasons. Normally, the beauty of nature and the fresh air and exercise brought a sense of peace, but today, every step was a fierce battle against those gloomy, familiar thoughts that threatened to take her down into the depths of despair. As soon as the steeple of the Gospel Church emerged from the border of thick pines and live oaks, her mood lifted and a surge of hope rushed back through her. "Reverend? Reverend Thomas?" she called, running all the way to the front door.

The church was dark and empty, but Cadie shuffled inside anyway and knelt in front of the wooden cross on the hard floor. "Oh, Lord," she moaned. "I need you, I do!" She bowed her head in prayer, but despite the warmth from a ray of sun streaming in through the windows, there was a chill around her, like she was talking to a piece of wood instead of an almighty God. An image darted through her mind of Boy standing in the road wearing a waistcoat and hat and leaning on a cane, and with it came a fresh dose of fear. "Lord, don't leave me. Don't leave me now," she sobbed. "I need to know—I need to know what to do." She closed her eyes tightly and saw the look on Boy's face, just as clear as day. He wanted her back. She knew it like she knew her own name. It was there in his eyes—he still loved her. "Lord!" Cadie cried, no longer able to hold her emotions inside. She fell flat on her face with her arms outstretched, just like she'd seen the reverend do that night in the woods. All she could do was repeat, "Lord, Lord, Lord" over and over again as the tears streamed down her cheeks while she cried out for Him in some unknown language. She dozed off and dreamt of the prince sitting on the rock high above the riverbank, whispering to her, *"Come, come . . ."*

A bird called in the distance, startling her back to reality. After a few more minutes, Cadie rose to her knees and wiped her face, feeling cleansed and clearheaded, yet not having the slightest idea what to do. She made her way outside, still deep in thought, when a familiar laugh drew her attention to the blackened oak. There stood the reverend gazing into the sky as he shielded his eyes with his palm. She joined him and looked up at the top of the burnt tree, toward the upper limb where the fragments of the tattered rope dangled like Spanish moss. "Looka there," he said, pointing at something. Cadie squinted into the sun and saw what he was referring to—a sprig of green protruding from the charred limb. "After all this time," he said, giving a slight chuckle. "I always knew the Lord would bring it new life." He smiled at her, focusing on the red welt on her cheek. He placed his palm over the mark and gently caressed it with his thumb.

"You been out here the whole time, Reverend?"

"I have." He removed his hand and looked back at the green sprig as it fluttered in the breeze. "Waitin' on you to finish talkin' to the Lord."

"Well, I need your help with somethin'. I need some answers."

He spoke in his usual deep, baritone voice as he stared at the little sprig like it was a newborn babe. "They that wait upon the Lord shall renew their strength. They shall mount up with wings as eagles. They shall run and not be weary, and they shall walk and not faint."

The fire returned to his eyes, making her nervous, as usual. "You sayin' I gotta wait on the Lord?" she asked.

"I'm not sayin' anything. Just quotin' the Word."

"Reverend, don't you ever speak plain to anyone? Does everything have to be in stories or Bible verses?"

"Miz McLain, I'll tell you somethin'. There's a buncha devil talk that goes on in this world every single day, and none of it makes one bit of sense. But when a man switches over and starts talkin' the way the Lord talks, things start to clear up real quick. And if he keeps at it and don't quit, he'll find everything becomes 'bout as plain as day."

"That's easy for you, bein' a reverend."

"Nope, God don't know me as a reverend. He knows me as his child, same as you, 'cause you trust in Jesus, same as me. I've been trustin' a little longer, that's all."

"I guess He's sayin' I gotta wait on Him, huh?"

"May be. Sure sounds like somethin' He'd say." He flashed another wide smile and winked at her.

Cadie gazed at the sprig growing from the blackened tree limb, letting a sense of peace fall on her like a soft, spring rain. The wind rushed through the leaves of the surrounding live oaks and sang a rustling tune, telling her it was time to go home. "Bye, Reverend." She rose up on her tiptoes and kissed him on the cheek. "I do thank you."

"Anytime, Miz McLain," he said. "Anytime."

Cadie wrapped her shawl around her shoulders and waved to him once more as she prepared to make the long trudge home. And with every step, she could still hear his bold, rich voice ringing in her ears.

Chapter 33

Boy rode Holiday at a pace that rivaled the speed of the howling wind. Under normal circumstances, his leg would have been writhing in pain, but today he felt nothing other than a consuming rage. He hated his uncle for what he had done and was angry at Mattie for trying to prevent him from seeing Cadie. She had been right there beside him after Boy stormed out of the plantation house, hot on his trail and clucking all sorts of advice like a mother hen. "Come on back inside, Mr. Robert, and eat some supper 'fore you waste away."

"I ain't hungry."

"Don't be talkin' that white trash slang. You speak proper, like you learned it."

"I'm not hungry, Mattie."

"It's not right for a grown man like you not to eat. Never seen you lookin' so skinny. Come on, now, Mr. Robert. You can deal with Mr. Stephens and them letters later. You come on, now, and eat some of my braised pork chops and sweetfruit salad. I know you like it. And I got hot biscuits, too, tall and flaky, just the way you like 'em. And some of that chocolate pecan pie for dessert."

"I ain't hungry!"

Boy winced at the memory of Mattie's eyes enlarging like two dark saucers. "Looord have mercy! I don't believe you just said that to me. I've a good mind to give you a whippin', you know that?" She had wagged her finger in the air as she followed him inside the barn. "Lord knows you're not too old for it, neither. Why, my daddy used to whoop my brothers good when they was bad, all the way up to the day 'fore they was married. You listenin' to me?"

"No, I'm goin' for a ride."

"Where you ridin' to? Not over to Miss Cadie's? You know you don't belong over there. She belongs to the Lord now, and she's doin' right by her husband, and you don't need to go messin' it up."

"You stay out of this, Mattie."

"I won't. That child's like a daughter to me, like a sister to Zena now. You done broke her heart once, don't you go doin' it again."

"I didn't break her heart. It was him. He did it—"

"That don't matter now. Your uncle's as mean as they come, you've always known it, and I'm sorry for what he's done to you, but she's not yours now. She belongs to Mr. Norman."

The truth of these words had pierced Boy's heart, yet he refused to believe it. Instead of lashing out at Mattie, he had held his tongue, walked Holiday out of the barn, and hoisted himself into the saddle. "Boy, don't do nothin' you gonna regret. God's given you a second chance at life with that leg of yours. Don't go throwin' it away on somethin' that's never gonna be."

"I love you Mattie, you know that," he had said, his voice clear and deliberate. "But I ain't your Boy, and you ain't my mama." Then with a swift kick to Holiday's ribs, he had disappeared into the woods.

The image of Mattie's hurt expression loomed in Boy's mind, taunting him with guilt and condemnation. He rode Holiday that much harder and faster to the McLain house, hoping to free himself from these terrible thoughts, and sure enough, as soon as the top of the roof came into view, the guilt dissipated like spit on a hot summer's day. He slowed to a trot and quickly dismounted, putting all of the pressure on his good leg before tethering the horse to a tall, spindly pine. He then crept through the foliage, listening for any movement in the yard. All was quiet, except for the chirping of the birds and the gentle flap of a bed sheet hanging on the clothesline.

Boy buttoned his waistcoat and adjusted his fedora as he walked with a steady and defined limp toward the door. His heart sank at the size of the house, but upon closer inspection, he couldn't help but notice how attractive and well-maintained it was. Everything looked fresh and new and was complimented by a front flower garden of snapdragons, vinca, and marigolds in full bloom. In the back yard, a vegetable garden grew alongside a little woodshed and outhouse. He took a deep breath, limped up the porch steps, and opened the screen door.

"You lookin' for me?" Cadie stared at him from the yard with her shawl wrapped around her shoulders. Her golden hair had fallen loose from its coif and hung in small ringlets around her neck, and her cheeks had a rosy glow from being out in the sun. He stared back, and her blue eyes seemed to pierce his. Immediately, something flamed up from deep inside of him, igniting his whole being. She was just as breathtaking as he remembered.

Boy limped off the porch, never taking his eyes off hers. "Cadie—" He drew near and then halted, noticing the welt on her cheek. "Did he do that?"

"No. I just got in a little tussle with Mrs. Williamson—you remember her. It's a long story, but it's all fine now . . ." His ears didn't hear another word, other than his mind demanding him to take what was his, to claim it, and do it now before the moment passed. He pulled her toward him, anticipating the reality of everything that had been a mere dream for the past two years, but she nudged free, sending his heart back down into the pit of his stomach.

"I'm fixin' to brew up some coffee. You wanna cup?" She clomped up the porch steps, pulled the screen door open, and disappeared inside the house.

Boy hesitated a moment before following her inside. He watched her light the stove and fill the coffee pot with water. "You can have a seat," she said, motioning toward the kitchen table. He removed his hat and sat down as she set a porcelain cup and saucer in front of him along with a silver-plated spoon. "You still take sugar?"

He cleared his throat and said, "No, I drink it black now."

She took the spoon away and lifted the lid off the cookie jar, placing four ginger snaps on a plate in front of him. "Made 'em fresh yesterday. They're Zena's recipe, so I know you'll like 'em."

"I'm sure they're real good."

Cadie pulled a chair out from the opposite end of the table which created an irritating noise as it scraped against the wooden floor. Neither of them said a word while the coffee pot began to heat. "This's a nice house," Boy said, casting a glance around the room.

He smiled, but an awkward silence had descended on them, condemning this statement as the obvious lie that it was. Cadie stared at him without reaction, making the quiet even more uncomfortable. "You gonna tell me what happened to your leg?"

Boy cleared his throat again and fiddled with the brim of his hat. "Had a little accident on a train."

"What kind of accident?"

"Well, I decided I needed to get home before that Christmas, like we planned. I wanted to see you somethin' bad, but I didn't have the money for the fare, so—I thought I'd jump the train."

"You jumped the train?"

"Yeah, done it all my life, 'cept this time it was goin' a little faster than I thought." He grinned, hoping to soften the seriousness of the moment. "Broke my leg in three places."

She nodded without reaction. "I thought your uncle paid for your schoolin' and travelin' and all."

"You know how I liked to gamble. But that's all in the past. I'm a new man now. May not look like it, but after bein' laid up in the hospital for almost a year—well—I had a lot of time to think about things. About my life. About us."

The coffee pot let out a whistle, prompting Cadie to rise and turn down the stove. She wiped her hands on a dishrag and hung her head. "Robert—"

"No, let me speak." He rose from his chair and stood behind her, using every ounce of strength not to reach out and touch the place on her neck where a row of miniature curls lined the edge of her hairline. "I know what you're gonna say, and you're wrong." His mouth hovered near her ear where her distinctive scent of lilac and sweat ignited his senses, making his whole body ache. "I wrote you almost every day I was in that hospital, I did—even when I heard about you and Norman. But my uncle, he stopped the letters from getting to you somehow, and I never got another one of yours till today—from Molly." He pulled the letter out of his pocket and handed it to her. "See? It was never postmarked." Cadie took the letter and looked at the front of the envelope. "He told me you couldn't wait—that you didn't wanna wait. That you loved Norman, after all. And that you didn't wanna be with a cripple."

"I never woulda said that."

"I know. He's a liar, he always has been. I've known that all my life. I just never thought he'd go this far."

Cadie fingered the crumpled letter, caressing the name *Robert Morgan* etched in her own hand. "I'm a married woman now. I'm Norman's wife, been that for well over a year now." Her eyes welled up as she whispered, "We've had a baby together."

"A little girl, I heard. I'm so sorry, Cadie." He grabbed her hand and pressed his thumb against the back of her palm where it bumped up against Norman's ring. She pulled it away and twirled the diamond to the backside of her finger. "You don't belong with him," he said. "You belong with me."

"You never came back."

"I wanted to. You'll never know how much I wanted to get up out of that hospital bed and come back to you." Boy pulled her into his arms as his eyes searched the depth of hers, hoping to latch on to something that would give him an indication of her heart. "Cadie—"

"It's too late." She pushed him away and sunk into the kitchen chair.

"No, Cadie." Boy fell to his knee, despite the pain in his leg. "I'll sell the plantation like I agreed. It was our arrangement for him payin' for the doctors and for fixin' up my leg. I'll take the money and start a business, make my own fortune. Then I'll come back and buy it back from him and make things right."

She shook her head and sobbed, "You and your dreams."

"It was our dream, remember? Yours and mine." He caressed her cheek and wiped a stream of tears away. "I know you still love me," he said. "I know you do."

"You don't know anything about me!" she cried, wrenching free, but then she was in his arms again, surrendering to his embrace. "No," she said, as his lips grazed her cheek. "No, Robert." She rose to her feet and moved toward the door, opening it wide.

Boy expected her to fall into his arms once more, but she stood firm with her hand on the door knob. "Tell me you don't love me, and I'll leave," Boy said. "Look me in the eye and tell me."

Cadie waited a moment and then lifted her eyes to meet his. They stared at each other for the longest time, peering into each other's souls. "This is my home now," she said with a cold look in her expression. "This is my place. I'm Mrs. Norman McLain, and that's the way it's gonna stay." She stepped back and grabbed the door handle even tighter. "Now, please leave before my husband gets home."

Time ticked away as Boy waited for her wavering gaze to buckle. "Say what you like, Cadie, but you and me both know the truth." He adjusted his waistcoat and grabbed his hat off the table. "I won't let you go. I mean it." Then brushing past her, he limped out the door, trying his best not to look back. After all these years, he still knew every detail about her hair, her skin, her small waist, and the delicate bones in her hands—but mostly the blue eyes and what he saw beneath the surface. He wouldn't give up, he couldn't. They had been cheated, robbed of what was theirs, and nothing or no one would stop him from taking it back. Especially Norman McLain.

Chapter 34

Despite the brightness of a full moon, a gloom hung in the air, reminding Cadie of a heavy, wool blanket caught in the tree limbs and nestled among the leaves. A light went on in the kitchen as Norman made his way through the house, clomping his boots against the wooden floor. Cadie ignored the sound and stared out the bedroom window, not caring that the torn bits of Boy's letters were scattered across the bed-covers. "Sorry I'm late," Norman said. "We had a delivery come in, some fabrics and the like. I brought home an old bolt of pink silk. Thought you could use it somehow."

"Thank you, Norman."

He leaned against the door frame and crossed his arms over his chest, reminding her of a chiseled statue. "Why're you layin' here in the dark?"

"I don't feel too good."

He cleared his throat and spoke in a hushed tone. "Was he here today?"

There was no use playing ignorant now, since they both knew who the *he* was. "Yes," she answered.

"What'd he want?"

"Just came by to say hello."

"Cadie, don't lie to me."

"Whadda you want me to say?" She grabbed the end of her quilt and tucked it under her chin. "I told him I was married, and that's that."

"You love him?" The tremor in his voice frightened her for some reason.

"I don't know."

Norman pushed Boy's letters aside and sat down on the end of the bed, making the bed frame creak in a ghostly whisper. The quiet between them was excruciating. "I love you Cadie, even though you don't love me."

"I never said I didn't love you, Norman."

"Well, you wouldn't be layin' here with all his letters 'round you if you did."

Cadie flinched, recalling the words "sweetness of your breath" staring back at her after she had ripped the letters to pieces and thrown them at the wooden cross over the fireplace mantle. "Is this what you want?" she had screamed, crying in wild hysterics. She shuddered at the memory and silently prayed God would forgive her for being so weak willed. "At least I tore 'em," she mumbled, more to the Lord than to Norman. "Don't that count for somethin'?"

He shrugged his shoulders and hung his head as another painful silence filled the room. "I've said it before—I've always known how I felt about you, even though I didn't realize it. Fact is, I love you more now than I ever did. And I love you enough to let you go."

"Let me go?"

He reached over and placed something on the bedside table. Cadie sat up, amazed at seeing her red coffee canister sitting there. "I've been savin' awhile and think it's 'bout time I gave you back what's rightfully yours." He nodded toward the canister. "Well, go on and open it."

Cadie removed the lid, turned it upside down, and pulled out a thick wad of cash. "Norman McLain!" she gasped, handling the bills with care. It was more than she had ever laid eyes on in her whole life. It looked like he had scooped up all the dollars from the mercantile cash drawer and crammed them inside!

"I want you to have your dream, Cadie. You take that money and go live the life you've always wanted. I don't wanna do nothin' to hold you back."

"Norman, no," she said. "No, I can't—"

"I won't hold you to our marriage no longer. I broke my vows more times than I care to remember, and you were willin' to forgive me. But we both know it wasn't real from the beginning. It never has been. I know you tried, we both did, but it just wasn't meant to be."

"What are you sayin'?"

"Divorce is what they call it. I know it's shameful, a sin even, but we'll both be happier. Truth is, I've got my pride, Cadie. I won't stay married to a woman who holds a candle for another man, especially if he's gonna strut around town, flauntin' his money and big white house across the river. If I'm gonna live in humiliation, I'd rather do it my way. I know business may suffer, I'll probably lose a customer or two, but in time, people'll forget. They always do."

"But Norman, I don't wanna divorce."

"You want him, don't you?"

Cadie stared into his eyes, not sure of how to answer. "I don't know what I want."

"You never have, that's the problem. You never wanted anything real, anything I could give you, that's for sure. You were always chasin' after somethin' else. Maybe he can give it to you. Maybe he can make you happy." Norman stood up and shoved his hands into his pockets as he leaned against the doorframe again. Cadie couldn't help but notice the muscles in his forearms and the length of his legs. "Truth is, I never thought he'd come back," he said, before turning and disappearing into the kitchen.

"Where're you goin?"

"I've said enough for one night," he answered back. "We can talk more in the mornin'."

Cadie stared at the money in the canister, trying to digest all he had told her. The truck motor cranked up, sending a wave of panic through her. "Norman?" She threw the bed-covers to the floor and ran into the kitchen, seeing the headlights disappear down the dirt drive. "Norman, you said you'd wait." She scurried down the porch steps and yelled, "You said you'd be here for me!" But her voice blended in with the roar of the truck and lifted into the wind like a duck feather floating in the breeze. *Lord, you've just gotta help me. You've gotta show me what to do.*

Within a few seconds, Cadie had her answer. She marched into the kitchen, hid the money and the canister inside the iron pot on the top shelf, and then went back to the bedroom and scooped up all the pieces of Boy's letters. Without hesitation, she dumped them into the opening in the kitchen stove where the fire still smoldered, slid another log in, and stoked the flame until it whooshed up into a blaze. An unspeakable peace surrounded her as she watched the torn papers burn brightly before crumpling into a mass of blackened ash. Something caught her eye, a word written in Boy's hand that read "home," before it disappeared into the red flame.

She went back to bed and snuggled under the covers, waiting up as long as she could for Norman to return. *I'll talk to him tomorrow*, she thought as she drifted off to sleep to the sounds of the crickets outside. *Tomorrow, I'll make him see.*

It was early morning when Cadie awoke to a boom of thunder rumbling in the distance, and with it, the sound of Norman's truck descending down the dirt drive. She had meant to ask him if she could use it to run into town to do a bit of shopping, but it didn't matter anyway, since they hadn't spoken to each other in over a week. In fact, there was no indication Norman wanted to speak to her again about anything, even the topic of divorce.

Cadie kicked the blankets to the floor and stared at the ceiling, planning her day. Food was a necessity, since there was barely enough in the pantry to get through breakfast, and her stomach was already howling with hunger. She had put off the marketing as long as possible, hoping to avoid running into Boy in town, or worse, enduring the looks and sneers from the Molly Wallaceses of the world and the fat Mrs. Williamsons who were certainly wagging their tongues with idle gossip. If she was to have any supper cooked for tonight, she had no choice but to brave her way to the mercantile and get what she needed.

After saying a quick prayer, she shuffled out of bed and fixed a cup of cream-laced coffee with the last grape jelly biscuit. She then slipped into a skirt she had sewn from the pink silk Norman brought home last week and paired it with a white, drop-waist blouse and gray linen jacket. For the finishing touch, she pinned her hair into a loose coif that resembled a bob and topped it off with a straw cloche hat trimmed with a matching pink sash. Tilting her head toward the dresser mirror, Cadie practiced how she might address her critics, should she run into any in town. They would consider her pretty, of course, and stylish, maybe not as fashionable as they, but attractive all the same. *But there's still somethin' missin'*, she thought, as her fingers touched the hollow in her throat where a strand of pearls might rest. She considered the money stashed away in the red canister in the kitchen, but that would not be spent on jewelry. Some of it would be used to pay for two leather-covered Bibles with gold-edged pages on order from the local bookshop, one for her and one for Zena, but other than that, the remainder of it would sit safely tucked away.

As Cadie stepped onto the porch, another rumble of thunder coursed through the clouds. The sky looked dark and gray, with no promise of clearing. Oh, she could just kick herself for leaving her umbrella in Norman's truck! She grabbed an old burlap potato sack from behind the kitchen door and tucked it under her arm just in case she needed something to protect her from the rain. Then taking a deep breath, she hurried down the dirt path and maintained a brisk walk on the road toward town.

By the time she made her way to the creek, the first drop of rain hit her on the shoulder, bringing back painful memories of a rainy day long ago. She swatted the image of Zoe in her little pink dress out of her mind and picked up her pace from a scurry to an outright run. The burlap sack covered her hat as splats of water ricocheted off her body, until suddenly, the bottom of the sky fell open. Cadie ran as fast as she could toward the trees, cringing at the rumbling of thunder and flash of lightning in the distance. By now, the rain was coming down in a deafening roar, drenching her from head to toe with its blinding sheets.

A bolt of lightning flashed across the sky, and the thunder erupted into a long, angry growl that echoed against the screams of a frightened animal. Cadie spun around and squinted into the woods. There, through the mist, a rider on a black horse raced toward her, moving through the forest at a fast canter. She backed up against a large live oak, and as the horse came closer, it reared on its hind legs, terrified by the storm. "Get on!" Boy yelled, extending his hand while water dripped off the end of his hat brim.

"No! I'm gonna wait here till it passes."

"It'll be hours, and besides, it isn't safe." The sky lit up as lightning flashed, causing Holiday to neigh and stomp its feet wildly. "Come on!" Boy screamed. Thunder shook the earth and the sky lit up once more, as a bolt of fire crackled in the distance. Without thinking, Cadie grabbed his hand and jumped on the back of Holiday. "Hold on!" he said.

She wrapped her arms around Boy's waist and clung to him for dear life as he nudged the horse forward in a steady gallop. They stopped some distance away, near the rope swing that dangled from the tree limbs like a noose waiting for its victim. "Quick, under there!" he said, pointing to the wooden lean-to. Cadie slid off the horse and scurried under the shelter where she huddled close to the ground with her skirt tucked around her legs, trying not to think about the predicament she was in. Her stomach gathered into a knot as she watched Boy's feet move around in the rain while he tethered the gelding to the tree trunk. He then scooted up under the lean-to next to her and shook the rain from his hat. "I'd say you picked a fine day to walk into town."

"And I'd say you picked a fine day to go ridin' through the woods," she said, sounding curt.

"Good thing, too, or you'd be soaked to the bone by now."

Cadie refused to say another word. Her elbow rubbed against his in the cramped quarters, sending a tingle down her spine, but she promptly pulled away. They sat still and quiet, listening to the rain beat upon the top of the shelter. "You thought about what I said?"

"Don't talk to me," she shushed, refusing to meet his gaze.

"Cadie—"

"Shh. I asked you not to talk."

"I have to talk to you."

"Then don't call me Cadie. I'm Mrs. McLain to you. Mrs. Norman McLain."

"I ain't ever gonna call you that."

"Suit yourself."

Boy smacked his wet hat against his hand and shook more water off the brim. "You're just as stubborn as you've always been."

"Me, stubborn?" Cadie chuckled, holding her stare on a crack in the wood and the blur of rain on the other side.

"Why're you so mad at me?" Boy asked.

"I ain't mad."

"You are, too."

"Well, don't I have a right to be?" She looked at him briefly and then snapped her eyes back to the crack in the wood.

He brushed the tip of his finger against the back of her neck and gently fondled a lock of wet hair that had fallen loose. "We both have a right to be mad at what he's done."

Shivers ran up and down her spine, but she wouldn't let them take control. "Don't touch me." Cadie shrugged away and hugged her knees to her chest. "I am mad at your uncle, but I'm more mad at you." She tore her eyes away from the crack and glared at him. "You were the one who gambled your money away. That was somethin' you did—not him. And then you go and do a stupid thing like hop a train like some hobo."

"You're right. I should've known better. I didn't see it then." He stroked the inside of her palm, and this time she didn't pull away. "I acted like a boy—not a man."

Time seemed to creep along as tears pricked her eyes while he gently caressed her hand. "I forgive you," she said, her voice trembling. "I'm a Christian now and gave my life to Jesus. Don't know if that woulda happened if you'd come back. So I guess some good did come of it, even if it doesn't feel like it."

"No good came of it, if you ask me." He brought her hand to his mouth and kissed it, just like she'd seen Dashing do a hundred times at all those Magnolia Hill garden parties. Instead of responding with a velvety laugh like the Darlene Bradshaws of the world, the tenderness of the gesture brought forth a sob that had been caught deep inside of her for days now. "I couldn't understand why you stopped writin'—" Cadie hung her head, trying to catch her breath. "I was just so sick with grief—I didn't know what to do. I guess I needed somebody," she sobbed. "And he was there."

"But I'm here now." Boy pulled her toward him and kissed her until her hat fell to her shoulders. "And I'm never gonna leave you, you hear? I'm gonna show you what kind of man I've become."

Cadie sunk into his arms like she had dreamed a thousand times before, with his hands on her face and neck as his mouth smothered hers, devouring her while whispering words of longing in her ear. It all sounded right and true—he loved her and she loved him, didn't she? She was bone of his bone and flesh of his flesh, and they were meant to be together, weren't they? Surely, God had brought him back to her after all this time. Surely, He wanted them to live out their future, to have a home and children . . .

Cadie listened as this discourse continued in her mind while her body gave way to the passion which swept the two of them into a wild frenzy. And yet, there was a still, small voice deep inside her consciousness whispering a word that echoed through the chambers of her heart, *No, no, no! No, this isn't right! Stop this! Stop!*

Cadie tried to fight what was happening like she had that day in her kitchen, but she was overpowered by the handsome, winsome gentleman in his brocade waistcoat and fedora filled with promises of a different life. They were caught up together, like sea creatures in a fisherman's net, squirming for freedom, yet struggling against the inevitable. Before long, she let Boy guide her to the wet, mucky ground, without caring what happened to her linen jacket and new pink skirt.

Images passed before her of her family, of Mattie and Zena smiling her beautiful smile, and the reverend with his fiery gaze—and then there was little Zoe with her soft skin and blonde curls—and lastly, the lopsided grin of her husband. A pang of anguish shot through her as she recalled the muscles in Norman's back gleaming in the sun the day he had fixed the fence, the lock of unruly hair over his brow as he had gazed at her after breaking her fall from the slippery floor, and then the power of his demeanor when he had confronted Mrs. Williamson and all those mean white ladies in the mercantile. Cadie closed her eyes and sunk further into Boy's kisses as they became Norman's. The strong arms pulling her close were now Norman's, the hair flowing through her fingers was Norman's, the distinctive taste of the lips she kissed and the freshness of shaving soap on the base of the neck and throat, all were Norman's. A wave of peace washed over her, releasing a surge of joy that made her giggle with delight. Instinctively, her lips found their way to Boy's ear, and she whispered, "I love you, Norman—"

A moment passed before she realized what she had said. "You don't mean that," Boy said coldly. She couldn't reply. Her mind was frozen and her tongue affixed to the roof of her mouth as if it had been sealed there with a wad of dry paste. "It's me you love. Not him."

"Robert, you'll always have a piece of my heart—"

"No," he said, his eyes filled with hurt. He pulled her close and pressed his body into hers. "Tell me you love me—like you said it to him."

"I've never told him I loved him," she said. "I never knew I loved him, not really—until now." After a long hesitation, she untangled herself from his arms and allowed her thoughts to settle for a moment. "No one can take away what we had, Robert. No one. But I'm not the same girl you fell in love with that summer. I'm a new person now, I'm different. Go make your fortune and come back to that house like you planned. And ask the Lord to heal your heart like he did mine. He'll do it if you ask. And then you'll be able to love again."

"I don't wanna love again."

"But you will."

Cadie placed her hat back on her head and stepped out into the rain. "Don't go, Cadie," Boy said, following behind.

"I have to." His arms enveloped her, preventing her escape while his eyes bore through the torment, as though he was burning her image into his consciousness. Cadie sealed the moment with a kiss on the mouth—a soft, gentle kiss mixed with the all the moisture from heaven pouring down on them. And then finally, Boy released his hold and let her go.

Chapter 35

Molly dropped her umbrella onto the mercantile porch and slithered into the store without being noticed. The place was empty because of the rumors spreading like wildfire that this could be a heavy storm. All of Pleasant Oaks were taking precautions, including Johnson's Jewelers and the Corner Pharmacy, who were boarding up their windows with storm shutters. Even her mother had started closing up Magnolia Hill, insisting that everyone come indoors and be ready to descend into the cellar at a moment's notice. Molly was staying with her parents while Lloyd was out of town on a supposed "business trip" and had managed to sneak away for a quick trip into town.

At the sound of Mr. McLain's voice, she scurried into the little corner storeroom and pulled the heavy curtain across the doorway. The smell of leather boots and dungaree overalls stacked on the shelves behind her brought back vivid memories of the day Norman had held her in his arms, growling his jealous passion in her ear. She closed her eyes and remembered every detail about it, word for word and breath by breath, savoring it like the culinary seasonings of a gourmet dish.

In the distance, there was a shout about "headin' home" and Norman's reply that he would be "closin' up soon," all of which made Molly snicker. She waited for the front door to slam and his father's motorcar to start before revealing herself. The full-length mirror propped up by the men's haberdashery section caught her reflection, making her pause. She did look as lovely as ever in her new, lemon yellow drop-waist dress made of soft muslin cotton with embroidered florets across the bodice, and of course, her matching felt cloche hat and tan leather pumps. On some girls, the yellow may have looked too pale, but on Molly it was luminous, giving her skin a peachy, golden glow and offsetting her hazel eyes so that they looked shiny and full of life. She surveyed herself one more time, touching the back of her curled bob that protruded just below the lip of her hat. Thankfully, the umbrella had kept most of her dry, except for a bit of moisture around the hem of her dress and a few mud stains on her shoes. Regardless of the imperfections, she knew she was irresistible.

She tiptoed through the store and hid behind the shelves of canned foods, lingering there for some time while she watched Norman stock boxes of fishing tackle and gardening tools on the back storeroom shelves. Sweat dripped off his brow and glistened on his chest where his opened shirt revealed the hardened muscles straining with each movement. Molly smiled to herself, letting her fingers drift to her neck where the double strand of creamy pearls nestled in the hollow of her throat. A wave of desire flashed over her like a ray of noonday sun passing through a dark cloud. She wanted him like she'd never wanted anything else, and he wanted her, too, he was just too prideful and stubborn to admit it. But she would change that.

With a quick jut of her chin and slight lowering of her head, she emerged from her hiding place. "Hey, Norman," she purred.

He continued his work, refusing to take notice. "Mrs. Wallace, we're closin' up 'cause of the storm. You best be gettin' home."

"I don't wanna go home. And stop calling me Mrs. Wallace." Molly sashayed into the back storeroom and leaned up against the wooden desk, trying her best to hold her head in such a way as to accentuate her shadowed eyes and full red lips. He ignored her, so she breathed in deeply and arched her back to reveal the embroidered flowers on her dress bodice. But still, there was no response. "Put those boxes down and talk to me."

"I need to finish this up, and then both of us need to get on home." He picked up a heavy box and slid it onto a wooden shelf. "This storm's movin' in fast."

"I don't wanna go home." She came up behind him and placed her hands on his shoulders. "This is the safest place I can think of right now."

"Mrs. Wallace," he said, gently pushing her away, "I'm sure your husband is wondering where you are."

"Oh, him," she said in a short, clipped tone as if having a husband were a minor nuisance. "He doesn't even know when I'm gone half the time. And anyway, I've never really cared for him." She waited for Norman to plop another box on the shelf and then stepped in front of him, smiling like a Cheshire cat. "Norman," she said with a slight tilt to her head and the bat of her eyes, "you know you're the only one for me." He stared down at her with that angry, frustrated look she knew all too well as a mask for hidden desire. "You ever think of me?" There was no reply as he continued to stare. "You remember all our times together?" She touched his glistening chest and wiped the sweat away with her fingers. "In the apple orchard, under the porch steps? Why, right in that little storeroom over there?" Her hand went to his face. "Don't you remember this?" She rose up on her tiptoes and strained forward for a kiss.

"Stop it," he said before her lips touched his.

"Norman, I can see it in your eyes. You still love me. You want me, don't you?"

"No—"

"You're lying, I can tell. I can always tell when you're not telling the truth." She brought her mouth close to his and whispered, "I'm yours now,

Norman. All yours."

"Stop it, I said." He grabbed her by the shoulders and shoved her hard. "Don't you hear me? I don't love you and I never have."

A twinge of hurt hit her in the gut, like she had received a stinging slap on the wrist. "What is it you want? Money? I can give you whatever, however much you want—"

"Don't cheapen yourself any more than you already have." He scooted the remaining boxes out of the way, snatched his raincoat off the coat rack, and made his way toward the front door. "I'm a married man—a happily married man."

"You sure your wife believes that?" As soon as the word "wife" left her lips, she cringed, wishing she could take it back.

"I'll say it one more time," he said, slowly and deliberately, "you better go on."

Molly searched his hard expression to see whether she had misread his intentions. "Maybe you better go on home yourself, Mr. McLain," she said, feeling a silky venom ooze from her pores. "Maybe you better check up on that little missus of yours and see what kinda trouble she may have gotten herself into. From what I hear, she may not be so fond of cooking your food and doing your laundry. Could be she's got her mind on something or someone else." She cozied up to Norman and rendered her most seductive look while the tips of her fingers found their way back to the solid muscles in his chest. "Maybe that's why she has you sleeping on the sofa every night, not providing for all your other needs like a good wife should."

"Don't you say a word about things you don't know nothin' about, you hear? Don't you say one word—"

Suddenly, the wind and rain broke through the front door as Cadie came bounding in the store, looking like a drowned rat. "Norman?" she said, her eyes flashing with excitement. On instinct, Molly pulled herself into Norman's arms and snuggled up close like she had done countless times before. She couldn't help but smile at seeing Cadie stop dead in her tracks and pull her eyes away as if she had been burned with a scalding iron.

"Cadie—" Norman pushed Molly aside, but Cadie wouldn't look at him. She paused for a moment and then bolted back out into the rain. Norman disappeared behind her, banging the door shut so that another gust of wind rattled the windows like the haunting of a tormented ghost.

Molly waited for a moment, thinking he would return, but the continual howling of the storm outside and the eerie creak of wind seeping through empty store said otherwise. For the first time that day, she felt the prickling sensation of alarm at the dramatic change in this weather.

Cadie jumped into Norman's truck and shut the door, trying to forget the image of Molly wrapped up in his arms with that haughty, condescending look she was so famous for. After all this time, he had lied about her—he did love Molly Stephens Wallace. In the end, he wasn't able to resist the money and fine clothes and pearls around the neck.

As soon as Cadie saw Norman running out of the store, she turned the key in the ignition and threw the truck in reverse. He was yelling something, but with the wind and rain, she couldn't hear a thing. She slammed her foot on the accelerator, backed up a few paces, and put the truck into drive before speeding away through the blinding rain. Her heart was numb with shock, but her mind reeled so fast, she couldn't even think. *How could he have had his arms around Molly? How could he?* Cadie's lip quivered uncontrollably until her entire mouth contorted in anguish. She wouldn't let Norman McLain make her cry, she wouldn't!

The wind howled through the trees, bending the trunks of the long leaf pines so that they swayed and danced with each moan of the storm. Cadie held the steering wheel as she fought to keep the truck from being pulled back and forth across the road. She didn't know where she was going, but she knew she had to keep driving. Before long, she turned onto a familiar dirt road and began a slow, bumpy journey toward the direction of Jackson's Creek. The live oaks reached toward her like long, jagged arms of an old woman whose muscles had pulled away from the bone, their ends like gnarled, broken fingers. The writhing of the wind through the trees surrounded Cadie and terrified her. It was as though she was going toward some dark and terrible place where a horrific, demonic creature was waiting to devour her. A vision of Zena's burnt Bible flashed before her, along with the reverend's words, *love never fails, love never fails, love never fails.* Cadie opened her mouth to pray, but only a sob came forth.

The truck came to a stop at the end of the muddy road where the creek flowed on the other side. Through each swipe of the windshield wipers, Cadie saw the faint outline of Old Hargett's Bridge. She hopped out of the truck into a puddle of mud, oblivious to the rain. Her clothes were beyond repair now, and the hat was long gone, having dropped onto the wet ground sometime before. As for her hair, there was no longer the slightest resemblance to a bob—only a wet, limp, stringy mess.

She fought her way to the bridge and gripped the railing, feeling the sway of the rotted pilings beneath her. The storm moaned as she maneuvered to the center and sat down with her legs straddling a guardrail so that her feet dangled above the rising water. The wind rushed down her throat, making her swallow unnaturally as it echoed her name in a slow, sad song, "Cadie, Ca-die . . ."

"I'm here, Lord! I'm here," she sobbed, not caring how foolish she looked sitting in the middle of the rain, crying like a mad woman. "I'm so sorry. I've been so blind and selfish. I didn't know what I had. I was just lookin' at everything that got taken away, and the things I got back, well I don't want 'em anymore. I just want one thing now." She closed her eyes and rested her head on the guardrail as she wept. "Just one thing." The wind blew violently before dying away in a long exhalation. "I want you, Lord," she whispered. "Just you."

She stared into the dark water and imagined the prince in the reverend's story rising up from the depths to claim her with arms extended, calling her name. "Cadie! Ca-die!" a faint voice echoed in the distance. Suddenly, Norman was there, at the edge of the bridge, yelling, "Cadie! Come on off of there, you hear?" She remained immobile, keeping her eyes on the movement of the creek that had risen to about the height and depth of the Cape Fear. "You gonna make me come out there and get you?" The storm inhaled deeply, causing the trees to bend in its direction and the bridge to creak and sway. There was a nervous pitch to Norman's voice as he called, "Cadie, I mean it! It isn't safe. Now, come on!"

The bridge wobbled as he made his way toward her. "You know how crazy you are, out in this rain? Sitting on this old rickety bridge?"

"You callin' me crazy, Norman McLain?"

"Cadie, what you saw, it wasn't what you thought. I've told you before, I don't want nothin' to do with Molly Stephens."

"She's Molly Stephens Wallace now."

"I know that."

"A married woman."

"Cadie—" He sat down next to her and gathered her in his arms, speaking above the storm. "What do I have to do to make you see? You're the only girl I've ever really loved. I've told you that a million times. Don't you know it by now?"

"I thought I did, it's just—when I saw you with her, I wasn't sure anymore."

He tightened his embrace and kissed her drenched eyelids and the tip of her nose. "I'd give anything to pull you inside of me so you'd know how

I feel, so you'd know how my heart runs a mile every time I see you or hear your voice or smell your sweet scent. Knowin' you're in the next room, cookin' or sewin' somethin' or even sleepin' so sweetly, with the moon on your face."

"Norman—" The heat flushed through Cadie and seized her heart, filling it with a gnawing hunger.

"You don't know how many nights I've laid there on that old lumpy sofa, wantin' to come in there where you are, knowin' if you were to love me, it wouldn't really be with me. That you'd be runnin' off some place in your mind." His gaze swept across her wet forehead as if he was surveying her thoughts trapped inside. "Runnin' off with him."

"No, Norman, no. That's what I came to tell you. I don't wanna go runnin' off or go live in that big, ole house. I thought I did, but I was wrong. I don't wanna love him, Norman. I wanna stay right here. I wanna stay with you."

Despite the rage from the wind and rain, the world seemed quiet to Cadie while she stared into his eyes. Moisture dripped off his lashes, framing the reflection in the brown of the iris which had become a beacon of hope amidst all the tumult surrounding them. "You mean that, Cadie?" he asked. "Don't be sayin' that 'less you mean it."

The wind blew with a hard rush, accompanied by the crack and pop of lightning above their heads and an immediate boom of thunder. Cadie jerked her head back in time to see the top of a tall pine tree come hurtling toward them. Her expression froze before she screamed, "Norman!"

What happened next occurred in a matter of seconds, but to Cadie, it was as though time slowed to a snail's pace. The tree hit the end of the bridge, jostling the pilings so that the entire thing bobbed up and down like an old river buoy. "Hang on!" Norman called, as a loud crack signaled the railing was giving way.

The bridge made a final sway, accepted its fate after lasting all these long years, and then broke in half, sending Cadie and Norman plunging into the swirling water with broken boards and exposed nails splashing down with them.

Chapter 36

Holiday whinnied at the clap of thunder, but Boy heard it in his mind long before the pine crashed into Old Hargett's Bridge. The flash of lightning and the loud boom of the falling tree were neither a shock to him nor a surprise, but corroboration of the truth that had pierced his soul—the arms wrapped around Cadie should've been his arms and the words whispered in her ear should've been his words.

"Cadie!" he screamed, seeing her head bob in the current and her arms flail about. Boy kicked Holiday in the ribs and raced toward the water, driving the gelding over the stones and into the deep, calling her name again and again. When the horse would go no further, he slipped off its back and swam as fast as he could. A broken board from the bridge swept past him, and he grabbed it, careful to avoid a protruding nail. "Cadie, grab hold!"

"Robert!" she sputtered, splashing toward the board and holding firm. "Where's Norman? Norman? NorMAN!" Boy looked around frantically, but there was no sign of him. "It was my fault!" she wailed. "It was my fault."

"Get over to shore." He kicked as hard as he could and swam diagonally to the current until they reached shallow water.

"Oh, God, Robert!" she cried.

"I'll find him, I promise," he said, regretting the words as soon as they left his mouth. "Just wait here."

He swam back into the water, floating on a broken piling, and called for Norman several times. The continual roar of the swollen creek and the steady downpour of rain hitting the surface muffled his voice, but he kept calling as loud as he could. The current moved him downstream toward a slight turn in the creek where he spotted a broken board wedged between two rocks and a dark mass flung across its side. Boy peered closely, swimming with all his might, until he made out the form of a human hand. "Norman!" he yelled. The water darkened as he drew close, mixed with the flow of blood from a deep gash on the side of Norman's head. *Leave him be,* a voice said in Boy's mind. *He's gonna die.*

Norman gasped deep gulps of air, one after another, while kicking his legs and thrashing about. "I've got you," Boy said, grabbing his arm and dislodging him from the rocks. "Just stay still, now. I'm gonna get you to shore. Just relax, and I'll swim us over." Norman took another breath and then another and became strangely quiet, with eyes wide open, as he stared at the sky. "That's it. Just relax. You're gonna be all right."

Boy wrapped his right arm across Norman's chest and kicked against the current, slowly making his way to where Cadie waited. He was just to the middle of the creek when a thunderous sound from upstream grew in volume until it reached a deafening roar. Cadie screamed his name before a broken section of Old Hargett's Bridge come rushing toward them and hit Boy square on the back, throwing him down into the depths of the dark, muddy water. He twisted and tumbled about, as if he was being trampled by a stampede of wild ponies, until an excruciating pain pierced the top of his arm from a nail that plunged deep into his flesh. He opened his mouth to scream, but his lungs quickly filled with water, sending waves of panic rippling through him. Yanking the nail free, he kicked his legs and ascended to the light above.

Boy erupted from the depths of the mire, coughing the muddy water out of his lungs. He was now in the Cape Fear River, where Jackson's Creek flowed past a cluster of live oaks that bordered the plantation house. He waved his arms through the water, calling Norman's name over and over. Cadie ran along the riverbank, calling in her own frantic way, while maneuvering around logs, tree stumps, and clumps of marsh grass. Suddenly, she stopped and pointed at something down river. Boy splashed through the water and moved toward it, feeling his heart plummet at the sight of Norman floating face down in the river.

He grabbed Norman by the back of the hair and turned him over onto his back. His face bore a pallor that brought back terrible memories. Boy had tried to forget his father forcing him into his mother's bedroom where she lay a withered, emaciated corpse between two bed sheets—having wasted away into a shell of a human being—but that image had stayed with him over the years, haunting his consciousness and dreams without warning. For many months, he had been free of these thoughts, but now the memory was as fresh and raw as it was that day so long ago. Despite the wind and rain, Boy smelled the stench of death all around him.

"Norman!" Cadie called, rushing into the current to meet them. She whispered Norman's name and then grew quiet as Boy pulled him out of the water and onto the muddy ground. "Norman, Norman—" She cradled his head in her lap and sopped up the flow of blood with her hands as she rocked back and forth, repeating his name over and over.

"I'm sorry, Cadie. I tried." Boy crouched beside her, dripping wet, having forgotten about the blood oozing from his arm and the throbbing from his back and leg. He wanted more than anything to take her in his arms and comfort her, and yet, he knew this was the last thing in the world she wanted. He felt powerless, like an impotent man who stood by like a scared, little boy. And he hated it.

"No, Lord!" Cadie sobbed and then did something that frightened Boy to the very core—she threw her head back, looked skyward, and opened her mouth, letting the rain fill it like she was drinking in the torrents of heaven. "No!" she cried, shaking her head violently. "You can't have him. You can't have him! I won't let you! You give him back!" She sobbed some more and then looked deep into the forest that bordered the plantation and stared at something or someone, Boy couldn't be sure. "You!" she hissed with a force that chilled Boy's blood. "In Jesus' name, you!" She shoved her finger into the air before her. "You give him back!"

The word "back" echoed over the river and absorbed into the density of the trees, rustling a bird from its perch. Boy shifted his glance over to the woods where Cadie was staring, half expecting to see the outline of a figure, but there was nothing other than the flutter of wings over the treetops accompanied by the call of a bird. She took another breath and yelled out, "Give him back, and then you get on outta here, you hear me?!" She continued to stare hard and fast at this invisible something in the woods, not moving a muscle. "Those that wait upon the Lord shall renew their strength. They shall mount up with wings like eagles. They shall run and not get weary, they shall walk and not faint."

"Cadie?" Boy touched her shoulder, hoping to free her from this strange emotion that had claimed her, but she recoiled, staring into the forest. "Come on, Cadie. We need to go get help."

"No, I'm waitin'," she said calmly. "He heard me, and now he's gotta do it."

"Who're you talkin' about?"

"He knows."

"You talkin' about God?"

"No."

Boy looked to where her eyes were fixed and thought he saw a shifting, shadowy movement. It was nothing, of course, but the swaying of a tree limb in the storm—yet, he couldn't stop the terror from creeping into his throat. "You're scarin' me, Cadie. Come on, and let's go."

But she wouldn't budge an inch. Boy tried to pull her to her feet, but her strength was astounding, like she had grown the deep roots of a live oak. She rested Norman's head to the ground and then lay next to him with her cheek on his chest as if they were a couple asleep in a marriage bed. "Cadie, I won't leave you like this. I won't."

"Get the reverend," she mumbled. "And tell 'em—tell 'em my husband and me wanna pray together. Tell 'em." Then she closed her eyes while her lips moved in a soft murmur.

It took every ounce of Boy's strength not to pick her up and shake some sense into her. Didn't she see Norman was dead? Didn't she see fate had brought the two of them together again—that she wasn't meant to live a life in that little ole house with the son of a mercantile owner, but with him, the heir to Magnolia Hill, a grand, plantation house?

Boy backed away toward the river, unable to look at Cadie and Norman any longer—not because of shame and disgust, but because of a sense he was intruding on a great mystery not destined for him. What was this power that had come over Cadie to make her speak to the forest with such authority or lie down in a puddle of mud with a man like Norman McLain? Boy couldn't fathom it—it was beyond his comprehension. It was something Mattie would surely understand, and Zena, too, but no one else. No one except the Reverend Thomas.

But what good would the reverend do her now? What possible good would come of it? He glanced back to where Cadie and Norman lay and stared at Norman's lifeless form and how Cadie had tucked her body close to his, like a glove molded to a hand. Her arm fell across Norman's torso, and her fingers crept towards his face, and then suddenly, her arm rose up with his chest, ever so slightly.

A prickly sensation rushed through Boy's extremities, down to his wounded leg and the tips of his fingers in his punctured arm. Had Norman breathed? Surely, it was his imagination. He crept closer, looked into Norman's still face, and then touched his forehead, which was still cold and clammy. There appeared to be no movement, and then, there it was—a slight rise of his chest. Boy placed his palm over Norman's heart, feeling a steady beat.

"Cadie, stay here—I'm gonna go get help!" He turned and splashed toward the mouth of Jackson's Creek where Holiday stood under the trees munching on a clump of wet grass. Then flying into the saddle, he rode in a fury toward the direction of the Gospel Church.

By the time Boy brought Reverend Thomas to the riverbank, the storm had lifted, and Norman had his eyes open and was able to speak in a soft whisper. Miraculously, his thick hair had allowed the blood to clot, which prevented his death, but Cadie thought otherwise, as did the reverend, and they both made their opinions known—God had intervened and brought Norman back from darkness.

Boy stood at a distance and watched, mesmerized by what had taken place. He would forever remember seeing the reverend kneel beside Norman, place his hand on Norman's brow, and then bow his head in prayer. He wondered what was said and why the reverend, of all people, seemed to have knowledge of this power of God beyond anyone else. What was the secret to it? Cadie embraced it, as well, for she knelt beside the reverend and prayed alongside him.

Boy blinked the tears away as he stared at Cadie, memorizing everything about her—the blonde curls caked with mud, her delicate, white fingers entwined in a clasp by her pale lips, her smooth, flawless skin streaked with dirt, yet flushed with passion and excitement, and the blue eyes full of fire but hidden away by folds of flesh trimmed with thick lashes. It was in that moment he realized this would be the last time he would ever see Cadie Hamilton McLean. Mattie was right—she didn't belong to him, after all. Looking at her the way he had these past weeks was like a covetous man gazing with longing on his neighbor's property, planning a way to get his hands on it—essentially a thief in violation of one of God's commandments. And so, there was no reason for him to stay in Pleasant Oaks any longer and certainly no reason to delay his departure.

Curiously, Boy felt an accompanying sense of relief at this revelation. The truth was, he had waited for this moment all of his life—when some unplanned event would force him into manhood. But he never anticipated it would occur in this cruel manner. Who would have known the powerful storm that had swept into town that day would dismantle Old Hargett's Bridge, as well as the life he had always known? In one swift and final moment, the elusive Robert Morgan sprung forth, not because of a conscious decision for him to be unleashed and set upon the world, but because the carefree, spirited "Boy" had come to an abrupt and momentous end.

Chapter 37

"We're goin' now, honey," Mama said, putting her arm around Cadie's shoulder and kissing her on the cheek. "And we'll take Mattie and Zena home."

Cadie mumbled a thank you as she continued to stare at Norman while he slept. He had been home twelve hours now and still had not awakened, as the doctor predicted. The wound had been cleaned and bandaged and a special tea brewed to prevent infection, but Cadie knew there would be none. The reverend had come, and the Lord had spared him, just as she had asked.

"I'll come by tomorrow and see how he's doin'."

Cadie nodded, refusing to look at her mama for fear she might erupt into a mass of tears. Today was the first time she had set foot in Cadie and Norman's house since its redecoration and improvements. Cadie had been meaning to invite her for supper once Tessie returned from college, but now that would have to wait. Tessie wasn't due home for another three weeks, and who knew when Norman would be well enough to entertain guests? And then there was the matter of her daddy.

Cadie tore her eyes away from Norman and looked back to the doorway where her father stood. He stared at the floor with his arms tucked behind his back, shifting from one foot to another. His face was gray and pensive and the few strands of hair on top of his head were greasy and mangled-looking from running his fingers through it. Cadie's heart swelled with a blend of love from the little girl she had once been and pity from the woman she had become. He looked old and broken, a defeated man whipped by the rules of life. He stood silently and said nothing, making no eye contact with anyone and refusing to pray with the reverend when he was here—even rejecting Mattie's delicious roasted chicken with cornbread and walnut stuffing. Cadie wondered what was going on in the depths of his mind. She'd probably never know, but did that matter? He had come to her home and seen where she and Norman lived, despite all that had happened.

Cadie kissed Mama on the cheek and approached her daddy. He kept his head down, but his feet suddenly quit their monotonous shifting. His strong, callused fingers worked the brim of his hat one way and then the other until she touched his hand to still their movement. The contrast between her pale skin and his rough hands darkened by dirt and the sun were striking. They were worlds apart in hopes, desires, thoughts, and yet, they had so many things in common.

"Daddy?" Cadie clasped her fingers over his until they entwined. "Daddy—" She embraced him, and in an instant, she was his Twiddle again, tucked in the folds of his arms where the familiar scent of coffee and tobacco greeted her after such a long absence.

He held her tight and gripped the back of her head with his strong palm like she was nestled in the bough of one of the Stephenses' apple trees. After the appropriate time for affection had run its course, Mama gently cleared her throat, indicating it was time for them to be going home. He pulled away and kissed Cadie on the top of her head. "You come on home anytime you want, you hear?" He kissed her again and then left without another word.

Cadie stood on the porch and waved good-bye to Daddy's truck with Mattie and Zena perched in the flatbed. Joy seeped through her heart at seeing Zena's smiling face and her hand waving as she called, "Night, Miss Cadie!"

"'Night, Miss Zena!" Cadie said, waving back.

"You get some sleep, now, you hear? The Lord'll take good care of Mr. Norman. Don't you worry none."

Zena's voice trailed off into the night with the taillights of the truck, blending in with the sounds of the crickets, bullfrogs, and the gentle creak of the porch rocker as it moved back and forth. The sound came from Mr. McLain, who puffed on a pipe that emitted a bluish, gray smoke that was strangely comforting. "Pa, can I get you some tea or a cup of coffee maybe?" Cadie asked.

"No, child," he replied.

In the dim light, she saw the exhaustion of grief on his face. She rested her hand on his shoulder in reassurance, and he responded by giving it a quick pat. He continued to rock, back and forth, staring into the night while the smoke swirled around him. "Well, I'll be right inside if you need me."

Cadie wandered into the bedroom to where Norman lay. It was the first time they had been alone since the accident happened, and the solitude was disquieting, like the first time a new mother is left alone to care for her baby. She gazed at him, realizing her feelings for Norman had started so long ago. Like a seed, it had grown in the garden of her heart, impervious to her efforts to snuff it out or rip it loose like a worthless weed. Despite all of her foolishness and stubborn ways, God had grown it into a healthy, fully-developed bloom.

Cadie tucked the blankets up over Norman's shoulders while humming something, she wasn't sure what, but she was sure it was a tune the reverend had sung one Sunday in church. His eyelids fluttered, and she grew quiet, waiting for him to awaken. "Norman?" After a few more flutters, he opened his eyes and looked up at the ceiling. "You awake?"

He looked at her and mustered a weak smile. "My eyes are opened, aren't they?"

"Norman McLain—" She smoothed his hair away from his brow and caressed his cheek. "How can you joke at a time like this?"

He smiled again as a lone tear slid down his face, wetting her fingers. "Makes life a lot easier, I reckon."

Cadie smiled back, fighting her own tears that threatened to flow. "You gave us quite a scare, you know that?"

"I woulda thought you'd be glad to be rid of me."

"Shh—don't say that."

"I know I haven't been the kinda husband you wanted."

"Stop, Norman. You're my husband." She brushed the stubborn lock of hair off his forehead once more, noticing the sharp planes of his face accentuated by the bristles of his beard. "My one and only husband."

He swallowed hard and stared into her eyes. "What you said on the bridge—I remember what you said—"

She laid a finger on his lips and silenced him. "You know I could never be with him."

He turned his face to the ceiling and looked straight ahead while the tears streamed down his cheeks. "'Blessed are the peacemakers, for they shall be called the children of God'," he said in a solemn voice. "'Blessed are they which are persecuted for righteousness' sake, for theirs is the kingdom of heaven.' You remember that? The night we fought?"

"That's all in the past, Norman."

"Will you read it to me?"

Cadie followed his gaze to the top drawer of the bedside table. She pulled it open, ever so slowly, and found a scorched, blackened rectangle of a book with a missing cover and pages burned around the edges. "Norman McLain," she said with a note of wonder and awe. "It's Zena's Bible." She carefully lifted it out of the drawer and flipped through it, amazed that most of it was still intact. "I thought it got burned up."

"Not all of it. Hope she won't mind that I've kept it awhile."

Cadie cut him a mischievous look. "Is this what you've been lookin' at in secret, makin' me think it was one of those girlie books?"

"I don't need no girlie books. Not when I've got you."

"Norman—" Cadie's face flushed in a way that replaced the shame she used to experience when these topics were mentioned. "Does this mean you might be goin' to church with me now?"

He took a deep breath before answering. "Cadie, the truth is, I don't think the reverend would want me there."

"Of course he would. He said there's nothin' the Lord wants more than for you and me to come to Him—together, as a couple."

"You don't know what I've done."

"All of us 've done bad things."

"Not like this. Not like what I've done."

"What on earth do you mean?"

"That night—" he said, his voice barely above a whisper. His eyes searched hers, seeking permission to reveal some deep, dark secret. "I was there, Cadie. I ain't never told anyone before." The fear in his expression was frightening, but he kept on. "The reverend—he saw me hidin' behind a pile of wood there by the church—and I saw it in his eyes. He knew it was me."

"But that was years ago," Cadie said. "You were just a boy."

"But I knew better. I knew it was wrong. And I did nothin'. Pa told me to stay home, but I couldn't. I wanted to see what they'd do."

"Oh, Norman—the reverend says he's forgiven all that."

"How could he? You don't know, Cadie. You don't know what I saw. I saw somethin' I ain't never seen before." He stared at the ceiling again as his words and thoughts drifted away into another world. "I saw an evil that scared me. And you wanna know why? 'Cause it's the same evil that's been in my heart all this time, I can't deny it. Maybe I was a boy, but I realized I wasn't no different from those men, even my own pa. I've got his blood runnin' through my veins, the blood of a man who would do such a thing." He sucked in a ragged breath and continued, "We deserved to get burned up for what we done, every last one of us—even if some of us did it in our hearts only. I ain't never seen the sky open up like that—it just opened up and lit up that tree like a torch, burnt it all the way to the root, and popped that rope right in two. Didn't burn nothin' else, neither, except those men who tried to put their hands on the reverend again. They screamed like someone'd taken a knife to 'em. And the reverend, he didn't even have a mark on him except what's on his neck."

Cadie breathed in deeply, carefully weighing her words. "You and I may not understand it all, but the reverend knows why our pas and those other men did what they did."

"They persecuted a righteous man who didn't want nothin' but God's peace, I can see that. And God rescued him." Norman's eyes bolted to and fro, indicating he was in a deep, unspeakable struggle. "But I've probably read that passage and others a dozen times or more, and I still don't understand how it applies to someone like me. I don't understand how I can make peace with my past, just like that, how God's gonna forgive me for all I've done. How's He gonna forgive me for all I've done to you?"

She stroked his cheek again, running the back of her hand against the bristles. "Do you have to understand it? Can't you just believe what it says?"

Her words pierced the air, bringing with them a heavy silence. Norman resumed his deep stare at the ceiling, not moving other than to blink his eyes. Cadie sensed his mind was churning at a furious pace as he sought to decipher this simple, benign statement—so profound that its notion would've never entered his thoughts had she not spoken it. She waited patiently, saying nothing, allowing the truth to cast out all doubts dividing them. He let out another sigh, but this one was different—not born out of frustration, but acceptance. "I shoulda died in that river, I know that. But for some reason, that same power that was on the reverend came on me. I don't know how I know, but I just do. I felt it runnin' all over me, inside and out, and it scared me, Cadie, I won't lie to you. It's got me scared real bad."

"There's no need to be scared, Norman," she said through her tears. "No need at all."

He looked at her, seeking assurance as his eyes lingered over her face, indicating the old Norman was still there to claim what was his. "Come here," he whispered.

Cadie leaned over the bed and adjusted his blankets again. "I'm here, Norman. And I'm never gonna leave. Not ever."

"Closer," he whispered again. His mouth strained to meet hers until they joined together in a gentle kiss. This time, Cadie felt something much deeper than what she had experienced in the apple orchard forever ago—it was a profound sensation that bypassed the body altogether and touched the spirit. It was the branding of her heart, the searing of her mind, and the filling of her entire being with the missing ingredient that had eluded her for so long. She was part of something inexplicable. She was home.

As Cadie melted into Norman's embrace, she thought of the prince rising out of the river with arms extended, lifting her up and up, higher and higher, into the safety of the clouds. Norman wrapped his arms around her waist and pulled her onto the bed next to him, making her giggle. "Be careful," she said. "The doctor says you're not supposed to move."

"I don't care what the doctor says. I want you with me."

Cadie snuggled next to him with her head on his chest, holding Zena's Bible near their hearts. "Oh, Norman, I do love you. More than you'll ever know." His body tightened as his fingers dug into her back, pulling her so close, she could barely breathe. But she didn't mind. Not one little bit.

Chapter 38

Poor thing, Zena thought, as she huddled next to Miss Cadie behind the shelves of canned food and listened to Jack Reynolds answer a litany of questions from old Mr. McLain. Because it was Sunday, the mercantile was closed, and there was no one else around, which didn't seem to make it any easier on Jack. His fingers worked the brim of his felt fedora, like an old lady furiously knitting a sweater before the cold of winter set in, stinking up the air with the spicy scent of nervousness—a clear signal he was sweating right through his clean shirt. Zena wished there were some way to relieve the tension. If he only knew Miss Cadie had already persuaded Mr. McLain to hire him while Mr. Norman was recovering from his accident, he wouldn't be the least bit nervous, and he certainly wouldn't be tearing up his nice hat.

"All right, you be here tomorrow, bright and early, you hear?" Mr. McLain glared at him under a pair of white, bushy eyebrows.

Jack stopped his fidgeting and broke into an enormous smile. "Yes, sir."

"And don't you be late," Mr. McLain said, shaking his finger for good measure.

"No, sir."

"I won't tolerate lateness. And you make sure you're clean and look respectable."

"Yes, sir, Mr. McLain, sir."

"All right then, go on."

"Yes, sir. Thank you, sir," Jack said, scurrying out of the store like a man on his way out of a burning building.

Zena clapped her hands, ignoring Miss Cadie's scolding glare to keep quiet. She didn't care if everyone in the world could hear—she could just pinch herself for what she had just witnessed. Without hesitation, she leaned over and kissed Miss Cadie on the cheek.

"Now, what was that for?"

"For you, 'cause of what you've done." She gazed at Miss Cadie, marveling at how her skin glowed like the dew of the early morning and how her eyes shone as bright as stars under her fashionable hat that seemed to crown her hair like a halo. She was like an angel to Zena, a lovely and beautiful angel.

"Oh, hush, now, Zena," Miss Cadie said. "I only did what any other decent person would've done." She winked at Zena and giggled. "Come on, let's have some fun."

Miss Cadie snuck up behind Mr. McLain and kissed his cheek, just like Zena had imagined doing herself. He blushed beet red, but refused to give up his cold, stiff demeanor. "You happy now?"

"Yes, I am," she said with a charming grin and slight tilt to her head. "And just for that, Zena and I are gonna cook you the best supper you've ever tasted. Right, Zena?"

"Right." Zena smiled, deciding she'd like to join in on the fun Miss Cadie was having. She propped her hand on her hip and wagged a finger at him in an exaggerated way. "But don't you be late, now."

Miss Cadie followed suit, giving him one of her sassy looks. "Yes, and make sure you're clean and look respectable."

"All right, all right," he said, rolling eyes with impatience, even though it was clear from the look on his face he was enjoying every minute of their attention. "Just go on, the two of you. Go on."

Zena grabbed Miss Cadie under the arm, and they both scurried out of the store, laughing like school girls. Mama was waiting for them at the end of the street, dressed in her burgundy silk hat and matching poplin coat—another one of Mrs. Stephens's hand-me-downs. "Where've you two been?" she said with a scolding look. "I've been waitin' a good twenty minutes."

"We was just takin' care of some business," Zena said with another giggle.

"On the Sabbath?"

"God's business," Miss Cadie said.

Her mama shot them a suspicious glare and sighed. "Well, all right, but I got my eye on you two. You better behave yourselves in the service today. I don't want any cuttin' up, you hear?"

"Yes, ma'am," Zena said in unison with Miss Cadie.

"The two of you can be a mess sometimes." She held her head up high as she guided them down the street like a mother hen protecting her two chicks. But then suddenly, she stopped in midstride and stared into the distance. "Lord 've mercy."

"What is it, Mama?" Zena asked.

The Duisenberg headed straight toward them with Mrs. Stephens at the wheel. "She's done seen us now," Mama said, her mouth hardening in a straight line.

The motorcar pulled up to a jerky stop, and Mrs. Stephens leaned out of the window. "Mattie, thank God," she exclaimed, out of breath. "I've been looking all over for you."

"Miz Stephens, what's wrong?"

"Get in. I've got a heap of people coming over for lunch, and that new girl, well, she's just no help at all." She reached behind her and opened the back passenger door, but Mama stood as solid as stone, with her chin higher, back straighter, and shoulders more square than Zena had ever seen. "Well, come on. Get in," Mrs. Stephens huffed.

"No, ma'am."

"What do you mean, no? I'm in a bind, and I need you."

"I don't work on Sundees anymore, remember? I'm goin' to church now, to worship the Lord. That's what we do on Sundees."

Mrs. Stephens' mouth fell open. "But—"

"You've got Ruby and Henry. They'll take good care of you."

"Matilda," she pleaded in a pathetic, desperate tone. "Please—"

But Mama simply closed the passenger door, like she hadn't heard a word. "Now, I'll be seein' you tomorrow mornin', bright and early. You have a blessed day. Come on, girls." Then grabbing Zena's elbow in one hand and Miss Cadie's in the other, she pulled them down the street, out of harm's way.

Zena continued to watch her mama's reaction, wondering what on earth had possessed her to stand up to Mrs. Stephens after all this time, especially after she had gone and used Mama's Christian name like that. Zena didn't have a clue, but she sure was glad. Mama never once looked back, but Zena couldn't help herself. She caught Miss Cadie's eye and then turned around and saw Mrs. Stephens watching through the windshield of her fancy motorcar with her mouth still hanging wide open.

For some reason, Cadie felt sorry for Mrs. Stephens, even pity. With all of her money and finery and beautiful home on the river, she was just a prisoner of her own making and didn't know it. As the Cape Fear came into view, Cadie stopped and stared at the great expanse of water, wondering if she would have suffered a similar fate had she chosen differently.

A riverboat sounded its horn, sending her spirits back up to the clouds. "Look, Zena!" she cried, pointing at the boat. "Come on!" Ignoring Mattie's complaints, she raced toward the riverbank with Zena close behind.

"Don't you be long, now," Mattie called. "Service's startin'!"

"Okay, Mama!" Zena replied.

Cadie plopped down on the grass and gazed at the boat in all of its detail, especially the outline of several passengers leaning over the railing. She strained her eyes and saw a young man with waistcoat and gray trousers and a rumple of blond hair. A thick lock blew across his forehead, and immediately, she knew who he was.

"Wonder where he's goin'?" Zena asked as she sat down next to Cadie.

"Don't know."

"Some place far off, I reckon."

"Reckon so." He looked their way, and Cadie gave a hearty wave—but he didn't respond. She sighed and stared out at the movement of the river, marveling at its flow. "It never stops, does it?" she asked dreamily.

"Nope," Zena agreed. "Sure is beautiful."

"It sure is."

A peace fell over them as they watched the boat disappear into the distance. Within minutes, the wind blew across the water, carrying the sound of Mattie's voice. "Come on," Cadie said, jumping to her feet. "I'll race you."

She turned and ran along the riverbank toward Jackson's Creek, giggling and squealing, with Zena hot on her trail. They breezed past Mattie and made their way to the Gospel Church, bounding up the porch steps to where Old Man Jackson sat in his rocker.

Reverend Thomas was already preaching fast and furious to a packed house, so Cadie inched the front door open, and they slipped inside, trying their best not to disturb his sermon. ". . . and Lord, I pray that all of us here, all of us be given the power to understand just how much you love us," he exclaimed in his typical, passionate style. He swept his arm across the congregation in one, grand motion, and said, "Help us to understand just how WIDE, Hallelujah! And LONG, Glory to God! And HIGH, Praise God! And DEEP—is the love of Christ."

Cadie tip-toed alongside Zena to the front pew, suddenly stopping cold as the word "Christ" filled every nook and cranny of the crowded room. There sat Norman, pale and bruised and sporting a bandage on his head. "Norman?" Cadie asked in a hushed voice.

He cast his eyes down at his feet while the congregation grew quiet, except for a whispering that came from above. Cadie glanced up and saw the dark face of a little boy perched outside her steeple window, staring. A flash of red ribbons in her peripheral vision told her Nettie Reynolds sat at the end of the pew and was staring at them, too, with eyes wider than the little boy's above.

Cadie slid next to Norman and slunk down in the pew, feeling the scrutiny of every member of the congregation, including Zena. For the first time in a long time, she sensed how *white* she and her husband must look among a sea of black faces, all of whom had every right to hate them. Fear gripped her, and it took all the courage she could muster to look into the reverend's gentle expression where the tip of the scar snaked up from behind the collar, trying to taunt her into accepting rejection and condemnation. But the reverend's loving gaze spoke another message, reassuring her that the scar was nothing more than a mere battle wound from a simple, uneventful brawl between the man of God and a group of wayward tomcats who were told to scat—with no record of time or date— just that it had happened on that spring night some seven years ago, now, and would one day be forgotten.

"It's all right, Miz McLain." The reverend placed his strong, black hand on the shoulder of Norman's crisp, white shirt and gently squeezed. "Everything's gonna be all right."

Cadie entwined her fingers in Norman's, holding tight. Their bodies were as one, sealed together with his mama's ring which sparkled in the light. Norman responded by tucking her arm under his while keeping his head low and his eyes away from the reverend's fiery gaze. She snuggled close and whispered something in his ear, words she would say many times over the coming years. Reverend Thomas winked at her and flashed his gleaming smile, for he had heard it, too—not with his natural ears, but with that special *something* he possessed. "His love flows," he said with that fervent look in his eye. "I said it flows, like a river. Just like that river out there . . ."

The wind swept the reverend's voice through the open window of the Gospel Church, past the blackened oak with its sprig of new growth, and toward Jackson's Creek, mixing together with the screech of the golden eagle and the congregation's enthusiastic response. The sound bobbed along the water's surface, hovering below the flap of the bird's mighty wings as it passed another grand garden party being held on the lawn of Magnolia Hill. Finally, it dispersed into the expanse of the Cape Fear and faded into the horizon, where a young man with tousled blond hair and brocade waistcoat traveled on a riverboat toward someplace—far off.

The End

About the Author

Caroline Friday is a novelist, screenwriter, illustrator, bible study teacher, and monthly columnist for christianfictiononlinemagazine.com. In 2008, she was a winner of the prestigious Kairos Screenwriting Prize for spiritually uplifting screenplays, sponsored by the John Templeton Foundation. Caroline currently serves as EVP of Sixth Day Media, LLC, which is headquartered in the Atlanta area. She lives in Marietta, Georgia, with her husband and three children and can be found at www.carolinefriday.com and carolinefriday.blogspot.com.

BOOKS BY CAROLINE FRIDAY

MAGNOLIA HILL

THE VELVET BOX

WHERE LOVE RUNS FREE

THE LOST PRINCESS

Made in the USA
Columbia, SC
26 December 2017